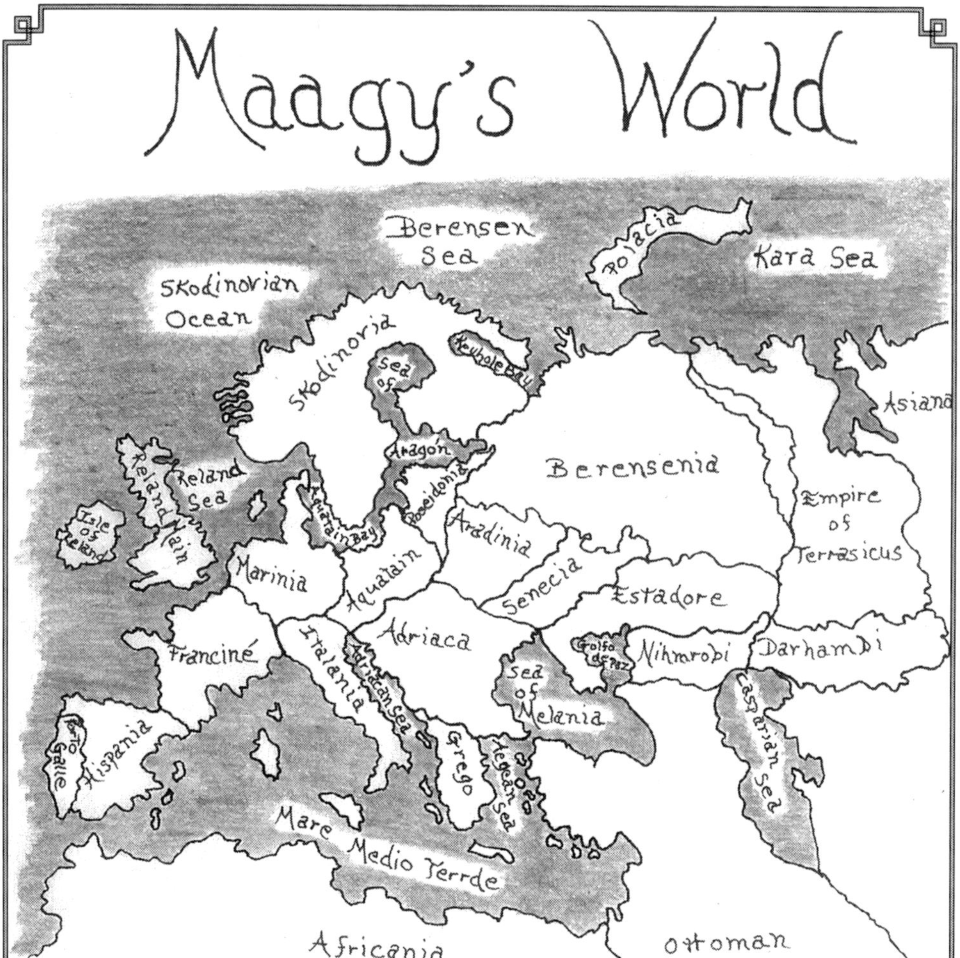

Maagy's World

Berensen Sea
Kara Sea
Skodinovian Ocean
Skodinoria
Sea of Aragón
Keyhole Bay
Asiana
Reland Sea
Reland Main
Isle of Reland
Aquatain Bay
Poseidonia
Berensenia
Empire of Terrasicus
Aradinia
Marinia
Aquatain
Senecia
Estadore
Franciné
Italania
Adriacan Sea
Adriaca
Sea of Melania
Golfo de Paz
Nihmrobi
Darhamdi
Caspanian Sea
Porto Galle
Hispania
Grego
Aegean Sea
Mare Medio Terrde
Africania
Ottoman

Just Maagy

VIRGINIA BURTON STRINGER

Illustrated by Lauren Abernathy

ARCHWAY PUBLISHING

Archway Publishing books may be ordered through booksellers or by contacting:

Archway Publishing
1663 Liberty Drive
Bloomington, IN 47403
www.archwaypublishing.com
1-(888)-242-5904

ISBN: 978-1-4808-1121-8 (sc)
ISBN: 978-1-4808-1119-5 (hc)
ISBN: 978-1-4808-1120-1 (e)

Library of Congress Control Number: 2014916677

Printed in the United States of America.

Archway Publishing rev. date: 10/02/2014

TO: CATHERINE—

ENJOY MAAGY'S JOURNEY!!!

Love

Virginia [illegible]

09/05/15

Contents

Author's Notes

Welcome to Maagy's world. The process of bringing this character to life and this book to you, the reader, has been a ten-year journey of exploration, exasperation, discovery, and best of all, a true labor of great love. My inspiration was mothering my own two daughters, now grown; and watching my son, David, raise his two daughters, now in the midst of teenage bad-land. It occurred to me that, no matter the era… no matter the century… young women have milestones. The first big one is at thirteen. In today's society, the lines are somewhat blurred for many girls, as they are allowed… or pushed… to grow up way too fast, but for the overwhelming majority of girls worldwide, twelve/thirteen signifies the first step into womanhood. They grow… almost overnight. Their bodies take shape… their chemistry changes, as do their moods. Some get braces, glasses, pimples, and dare I say it, breasts. They enter an awkward, gangly, clumsy-puppy phase, which lasts about two more years. Then suddenly… and it seems, again, over night… the butterflies, with all their myriads of colors, emerge from the cocoons and… *voila...* they are sixteen-year-old sophomores, working first jobs, asking for car keys and accepting dates to the prom. The next big step is eighteen, that magical age when society deems these creatures have reached majority and we call them adults… I'm not sure I agree. Nonetheless, they graduate high school, go off to college and embark upon the next journey. They become wives, mothers, executives… or soldiers… or venture from our grasps in other ways. If we are lucky, they take on responsibility and maturity. It's a beautiful thing, watching these butterflies flit through our gardens, as they grow.

The ***Maagy*** series of chapter books, set in a mythical fairytale time, chronicles the journey of Princess *Melania* (daughter, Melanie) *Abigail* (granddaughter) *Alice* (daughter) *Grace* (granddaughter) (thus, the name *M-A-A-G-Y*… with a hard G sound… as in Grace), as she navigates the milestones in her life and learns to be a decisive, tenacious, brave, gentle, patient and responsible queen. I started, in 2004, writing a fifty-minute children's play about an impetuous little princess, as my background is in theatre and I have spent thirty years teaching, directing and writing for children's theatre. However, I quickly realized I had more stage directions and set description than dialogue. I decided it was a short story. By 2011 there were three more books… close to a thousand pages in all… and here we are… 2014… with a series of chapter books appropriate for tweens and teens.

I would be remise if I didn't mention and give special thanks to a few people, without whose help this project could not have come to fruition. First and foremost, Bill Stringer, my husband of thirty-four years, who has been patient and supportive… and cooked dinner way more times than he would have liked… to allow me to immerse myself in my writing. He once said, after reading, "What do I know? I'm a fifty-something man, not the target audience, but I loved it!" I love you, too, Honey. Then there are my three children, who have read and given editorial advice, but most of all, who have been my biggest cheerleaders. A huge thank you to Mick Mahone, a high school friend and scholar of literature, who read with an objective eye in the early draft stages and gave me gentle nudges, which opened up a world of yet unexplored ideas for Maagy's growth. My dear friends, Margaret Dozier, Susan Bishop, Reva Payne, Michele Raddin, and Kathy Gylfe all read rough drafts of Maagy and each gave me solid and intelligent critique… not just "atta-girls" because they're my friends. Last, but not least, thanks to Dagmara Dominczyk, my niece, for her expert advice and undying support when I was ready to hit delete. So, there you have it… here it is… please enjoy the adventure! Cheers, *Virginia Burton Stringer*

Prologue

Once upon a time, in a kingdom nestled in a green valley between two tall mountain ranges, there lived a beautiful little princess with her loving, but aging father. She was the only child of the beloved King Henry and had come to him and his darling Queen Melania at a time when most couples were welcoming grandchildren. They were thrilled, nonetheless, and he had given his daughter everything her heart desired. This is not always the best way to love a child.

Melania Abigail Alice Grace, Maagy, as she was called, was willful and spoiled and tempestuous* outbursts were a given several times each day. The kindly king did what he could to guide her toward good behavior, but he was loath to scold his precious child. He was quite certain her mother… were she still alive… would have known how to handle the laziness and the sulking and the tantrums. The gentle father recognized the huge responsibility he bore for the welfare of his entire kingdom and she would be of age far too soon for his liking. He realized he had little time left in which to teach the young princess to take his place as the ruling monarch, as Maagy would ascend the throne while in her teens. The absence of his queen and advancing age weighed heavily on His Majesty and he longed to retire and spend his later years welcoming grandchildren before he joined his queen. He knew he had to take drastic steps to insure his daughter was fit to be queen and his kingdom would thrive in his absence.

Chapter 1
Birthday Fiasco*

Maagy awakened early that morning, knowing it was a special day. It was her birthday. She felt it immediately. She had grown overnight and was much more mature. After all, she was now *thirteen*! She sat up, propped herself with pillows and tugged hard on the bell cord. The kind voice of Head Chef, Persephone Fendlwart, floated into the room.

"Good morning, Your Grace, and a very happy birthday to you. What shall I prepare for your breakfast?"

"Whatever you do, *don't* send me any of those nasty gooseberries. I hate gooseberries and now that I'm thirteen, I'm old enough to eat what I want. Send me chocolate chip pancakes with lots of whipped cream and two cherries… and a bowl of spumoni ice cream*[1]," she demanded, as she sat, arms folded across her chest; her mouth pursed in the hint of a smile, proud of her decisiveness.

"Begging your pardon, Your Highness," Missus Fendlwart replied, after a long pause, "I believe you finished the spumoni ice cream for dinner last evening. I've already…"

1 Where * appears, please see Glossary; Words and Terms, for definitions and explanations

"If I want spumoni ice cream, you have to give me spumoni ice cream. I am Crown Princess Maagy, future Queen Maagy, and it's my birthday!" She screamed, as she began to cry and kick her feet and throw pillows round the room. *"I want spumoni ice cream! I want spumoni ice cream!"*

The door opened abruptly and in marched a rather out-of-patience king.

"What is all of this racket about? The horses in the stables can hear you, Child."

The pouty little princess… arms still folded and chin set sideways… told him what she had ordered for breakfast *and* the kitchen was out of her favorite ice cream *and*, since it was her birthday, she was entitled to whatever she wanted *and* the staff should comply.

"Maagy, Dear, it takes time for ice cream to freeze," he explained calmly. "I've spoken with Missus Fendlwart and more spumoni has been made for your party this afternoon. Won't that do, Darling?"

"I want it *now*!"

"Well, it isn't ready *now*… my dear…" he said, using all his might to hold his temper. "You'll have to be patient."

"Oh bother! Then I won't eat anything! I'll just go hungry! No one cares if I'm hungry, anyway."

"Now, Darling, that isn't true. Everyone loves you. You're Crown Princess Maagy."

"Then why can't I have spumoni ice cream for breakfast? It's my birthday," she wailed.

At that moment, a young chambermaid, Miss Samantha Payne, entered with a tray of chocolate chip pancakes with whipped cream and two cherries, a cup of hot chocolate and a bowl of strawberry ice cream… her second favorite flavor. She saw the strawberry ice cream and let out a tremendous caterwaul*. The noise so shocked Samantha that she dropped the tray, which made a tremendous clang, and food went everywhere. Maagy began throwing things at the poor girl, as she cried, apologized and tried to clean up the mess through a barrage of pillows and hapless* inanimate* fuzzy bears

and rabbits. The bewildered* father sank to the bench by the door in complete exasperation*. There was no question he needed help.

The rest of the morning went accordingly. She refused to eat anything, which made her even more cross than usual. Lady Periwinkle, the Palace Social Mistress, had planned an elaborate birthday party with more than fifty of society's most well heeled* children expected to attend. The grand ballroom was decorated to the hilt with bows and ribbons of lavender, purple, pink and green, Maagy's favorite colors… at least, everyone *assumed* those were her favorite colors… since she always wore pastels. The truth was no one had ever asked her what colors she preferred. Had anyone bothered, they would have learned the more vibrant hues where her favorites. Red, in particular, was her secret obsession.

Her birthday cake was a luscious creation of one chocolate fudge layer, one of raspberry, one vanilla and one banana layer. The icing was butter cream and tinted soft lavender with green icing vines and pink roses from top to bottom… she would have rather they were red. There were a number of delicacies, which included finger sandwiches and fresh fruit trays. Lady Periwinkle had sought approval from Her Highness on several last minute items on the agenda, such as when to open presents… before or after cake and ice cream… spumoni ice cream, of course.

"If you'll allow me, Your Highness, I believe it is accepted practice to feed one's guests first, before indulging one's self in opening presents."

"Well, I don't care! It's my birthday… my party… and I'm the Crown Princess. I can do what I wish. And I wish to open my presents first… as soon as everyone arrives."

"Begging your pardon, Your Grace, but the guests are scheduled to arrive at three o'clock. There is a magic show scheduled at four. I thought if we served refreshments at three-thirty, it would coincide nicely with tea time and the guests could have their goodies whilst watching the magician…"

"*NO, NO, NO*! I will open my presents first! Then we'll play croquet and hide and seek. Then we'll have cake and ice cream and magic so everyone can rest."

"Again… begging your pardon…"

"No, you do *not* have my pardon!" She screamed and stomped her feet. "*No, no, no…* it is *my* party… we will do it *my* way!"

King Henry happened to be walking past and over heard the exchange. He went into the parlor.

"Princess Maagy, might I have a private word with you?" He said with authority, as he ushered her aside and then whispered. "You will not speak to Lady Periwinkle in that tone. Do you understand, Child? Lady Periwinkle, thank you for your indulgence in this tedious matter. You are the social planner, so plan and my daughter will do it your way, won't you Maagy?"

"Yes, Father," she returned, reluctantly. "Whatever you say."

"Now, do apologize for your tone… go on… *now*, Maagy!"

"Sorry, Lady Periwinkle."

"Of course, apology accepted."

"Very well," he said, "Now go and eat something… and calm yourself before continuing this conversation."

She did as she was told, knowing he meant business. The rest of the meeting was relatively calm, considering she pitched only four more minor tantrums, mostly over which games would be played. She was in a better mood, once she had eaten something.

The afternoon seemed to drag on as last minute details were accomplished and Maagy occupied her time primping for the festivities. Her Lady-in-Waiting*, Lady Cecily Greymiller, helped her choose a party dress for the occasion. It was tea-length and fluffy… albeit lavender and not deep purple. Aristocratic young girls were not allowed to wear bold colors, so she settled for lavender. She chose white stockings and white shiny slippers. Lady Cecily pinned her long, blond hair up in curls on top of her head and she wore a stunning diamond tiara her father had given her as a birthday gift.

Lady Cecily was the only person who seemed able to tolerate her nasty moods, despite her unkind treatment of the gentle girl. She was just over a year older than the princess and had returned to the palace court, several years earlier, to become her Lady-in-Waiting. The king thought it would be good for his daughter to have a young female companion.

Finally, it was time for the guests to arrive. The first one through the door was Lord Wesley Applegate, the young Duke of Kent; a somewhat round, red-faced lad of fourteen. It was no secret the chap was smitten with Princess Maagy, so it came as no surprise he was the first to arrive. In fact, he had been waiting to enter for over an hour. He brought with him a large box wrapped in pastel green silk material tied with a white satin ribbon. He was ever so proud, as he presented the box to Lady Periwinkle for placement on the gift table. He surely expected his gift to be the most treasured. Next to arrive were Ladies Millicent and Elizabeth Smythe. Their parents, Baron Bullington Smythe and Baroness Jacqueline, were members of the King's Court and Baron Smythe was a close friend of the king as well as a financial advisor to Parliament. Maagy did not particularly enjoy the Smythe girls' company nor did they enjoy hers. She felt as if they constantly conspired against her. They considered her to be a bit haughty. Had it been left to Maagy, she would not have invited them. Left to them, they would not have come. The truth is she had many acquaintances, but no real friends.

Children continued to trickle into the grand ballroom, welcomed elegantly by Lady Periwinkle. Rather than greeting her own guests as they came, Maagy decided to wait until all were present and then make a grand entrance to applause and shouts of "*Happy Birthday, Your Royal Highness*". She insisted upon being announced with trumpets and flourishes. But to her dismay, only half the children invited were in attendance and none applauded her entrance. It immediately put her into a royal snit and things only went downhill from there. She complained about the watercress sandwiches and refused to eat them. The bacon-wrapped escargot* went virtually untouched and the spinach soufflé deflated. Poor Wesley was so nervous, when he bowed elegantly to his Muse*, he spilled his red cherry jubilee drink on her ever-so-white legs and feet… purely by accident, of course. She screamed and shoved her large bowl of spumoni ice cream in his face. He retaliated by dumping a plate of chocolate mousse with whipped cream on her head, which caused a rather nasty food fight to ensue. The bits of escargot were used effectively as missiles, hurled by several of the boys. The spinach soufflé found a home in Lady Elizabeth's lap. The event deteriorated into chaos until His Majesty entered the room and put a stop to it. Wesley was mortified and felt his chances with the impetuous* princess were surely dashed. His face was even redder than usual. The Smythe girls left crying and Maagy and Cecily had to completely change their clothes and redo hair before anything could continue. In fact, all the children needed cleaning off before the magic show could be presented.

Lady Periwinkle managed to get the party somewhat back on track… good thing there was a generous supply of Spumoni. She enticed them to take seats in front of the stage, as they were served cake and ice cream. The magician, who called himself Merlin The Great, had a number of clever tricks to perform. Audible groans drifted from the audience, as Her Royal Highness took her place beside him.

"I shall be your assistant," she announced. "You're Merlin The Great, so I shall be The Magnificent Princess Maagy."

The first sleight-of-hand* involved pulling birds out of a seemingly empty hat. She jammed her hand into it, before Merlin could stop her, and pulled out a false bottom prematurely. The birds poked their heads up at the wrong time and the trick was ruined. He continued his show, but all his best prestidigitation* came to a similar end. As the children grew more fidgety and exasperated, the poor man gave up and went right to the finale. He rolled a large, elaborately painted wooden cart onto the stage. The impressive box drew gasps from the crowd. The children were immediately intrigued and he, once again, had their undivided attention. He asked for a volunteer to step into the box and vanish.

"It's my birthday and I'm the Crown Princess so I shall be the one!"

Against his better judgment, he went along with her wishes and opened the front, helped her in and closed it. Upon doing so, she straightaway screamed to be let out. She proceeded to give a detailed description of the inside and promptly burst out the back of the box and plopped onto the floor, which totally ruined the moment for everyone. The children moaned in unison and one or two stormed out in disgust. Maagy's tempestuous behavior made it difficult for anyone to accommodate her demands. The king apologized to the magician and staff for the mayhem and tried to cajole* the remaining children into staying for more fun, but they all left, tired of her selfishness and sulking. He finally sent her to her room to ponder her bad behavior. She opened most of her presents alone, then gave up and fell asleep. As he climbed the stairs, weary from the disastrous day, he wished his queen were still with him.

"She would know how to handle this," he thought. "I must do something to set my little girl upon the right path."

The next morning, the king rose before dawn. As his *Gentleman of the Bedchamber** packed his bags for travel, he went to his daughter's room and tapped lightly on the door.

"Maagy, Dear, it's Daddy. Wake up. We must get an early start."

She opened her sleepy eyes to see the sun had not yet risen.

"Daddy, why did you wake me? The sun isn't even awake."

He took a deep breath to strengthen his resolve and began to speak slowly, but in a serious manner he was loath* to use on her. It was as if he'd practiced it all night.

"Today is the day you begin your journey toward the throne of this kingdom. Your behavior yesterday was unacceptable. It was

willful, spoiled, rude and self-centered. Raising you without your mother… rest her soul… has been difficult. I fear I've failed you, my child. But, you shall not fail your mother or me. In only a few short years you will ascend the throne and have decisions for the entire Commonwealth resting in your palms. You must be prepared."

As she listened to his words her heart began to pound. She had never heard him speak in that tone of voice. She slowly opened the door and saw him as she had never seen him before. He was serious and worried… and it frightened her.

"But Daddy, you have many chancellors and advisors who will tell me what to do. And I can *always* ask you. I only have to preside at state meetings and wear Mummy's crown and look official."

The king saw his little girl as he had seen her many times before. She was spoiled, to be sure, but she was innocent and full of wonder, as any child should be, and it pleased him immensely. He saw the glimmer of his belovéd queen in her sweet smile. He was even more resolute on the task ahead.

"Get dressed, Child. I've summoned Lady Cecily to help you pack a few things in a travel bag. You'll be gone for several months. We'll send for the rest of what you need."

"Several months? Are you joking? Where are we going, Timbuktu?"

"We're going to the Summer Castle where I should have been taking you all along. I have a League of Kingdoms Summit meeting there next month so it's the perfect time. The caretakers are a wonderful couple who can teach you many lessons, which I have not. They will help you become the woman I know you can be."

Maagy groaned… and grumbled… and whined… and threw things… and stomped her feet… as she and Lady Cecily packed. Her father sat and waited patiently.

"Aren't you coming with me, Cecily?"

"No," the king replied. "I thought it best we go alone… just the two of us. I've given her permission to spend time with her mother for the summer. Is that acceptable to you, Lady Cecily?"

"Oh, yes, Your Majesty! I do miss my mum and will enjoy the summer with her. Thank you, for your kindness. Have a safe and enjoyable journey, Princess Maagy," she said, as she curtsied and was gone.

"But who will play with me and do my hair? Who will help me choose my frock* for the day?"

"I'm sure you'll manage. Now finish up, will you? We must be going."

Avington Palace was the official home of the royal family. It was built on top of Aving Mountain, which stood alone in a vast plain region in the east central portion of the kingdom. The capital city was at the base of the "*mountain in the clearing*", thus the name, Montclair. North of the royal palace, in the foothills just below the apex of where the Depopulo and Sagamathia mountain ranges met[2], stood the magnificent Whitmore Castle at the center of a sprawling estate, the childhood summer home of King Henry. Several quaint and charming villages surrounded the base of the estate. Among them were Winter Garden, Berryville and Summer Valley. His Royal Majesty had fond memories of his days at Whitmore. He had even taken Maagy there when she was a baby, but she had no recollection if it. The caretakers of the castle, Grandpa Kris and Grandma Polly, were a rather elderly couple, thought by many to be enchanters. Rumors had spread for generations about the pair and no one could remember anyone else ever caring for the place. Even the oldest citizens remembered… from their childhood days… the same two people living on the estate… a most curious situation… as it would have made them well over one hundred years old. Nevertheless, the king knew the couple to be both wise and kind. They were, after all, there when he was a boy, and given his father was *not* so kind, they had been a welcome influence in his life.

2 Please refer to Glossary; Maps

The old man had taught the young prince to fish and lawn bowl. He had also taught him horsemanship and agriculture. The old woman had baked delicious confections and let him lick the spoons and hang on her apron strings when the summer storms raged outside. These distractions had helped to pass the endless, hot summer days and had taken the sad little fellow's mind off the fact his own father was so cold and unfeeling. Henry's mother was the one who insisted he spend his summers there, in spite of his father's objections, so he was sure the two could help him prepare the spoiled princess to be a wise and kind queen.

As the royal entourage approached Whitmore Estate, he could see nothing had changed. The huge Fir trees he darted between as a boy, playing Knights and Dragons, still lined the lane. He had spent many hours swinging on the iron gate in the wall surrounding the farmland and forests at the base of the hill where the castle was perched. The climbing roses still made an archway at the beginning of the cobblestone path leading to the main entrance. He had picked many a blossom from those bushes for his own dear mother and for a beautiful young princess before he married her. The fishing pond and the archery range were still there and just as inviting as they were when he first saw them. The smell of morning pastries filled the warm summer air. Maagy opened a sleepy eye and realized she was in the carriage. She began to remember being awakened by her father for an early morning journey. She hardly had time for tea and toast when she climbed into the seat and snuggled into a soft pillow in her daddy's lap for the predawn adventure. Now, it was light and she could see the sun was up. It was a beautiful day with blue sky and not a cloud in it. She sat up and rubbed her eyes and yawned.

"Well, hello, my sleeping beauty. How is Her Royal Highness today?"

"Very well, thank you. Where are we, Daddy?"

"We are just arriving at the Summer Castle, and I'll bet we're in time for breakfast."

Just then, she smelled the delicious aromas that always surrounded the castle, the fresh breads and blueberry muffins. The smell of bacon cooking was almost too much to bear. She realized tea and toast had long since gone from her tummy and she was quite hungry. As the carriage rumbled up the long, winding road, she wondered why it was so important to rush there… before dawn. After all, she had only just turned thirteen. She hadn't even had time to open all her birthday presents.

"What if someone gave me a puppy in one of those unopened packages?" She thought.

Then her mind wandered back to the conversation before the journey began and she remembered the worried look on her father's face. She got the same scared feeling she had when she saw that look.

"Daddy," she said, gently, "why did we come here… now… this very day? Is there something wrong? Have I done something wrong? Is there something wrong with you? Are you sick, Daddy?"

The sudden rush of seriousness from his daughter took him by surprise.

"Oh, no, my child… I'm well… never better. You haven't done anything wrong. Everything is fine. Why would you think otherwise?"

"Because you scolded me and said I was spoiled and self-centered and that's when you said we were coming here. Are you tired of me, Daddy? Did I make you angry? Are you going to leave me here forever?"

It was then he felt as he hadn't felt in years and remembered how hurtful it had been when his father had said unkind things to him. He realized the impact of his harsh words on the tender heart of his child. He wrapped his arms round her and held her close.

"Oh… my darling child… I deeply regret hurting your feelings. What I said was your *behavior* was spoiled and self-centered. I must admit, I *was* angry, but I'm not anymore and I would *never* leave you *anywhere* forever. You're my beautiful little girl and I love you more than life. Sometimes, when we say things in a moment of weakness… or anger… we don't comprehend how our words affect the other person. When I said your behavior was unacceptable, I was reacting to your rudeness to the kitchen staff and your birthday guests. I was, also, thinking how angry I was with myself for not starting earlier teaching you the life lessons you'll need to be a well-respected person and a beloved queen. So I thought, 'There's no time like the present!' Besides, we haven't been here in years. I've missed it terribly and kept you from the joy of knowing this place. We are not here as punishment, but rather, to enjoy holiday together. Does that answer your questions? Are you still frightened?"

The little girl looked hard into her father's eyes.

"And you're *really* not angry with me?"

"No, I'm *really* not angry with you."

The carriage made one last turn through the gates of the castle grounds. It was a good thing, too, for she could hardly contain her distress from hunger. The smell of bacon and muffins and coffee was even more intense, and the earlier conversation had left her with an even bigger appetite. As the carriage came to a stop, one of the giant wooden doors of the castle creaked open. An elderly couple, with great smiles on their faces, emerged with open arms.

"Henry!" The old woman shouted.

"Henry, My boy!" The old man echoed.

Both ran down the castle steps like youngsters waving their arms and laughing all the way. She had never heard anyone call her father anything except, Your Majesty, Your Royal Majesty, Your Royal Highness or Sir. But here were two strangers calling him "*Henry*". This was odd, indeed. He flung open the carriage door and sprang to the ground like a man half his age and dashed up the steps… two at a time… with arms wide. Maagy watched in amazement as the three hugged each other… and laughed… and cried… all at once. She wasn't sure what to do. She was accustomed to meeting people, for the first time, in a much more formal way. They bowed and curtsied to her. How should she handle this situation? Since she was still a little uneasy about all the events and conversations of the morning, she did not want to make a mistake and upset her father. Now was not the time to be a spoiled little princess. So with great dignity and all the maturity a thirteen-year-old girl can muster, Princess Maagy emerged from the carriage and stood straight and tall. She hoped no one could see her knees shaking or hear her teeth chattering. The woman suddenly broke from the two men and headed down the steps toward her. She felt a wave of weakness and an impulse to run as fast as she could in the opposite direction, but her feet were nailed to the ground. The woman was upon her in a heartbeat. She stopped short and stared for a second and then let out a tremendous laugh that took Maagy quite by surprise.

"Oh my goodness!" The woman said, joyfully. "You are the *spitting image* of your mother and just as beautiful!"

Tears began running down Maagy's face and she was frozen in fear. That's when the lady stopped laughing.

"Oh, my dear, I've frightened you to death. There's no need to cry. I won't come any closer."

Maagy didn't know what she would have done if the woman hugged her the way she had hugged her father. She couldn't remember anyone ever hugging her… except him. She was not accustomed to people touching her… showing her affection… or running toward her and laughing… or speaking of her mother. Somehow, the lady must have understood and, instead, held out her hand.

"Welcome, Your Darling Highness. What a beautiful young lady you have grown up to be."

Maagy timidly reached for the hand and was surprised to find it so warm and soft and gentle. She knew, immediately, she had nothing to fear. In all the excitement, she had forgot how hungry she was, but before she could address the subject, the two men came down the steps.

"Maagy, I am pleased to introduce you to the caretakers of this castle, Grandma Polly and Grandpa Kris. This is my daughter, Princess Melania Abigail Alice Grace… Maagy for short."

Grandpa Kris bowed graciously and Grandma Polly curtsied.

"It is a pleasure to see you again, Your Grace," he said. "You were but a tiny thing when you were last here. You've grown up to be a charming young lady."

"Thank you, Sir. It is my pleasure to make your acquaintance. But could we please eat? I'm quite hungry. All I've had were tea and toast before dawn."

"Maagy, Please don't be rude," her father whispered.

"Nonsense," Grandma Polly spoke up quickly. "The girl is hungry and we have breakfast ready. Let's not stand on ceremony. Come in and eat!"

Maagy instinctively grabbed her father's arm, as they all ascended the stone steps to the portico*. She felt small, indeed, approaching the massive doors. Her breath was taken away when she entered the cavernous* foyer with the white marble floors and gold framed mirrors that reflected the sunlight pouring in from the rotunda* windows high above. It was a spectacular scene. Her eyes were wide with wonder and her little hands gripped even tighter to her father's arm.

"Isn't it magnificent? This is where I spent my summers as a child."

"Did Mummy come here with us?"

Before he could answer, Grandma Polly burst into the hallway and flung the doors open wide.

"Come, come, the food is ready to be served."

As they entered the family dining room, the delicious smells and the exquisitely cozy and inviting dining room stopped her in her tracks… she completely forgot she'd asked the question. She loved Avington Palace, but it was darker and more formal. Grandma Polly gently took her hand, led her to a chair and put a white linen napkin in her lap. When King Henry took his seat, Grandma Polly and

Grandpa Kris served the food and then joined them for the absolute best breakfast she had ever eaten.

Maagy settled into her room full of all the things a young girl could want at her disposal. The closet was well appointed with everything from white blouses and casual skirts and dresses in bold shades of green, orange, yellow, blue and purple... even floral prints... to ball gowns... also in brilliant hues... none of which she recognized, but looked as if they would fit her perfectly. Nothing was pastel.

Her bed was large and soft with snow-white linens. The ample pillows were adorned with delicate lace. Her duvet* was white linen with goose down stuffing. Soft gauze curtains surrounded her substantial canopy bed and were tied back to each of the four ornately carved posts. White lace curtains hung long and flowing from three tall windows, which were open so a gentle breeze wafted through the room. All the white was in sharp contrast to Avington Palace. There, she was surrounded by dark-colored, brocade bedding and heavy velvet drapes that blocked the sun most of the time. She never realized how dark it was until she entered this room.

A chaise longue*, covered in purple satin brocade, sat in the corner by the window and the curtains brushed it, back and forth. There was a stripped couch with all her favorite colors in front of the fireplace across from the foot of her bed. She thought it looked cozy and would be a good place to curl up, since there would be chilly nights so early in the summer. A full-length, freestanding mirror was by the door and a dressing table and purple, tufted stool rounded out the furnishings. Her private lavatory* featured a tub carved from a huge piece of marble and polished to a brilliant shine, which dwarfed any she had seen at Avington Palace. She couldn't wait to try it out. There was a large pedestal sink, also carved from marble. Each vessel had its own pump to offer all the fresh bath water she would need. A small wood stove sat inconspicuously* in the corner to both warm the room and heat buckets of bath water.

"Brilliant!" She thought.

Soaps, fragrant oils and perfumes were plentiful and fit for a princess. As she placed her toiletries in the lavatory, the upstairs chambermaid, Estelí Barrineau, unpacked and put away the things from her travel bag. She was a girl of fifteen with a heavy Francinése* accent. She was petite and willowy, with light brown hair and green eyes. Maagy kindly thanked her for helping and she was on her own. She felt safe at Whitmore Castle.

She was pleased to discover her father had brought along all her birthday gifts, including the ones she had not yet opened. She enjoyed seeing the unexpected kindness her guests had extended and was remorseful for having been so unpleasant to them. She was relieved none of the unopened packages contained a puppy. Wesley's gift in the exquisite package was among those brought still wrapped. She saved it for last, since it was the biggest and prettiest. The contents, however, were not nearly so enjoyable. It seems Wesley had recently taken up oil painting and had decided to give her a large self-portrait. Unfortunately, his skill… and, dare say, talent… left much to be desired. She broke into hysterical laughter when she saw a more red-faced than usual, round figure staring at her from the canvas. There stood Wesley in full riding gear, next to an even rounder creature that was surely supposed to be a horse, but looked more like a well-fed Wildebeest. She couldn't stop laughing and thought how fortuitous* to have opened this one in private, avoiding the awkwardness of her outburst. Once she composed herself, she arranged the gifts neatly in the corner with each card carefully attached so as to write her 'Thank You' notes promptly. Wesley's gift, however, was tucked under the bed, to be pulled out only if she needed a good laugh.

Chapter 2
Self Portraits

After changing out of her travel clothes into casual attire, Maagy decided to go exploring in the enormous castle. Her room was the first one, at the top of the grand staircase. Large pocket doors closed off the entire end of the second floor hallway closest to her room. She was ever so curious and tried to pry them open, but to no avail, so she knocked. Estelí unlocked and opened the doors.

"Oui, Mademoiselle, Your Royal Highness? How may I be of service?"

"Oh! I… I don't need anything, thank you. I just wanted to know what was behind these doors."

"These are the household staff quarters, Madam. We live here so as to be of service to the family immediately, anytime of day or night. One need only to pull the cord and someone will respond, straightaway."

"I… I see. I didn't mean to disturb anyone."

"No disturbance at all. It is our pleasure to serve you. Is there nothing I can do for you?"

"No, thank you."

"My room is here, the first one, Your Grace. Our rooms share a common wall, so I am very close, if you need me."

"Thank you," Maagy said, as she tried to see down the hall behind Estelí. "I'm exploring the castle and I was curious, that's all."

"Well, enjoy your adventure, Your Royal Highness."

"Yes… of course… you may go back to… whatever you were doing…"

She continued to gawk past the chambermaid for another awkward moment and then realized she was being rude. What she could see looked mostly like the other end of the corridor, which wasn't closed off, so she decided to give up.

"Well, that's it then. So long."

She quickly turned and headed the other way as Estelí closed the doors. It was then she was stopped in her tracks by the massive chandelier hanging above the foyer across from the second floor landing. Sunlight shone in the windows at the top of the rotunda and reflected off the crystals, bouncing rainbow colors over the pale walls. It was captivating. The tiniest movement of the crystals in the slight breeze drifting through the house sent wildly dancing prisms in every direction. As she twisted and turned to watch the kaleidoscope*, she noticed the large double doors… flanked by stained glass panels… to the only room between King Henry's and her bedchambers. She tried to look through the wavy colored glass, but could make out nothing. Curiosity got the best of her and she eased one of the doors open to have a peek. What she saw made her mouth flop open. Directly across the large room from the double doors were four spectacular windows, which made up the entire far wall and extended upward two-story to the ceiling. The top half of each window was crafted with stained panels depicting familiar stories she remembered from childhood. *Le Petit Poucet* * was on one, *Little Red Riding Hood* on another, *Cendrillon** on a third and *Hansel and Gretel* on the last. She couldn't help but go into this intriguing place to have a better look round.

A staircase, which seemed to float in thin air with no apparent means of support, curved gently up in front of the windows to a balcony, underneath which, there was a stone fireplace with a wide hearth. Popcorn baskets stood guard at either side. She could envision herself enjoying the treats those trusty centurions would yield. There was an overstuffed couch, two large chairs and a low table in front of the fireplace. A woven rug covered part of the slate floor, making it ever so cozy. Bookshelves, two stories high, occupied the other end of the room, with the wall of books curving round toward the center and in front of the lower part of the staircase. Pillows were arranged on a thick, soft rug in front for a reading circle. She remembered her reading circles at home in the palace. She looked forward to being read to by her tutors, as a small child, and then learning to read on her own. There was a ladder, for access to the higher shelves, attached to a track that ran end to end along the ceiling and had wheels on the bottom. Maagy couldn't resist… she jumped on and gave a mighty push. Sure enough, it rolled easily and zipped along, giving her a good giggle all the way. As she breezed past, she perused* the many volumes and noticed all the titles she could see were stories for youngsters.

"This is a library devoted entirely to children," she whispered to herself. "What a perfect idea."

She jumped off the ladder and was so enthralled* by the floating stairs she couldn't resist climbing them. Halfway up, she stopped and surveyed the entire scene. Large window seats with cushions and pillows made for cozy reading spots. She looked toward the curved bookshelves and down onto the reading circle. She looked out the windows and saw the meadow… and beyond, the forest outside the estate wall. She could see the mountains in the distance. She looked forward and up at the balcony with its mysterious darkness beckoning her. Then she looked down at the foot of the stairs behind the curved wall. It was devoted entirely to afternoon tea. Half-size tables and chairs with linen napkins and miniature china cups and saucers were pristine* and ready for half-sized party guests. Cloth fuzzy bears and bunnies and immaculately* dressed porcelain dolls sat patiently waiting for companionship. It was so inviting she forgot about the balcony and descended to reminisce about the tea parties she and her father had shared so many times when she was younger. She wondered when… or if… they would "tea party", again.

With a melancholy sigh and one last look round, she made her way back to the double doors and exited, closing them quietly. She knew she would spend many hours in that room, but was anxious to continue her mission of exploration. She continued down the hallway, past her father's room to the end where it intersected another corridor. She knew the other bedchambers on that level would be unoccupied, as it was customary for only the royal family to have their living quarters on the second floor, as it was at Avington Palace. Each room was lavishly appointed, but she was curious to see them, anyway. The long, wide passage was lined in both directions with ornate* mirrors and elaborately framed portraits. Light streamed in from both ends, as the tower doors were open and it was early in the day. She looked one way then the other, intrigued by the possibilities. She chose a direction and set off, heart pounding with excitement.

Handrails along the walls were beautifully carved and polished to the hilt. She thought the slick marble floors would be wonderful for sliding in her sock feet or for rug racing. Rug racing was where one person sat on a rug and another person pulled it on a slick floor as fast as possible. The object of the game was to cross the finish line ahead of the other team… with no one falling down. She had played it often with the children in the palace court, but decided… since none of them were there… she would give sock-sliding a go. The playful princess slid from door to door peeking into the bedrooms along the hall. Each was beautifully decorated in lightweight materials and cheerful colors. She thought the massive furniture was far less imposing with those delicate touches. Still, they did seem lonely…

all perfect and unoccupied… it made her a little sad, really, so she made sure to close each door completely.

In addition to the unlocked bedroom doors, there were two other doors, which were locked tight. She was quite intrigued by what might have been behind those mysterious doors, but could find no key or secret way to release the contents. She tried peeking through the keyholes, but her eyes were met with only darkness. What were these doors hiding? Why were they locked? She was the royal child; was she not worthy of entry? She tried reaching her hand under one of the doors, but quickly abandoned that idea as it popped into her head something might grab it from the other side. She soon realized her best efforts were yielding nothing and gave up the quest, vowing to return and conquer another day. The corridor ended in the northwest tower with a large parlor. There were cozy couches with soft pillows and a huge fireplace that looked as if it were used often in the winter… a good place to read… or have a nap. There were tall windows on all sides, thus the brightly lit hallway. She walked round the room taking in the view. She could see pastures, farmland and a small village at the bottom of the hill. The mountains were always in the distance. As she continued, she looked out over a meadow and beyond the wall toward the forests with more mountains in the backdrop. Below, she looked out over the courtyard and toward the northeast tower. She marveled at the spectacular view. As she turned to leave, she caught sight of a narrow, spiral staircase that apparently wound its way from top to bottom of the tower. She peered in and looked it up and down. Castle towers were a bit mysterious for Maagy, as she was never allowed in the two main ones at Avington palace. There always seemed something foreboding about the ever-locked doors, so she chose *not* to venture too far in, but rather, continued her hallway expedition… and save those tower steps for another day. The other end of the corridor had more bedchambers and two more locked doors.

"Ah-ha!" She thought, "more mysteries to solve. I shall be far less bored than I had anticipated."

It had crossed her mind, with Lady Cecily at her mum's and none of the palace children to play with, she might find herself with nothing to do for the long summer months. As she made her way toward the opposite end of the corridor, she amused herself by making faces in the mirrors. She was pleasantly surprised to find a balcony at the end with an ornately carved railing. She looked over it and down onto a shiny wooden dance floor. It was the grand ballroom. Two more crystal chandeliers, matching the one in the foyer, hung directly in front of her and beyond it were tall windows letting in the sunlight. As she peered down and across the abyss, she imagined kings and queens in their finery, gliding as if ice-skating to music. As she meandered* round the railing… still watching the imaginary dance… she caught sight of a set of double door across the hall. Upon entering, she discovered it was yet another library. This one had not only floor to ceiling bookshelves… with a rather inviting ladder of its own… but was also outfitted with science equipment, complete with a workbench, beakers and bottles of mysterious liquids of all colors. In addition, there were large, detailed maps, hanging from the ceiling, and chalkboards with references to latitudes and longitudes. She thought this might be the area where school was held… though she had not seen any other children, as yet. There were, however, many things she was not familiar with and, since science was *not* her forte, she thought it best to leave that area alone. As she continued to look round, she discovered a spiral staircase. Curiously though, this one went up, but not down below the second floor. Unlike the staircase in the parlor at the other end, this one was brightly lit from above… not at all mysterious, but rather alluring. She cautiously began to ascend the steps. She went all the way to the top, four stories from the science library, to find it led into an observatory, complete with a monstrous contraption in the center of the floor and star charts hanging round the room.

"Oh my goodness! I believe this is a telescope," she thought, her mind racing. "It makes far-away stars seem close enough to touch. I've heard of it in school. I shall have to ask about this."

She descended the stairs, her head still spinning with excitement. This was a significant finding and she would surely return. As she left the science library, backtracking along the corridor, she paid more attention to the portraits she had seen the first time through. Most were of rather scary looking men… whom she hoped were *not* her relatives. One of the paintings, however, caught her eye. It was of a strikingly beautiful blond woman in full battle gear, complete with chain mail, breastplate, shield and sword… and a *red* cape. She pondered it for a long time. To her knowledge, no women were allowed to serve in Her Majesty's Royal Guard*, other than as security details for her personal safety… and *none* of them wore chain… or carried swords… so *who was this* looking at her from canvas? She could see the resemblances to herself and surmised* it must have been a portrait of an ancestor. Was it her grandmother… or perhaps… her mother? Were there things her father had not told her? She had only snippets of memory of her mother and all were more like dreams, fuzzy and out of sequence. She knew it was a delicate subject for her father. His grief was still palpable* and very little was ever spoken of the deceased queen. She knew to tread lightly, since she had already upset him with bad behavior at her party. Being a curious girl, however, she was anxious to learn this warrior woman's history… as well as more about her mother.

The third floor was accessible by another grand staircase, which wound round the front of the foyer past the massively tall windows. The view from the steps so high above ground, toward the entrance to the estate, was spectacular. There were no rooms on the front hallway overlooking the foyer, as the two-story children's library was on the other side of that wall. Instead, it was adorned with an ancient tapestry depicting a mythical-looking scene of a fierce battle. At the center was a woman on horseback with a sword thrust high in the air.

Maagy thought the warrior woman resembled the portrait, but the tapestry was too old and worn to be sure. She would examine it more thoroughly, later. This floor was much the same as the second in that the corridors held private bedchambers equal in adornments to the royal suites. The difference, however, was there were no pocket doors closing off the east wing hallways. This floor was reserved for visiting dignitaries and would be fully occupied soon. Now, however, it was quiet and abandoned. The hallways were not as brightly lit, either, because the doors to both east towers were closed making it a bit spooky. Maagy knew there was a fourth story, however, her dilemma* was she couldn't find steps leading to it. The circular staircase between the second and third didn't continue. She thought about searching out the illusive stairs… perhaps in the towers… but, as she was wary of towers and it was getting on toward midday, she decided to save that adventure for another time. She made her way back down to the foyer and went into the dining room where she had eaten breakfast. There was no one there, so she continued through into the kitchen and found Grandma Polly. She stopped just inside the door.

"Excuse me, do you know where my father is?"

"There you are," was the cheery response. "I see you found the dresses. I hope you like the colors."

"Yes, I do like them… very much. I hope it was all right to change into one."

"Well, of course. They're yours, my dear."

"The colors are my favorites. How did you know?"

"Oh… perhaps your father told me."

"I see. Do you know where he is?"

"Yes I do. He's gone for a walk with Grandpa Kris. I'm sure they'll be back soon. Is there anything I can do for you, my dear?"

"Um, no… thank you… I suppose not."

She was surprised to find she was rather uneasy in the situation, without her father present. She wasn't sure of her boundaries. She didn't know if she could ask for something to eat or if she should wait for him to return. She started back to her room when Grandma Polly spoke, again.

"Have you had fun exploring, Princess Dear?"

"Yes, the castle is beautiful."

"Well then, you must have worked up quite an appetite. How about a bite to eat? I'll bet you're famished*."

There could have been no words spoken more welcomed, at that moment.

"Oh, yes, please. I am rather peckish *... and thirsty... if you don't mind."

"Of course I don't mind. I'm delighted! Come, sit, I'll get you some nice cold peach tea. What would you like to eat?"

She was relieved and apprehensive at the same time. Peach tea was her favorite. However, now she faced another quandary*... how to say politely she was a rather finicky eater and didn't like most foods... except breakfast... she loved breakfast. Just then, Grandma Polly began to mention various choices.

"How about various cheeses... do you like cheese?"

"Oh, yes, thank you. I like all sorts of cheese."

"And cucumber, do you like cucumber?"

"In fact, I do!"

She was getting excited about the possibilities and was beginning to relax. Grandma set a tall glass of the delicious nectar in front of her. She took a polite sip to make sure it was to her liking.

"Then how about cream cheese and cucumber sandwiches? It's such a hot day. They'll be cool and refreshing. What about strawberries? I'll bet you like those."

As Grandma spoke, Maagy guzzled the entire glass of tea at once. Before she could stop it, a loud belch jumped out her mouth and she clapped her hand over it quickly, eyes wide with surprise.

"Oh! Pardon me! That was unexpected!"

"No worries, Dear. It's just the two of us and I didn't hear a thing.

Here, you have a little drop on your chin," was the nonchalant* reply, as a linen napkin dabbed.

She was taken aback by this odd display of affection, but strangely, not offended by the gesture. No one… *but no one*… touched her except the king. This was a new experience she would have to process.

"Yes, I love strawberries… and cucumber sandwiches would be lovely… thank you. May I please have more peach tea? It's quite nice."

"By all means, you may have all you want. We make it from the best tea imported from the south and fresh peaches. Here, I'll put a slice in for you."

She could tell she was growing fond of this round, cherub-faced woman and could already understand how her father could be so attached to her and to this place. She ate several of the sweet sandwiches and enjoyed the fruit and yet another glass of peach tea. Then Grandma Polly lifted the cake dome to reveal the most sumptuous chocolate layer cake she had ever seen.

"How about a little dessert? Is there room for a piece of cake?"

"Oh my goodness! That is the most luscious cake I've ever seen! Chocolate is my favorite! Maybe just a tiny piece."

"Chocolate cake was your mother's favorite, too," Grandma said gently. "Did you know that?"

"No… I didn't…"

As she ate the confection*, she tried to imagine her mother sitting there.

"Did you know her well?" She asked softly.

"Yes. She was a dear soul."

Maagy couldn't bring herself to ask anything else and Grandma Polly instinctively knew to leave the subject alone. By the time Grandpa Kris and King Henry returned from their walk, Grandma Polly and Princess Maagy were laughing and sharing stories about birthdays and Krispens* past. She was curious as to just how many birthdays and Krispens Grandma had celebrated, but knew it would be rude to bring up the subject, so she let it go… for the time being. When Henry came into the kitchen and saw his daughter at the sink with the elderly woman shelling peas for dinner, he reflected on his conversation with Grandpa, and knew he had made the right decision.

Maagy spent the afternoon continuing her exploration of the castle's first floor and discovered there were several dining rooms… the smaller one where they had eaten breakfast… and an enormous, elaborately decorated one across the hall. The table could seat at least fifty guests easily, many more with all the leaves in place. It was similar to the state dining room at Avington. There was, also, a cozy area on the other side of the kitchen for service persons and two more intimate settings for very small gatherings. There was, of course, the grand ballroom, which she had already seen from above, located through the large dining room on the west side of the castle and another library on the ground floor with a fireplace and books of all types… also with a rolling ladder. There were various comfortable rooms for relaxing, a room dedicated to hunting and steeplechase and a music room for concerts. There was a chapel and a large meeting room… and a playroom… with toys neatly arranged on shelves, none of which looked recently used. This room made her a little sad. She wasn't sure if she was sad for the toys, which were not being played with, or for herself, because she was too old to play with them. She thought about the past and wondered if her mother had played with those toys… or her father… and about the future… if her children would play with them. These were serious thoughts, indeed. Maagy couldn't remember ever thinking about such serious things… except for that morning when she had worried about coming there… and about her father.

She noticed discrete hinges along the side of a bookshelf in the foyer. Upon closer examination, she uncovered a hidden door, which led to a maze of rooms along the front hallway, under the grand staircase and second floor corridors. They were service rooms for

storage of china, glassware and serving items; some held stacks of chairs and more tables. There were long wooden tables on wheels and flat warming stones neatly stacked on the hearth beside a fireplace. The stones were heated in the fire and laid out on the tables. Covered dishes were set on them to keep food piping hot while servers rolled them straight to the table. She was fascinated by the ingenuity. There were passage doors hidden in the tall wainscoting that were not visible from the grand dining room. The doors magically opened and closed, without being touched, when the staff approached. She was captured by these phenomena* and amused herself by going in and out of them, while hoping to uncover the secret. She found another door from the service hall, which led into a large coat closet directly under the upstairs balcony. It was full of heavy winter garments, but when she pushed through them, she discovered the door into the foyer. She thought it would be a fabulous place for hide-and-go-seek on a rainy day… if she could find someone to play. All these halls and closets with the mysterious doors added to the intrigue of her adventures.

The afternoon sun began to sink over the mountaintops and wonderful aromas drifted from the kitchen. Dinner would be served shortly, and none too soon for Maagy. She found her way back to the main entrance where she heard the two men talking. She followed the sound of their voices and discovered a sun porch off the ballroom. There they were, both dressed in overalls and soft white work shirts. They looked almost like father and son. She had never seen her dad dressed so casually. They were watching the sun set over the mountain and reminiscing about past sunsets. She stood quietly for a moment and took in the sight… then spoke softly.

"Excuse me, I don't wish to intrude."

"Nonsense, Child. You couldn't intrude if you tried!" King Henry said. "Come and watch the sun go to bed. He's almost asleep."

She climbed onto her daddy's knee and laid her head on his chest. She felt safe when she was close to him. They watched in silence as the sun slowly sank behind the blue-gray mountain ridge. The sky was ablaze with color and there was nothing to do but relish the moment. Finally, the show was over and dusk fell quickly over the garden and the night birds and crickets began their evening serenade. From the pond, far down the lawn, below the garden, the frogs began their nightly ritual of gossip from one lily pad to another. She had never heard such beautiful music. At home, there were too many people and carriages and dogs barking and industrial sounds to hear the creatures that really own the night. It was an awesome symphony. Maagy suddenly sat up, as her eye caught sight of something she had never seen.

"Oh!" She exclaimed. "What was that?"

"What was what, my dear?" King Henry said, slightly startled.

"That… there it is again… and another there… that blinking… are they falling star?"

"No, dear princess," Grandpa chuckled. "They're fireflies*… lightning bugs*."

"Fireflies? Lightning bugs?"

"Yes, Darling," her father confirmed.

"They are tiny bugs that flit round attracting mates with their displays of colorful light," Grandpa Kris explained. "Their bodies have chemicals, which combine periodically and give off light… their larvae are called glowworms. Lovely, aren't they?"

"Quite… and fascinating… I've never seen them before."

"That's why I brought you here… to experience new things," Henry said, as he reached out and caught a bug. "Here… hold him in your hands. Cup them round him so he won't fly away and peek through your fingers."

"Will he bite me?"

"Heavens, no, child," Grandpa said, as excitedly as a child, himself. "They're completely harmless little beetles."

She took the creature and gently cupped her hands and giggled as it lit up its abdomen to a greenish yellow glow. She opened her hands and the little fellow crawled on her for another moment, blinking several more times, and then taking flight to freedom.

"The city is no place for frogs croaking… or night birds singing… or fireflies blinking," King Henry said with a slightly melancholy tone.

"I think I'm going to like it here," she whispered in his ear.

He smiled and winked, as the dinner bell tinkled its summons.

"Ah… that's the music I want to hear. Polly is ready for us," Grandpa Kris said cheerfully.

The three rose without another word and walked slowly through the castle, Maagy and her father arm-in-arm. As they approached the dining room, the delicious smells were most inviting.

"There you are," Grandma Polly said cheerfully. "Go wash your hands and hurry back. Dinner is almost on the table."

"Yes mam."

She flew to her room and washed up. She brushed her hair and quickly returned to the dining room. As expected, the meal was marvelous. She actually tried two foods she, heretofore, thought she did not like; mushy peas, which she helped shell, and sweet potatoes, with cinnamon butter. She was surprised to discover she liked them both. King Henry was proud of her for both trying the foods and not making a scene doing it. It was even more rewarding she liked them. After dinner, she realized just how tired she was, having arisen before dawn.

"Thank you, Grandma Polly. The meal was scrumptious and I even enjoyed the mushy peas."

"The pleasure was all mine, Dear Child. I'm glad you discovered something new today!"

"I don't mean to be rude. I do enjoy your company, but I'm frightfully tired. Would anyone mind if I went to bed now?"

"*Not at all, Darling…*" "*No, Your Dear Highness…*" "*Not in the least, Princess,*" were the unanimous replies from all three adults.

"Good night, then."

"Good night, sweet dreams, sleep tight and don't let the bedbugs bite," the king chimed, as he kissed her on the forehead with each jovial phrase.

She climbed the stairs slowly, reflecting on the day's events. She felt peacefulness like none she had ever experienced. It was as if a calming spell had befallen her and she did, *indeed*, have sweet dreams.

Chapter 3
Hard Work

Maagy slept and dreamed among a mountain of feather pillows and was still enjoying her repose* when Grandma Polly called her name.

"Maagy, Darling. Wake up. It's time to start your lessons."

She opened a sleepy eye to see the room bathed in warm morning light and the crystals hanging in the window tossing streams of color across the ceiling. She didn't even mind waking.

"Good morning, Grandma. I'm awake."

"Good. Come down soon and have breakfast. We're going to start making your coronation* gown today."

She heard footsteps go downstairs.

"Make my coronation gown? *Make* my coronation gown? We have royal seamstresses and tailors for that sort of thing. Why in the world would I want to make my coronation gown? I can't even sew," she mumbled under her breath, the idea never having crossed her mind.

Thoughts of breakfast overtook thoughts of sewing and she freshened up, dressed quickly in a pretty cotton dress with floral print, which flowed round her ankles in soft swirls, and ever-so-feminine white leather pumps, then joined her father and Grandpa with cheery greetings.

"After we eat you might want to go and change your clothes into something more suitable," Grandpa said.

"More suitable? What do you mean?"

"Well, it's going to be a busy morning... busy week really. First, we're going to the barn where you'll learn to clean out stables and milk cows. Then, we're going to curry the horses and you'll learn to braid manes and tails. Later, I'll show you the silk worms and teach you how to care for them. I shouldn't think you'd want to muck up that pretty dress. Maybe work clothes would be better."

She was speechless, but her thoughts were screaming in protest.

"This is supposed to be holiday. I am the Crown Princess*, soon to be queen. I am here to learn lessons about running the kingdom, not slopping round a barnyard. How dare..."

"Doesn't that all sound like fun, Darling?" King Henry said, enthusiastically, interrupting her silent tirade.

"*Fun*? What could possibly be fun about worms and horse manure? Grandma Polly said we were going to sew today."

"No, Child. I said we were going to *start* making your coronation gown. There is much to do before we begin cutting and sewing."

"Maagy, please don't be rude," the king chided. "This is all part of your education."

"But..."

"No but..."

"Yes Father."

After breakfast, she went to change clothes and on her bed were overalls, a white cotton blouse and a pair of socks, but no shoes. She had no idea where they came from, but she put them on and they fit her perfectly. She went downstairs, reluctantly. Grandma Polly met her at the foot of the steps and gave her work gloves, a burlap gunnysack* and a pair of boots that came to her knees.

"What are these for?"

"You'll see. Run along now… they're waiting for you at the barn."

"Yes, Mam."

Bewildered as she was, she put the gloves in her back pocket, slipped her feet into the boots…which fit perfectly… draped the sack over her shoulder and exited through the main entrance. She circled round the entire castle to prolong her arrival at the barn, dreading what might be in store. Thus began another journey for the spoiled little princess.

She did *not* like the smell of the barnyard one bit. She drew her face into a prune-ish grimace, grabbed her nose and pinched it shut so as not to smell the foul odor. Her father and Grandpa Kris just laughed.

"You'll get used to it," King Henry said. "I did."

"I don't want to get used to it," she whined. "I don't want to be here."

Both men ignored her and continued into the barn. She followed on tiptoes to avoid soiling her boots.

"Grab a pitchfork, Maagy," Grandpa Kris said.

She was practically in tears. She was in the middle of a smelly barn, standing in cow manure with many sets of eyes staring at her, and she had no idea what a pitchfork was. This was not how she had planned to spend her first summer days as a stripling*. The men each took one of the pronged tools from the rack and began scooping manure and wet bedding and tossing it into the wheelbarrow. She knew what that was. The gardener at home had given her rides in their wheelbarrow, but it had only held sweet Pine needles… *never* cow manure.

"Hustle up, Maagy. There's lots of work to be done," Henry reiterated.

She thought about running away or crying, but realized neither tactic would accomplish much, so she put on her work gloves and chose the fork with the shortest handle and began scooping and tossing.

"That a Girl!" Grandpa Kris praised. "You'll get the hang of this in no time."

Sure enough, she soon forgot she was an impetuous princess and instead, became enthralled with the stories and memories the two men recalled. She had never seen her father laugh so much or seem so comfortable in a situation. And here he was, *The King...* in a barn... shoveling manure and having a marvelous time. Before she knew it, the mess was all gone and they were replacing it with clean, dry bedding straw that smelled sweet. Then Grandpa showed her how much hay to put in each manger from the feed room side of the barn. She felt a great sense of pride when the job was done. It was a new experience for her.

She had been so involved in the work she forgot all the sets of eyes that had been watching her so intently. She thought they would be more intimidating, but their soft noses and big brown eyes seemed friendly, so she decided to *like* the cows. She especially liked the one called Julie, who was the color of toffee candy, with a white heart-shaped mark on her face and legs that looked as if she were wearing white stockings. Her eyes were large and round. Her lashes were long, as if someone had curled them. One look into those beautiful eyes and she was happy to have made Julie comfortable. The milking part was just plain disgusting, at first, but Grandpa Kris was patient and she soon learned the proper technique for extracting the milk without hurting the cow. Who knew milk was so hard to get? All she knew was it came in jugs and the nice man on the milk wagon delivered it. She never thought about where the milk actually came from or the gentle creatures that made it... nor did she think about all the people it took to get it to her, fresh and cold.

Once the milk was collected and sent to Grandma, it was time to move on to the horses. Maagy was definitely afraid, at first, and refused to enter the stalls. Her only contact with horses had been watching them pull the royal carriages. She had wanted to get closer, but no one had ever allowed it. After all, she was a princess and a little girl. She had a few of her tantrum moments, but Grandpa Kris was neither impressed nor intimidated by the behavior. He assured her the horses were gentle and she would eventually have to do the job. She was a bit nervous… and another bit perturbed… but finally… gave in and despite her continued stubborn protests, he was right… and she completed the task just fine. It only took a few days for her to feel comfortable round the horses and she took more and more responsibility for their care.

There was one horse to which she was particularly drawn… a young filly named Cupid. She was still growing… lanky and feisty… and didn't always cooperate with her handlers. At first, Maagy was afraid of the head bobbing and hoof stomping, but then… perhaps… she saw a bit of herself in the horse and they became fast friends. Like her human counterpart, Cupid was blond, a color called palomino. She was light golden and her almost-white mane and tail were unusually long for one so young. Grandpa Kris showed Maagy how to groom her and then said a curious thing; he said to collect the mane and tail hair from the currycomb and place it in the gunnysack Grandma Polly had given her at the beginning of the week. When she asked why, he simply said, "*You'll see*". She especially enjoyed caring for Cupid… feeding, grooming and pampering her. Maagy spent hours braiding her tail and mane with ribbons and beads and Cupid seemed to like the attention. She was careful to do as she was instructed with the curried mane and tail hair and by week's end had a gunnysack full of long, golden strands.

She looked forward to the next Festival Day. King Henry had told her about them, but they had just missed the first one, which was on her birthday. Festival Days were the third Saturdays in each of the summer months, when people from the surrounding villages stopped working and came to the castle grounds with picnic baskets to share and wares to sell. He told her about the parade where children actually dressed their pets in outlandish costumes and led them all through the gardens to the delight of everyone who witnessed it. She hoped she and Cupid could participate in the next one, now that her braiding skills were so advanced.

On her first morning as a stable hand, Maagy had been introduced to Jorge Corrales, the stable manager and John Miles, horse trainer, farrier and animal medicine expert. She had also met Claude Wickham and several other stable hands and was comfortable working round them. Under Jorge's tutelage* and watchful eye, each morning seemed easier than the one before. She greeted Julie first and discovered she was actually eager to clean her stall and feed her. The milking got easier, too, when she discovered the cows were relieved at having their utters emptied and the buckets of sweet milk became her reward for a job well done. Unfortunately, there was an incident with the cows on the fourth morning of her newfound vocation. She mistakenly put bedding straw in the mangers and used the prime, sweet hay for bedding. When Jorge discovered the misstep, he became incensed* and scolded her for doing such a foolish thing and causing him much more work. He had to throw away all the feed hay the cows had walked on and could not eat. He had to clean out each manger, put that straw down for bedding, and then fill each one with edible hay. The extra work put the morning milking schedule two hours behind, which caused the cows discomfort and could have affected milk production in the future.

"And most important," Jorge said, "If any of the girls had eaten the straw, it could have caused them gastric distress, since it is not food quality!"

As he chided Maagy, his agitation amplified. He was quite attached to the animals... as evidenced by his calling them "*the girls*"... and he began to shout at her in a language she was not familiar with, but understood the meaning of, nonetheless. She was not accustomed to being reprimanded by anyone other than her father and took great offense. Being the plucky little girl she was, she fired back with a reprimand of her own.

"You, Sir, have no right to speak to your future queen in such a manner! You shall apologize immediately or suffer the consequences! I am the daughter of your king!"

She stomped her foot and threw a water bucket, which made a terrible clamor. Just as it hit a wall of hanging tools, Grandpa Kris and King Henry came round the barn and heard the commotion. Poor Jorge was frozen in his shoes… his eyes wide and his mouth open… he was terrified of what might come next.

"Maagy, what's going on?" Her father asked.

"Oh! Father! Um… I… um… I made a little mistake… in the feeding this morning… and this horrible man is screaming at me in an unknown language."

Upon seeing the king, Jorge gasped and fell to his knees, his face to the ground. Unfortunately, Maagy had been introduced to him as simply "Maagy" and not Her Royal Highness Princess Maagy. King Henry wanted her to enjoy the learning experience without worrying about special treatment. He never dreamed this would happen.

"Stand up, man, and explain."

Jorge was so befuddled he could barely speak. He remained on the ground with his head on his chest and mumbled several unintelligible phrases in what sounded like at least *three* languages, this time. King Henry reached a calming hand and placed it on his shoulder.

"Calm down, Jorge, and stand up! I can't understand a thing you're saying. Take a breath and collect yourself."

"I… most… humbly… beg your forgiveness… Your Royal Majesty. I did not know… the child was… Her Royal Highness

Princess Maagy," he explained, not daring to make eye contact with King Henry.

"Oh dear..." he admitted, "I'm afraid that is my fault."

"I will... collect my things... and leave the castle... immediately. I... I... am your grateful... and loyal... servant... and would *never*... presume to offend. I will be gone... within the hour... if you will spare me... most kind Majesty."

"Spare you from what? And why would you leave? Did my daughter do something wrong that needed correcting? Speak up, Jorge!"

"I... I... I do not... wish to cause trouble... Your Majesty."

Maagy stood by listening quietly and feeling guilty. After all, she *had* made a terrible error. She had also thrown a tantrum and startled the cows with the bucket. She didn't want to see Jorge, now, lose his job by protecting her with silence. She stepped forward bravely and addressed her father.

"Father, I *did* do something wrong and it made more work for Jorge... *and*... I upset the cows," she said, trembling, her voice thin and shaky. "I gave them straw in their mangers and put feed hay down for bedding. He had to fix it quickly before the cows ate any of the straw. It was a huge mess and it cost two hours of precious time. The cows had to wait to be milked... and then... I got angry... and threw a bucket... and made a great clamor. I didn't even say I was sorry. He wasn't out of line, Daddy... *I was*. I'm so sorry, Jorge."

King Henry stood silently for a moment to collect his thoughts. Jorge did not move a muscle... except to tremble.

"I can understand your anger at her blunder, however, perhaps you could have reacted more calmly to the situation. After all, she is only a child, whether a princess or not, and children do make mistakes."

"Yes, Your Majesty... you are correct. I *do* regret raising my voice."

"And Maagy, you, my dear, should not have treated Jorge in such a disrespectful manor by pitching a tantrum, especially since it was your error. I hope you have both learnt something from this. Jorge, please continue about your business and don't even think of leaving us. You are much too valuable."

"But Sir..."

"No buts..."

"Thank you, Sir, for your kind generosity."

"I'm sorry I caused so much trouble," she added timidly. "Next time I'll be much more careful, I promise."

"Thank you, Your Royal Highness. I humbly accept your apology... and please accept my regrets for my behavior."

"Of course... Sir," she replied, as Jorge returned to work.

"Maagy, come here."

"Yes Father?"

He put his arm round her shoulders and they began to walk toward the castle with Grandpa Kris as they talked.

"I'm proud of you, Maagy... owning up to your fault... willingly. I believe it may be the first time. It shows the true nature of your heart and that gives me great joy. It proves we did the right thing... coming here for the summer."

Grandpa Kris gave her a wink of approval.

Maagy quickly grew accustomed to rising early with a smile and eager anticipation for the day. She made her bed, washed her face and cleaned her teeth before going down to a cheerful breakfast with family. She and Estelí were becoming quite friendly, as the chambermaid's personality was warm with a great sense of humor, which Maagy found refreshing... unlike the stuffy Courtier girls she knew at Avington Palace.

"Madam, I will be most pleased to make your bed. You are not expected to do it for yourself."

"Nonsense! It's fun… I never knew how nice it could feel to do something so simple. Thank you, just the same, Estelí."

When Jorge noticed her dedication to the barnyard tasks, he assigned her more and more responsibility. She worked tirelessly and found herself quite proud to stand back and survey her accomplishments. Her milking skills improved drastically over the first week and she made fast friends with her four-legged charges. Luncheons with Grandpa, Grandma and her father were always adventures, with occasional picnics by the pond and the endless stories of by-gone days. Afternoons were filled playing tag with Cupid in the pastures or exploring the massive fields with the farmhands taking her under their wings and teaching her planting techniques. She learned to climb the giant, ancient tree at the back gate… the one with huge routes taller than she. King Henry taught her to catch frogs and stand still so a butterfly would land on her head. Grandma Polly kept her occupied with indoor things, as well, like cooking and knitting and polishing silver and setting tables. Each night of welcome sleep brought her peaceful dreams and in some of them, she even imagined her mother was there, too.

Chapter 4
Locked Doors

Gram-P and Poppy… affectionate names Maagy chose for her newly adopted grandparents… had definitely kept her busy since arriving at Whitmore Estate. She hadn't had a spare minute the entire first week to satisfy her curiosity about the locked doors on the second floor. Finally, on Tuesday of the second week, a small rainstorm rolled through the valley and she was stuck inside for the afternoon. King Henry took the occasion to hole up in his bedchamber and work on plans for the up-coming League of Kingdoms Summit. Luncheon was over and the castle seemed deserted. Maagy was intrigued by the noise her heels made on the marble floor in the foyer. It echoed all the way to the top. She occupied herself by stomping out various rhythms and listening to the ricochet off the rotunda ceiling, but it lasted only a few minutes until she was bored. She climbed the stairs, tapping her toe on each step just to make a racket. She stomped back and forth in the second floor hallway for the same purpose. A voice called out from behind the closed door and startled her.

"Maagy, what are you doing out there? Have you brought Cupid upstairs with you?"

"Oh, sorry Daddy. I didn't know you were in there. What are you doing? May I come in?"

She had peeked inside all the other bedchambers, but his remained a mystery. She was still curious to see in and thought it might be the perfect opportunity.

"I'm working on the Summit, but you may come in for a moment."

She pushed open the door and discovered she was a bit nervous about intruding on his privacy. She entered slowly and stopped just inside.

"Come on in, Darling. It's all right. I'm not too busy."

She went next to him and put her arm round his shoulder. She looked at the papers on the desk.

"What is all that?"

"A lot of mumbo-jumbo, I'm afraid. These are reports of various activities by one of our members. He's causing a great deal of trouble and that's why we're meeting next week. By the way, I want you present in the sessions. You should become familiar with the way these things work. What can I do for you, My Dear?"

She looked round and recognized the layout was similar to her room, but not at all what she expected the king's quarters to look like. The furniture was plain and roughly carved. A patchwork quilt was his coverlet. The sheets and pillowcases were white linen with no adornments. The upholstered chair in the corner was worn and frayed, but looked ever so comfortable. The curtains were of the same gauze material as those on her bed.

"Is there something on your mind, Maagy?"

"Um… no… not really. I just wanted to know what your room looked like."

"And?"

"And… well… I'm a bit surprised… it's not more… grand."

"Grand?" He queried with a chuckle. "Why should it be grand?"

"Because you're King and kings are supposed to have grand surroundings."

"These *surroundings*, as you say, are exactly what I need. I come here to get away from all the pomp and grandeur. This is where I can relax and be myself. These things bring me comfort."

"Why?"

"Well, the bed for instance, I whittled it myself… when I was young… I built it as a wedding gift for your mother. She loved it. So I keep it here. My Francinése grandmother made the quilt from bits of fabric from my childhood clothing, table clothes, curtains, my grandfather's uniform… all of which I remember. So when I sleep under it, I feel a special kind of warmth. That old chair was my mother's favorite reading chair. She sat right there and read poetry to me while I looked out onto the meadow. So you see, this is all the 'grand' I need."

"You built the bed for Mummy?"

"I did."

"Daddy, why don't you ever talk about her?"

"Because it hurts."

His blunt statement stunned her. A flood of emotion overtook her.

"Does it hurt to look at me? You always say I look like her."

"Oh, My Darling, no! Looking at you is the greatest joy of my life. You *do* look like her and I live to see her in you, every day. That is not what hurts… but I really can't explain any further. I do have work to do, so perhaps you should run along and play," he added quickly.

Once again, as many times before, she recognized the sadness in his eyes and knew to press no further. She diverted his thoughts with a question, which had been bothering her for a while.

"Daddy… do I have a surname? Everyone else in school has one, as well as their noble titles, but I don't know mine."

"Officially, the answer is no. Since you are a royal, a surname is not necessary. Surnames are for connection to family roots… lineage. As the Crown Princess, your lineage is of the royal line and well known. You are Her Royal Highness Princess Maagy, Duchess of Wentworth, as was your mother, but if you wish to use a surname it could be Wentworth. You may be Duchess Wentworth or Princess Maagy Wentworth, if you choose."

"But… you're Duke of Covington. Does that count?"

"I am Duke of Covington in Aradinia, where our estate, Auburndale, is located… Covington Province. So, I suppose you could use either name… Covington or Wentworth. They are both your heritage."

"Why don't royals have surnames?"

"It goes back many centuries when people had only one name and they were associated with a location, such as… oh say… John of Avon… or Margaret of Stanley. People were distinguished by their village or county. Well… then, as there were more Johns and Margarets, they became known by their skill or their job. Back then, John Miles… and who knows where Miles originated… might have been John the Farrier… his family might have then evolved to present day as the Farriers… John and Rebecca Farrier. Do you understand now?"

"I suppose… I still wish I had a proper surname."

He chuckled at her consternation*. She noticed a closed door not like the others. She knew which were the closet and the lavatory, but this one was extra.

"Daddy, where does that door lead?"

"I forgot about that room, it hasn't been used in so long. Open it."

She did and found an immaculate nursery.

"Who lived in here?"

"You did, the few times I brought you here, when you were a baby. That's where you slept. That door through there goes into the hallway. I kept it locked so you wouldn't escape. Do you remember it?"

"No. I wish I did. It's lovely and sweet," she said as she dragged her finger along the railing of the crib. "Did Mummy come, too?"

"I must get back to my work…"

"So this is one of the locked doors on that corridor?" She said quickly, changing the subject.

"Yes, why?"

"There are two doors locked… what's inside the other one?"

"I'm not sure. I think it's just a storage closet. Some old books and rubbish are in there… I really don't remember. Maagy, darling, I really must…"

"Where is the key? May I have it?"

"I've no idea where the key might be, it's been so long."

"If I find it, may I use it and have a look?"

"I suppose," he shrugged, giving in to her persistence. "What a curious little soul you are. Go on, have your adventure. Look for the key to the mysterious locked door. I do *need* to get back to work."

"Don't work too hard. After all, we are on holiday," she said as she turned for the door and then stopped. "I didn't mean to make you sad, Daddy."

"Maagy… *you*… do not make me sad. Now come give Daddy a hug."

She threw her arms round him and held on tight for a few extra moments, then kissed his cheek and left, closing the door behind her. Her mission was set. She would find that key before sundown. She turned down the hallway with the two locked doors. She figured out which one was the nursery attached to her father's room and left it alone. She checked the other to see if someone had unlocked it during the week when she wasn't looking, but found it still unwilling to give her access.

"Now, if I were a key to a mysterious lock, where would I be hiding?"

She pulled a chair over and stood on it to feel above the facing, but it wasn't hiding there. She looked under a vase of flowers, but it wasn't there, either. She sat down on the floor and thought for a moment.

"When I hide something small, I put it in something bigger so no one will suspect it's there."

She strolled down the hallway looking into each of the rooms until she saw a china box with a top on a dressing table.

"That's it! It has to be in there!"

She went to the box and opened it and *found a key*. She ran to the mystery door and put it in the keyhole, her hands shaking with anticipation, and gave it a mighty turn… nothing. It didn't budge. It was not the right one.

"Horse feathers!"

She continued her quest looking in every box, under every lamp and rug and into every drawer in every room on the hall. She was fully occupied for several hours. She worked her way to the end of the corridor, into the tower parlor and back, again. As she meandered past the portraits, a thought struck her. She had found notes, necklaces and various other sundries hung on hooks on the backs of some of the wooden picture frames along the family hall at Avington Palace. She began to run her hand behind first, this one… then, that one… with no luck… until low and behold… she discovered another key… hanging about half way up one of the frames.

"This must be it! It's the only other key on the entire floor!" She exclaimed, forgetting she was talking to herself.

She raced to the door, put it in and turned. *Voil*à*! The latch surrendered. Her heart pounded. She turned the knob and pulled the door with a flourish. Cobwebs dangled and dust billowed out. She squealed and coughed and waved away the flying debris. The rain had stopped and the clouds had lifted, however, the hallway was still steeped in shadows as it was getting on to evening. She had trouble seeing what was in the dark hole. With some trepidation, she reached in and felt round, hoping she wouldn't encounter a spider angry for having her web destroyed.

What she discovered was her father was right. There was nothing but several cedar boxes containing some very old, tattered books. She pulled one box out into the hall. The books looked like personal records of some sort. She picked one up and opened it carefully, as it was fragile. The writing was nothing she recognized. She couldn't make heads or tails of it and, as they were so dusty, decided they weren't worth her time. There were a few other things piled in with the boxes, but it was too dark to really see them, so she gave up the quest, ever so disappointed the secrets were not more interesting. She shut the door, replaced the key… and only then realized *which* portrait it was… *the warrior woman*! Determined to know her name, she ran to her father's door and knocked.

"Daddy, can you come here, please?"

"What is it? I'm rather busy at the moment."

"Please, Daddy? It'll only take a minute."

When he came to the door, she grabbed his hand and pulled him round the corner and down the hall.

"Did you find the Key? Was there something wonderful in the closet?"

"Yes… and no… just some dusty, old tattered books," she said as she reached the portrait. "Who is that, Daddy? Is it my mother?"

"I've no idea who she is. It's definitely *not* your mother. She was a queen, not a warrior. That portrait has been here for centuries, I suppose. I remember it as a child. I doubt if anyone knows who she is."

"Could it have been my grandmother or great grandmother?"

"I don't know. Why so much interest in the portrait?"

"Daddy, don't you see the resemblance? Don't you think I look like her?"

She struck a pose similar to the mysterious Muse*, minus the sword and shield. He couldn't help but chuckle.

"Don't laugh, Daddy… I want to know who she is."

"Maagy, I've told you, I don't know. Now, I must get back to what I was doing."

"Would Gram-P or Poppy know? After all, they've been here a *long* time, haven't they?"

"They have, but I don't think *that* long."

"How long, Father? Do you know?"

"Maagy!"

"It's just that no one remembers anyone else being here… that's what everyone *says*, anyway. I find that intriguing, don't you?"

"All I know for certain is they were here for me and now they're here for you. Some things we must accept without question. And now you must accept I have work to do. Have fun, Darling," he said as he disappeared round the corner.

"But, Daddy… oh… all right. So many questions without answers… why am I the only one who wants to know?"

She took one last look at the woman on the canvas and drifted slowly along the hallway, dragging her hand on the wall, to the balcony overlooking the grand ballroom. She rested her elbows on the polished railing with her chin in both hands and stared at the cavern below. She pondered the fact her father was more concerned about the meetings taking place there, soon, than he was about his own daughter. She sat quietly for a while longer, not noticing dusk had fallen. Her melancholy* was interrupted by the dinner bell and she decided hunger was stronger than self-pity and started down to the dining room. King Henry was emerging from his bedchamber to do the same when they met in the hall.

"So… you found the key?" He asked jovially. "But no great secrets to discover?"

"Yes, I found it. And, no, there were no great secrets… just some dusty old boxes of ancient-looking books… as you predicted. It was too dark to see the rest of what was in there, so I put the key back… where I found it."

"Why so glum? You'd think someone had stolen your spumoni ice cream!"

"Just tired, I suppose… and hungry."

"Well, we can fix both of those problems. It smells like another tasty dinner is imminent and your fluffy pillows will solve the rest," he said as he put his arm round her and they descended the stairs.

The meal was delicious, as always. She looked round the table at her new family and the doldrums lifted. They enjoyed good food and shared stories and news of the day. She mentioned the portrait, nonchalantly, and asked Gram-P and Poppy if they knew anything about it. They said it had been there since before they came. The king gave his daughter a look that told her to drop the discussion. After a scrumptious dessert, She excused herself and went up to join those fluffy pillows.

Now it was Friday, again, and Maagy had just finished grooming Cupid and walking her round the paddock with a halter and lead. She could hardly believe it had been almost two weeks since she first arrived. She was turning the filly loose in the pasture when Grandpa Kris called to her from the barn.

"Maagy, come here, child. I've saved the best for last."

She could only imagine what he had in store. After all, she had milked cows, collected horsehair and been knee deep in manure. What more could there be?

"Are you coming?"

"I'm on my way," she called, as she gave Cupid one last bit of carrot and released her with a gentle pat on the neck. "I'll see you later, my lovely friend."

She turned and trudged up the path to the barn. She must have had a sour expression, because Grandpa Kris took one look at her and burst into laughter.

"What a face! You'd think I was sending you into battle!"

"Oh, I'm so sorry, Poppy," she said, embarrassed he might think she was not enjoying her experiences. "I was just thinking I would miss Cupid today."

"Not to worry, Dear. You'll be back in no time. You're going to love what I have in store for you now!"

Maagy saw in his face the excitement of a child on Krispen

morning and hoped she would be as enthusiastic. He began walking fast down a path that led into a grove of fruit trees. She could hardly keep up. They cleared the orchard and continued into a sprawling grove of Mulberry trees, full of lush green leaves. As they moved through the grove nearly running, she could see a large greenhouse just in front of them. As they approached the door, Grandpa Kris stopped and caught his breath as she caught up.

"This is the most amazing thing in the kingdom!"

He slowly opened the door to reveal thousands... hundreds of thousands... of moths and cocoons and web-like structures all over the inside. She gasped in surprise.

"What is this?" She asked, her eyes wide with apprehension.

"This is our silk worm farm! Isn't it magnificent?"

She wasn't sure what to say. It looked creepy, in her opinion, with all the webs and cocoons hanging everywhere. The large moths were certainly beautiful, but she wondered what they were doing in there.

"Um, sure... magnificent... actually, I have no idea what I'm looking at, Poppy."

"Oh, well, of course you wouldn't know, would you? How foolish of me to think. Let me explain. This is where the silk worms manufacture silk threads."

"*Worms*? *Thread*? *Silk*? Poppy, what are you talking about? We *buy* silk from the East... what do *worms* have to do with it?

"Everything! But silk worms are not actually worms in the true sense of the term... *worm*. They are actually the larval stage in the life cycle of moths. They just happen to produce incredibly strong fibers while spinning their chrysalises*."

"Poppy... I simply do not understand... what you're telling me."

"Let me start from the beginning. You see the moths flying round? Well, they have one purpose in life... to make other moths. Once a moth emerges from the cocoon, it has only twelve hours to find a mate and another twelve hours to lay eggs."

"That's only one full day!"

"Exactly! The eggs take about twelve days to hatch, then another twenty-four days to grow into big, fat, mature silk worms."

"Oh, those... creatures," she said, pointing to one on a leaf. "I've seen them crawling in trees! I thought they were butterfly caterpillars."

"Some of them probably were, as the two are quite similar, depending upon the species."

"Fascinating... but what does it have to do with..."

"I'm getting to it. During those twenty-four days, they eat voraciously*. We feed them lots of freshly cut Mulberry leaves. We keep them fat and happy inside the greenhouse or worm house, if you like, to protect them from predators, like birds and insects. Then they spin their cocoons. Ah, the cocoons!" He continued as he led her to one on a branch and caressed it. "These are what we are waiting for. Each chrysalis can yield up to *thirty-six hundred feet* of raw silk fibers."

"Wait... did you say the *chrysalis* is made of silk fibers?"

"That is precisely what I said! And each one can yield twelve hundred yards."

"Incredible... absolutely incredible!"

"Didn't I tell you it was the best? In five days they emerge as moths and the process begins again. We harvest the empty cocoons, begin unraveling them and spin them into thread. Do you follow me, so far?"

"How on Earth do you unravel them?"

"They are soaked in warm water and then tiny delicate fingers patiently unwind them."

"So you're saying these tiny creatures are responsible for all the real silk?"

"Well, these and a few billion others round the world. It's a process that has been going on since ancient times; a great example of how even the tiniest of creatures can have a huge impact on the world. Now the story doesn't end there. Once the cocoons are unraveled, the fibers must be separated, combed, cleaned, spun together for strength into fine thread, dyed, dried, and woven. The whole process takes anywhere from two to four months from harvest to cloth. It takes many dedicated workers to care for the creatures, harvest, spin and weave. All must do their jobs perfectly to produce fine silk."

She was speechless. She had never before received so much interesting information in such a short time. This certainly overshadowed the disappointment of the locked closet, earlier in the week. The two spent several more delightful and informative hours in the silkworm house. By the time they got up the path and through the groves, she was quite exhausted and still had evening chores. Of course, she had to see her beloved Cupid. As she combed and curried her, she couldn't help but think about the silk worms and all the work it would take to make enough material for her coronation gown. She realized she was beginning to think more about other people and creatures and less about herself. She spent considerable time contemplating this revelation. They walked round the paddock once more before Maagy led the filly into her stall and gave her a generous portion of hay, kissed her goodnight and headed back to the castle.

The sun was on its way behind the mountaintop. She knew dusk would be spectacular. There were just enough clouds to reflect the sunset colors. The fireflies would be out soon and the whip-poor-wills* would start calling to each other. It was time for dinner and the aromas were especially wonderful. She entered through the kitchen door.

"Hello, Josephine," she greeted the kind lady who helped Gram-P.

"Oh, Your Grace!"

She dropped to her knees and bowed her head. Maagy was

surprised and stopped dead in her tracks, forgetting for a moment what to do next.

"You must tell her she can get up and go about her business," Grandma whispered, as she came to her rescue.

The dear, sweet lady could hardly walk and there she was, on her knees. Maagy leaned down and gently took her hands.

"Josephine, you may get up now and I will help you. You may go about your business. And Josephine, you must never kneel before me again. You have earned a place of honor in this kingdom and you shall remain on your feet whenever I am in your presence, even when I am Queen."

She looked to Grandma Polly to see if she had overstepped her authority. The proud grandmother was looking back with a warm smile of approval and she knew she had done the right thing. She poured a cool glass of tea, thanked the ladies for their work and went to the veranda to watch the sunset. As she sat in silence watching the show, she reflected on her time at the Summer Castle. It seemed only yesterday she had arrived in all her finery and pomp. She went back to that very first morning in the barn among the animals with Grandpa Kris and her father. She marveled at how peaceful she found it, now.

Maagy felt proud of how far she had come with mucking stables and feeding livestock and milking cows. She was learning to train Cupid and Mister Miles had given permission to begin using a training bridle on her. Her bones were still soft and growing, but he saw no harm in getting her used to the tack. Suddenly, a large moth appeared in the dusk, flying circles round the lantern on the porch. Maagy couldn't help but chuckle and wonder if this big fellow had escaped. She reflected on her work inside the castle, as well. Grandma Polly had taught her to separate cream from milk to churn butter. She was fascinated to learn milk could be transformed into so many tasty foods. They made cottage cheese, yogurt and sour cream. She whipped sweet cream for the berries at dinner.

She couldn't wait for all the various cheeses to be complete, as they wouldn't be ready until Krispen. Gram had promised to send some for the holidays. She would have to exercise patience and wait, which was something she was not accustomed to doing. She had made her own bed every day and had learned how to do laundry and ironing, despite Estelí's gentle protest.

Grandma had started sewing lessons by teaching her to sew on buttons. There were always buttons to be sewn; large buttons on overalls, small buttons on shirts. With all the people working at the castle, someone always needed a button sewn back. Those lessons were not without incident. She had stuck herself with a needle on more than one occasion and, finally, had a complete breakdown. She tried to use the "*I'm-a-princess-and-you-can't-tell-me-what-to-do*" tactic, but to no avail. Grandma Polly let her know, under no uncertain terms, that she *could* tell a princess what to do because the *king* said so. These little reminders gave her a better perspective and the rest of the sewing lessons were much more pleasant. Grandma Polly finally revealed what she had planned for the mane and tail hair Maagy had collected. She taught her to carefully separate the hair, sort it by length, brush it smooth and wash it. There was an antique spinning wheel in the sewing room just off the kitchen. She taught her to spin a few hairs at a time into fine thread with flakes of actual gold. Then these threads would be twisted into piping that would adorn her coronation gown. It was tedious and sometimes frustrating work. She frequently pricked her fingers on the spindle and the "*Impetuous Princess*" appeared more than once. Nevertheless, she persevered and gained skill by the day.

One might think a princess would be out of sorts at having to do so many chores. But, actually, Maagy was quite pleased to learn so much. She had gained not only skills, but also life lessons from her experiences. Most of all, she had come to appreciate the many people who worked for her and her father. She thought about the kitchen staff, the morning of her birthday, Lady Periwinkle and her guests at her party, and truly regretted her rudeness. Once again, the familiar dinner bell tinkled just as the last of the big red ball disappeared behind the mountain. She sighed in contentment and headed to the dining room. After the usual wonderful evening meal, she climbed the stairs with a sense of pride and peace. She crawled into her welcoming bed and went fast asleep.

Chapter 5
Devine Confections

Maagy had discovered Saturday mornings were not really so different from Monday through Friday mornings. There were stables to clean, cows to milk and mouths to feed. After all, these were living creatures that needed care, no matter what day of the week. This was a new concept for her. At home, she had school Monday to Friday, but on the weekends she slept late and did only what she wanted. She was waited on, hand and foot, and pampered with manicures, pedicures, hair washing and curlers. Her clothes were laid out and she even had help putting them on. But here, she was treated like a regular person and was the one *doing* the pampering.

She made her own bed on *Saturday* morning… just like every other day… and picked up the clothes she was too tired to put in the laundry hamper the night before. Her nails were dirty and the soles of her feet were rough and calloused from running barefoot in the fields. Her skin was beginning to show a healthy tan and freckles danced across her nose. Her long, golden hair… while washed daily… was pulled back in a ponytail to look more like Cupid and hadn't seen a curler in weeks. She had become accustomed to wearing men's long pants or overalls with soft cotton blouses and boots rather than frilly dresses and shiny leather slippers. She wasn't sure how this new fashion sense would be received at home, but she had plenty of time to figure it out before the end of summer. For now, she was confident and happy. After morning chores and the milk had been delivered, Grandma Polly told her to come in as soon she finished with Cupid's morning exercise.

"I have a surprise for you," she teased.

Maagy could hardly wait to find out what it was. She loved surprises and usually whined and begged until the person giving it was so annoyed they gave it to her, straightway. Not this time. She knew she had a responsibility to Cupid. The young horse seemed to look forward to their romps in the meadow and she had been told the workouts were essential for a smooth transition to having a saddle. So, even though she was bursting with curiosity and impatience, she gave the filly her full attention. Once done, she raced from the barn, flung open the kitchen door, and bounced in, her face red and beaded with sweat. She went straight to Grandma Polly.

"I'm ready for my surprise now, Gram-P!"

"Oh, you are most certainly not! You smell like a horse and you are sweaty and red-faced. You need a bath, clean hair and clean clothes. You might want to wear a dress; and you should clean your fingernails. Then, you'll be ready to go."

"Go? Go where?"

"That is for me to know and for you to find out!"

She could hardly bathe fast enough. It seemed to take forever to get the suds out of her hair. Without Lady Cecily to help, she took way too much time choosing her dress. Then she noticed her dirty fingernails and returned to the lavatory and scrubbed them clean. Finally, bathed, dressed, hair clean and in a ponytail, nails scrubbed and teeth cleaned… she remembered that on her own… she emerged from her room and bounded down the stairs, to find the sweet lady waiting with a big smile.

"You look lovely, my dear, and you smell much better. Are you ready to go?"

"Oh, yes! Where are we going?"

"Into town to shop."

She was thrilled. She loved shopping, but at home, it was usually such a process, with guards and escorts and footmen, *et cetera**, it sometimes wasn't worth the trouble. This time, however, she was sure it would be much more fun. They climbed into the waiting carriage and were off with no one but the driver to accompany them. Maagy felt quite grown up. She couldn't help but wonder what this trip would have been like with her mother. She had been thinking about her a lot, during the last month, because of the words her father had said:

"Your behavior... was willful, spoiled, rude and self-centered... Raising you without your mother... has been difficult... I fear I've failed you... But, you shall not fail your mother or me. In only a few short years, you will ascend the throne and have decisions for the entire kingdom... You must be ready..."

She certainly did not want to disappoint him and wondered what her mother would think of her progress since coming to Whitmore Castle. She had tried to be less willful and self absorbed, even though there had been a few impulsive moments. Her thoughts quickly faded to happier ones as she rode through the scenic countryside toward the little town of Berryville.

"Why did they name the town Berryville, Gram-P?"

"Because the land all round is particularly good for growing all sorts of berries... strawberries... blueberries... raspberries... gooseberries. For decades, the local farmers have brought their crops to town to be sold all over the world. Back when it all started, they called the township the berry village. Finally, it was officially named Berryville about a hundred years ago."

Maagy thought about the rumors of the old couple having been at the Summer Castle for over a hundred years. She couldn't help wondering if Grandma Polly had been present at the ceremony when the town was officially named. She did seem to have first-hand knowledge of the events. However, she thought it might be rude to ask and was working on *not* being rude, so she wondered in silence. The carriage finally rocked to a stop in the middle of the town square. There were people strolling across the lawn of the Courthouse, where official records were held and legal matters were attended. Others rushed to and fro, as if late for something or they had a mission in mind. The shop doors were open and merchandise was displayed on the streets like a grand celebration.

"Gram, is something special happening today?"

"No, why?"

"In Montclair, when the shops have all their wares out on the street like this, it's usually a festival or holiday."

"No, this is just a normal Saturday. I guess you'd say it's always a holiday atmosphere in Berryville."

It was so charming she found herself standing in the middle of the street gazing at it. Grandma Polly took her hand and gave her a gentle tug to avoid the carriage coming toward them. As they walked toward the market, she noticed no one seemed to be aware royalty was present. Everyone was pleasant enough and greeted them with smiles and tipped hats, but no one bowed or curtsied or called her "Your Royal Highness". She suddenly felt the urge to stomp her foot and scream. She thought it quite rude of these *peasants* not to acknowledge her with proper respect. After all, she was their Crown Princess. Someday, she would be their queen. How dare they ignore her?

"Gram-P, why are these people ignoring me? Do they not know how to address their Crown Princess?"

"Well, of course they know, but they don't know you *are* their Crown Princess. How could they? You came into town with me, not a royal entourage. You are dressed as any other young girl here, not as a princess. Would you like them to drop to their knees and call you '*Your Royal Highness*' and then follow you round like puppies or would you rather stay incognito* and move through the town as you wish, going in and out of shops enjoying your day?"

She appreciated the wisdom and chose to stay a regular girl. However, she was concerned about her personal safety. She had been warned, many times, not to go outside the palace walls without proper security. She had not thought of it before at Whitmore, because staff had constantly surrounded her and the entire estate was inside a great stone wall. Here, she was out in the open and had no guards or soldiers surrounding her. For the first time in her life, she felt a strange uneasiness in the pit of her stomach.

"Will I be safe here… on my own?"

"Of course, you will. There are several guards watching you at all times. Your father would never allow me to take you out of the castle unprotected. There are at least four armed men and women in disguise watching over you. So, yes, you are safe and may explore the entire town if you like."

"There are women… *armed women*… watching me?"

"Absolutely. I see at least one that I know… a Master in the ancient martial arts… quite capable of defending you, should the need arise."

"Oh… I see… that puts me at ease."

She could explore and stroll and shop on her own. She felt ever so grown up.

"I must go to farmers' market, first," Grandma Polly said. "I need some nice fresh peaches to make a cobbler for our guests tonight."

"Oh, goodie, we're having peach cobbler? We're having guests?"

"Oh yes, lots of guests. The representatives from the surrounding kingdoms are arriving for the League of Kingdoms Summit meeting to begin on Monday. It's a huge night of dinner and dancing afterwards… very busy. Also, the son of your father's good friend, King Rafael, is here to attend in his father's place. Henry and King Rafael have been close friends since boyhood. We're all anxious to see Rudy, all grown up."

"Oh… I didn't realize so much was happening… might I go with you to farmers' market? I've never been to one."

"Of course, you may, but then I must go to Courthouse for a bit. You might want to explore the town then."

The farmers' market was fascinating. All the vendors had samples of their best fruits, nuts and vegetables out on trays for customers to try. She was uncharacteristically brave and tasted cantaloupe, kiwi, casaba melons, macadamia nuts, radishes, beets, and asparagus; she sampled hearts of palm, pine nuts and raw chickpeas. She had never heard of chickpeas, but they were quite good. She had homemade granola and boiled peanuts and rhubarb pie. She tried tomato preserves and tasted clover honey. There were fresh breads and cheeses and some vendors had wine from their vineyards. She didn't know wine could be made from dandelions… but there it was… dandelion wine. The strangest thing, however, was the worm farmer with many buckets of live earthworms to sell to farmers whose soil needed aerating.

She had a wonderful time following Gram up one aisle and down the other, but she was ready to strike out on her own and explore other areas of the town square. She walked back to where the carriage had left them. As she approached the center of town, a wonderful fragrance drew her attention. She followed her nose to the *Creamery and Confections Shoppe.* Once inside, she could hardly believe her eyes. It was a brightly lit, colorful wonderland of candies, cookies, pies and cakes to rival those produced at Whitmore Estate. A vat of hot caramel candy stood near the door with the candy maker stirring in pecans. A pastry chef emerged from the kitchen with a tray of cherry tarts for the display case. Then she saw the ice cream counter with more flavors than she had fingers and toes to count them. Best of all, they had spumoni, her favorite. When she left the market, her tummy felt quit full from all the sampling. Now, however, there was spumoni ice cream right in front of her and she had to have a dish. She strode to the counter.

"I'll have two scoops of spumoni, please."

"Hey you… Girlly… who do you think you are, a princess or something? You just cut the line," a voice shouted.

The loud, unpleasant person took her aback. She turned round to see several people standing behind her, glaring as if she had done something offensive.

"Excuse me," she said, in an authoritative voice. "Are you speaking to me?"

"Yeah, I'm speakin' to you. You cut in line and we been standin' here forever waitin' our turn. You come strollin' in here, actin' like royalty and just cut in line."

She was thoroughly insulted. She most certainly *was* royalty and had every right, as such, *to cut in line.*

"Do you know who you are addressing, Sir?" She fired back. "I am Princess Melania Abigail Alice Grace, Duchess of Wentworth, Crown Princess of Berensenia. You will address me as Your Royal Highness and you will kneel and bow your head in my presence!"

She crossed her arms and set her jaw, waiting for response. Everyone in the shop burst into laughter.

"And I'm Cendrillon's Fairy Godmother," squealed an elderly lady.

"Pardon us all to heck, *Duchess*!" Someone else chimed in.

"You don't look like no princess I've ever seen, with your ponytail and suntan," the clerk sneered.

She realized, indeed, she did not look like herself and remembered what Grandma Polly had said about no one knowing she *was* a princess. Did she really want to make a fuss and get the security personnel involved or did she want to continue incognito and explore on her own? She made the wise choice.

"Begging your pardon, I was just… just… being… foolish."

The chagrined* child backed away from the counter and went to the end of the line to wait her turn, like all the other ordinary people. She was embarrassed at everyone looking at her so hatefully… and furious at the thought she had backed down. It was not her nature. She was accustomed to getting everything she wanted even if she had to throw a tantrum to do so. She folded her arms across her chest and sulked. Finally, everyone had ordered and it was her turn.

"I'll have two scoops of spumoni, please."

"That'll be one and twenty," said the clerk.

"One and twenty what?"

"You know, a buck and twenty pence."

"Oh, you mean money."

"Yeah, I mean money! No money, no spumoni! Hurry it up, Girlly. I got customers."

"I don't have money. My father always pays for whatever I want."

"Well, if your pappy ain't with ya', ya' gotta move out of the way," he said, annoyed.

"But I want my ice cream. I must have it! I want it! I want it! I want it! Give me my ice cream!"

She was on the verge of a full-blown tantrum and her guards were approaching, when a handsome young man stepped up to the counter.

"Please, give the young lady what she wants and charge it to my account."

"Yes, Sir… absolutely, Sir… right away, Sir."

With that, the clerk dug deep into the frozen concoction and plopped two giant scoops of spumoni ice cream into a dish. He added two sugar cookies and a long spoon and set the dish on the counter in front of her.

"The usual for you, Sir?"

"Yes, thank you and please bring it to my table."

It happened so fast Maagy's head was spinning.

"Will you join me?" The gallant youth asked, as he picked up her dish and motioned to a table in the back of the shop.

"Yes… thank you," she said breathlessly, without taking her eyes off him.

She followed him to the table. He put down the ice cream and pulled out the chair for her to sit.

"Thank you."

She could hardly breathe. She had never felt like this before. She was giddy and nervous. Her stomach was fluttering as if she'd swallowed the moths in the silkworm house. She couldn't take her eyes off this beautiful human being in front of her. He was tall with tanned skin. His hair was silky and raven black and his eyes as dark brown as coffee beans. He was slim with fine chiseled features and spoke as gently as a spring rain. His voice was like music and he smelled wonderful. He was well dressed, but not pretentious. She had never before felt such a connection to anyone… other than her father. She was confused, yet strangely happy and contented. She wondered what was happening to her.

"Who… are you? I mean, wh… what is your name."

"My name is Rudolpho, and you?"

"Prin… um… my name… is Mel… um… Ma… my name is… Maagy."

"Your ice cream is melting. You seemed to want it rather badly. Now you're letting it melt."

The clerk set a tall glass of foaming confection in front of him.

"Oh, yes… I… I… do want it. And thank you. My father will pay you back… several times over."

Then she stopped short of saying he was the king. She didn't want to be laughed at again.

"Do you live here?" She asked, putting a spoonful of ice cream in her mouth.

"No. I live in Estadore. I'm here on business."

She wondered what business such a young man could have. She concluded he was trying to impress her by saying he had "*business*" in Berryville.

"Yes, I have business here as well. I live in Berensenia. I come to this quaint little town often," her mouth rattled on before she could stop it.

She took another bite of her half melted spumoni and he took a sip of his sarsaparilla* float. She looked down at the table, but could feel his eyes fixed on her. She looked up to see him… elbow propped on the table, his chin in hand… smiling at her.

"Why are you smiling?"

"Because I like you. You're all spit and vinegar. I like people who speak up for themselves. Are you really Princess Melania Abigail Alice Grace?"

She almost choked. She was mortified he had heard her outburst and witnessed her causing such a scene. She didn't want this *ordinary* boy to feel intimidated by her social status, so she did *not* tell the truth.

"No… not really…. I just wanted to… oh… never mind. How old are you?"

"Seventeen," he answered, still grinning, "and you?"

"Me? Um… seventeen," she blurted out, as she shoveled in a big sloppy spoonful of ice cream. "No, actually sixteen."

She found herself stammering and telling wild tales. She didn't even know why she wouldn't tell him her real age.

"So how old are you, really, Miss Maagy?" He said, reaching across the table and dabbing the corner of her mouth with a napkin. "You missed."

"I just turned thirteen!"

She was doomed. He would surely think her foolish, now he knew she was so young… and had been less than candid about it.

"Happy Birthday. You're quit mature for thirteen. I thought you to be at least… fourteen."

"Really? Thank you for the compliment."

For an undetermined, enchanted period of time, the two sat in silence eating their treats and sneaking peeks at each other. Inevitably, they both looked at the same time and were mesmerized… and embarrassed. Just then, a rather large man in uniform entered the shop and approached the table, interrupting what seemed like time standing still. She instinctively thought he was one of her father's guards and tried to wave him away, but the soldier took no notice of her and addressed Rudolpho.

"Sir, I have seen to those details. Shall we go?"

"Yes, I'm ready. By the way, Maagy, this is Captain Makubar Sistrunk. Mak, meet Maagy… my new friend."

"Pleased to make your acquaintance, Madam."

"How do you do, Captain Sistrunk? I'm please to meet you, as well."

She was reeling. Who *was* this boy? What had she missed? Before another thought could pop into her head, he took hold of her hand and knelt on one knee. He was now at eye level with her… and she couldn't breathe.

"It has been my pleasure to share ice cream with you, My Lady. Perhaps our paths will cross again… soon."

He kissed her hand gently and then stood tall, *very* tall, bowed at the waist and backed toward the door.

"Until next time… Come, Captain, let us be about our business."

He turned and was gone. Her heart was pounding. It was the first time anyone had *ever* kissed her hand. She wanted to follow him, but couldn't move from her chair. Finally, she rose and with shaky knees, went to the counter and addressed the clerk.

"Who was that?"

"Foolish child! That was His Royal Highness Prince Rudolpho of Estadore. Did you really not know?"

He burst into laughter. She was speechless. Grandma Polly entered the ice cream shop and found her still staring out the door.

"Hello, Dear. I thought I might find you here, knowing your fondness for spumoni. Have you had a nice day?"

Maagy didn't respond, but stood… with her mouth wide open… gazing in the distance.

"Maagy? Maagy Dear, are you all right?"

"Yes, Gram-P, I am wonderful! I made a new friend… a *boy*!"

"That's nice, Dear. You can tell your father all about it. In the mean time, we must get home so I can begin dinner preparations for our guests."

"Really? Who?"

She wasn't actually interested in the answer. She was searching the streets for a glimpse of Rudolpho.

"I told you, heads of state and the Prince of Estadore are coming. Did you hear me, Maagy?"

"Sure, a prince... *The Prince... of Estadore?* You mean *Rudolpho? That's who you called Rudy?*"

"Yes, Dear... I did tell you already. Hurry along... we must begin the journey home if we are to be proper hosts."

Maagy's heart raced as she and Grandma Polly hurried back to meet the carriage and driver. She continued to search for the illusive prince, but he was nowhere to be found. She had never experienced such feelings... a combination of fear and shear joy; anticipation like Krispen morning, but tinged with uncertainty; she wanted to laugh and cry at the same time; she wanted to hurry home, but run the other way; the jumble of emotions was unique... and marvelous. What could this mean?

She boarded the carriage and settled in for the ride. Her mind went back to the confectionary and she replayed, over and over, the moment she first saw the handsome youth. She relived every word of their conversation. Each time she did so, the flutters in her stomach returned. Her heart raced and her face flushed with excitement. How would she maintain her dignity? This fellow who made her giddy... made her shiver... was to be her guest for dinner. She would be seated next to him at the table, as per custom. She would surely spill something on him if she continued to tremble so. She worried about not being honest when asked if she were Princess Maagy. She feared he would think unkindly of her.

"He didn't tell me who he was either, so he wasn't completely honest with me," she reasoned under her breath.

"Did you say something, Dear?"

"No, Gram."

Then she remembered she hadn't asked him if he were a prince. She had only asked him his name and he said, "*Rudolpho*".

A feeling of foreboding overtook her. She was ashamed of herself. How would she face him now, as Her Royal Highness, The Crown Princess of Berensenia, as she would be formally introduced? Perhaps she could say she had eaten too much ice cream and had a tummy ache and could not possibly come down for dinner. It would solve one problem, but create another. It would be another lie to cover the first to say she had eaten too much ice cream, since she had eaten hardly any… because she couldn't stop looking at Rudolpho. She could eat a lot of ice cream… especially spumoni… without any ill effects and her father knew it. This was the trouble with lying, as her father had always cautioned:

"Always tell the truth, even if you think there is a good reason to lie. Lying is like a spider's web. It binds you up and holds you captive. The more lies you tell, the tighter the strings. Never tell the first and you won't feel the need for the second."

Now, here she was, in the web, thinking she had a good reason to spin it tighter. Her thoughts were interrupted by the carriage coming to a stop outside the kitchen entrance.

"You've been mighty quiet all the way home. Is something troubling you, my dear?"

"Yes… No! Well… I've just been lost in my thoughts. I have a big decision to make. Can I help you carry?"

"No, the kitchen staff will do it, but thank you for offering. You should go up and choose your formal gown for this evening. Your father wants everything to be perfect. There is a lot at stake. Run along now."

Her wonderful feelings of euphoria were turning to dread. She had fibbed about her identity to, of all people, the son of her father's close friend. It dominated her thoughts. She could hardly enjoy the anticipation of seeing Rudolpho again. She pondered over every dress in her wardrobe, putting on each one several time. Try as she might, Estelí couldn't help. This was so unlike Maagy. Her father said she inherited her eye for fashion from her mother. He spoke so fondly of Queen Melania and how she was always the most beautiful woman in any room. She wondered if he would say the same about her. Would he immediately see the lie on her face? Would it make her ugly in his eyes? She could live with it no longer. She had to tell her father what she had done and apologize for ruining the entire event. The walk down the hall was the longest ever. With each step, her heart pounded faster. Her hands were clammy and her knees felt like jelly. She could barely breathe and tears welled in her eyes as she tapped, timidly, on the door.

"Who is it?" was the cheery reply.

"It's Maagy, Daddy. May I come in?"

"Of course, my precious. You're welcome anytime."

She took a deep breath… wiped her eyes… pushed open the door… and entered slowly. She was looking at the floor, as she couldn't bear to look him in the eye. The lump in her throat grew bigger and the tears streamed down her cheeks.

"Oh, my! What in the world is the matter? Are you all right, Child?"

She collapsed in his arms in great wailing sobs. She could hardly talk between the gasps of breath, but managed to pour the entire business out in a tidal wave of simultaneous explanations and apologies. Finally, she regained her composure. She took one more deep breath and gave one last apology and waited for him to speak.

King Henry had a reputation for being one of the kindest and most caring monarchs in all the kingdoms. He was especially loving and gentle with his daughter; some would say, to a fault. He could see she was truly contrite* and had punished herself far worse than he could do. So, instead of scolding her, he wrapped her in his arms.

"Maagy, I think this lesson speaks for itself. I have no words as powerful as your own conscience. I'm proud you have such a strong sense of what is right and you've listened to that small voice within you. If you always listen and do as the voice tells you, you'll be a wise and honorable queen. Now dry your tears and get dressed. Our guests have arrived and opening ceremonies are in one hour. I shall be proud to have you at my side."

"But, Father..."

"No *but Father.* You must now be a woman and face your fears head-on. You will be introduced with all the pomp and ceremony of a formal state event and Prince Rudolpho *will* recognize you and you *will* have to manage the consequences. Trust me, my dear. It will not be nearly as bad as you anticipate. Now off with you, I must finish rehearsing my speech."

She felt closer to him than ever and was determined to earn his trust and pride once again, so she kissed him on the cheek and marched back to her room with renewed purpose. She chose the red, taffeta ball gown, which had found its way mysteriously into her closet. It would surely shock the guests who would expect the young princess to be clad in more conservative pastel attire. In fact, there was that silly rule of etiquette that young girls were only allowed to wear pastel garments until age thirteen, but red had always been Maagy's favorite color. She had appeased her bold preference with red nightgowns, since only her father and the house staff saw them in her bedchamber, but on this night... since she *was* thirteen... she would wear the glimmering red dress. She chose matching satin slippers with low heels for comfort... also mysterious in origin... since the night would certainly be long. She pulled the cord next to her dressing table and politely requested help fixing her hair, since all she could do was pull it into a ponytail. Estelí responded immediately and pinned it up in lovely soft curls so her tiara fit perfectly. The hour flew by so fast Rudolpho had not crossed her mind.

Chapter 6
Breathless Dance

King Henry knocked on the door. It was time to go downstairs. Images of her dashing new acquaintance engulfed her. Flutters and jitters poured over her. She hung onto her father's arm as they waited at the top of the stairs for the formal introduction. Finally, the trumpets pealed and the drums rolled and the announcement came.

"Ladies and Lords and all subjects of this kingdom and peoples here present, give your full attention. Descending the stairs, please give homage and due respect to His Royal Majesty King Henry David Charles Edward, Supreme Monarch of the Commonwealth of Realms including Berensenia, Marinia, Aquatain, Poseidonia and Polacia; Guardian of the List; Duke of Covington of Aradinia; Knight of the Commonwealth of Realms; Presiding Parliamentary Officer for the Commonwealth of Realms; Chief Ambassador of the Commonwealth of Realms; and accompanying His Majesty, Her Royal Highness Princess Melania Abigail Alice Grace, Duchess of Wentworth, Crown Princess of the sovereign kingdom of Berensenia and future monarch of the Commonwealth of Realms. Long live the King and long live the Crown Princess."*

"Daddy, I never knew you had so many titles," she whispered.

"Here, Here! Long live the King! Long live the Crown Princess!"

Maagy heard the melody of a familiar voice. She looked down at the crowd assembled at the bottom of the stairs and her eyes immediately fell on Rudolpho. His eyes met hers and she almost fell down the steps. Her father caught her arm and avoided disaster, which just made it even more difficult to face the young prince. As the two reached the landing, Prince Rudolpho stepped forward and bowed at the waist, with one hand on his sword handle and the other behind his back, first to King Henry.

"Your Royal Majesty, it is truly an honor to be in your presence. My father speaks so highly of you."

"Welcome, Prince Rudolpho," the king said, as he gave him a formal salute and then leaned close and whispered, as they shook hands. "Rudy, my boy, I can't believe how much you've grown since I saw you last!"

"Thank you, Sir."

"Have you seen the Emperor?"

"No Sir. I don't believe he's arrived as yet."

"Do you know why? Have you heard anything? Has Mak gotten any intelligence from his sources?"

"No, Your Majesty. Zinrahwi is an odd fellow, quite secretive. He could have something up his sleeve. Beware of him, Sir."

"Thank you for the insight, Rudy."

Maagy overheard bits and pieces, but couldn't glean* any sense from it.

"And this is your daughter," he chortled, as he bowed and presented his hand for hers. "Princess Melania Abigail Alice Grace, I believe. I feel as if we've met already. Is that possible?"

Once again, she could hardly breathe. Her knees were trembling under her dress and her mouth was as dry as Cupid's hay. Was he teasing her or did he *not* recognize her? Could he be so gallant as to save her embarrassment by not *acknowledging* that he recognized her? Either way, she was not humiliated and no one, but her father and she… and possibly Prince Rudolpho… knew the truth of what had happened earlier in the day. She could relax and enjoy the moment. She placed a clammy hand in his.

"It is truly a pleasure to be in your company, Your Grace," he continued, as he kissed her hand gently and looked deep into her eyes. "I look forward to our first dance together if you will so honor me."

She felt her face go bright red. She was sure he could feel her hand trembling, but tried to maintain her dignity and speak. All that came out was a faint squeak. How embarrassing. She tried again and this time managed to utter a few intelligible words.

"Yes… Your Highness… It will be… my pleasure… to… dance with you."

Did he *really* not recognize her? After all, she had been dressed as an ordinary person in town. Her hair had been pulled back in a ponytail and she was not wearing her tiara. Maybe she would be spared the awkwardness of a plausible explanation of her behavior. The blaring of trumpets and rolling of drums summoning everyone's attention for the introductions of the honored guests interrupted the moment.

"Ladies and Lords and all subjects of this kingdom and peoples here present, please give your full attention. His Royal Majesty King Henry of Berensenia and the Commonwealth of Realms welcomes his honored guests from lands near and far to Whitmore Castle and to his dining table. Please acknowledge His Royal Highness Prince Rudolpho Eduardo Rafael Valente of the house of Santiago, of the sovereign kingdom of Estadore. Long Live the Prince."

"Here, here! Long Live the Prince!"

Prince Rudolpho stepped forward and raised his hand to greet the crowd.

"On behalf of my father, King Rafael, and my mother, Queen Marisol, we thank King Henry and Princess Maagy for their kind hospitality and we bring warm salutations to all good people here present."

Maagy, he called her *Maagy*! He knew. He recognized her. There was no question now. The Royal Crier continued to announce the visiting dignitaries. The introductions gave her time to consider how she would proceed, now that her worst fear had been confirmed. Finally, she decided to do as her father had advised and meet the problem head-on and put it behind her, so she could enjoy the rest of the evening. As each person moved down the receiving line, she gave polite acknowledgment, as was required by her position as Official Hostess. However, her thoughts were miles away, as she searched for the right words to say to Prince Rudolpho. As time went by, she gained strength, as she pondered her father's words. Finally, the line ended and everyone dispersed into small groups chatting and laughing as *hors d'oeuvre** and cool drinks were circulated. She took a deep breath, let it out and moved through the crowd toward him. As she approached, he turned in her direction and immediately broke into a broad smile. The smitten girl felt her heart flutter as she reached her destination. She curtsied politely.

"Your Highness, may I have a private word with you?"

She was proud of herself for maintaining her composure.

"Of course, Your Grace. It will be my pleasure."

The two stepped slightly away from the crowd and she began to speak softly, almost in a whisper.

"First, I would like to thank you, again, for the ice cream today. It was kind of you. Then I'd like to explain why I was not completely truthful about my identity. You see, no one in Berryville knew who I was. I chose to dress as an ordinary person so I could experience farmers' market and shopping without making the town's people uncomfortable. Then you came into the confectionary. You were dressed as an ordinary person, although somewhat more formally than the town's people, and naturally, I assumed you *were* ordinary. I didn't want to make you uncomfortable by telling you my true identity."

She realized she was spinning another web and quickly changed her direction.

"No… that's not true. The truth is… I was afraid you wouldn't believe I really was a princess… and you would laugh at me… as the patrons in line had done. So I chose to give you my *sobriquet**, Maagy. I'm sorry I was deceptive. I hope you don't think less of me for it. I also hope you won't hold this against my father during the negotiations at the Summit meeting. I do beg your forgiveness, Your Royal Highness."

"Are you saying you… and that plucky little girl in the confection shop earlier today… are one in the same?"

"Yes."

She had looked at the floor throughout her entire speech. She was sure, had she made eye contact, she would have lost her nerve and burst into tears. She continued to stare at the floor.

"I'm amazed! I didn't recognize you. You look much more grown up this evening."

"You Didn't? I do?"

"Not at all and yes… you do."

"Then how did you know I go by Maagy? You said King Henry and Princess Maagy."

"My father told me. It's common knowledge, you know."

"So, you really *didn't* recognize me?"

"No."

She looked up and straight into his eyes. She forgot how enamored she'd been and was instead, *rather annoyed.*

"Then why did you let me go on and on with my confession? Couldn't you have been gracious and interrupted me? Did you have to let me humiliate myself and grovel for your forgiveness?"

"Do you consider righting a wrong and telling the truth to be humiliating?"

"Well, no… I mean… I was *embarrassed*… and you could have saved me from some of it."

"It seems I have already saved you once today by paying for your ice cream. How many times must you be saved in one day?

Besides, you're the one who chose to lie. Why should I save you embarrassment?"

"How rude!"

"I see why you're called the Impetuous Princess Maagy," he said with an unflappable* chuckle.

"I see why you're called Rude-Dee!"

Prince Rudolpho could contain himself no longer. He began to smile. He was amused at her impudence*. She, however, was not amused at his smiling and became even more incensed.

"Stop smiling! You're making me angry! I can't believe I thought you to be charming. You're really quite annoying and *RUDE!*"

She realized the room full of people was unusually quiet. She turned round to see all eyes on the two of them. Apparently, she had been speaking somewhat louder than intended. She was humiliated and turned away quickly, her face bright red. Tears welled in her eyes and she began to tremble. The last thing she had meant to do was throw a tantrum. She had surely disgraced her father, which was the very thing she had feared doing the most. She could not seem to move or even breathe. Rudy was biting his bottom lip and looking at the floor trying desperately to contain laughter. Just then, the royal trumpeters signaled it was time to go into the dining room and be seated for dinner. Thankfully, attention was drawn away and the crowd began quietly conversing again, and moving toward the dining room. It was the custom in Berensenia for the ruling monarch and honored guests to enter last. This was a fortunate turn of luck for Maagy. She felt a familiar hand on her shoulder and looked up to see her father's eyes. He was kind, but firm when he took her by the arm and ushered her into the coat closet. He nodded for Rudolpho to follow. Once the door was shut to ensure privacy, she burst into tears and threw her arms round her father.

"Oh, Daddy, I'm so sorry! I didn't mean to have a tantrum! But Rudolpho is so annoying and rude! I just forgot myself!"

"Rudy? Rude? What's this? Have you been unkind to my daughter?"

"Begging your pardon, Your Majesty. I didn't intend to offend Her Royal Highness. I was only joking with her. She has such spunk; I thought she could take a little teasing. I never intended to hurt her feelings… or inspire anger."

"Maagy, what is this all about?"

"Well, Father, do you remember earlier this evening, I came to you and confessed I had been less than truthful? You said I would have to face Prince Rudolpho and be strong about it. So, I thought he recognized me immediately upon our introduction and was just trying to save my dignity by pretending not to recognize me. I decided he was being kind and deserved an apology. But when I poured out my soul, he said, in fact, he *hadn't* recognized me at all, but he let me go on and on groveling. Then he laughed at me!"

"Is this true Rudolpho? Did you laugh at my daughter's apology?"

The young prince now realized he was between a rock and a hard place.

"It is true, Sir… I smiled… but not at her apology… rather, her audacity*… I found it amusing, as I had already saved her dignity and her identity. I knew, immediately, she was Princess Maagy. So when she confessed to me, I decided to have some fun and deny I recognized her. I didn't expect her to be so hot-tempered and cause a scene," he related, trying desperately to keep a straight face. "I do most sincerely regret I caused you embarrassment and hurt your feelings, Duchess."

She had stood listening with arms folded in a pout. King Henry had listened intently to both sides of the story. He took a long pause and walked round the coat closet, obviously deep in thought. Maagy and Rudolpho stood silently… motionless… she not daring to look at him… he not able to take his eyes off her. Finally, the king spoke.

"Rudy, would you be so kind as to give us a private a moment?"

"Certainly, Your Majesty. And again, I am sorry, Princess Maagy."

Rudolpho exited the closet and closed the door, relieved to have a moment to collect his composure.

"Well, Maagy… once again… a lesson to be learnt. The tangled web I warned you about has spun round and round, today, don't you think? If you had been completely honest with Rudy, in the first place, there would have been no need for apologies. There would have been no teasing and no tantrum and my guests would not have experienced the Impetuous Princess Maagy. However, there is a bigger lesson here, even still. Maagy, when you make a mistake… and there will be many more before it's done… it is *yours* to own. It is *yours* to make right and it is *yours* to put behind you. You cannot blame others because you are ashamed of yourself for being in the wrong. It wasn't Rudy's place to save your feelings of humiliation and remorse. It is your place to be a mature woman and accept your punishment… in this case, it is embarrassment… with grace and dignity. I hope you understand that now, and will not hold a grudge against Prince Rudolpho for giving you a taste of your own medicine."

She stood quietly for a few more moments. He was right. She opened the closet door and asked Rudolpho to come in. She took a deep breath and spoke.

"Father, you are right. I have behaved badly today. I deeply regret my deception, my attempt to place blame on Rudolpho and especially embarrassing you. Prince Rudolpho, I have treated you badly and would understand if you choose not to speak to me ever again. Please accept my sincere apologies, both of you."

She felt the weight of the world lifted from her shoulders, as she contemplated the wisdom of '*own it, make it right and put it behind you*'.

"Your Royal Highness Princess Maagy, please accept my sincere apology for my crass behavior. I should have been more sensitive to your feelings. I should not have amused myself at your expense. I do admire your spirit and would be honored to be your friend. Your apology is humbly accepted."

"Likewise, Maagy. I forgive you for causing a scene and I'm sure you've punished yourself enough. There will be no further penance* for you. Now, we have hungry guests awaiting our presence. Shall we make our entrance? Rudy, you may escort my daughter, if you wish… if she agrees."

"It will be my pleasure, Your Royal Majesty."

Rudolpho bowed at the waist and offered his arm to Maagy. She accepted, but reached for her father's arm, as well. The three emerged from the coat closet and entered the dining room with heads held high.

"You thought I was charming?" He leaned down and whispered with a cheeky* grin.

Maagy cut her eyes at him, but refused to respond and kept a smile pasted on her lips. They were greeted with standing applause and wonderful food that only Grandma Polly and her kitchen magicians could create.

The meal was a true masterpiece of culinary art. There was an antipasto of delicacies, many of which were gifts from the foreign dignitaries at the table. The soup course was Salmon bisque. Maagy *really* didn't care for fish soup. She was polite, however, and dipped her spoon ever so slightly into the mix and moved it gingerly to her mouth; several tasty crackers followed the tiny sip. She made small talk with Prince Rudolpho, who was sat at her right, and was amazed he seemed to actually like the unpleasant concoction. He ate it all without a single cracker. A tasty salad followed accompanied by warm dinner rolls with honey butter. She could have stopped there and been perfectly happy with the meal. But the food kept coming; a main course of perfectly cooked roasted duck and vegetables. It was followed with cheese and fruit trays, accompanied by various teas and coffees. Maagy was a perfect lady throughout dinner and tried especially hard to be a good hostess. She occasionally looked at Grandma Polly for a nod or wink to indicate she was on task. King Henry was at the head of the table and Maagy was in the same position at the other end. He looked at her often and smiled, reassuringly. She was pleased Rudolpho was sat at her side. It was easier to sneak glances at him.

Among the dignitaries were Queen Haideh and Prince Shamir of Nihmrobi, and their daughter, Princess Asanna, the Heir-Apparent to the throne. Father-King Afarnae of Nihmrobi, who had abdicated* the monarchy to his daughter, and King Henry had met as young men at Academy of Her Majesty's Royal Guard*. They had been fast friends ever since and could share in each other's loss. King Henry had issued a special invitation to him as an honored adviser. He was sat at King Henry left and the two men were busy catching up, as they had not seen each other in a long while. It struck Maagy her father was the same age as Princess Asanna's grandfather. The miracle of her birth was not lost upon her. For the first time, she began to sense the magnitude of her responsibility, as she looked round the table at the leaders of the known world.

Officials representing Marinia, Aquatain, Aradinia, Senecia and Poseidonia were also present with their families and of course, Rudolpho represented Estadore[3]. Several chairs were vacant. Maagy didn't know who was missing, but got the impression there was gossip circulating about the absences. Finally, her favorite part of the meal was served, *dessert*! Grandma Polly's famous peach cobbler was featured along with a wide variety of *petits fours**, cookies, flan, custards, and pies. Everyone continued to chat and sip their beverages... in no hurry to leave the table.

The little ones were upstairs in the children's library for a puppet show and slumber party. King Henry always provided entertainment for the children of dignitaries and it seemed to Maagy that just yesterday, she was one of them. She remembered sneaking away from the nannies and peeking at the guests in their finery. She especially loved seeing her father in his ceremonial uniform with the shinny gold epaulets and the bright red sash across his chest, his polished sword at his side. From her youthful viewpoint, he was elderly. However,

3 Please see Glossary; Maps

he was actually in his middle years and still quite vital. He was taller than average and his wavy gray hair belied his robust, muscular frame. He had been a force to be reckoned with on the battlefield, in his day, and he was still feared by many and respected by most. His strong jaw and deep-set, piercing, gray-blue eyes made him quite handsome. As she continued to take in the scene, she thought about the exotic queen she looked for each time there was a State function; the one who wore the elaborately wrapped yards of fine silk with the golden threads woven through it. Now she realized it was Queen Haideh and she smiled to herself for making the connection. She kept these thoughts private as she looked round and realized she was in the midst of the same adults she spied on as a little child. She especially enjoyed meeting Princess Asanna, a tall slender sixteen-year-old… poised far beyond her years… who sat across from Rudolpho.

"Please, call me by my name without the title," the raven-haired beauty requested. "In this setting, it feels so pretentious. We are all royalty, so let us just be friends!"

"I agree," Rudolpho added. "So it's Maagy, Asanna and Rudy, from this minute on."

"I like that idea, as well," Maagy said. "Asanna, why have we never met before… or have we and I was too young to remember?"

"Sadly no, we haven't. My parents have strict policies about taking children in public, as they do not wish to expose us to possible danger as royal children. So I have never accompanied them and the younger children are still left at home."

"Younger children? You have siblings?"

"Yes, I have three sisters and a baby brother who is just two years old. He's adorable."

"Oh, so he is the Crown Prince, since he's the only boy."

"Actually, no. It is I who am in line for the throne. The royal ancestry dictates the first-born *female* of each generation is the Heir-Apparent. My grandfather, King Afarnae, had no sisters. He is the oldest of three males, so he ascended the throne. Had there been a girl, even one younger than he, she would have been the Heir-Apparent, you see?"

"I do. I'm honestly not sure how it works in Berensenia. All I know is my father is king and I'm an only child, so I'll be queen. I really don't know how things would be different if I had a brother... or a sister. I suppose I should ask my father about it. How old was your mother when she became queen? She looks quite young."

"She was fifteen and my father was sixteen, my age. My grandmother, Queen Ajeera, fell off her horse in a steeplechase* and died days later of her injuries. My grandfather was devastated and could no longer be an effective head-of-state, so he abdicated to my mother, who was already expecting me. She was only sixteen when I was born."

"Oh my! That is young!"

"Theirs was an arranged marriage, as was the custom for upper class and royal family at the time."

"Arranged? You mean *someone else* decided they would marry?"

"Yes. It was accepted practice. The process of choosing potential mates started when the babies were born. Based on the results, they would betroth their children to marry when the girl turned thirteen. My parents married two days after my mother turned thirteen. My father's fourteenth birthday was two months later."

Maagy's mind was boggled. She could not even imagine being married, much less to someone chosen by her father. She was quite sure she would want to choose her own husband... *husband! Yuck!*

"I can't begin to imagine that! Oh, I'm so sorry. I didn't mean to insult your parents."

"Don't bother about it," Asanna retorted. "It's no insult. They felt the same way. They've told us stories about their childhoods and how much they disliked each other, at first. Their families visited monthly so they got more acquainted and... hopefully... learn to *like* each other... they finally did. Fortunately, they fell very much in love."

"If I may ask... are you betrothed? If so, why aren't you married?"

"No, thank goodness! Mother put a stop to arranged marriages when I was born. A few upper class families enter into informal agreements even now, but the practice is officially banned."

Maagy's mind drifted back to those childhood days and her fascination with the beautiful young queen and realized how difficult it must have been for her to be so young and lose her own mother, while preparing to become a mother, and then queen.

"It must have been so difficult for your mother… she's quite amazing. I hope I'll be as strong."

"Why, Maagy, what a lovely thing to say. I'm sure you will be a fine leader. I'm glad we've met. I think we have a long friendship ahead of us… like my grandfather and your father."

The evening had been a great success. There were old friends catching up with news on the veranda; some were in the music room listening to a piano recital; Grandma Polly and her expert staff had been through the crowd several times with trays of refreshing drinks and cookies, fruit and cheese. Most of the younger guests had migrated to the ballroom. In addition to Prince Rudolpho, Princess Asanna and Princess Maagy, there were Emir Sistrunk, seventeen, and Ohno Sistrunk, fifteen; the sons of Rudolpho's guard, Makubar Sistrunk. Also present, his daughter, Lamalah, who was thirteen. There were a number of young people Maagy did not know, among them, Martha Chamberlaine, the sixteen-year-old daughter of the Premier of Senecia. She was quiet and seemed shy, but she was always near Asanna and Rudy. Maagy tried to make friends, but she wasn't personable*. Owanu Obuku was the fourteen-year-old son of one of the tribal chieftains of Darhambi. They had arrived late, just after dinner. Owanu was not friendly either and refused to mingle, but stayed in the ballroom and watched from the corner. The musicians had slowed things down with a waltz. Maagy and Lamalah had just got acquainted and were enjoying a cool drink, when Prince Rudolpho stepped beside them, one hand behind his back and the other extended, palm up.

"Greetings, Ladies… Lamalah, you look lovely this evening."

"Thank you, Prince Rudolpho," she responded, as she curtsied.

"Princess, I believe this dance is ours, if you will so honor me."

Maagy gulped a mouthful of drink and looked wide-eyed at Lamalah, who raised her eyebrows as if to say, "La-de-da", as she took her cup.

"Um… yes… of course… It will be… my pleasure, Prince Rudolpho."

"Will you excuse us, Lamalah?"

"Of course," she chortled and curtsied.

Maagy felt as if all the moths in the silkworm house were fluttering in her stomach. Her knees were weak and her mouth was like cotton, even though she had just drunk an entire glass of punch. She placed her trembling hand in his and he escorted her onto the dance floor. As he turned her toward him, and smiled, he slipped his right hand round to the center of her back. When he touched her, it took her breath away and her face went bright red.

"How embarrassing!" she thought. "Surely he can see me blushing!"

She placed her left hand on his shoulder, which was almost too high to reach without going on tiptoes, and they began to move in unison round the floor in perfect time with the music. He continued to smile and look into her eyes. She was mesmerized and quite forgot about blushing… and breathing.

"You're a marvelous dancer," he said.

"Thank you… you are, as well. And yes… I did think you charming in the confectionary."

He chuckled and pulled her a bit closer… she could barely feel her feet touching the floor, as he twirled her round in perfect time… and time… again… stood still. She was lost in his eyes… both were lost in the music… and the magic of the dance. He truly was a charming and elegant young man. She was pleased to have cleared up the misunderstandings of the day. This moment was too precious to have missed because of impetuous behavior. Finally, and sadly, the song ended, as did the dance. He let her go slowly and placed one hand behind his back and held on to hers with the other. He kissed it gently and bowed as she curtsied.

"Thank you, Your Grace," he said politely. "Perhaps we may… dance again… if you'd like."

"It was my pleasure," she replied as she curtsied, "and would be my pleasure… to dance with you again… if time permits."

The two stood for an awkward moment… hand in hand… neither quite sure of what to do next, when Asanna joined them.

"What a perfect dance couple you make!"

"Thank you," Maagy said, as she took back her hand and felt the redness return to her face.

"May I get you ladies a glass of punch?"

"Yes, please. That would be nice," Asanna responded with a smile.

"Yes, thank you."

"He's a nice boy, and quite handsome, too," Asanna whispered. "Don't you think?"

"Really? I… I… hadn't noticed."

"*'Really? I hadn't noticed'* indeed! How could you not! You silly girl, you noticed. I saw you blush!"

"Was it that obvious? I've never felt this way before. I'm usually fine meeting someone close to my age, but this is quite different. My knees shake, my stomach jitters and my mouth goes dry. I can't think straight. What's the matter with me?"

"Obviously… you have a crush," Asanna whispered.

"Oh… this is what it feels like… I've never had a crush. I don't even know any boys my age… other than Lord Wesley Applegate… and he certainly doesn't make me blush. Is it inappropriate? Will I get over it? Should I tell my father? Oh my, I wish I had my mother, right now. I'm at a loss."

Asanna was sympathetic. Maagy had no one to help process these overwhelming feelings. She thought it might be helpful to assume the "big-sister" role and give some counsel.

"No, it's completely normal. Rudolpho is handsome and charming… he's also a gentleman. That's why you are attracted to him. But that's also why he is a good friend. I've known Rudy since we were small children and he is one of my best friends. He's easy to talk to and mature for his age. He's also kind and thoughtful. I would be surprised if you *didn't* have a crush on him. He's obviously quite taken by you."

"Really? How can you tell?"

"By the way he looked at you the entire time you were dancing. If I were you, I would relax and just talk to him as if he were any other friend. Get to know him. Ask him questions about himself. And above all, *be yourself*, Maagy."

"Have… you… ever had a crush on him?"

She was almost afraid to hear the answer. Asanna was such a confident young woman she felt a little intimidated.

"I had a crush on Rudy when I was twelve. He was thirteen, almost fourteen and had just grown taller than I. As children, I was always taller and he hated it. Then he started to sprout and in one summer, he shot past me and wouldn't let me live it down. I found the banter* rather attractive. But then it became obnoxious and I soon lost interest. We have remained fast friends ever since. He's turning into a fine man."

Maagy was grateful for the advice. While she was surrounded by women and girls her age at home, and had Grandma Polly and Estelí here, she really had no one who was her social equal, and therefore, would speak freely and candidly to her.

"Should I tell my father I have a crush on him? Would that be the right thing to do?"

"Maagy, that's something you'll have to decide for yourself. Do you feel comfortable telling him other intimate things? Would you tell your mother if she were here? If so, your father is your only parent and, as such, must be both father and mother. A crush is not something to be embarrassed about. How you behave is what is important. If you maintain your dignity you'll have nothing to worry about. Listen to the small voice inside and you'll do the right thing."

"Shall we go out to the veranda and sit for a while?" Rudy said, returning with a tray of cookies and drinks.

"Yes, that would be nice. I'm ready for another of Grandma Polly's cookies. I've been learning to bake, you know," she said, glancing at Asanna, who smiled and gave a slight nod.

"Really? I didn't know impetuous princesses could learn such skills," he teased.

"Excuse me… Rude-Dee?" Maagy said playfully, as she gave back as good as she got. "I'll have you know I can also muck stables, milk a cow and braid a horse's tail. I do it every morning as part of my chores. So there, Mister Prince of Estadore."

"Now there's the girl for whom I bought spumoni ice cream! Welcome back, my feisty friend!"

The night was perfect. The whip-poor-wills were in full voice as was the frog chorus. The moon was full and high in the sky so it illuminated the meadow. They sat in silence for a while and enjoyed the refreshments and the evening.

"Can you really milk a cow?" Asanna asked, breaking the silence.

"Yes. I do it every morning," Maagy replied. "It's most rewarding."

"I'm envious! Will you teach me?"

"Absolutely, if it's all right with Grandpa Kris and Jorge… he's the stable manager. The cows are sensitive and they won't give milk if they're upset."

"It's excellent you're interest in everyday chores," Rudolpho said. "It's good to know how things are done."

"I wasn't always. When I first arrived, I didn't know anything. Father said he brought me here to learn how to be a good queen. He's anxious to retire and that means I must take the crown. I've learnt so much in such a short time. I've been introduced to a whole world I never knew before. I didn't know where milk came from… and I'd no idea how much work it was to feed a stable of horses. Did you know silk is made from fibers made by moth larvae? They're called silk *worms*, but they're not actually *worms* at all. Opps… I've been talking too much… haven't I? Neither of you has got a word in edgewise."

"Not at all. I could listen to you talk all night," Rudy said.

"Oh… my…"

"I'm quite impressed by what you've said, so far," Asanna spoke up to save Maagy. "Do you do these chores every morning, really?"

Maagy was still hanging onto, Rudy's last sentence and barely heard the question, but managed to respond anyway.

"I do… I get up early… dress in overalls and boots and off to the barn I go."

"Will you wake me in the morning, then? I'd really like to watch."

"I'll go, as well," Rudy said. "I haven't worked in a barn in two years. I miss it. I especially like working with horses."

"If you're both sure. I have a special friend I'll introduce to you. She is an adorable palomino filly named Cupid. I care for her every day. I'm training her to eventually have a bridle and saddle. She's really quite sweet. You're not teasing me, are you? You're sure you want to get up that early? It's barely day break."

"No teasing, quite sure," was Rudy's reply.

"I'm absolutely positive. I love watching the sunrise. So, since I'll have to scrounge up some appropriate clothing for the barnyard, I think I'll excuse myself and retire to my room. It was a long journey and I'm quite tired. Will you both excuse me?"

"Yes, of course. Sweet dreams, my friend," Rudy said, as he stood and gave her a kiss on her cheek.

"Yes, certainly, until morning then. I'll let Gram-P know there'll be two more for breakfast," she said, as she stood and hugged Asanna. "Thank you for your words of wisdom."

Maagy and Rudolpho were alone… but under watchful eyes… always.

"It's a beautiful evening, isn't it?"

"Yes, it is. I love coming out here after dark and listening to the night sounds. Daddy, Poppy, Gram-P and I come out… and just sit."

"You called your father 'Daddy'. That's sweet."

"He's a sweet man… at least, to me, anyway. I don't know how others see him. He's just my daddy."

"A secret? So is my father, Dad. We're quite close. Sometimes I almost forget he's a king. My mother is a bit more… imposing… shall I say. Don't get me wrong, she's a good mother, but not as… approachable as my dad, and much more formal, even in private settings."

"I don't know how my mother was. I don't remember anything about her. I only know her through my father and he says she was warm and loving. I have to take his word for it. Sometimes, in my dreams, a woman is there who I suppose is my mother. The dream is always of a picnic on the lawn, but I never quite see her face. I know it's a silly dream, because the woman has dark hair and Mummy was blond. I guess that's as close as I'll ever get to actually knowing her."

"I'm sorry, I didn't mean to make you sad talking about my mother. I should have been more aware."

"Oh, no, really… it's fine. I love thinking about her. I'm not sad at all. I guess I'm more curious than anything. Please don't apologize."

"Well… if you're sure… I've done enough today to be offensive. I shouldn't want to add insult to injury."

"You? Please! I pitched a tantrum in front of the leaders of the known world and thoroughly humiliated my father, *The King*. That tops it all!"

"That was rather funny, I must say."

"Hello, it was your fault, too, you know. Let's not forget that."

"*Touché,* Dear Lady. *Touché.*"

All the moths had flown away from her tummy and her knees no longer trembled in weakness. Asanna had been right in advising her to "be herself" and talk to Rudolpho as she would any other friend. Now, however, the long day was beginning to take its toll and she couldn't help but yawn. He did the same.

"Excuse me!" they both said in unison as they dissolved into giggles.

"It has been a long day, I suppose."

"Indeed, it has. My journey actually began yesterday. By the way, I do not recommend spending the night in a moving carriage. Sleep is elusive, at best. Then I had much business in Berryville, on behalf of my father, so I arrived here too late to rest before dinner. Ah… the responsibilities of being a prince."

"Let us not forget the rescue of a damsel in distress."

"Oh, yes! That, too!"

"So, I suppose we should find my father and bid him *adieu** for the evening."

"Brilliant… but… one more dance before we call the evening done?"

He stood and extended his hand to help her up and escorted her to the ballroom. She was again, breathless and mesmerized, as they glided round the floor, both lost in the moment. When the music ended… much too soon… they bowed and curtsied without speaking a word and again, he kissed her hand and held it a little longer. The butterflies flew back and her heart fluttered wildly as they began searching for King Henry. They found him ensconced* in the corner with Father-King Afarnae, Queen Haideh and Prince Shamir. The conversation looked serious, but when they saw Maagy and Rudolpho approaching, they broke into smiles.

"Rudolpho, what a fine young man you have grown up to be," Prince Shamir said.

"Thank you, Sir. Good evening, Your Majesties, and Your Royal Highness."

"Tell me, Dear boy, how is your father," asked Father-King Afarnae. "I've not spoke with him in way too long."

"Your Majesty, King Afarnae, I have a special message for you… a gift, really… from my father… if you'll allow me to deliver it."

"Well yes, of course, by all means."

Rudolpho moved toward him and gave him an affectionate hug. All seemed pleased at the gesture and applauded in approval.

"I also have a note he instructed me to deliver and wait for a response."

He reached into his uniform coat and retrieved a note sealed with wax in the royal coat-of-arms stamp. He handed it to King Afarnae, who seemed to know there would be humor enclosed. He opened the note cautiously with several comical flourishes and began to read aloud:

"'Dear Farnie', he always called me that and I don't know why."

"You never liked it much. That's why!" Chided King Henry, with a laugh.

"Hmmm… I suppose… *'Dear Farnie, Since you have abandoned Henry and me and passed the buck to your daughter… some of us still have to work for a living… you are no longer a king and therefore I am free to send you any gift I choose. I hope you liked the one I sent through Rudy and will pass it on to Henry for me. Take care, Old Man'*… old man indeed!" He mumbled aside. *"'And try to work a fishing trip with some old friends into your busy schedule, before too long. None of us is getting any younger… especially you!'* Hmm! *'Fondly, your friend and accomplice in foolishness, Rafie'*. Ha! That rascal! I'll fix him, when he least expects it! That's my reply… tell him… when he least expects it!"

He tucked the treasure into his pocket and then passed on the gift, as instructed, to Henry with a big bear hug, practically lifting him off the floor. Everyone present was thoroughly amused, but Maagy found it particularly appealing. She had never seen this side of her father or any other adult, for that matter. She had never been a part of their socialization. Now, she thought about all the little ones who had retired to the children's library much earlier in the evening, as she had always done. What do they know of their parents and grandparents? Do they understand what pleasant people they are? It occurred to her there might be two sides to everything and one should find out what the other side is all about, before making judgments.

"Prince Rudolpho, have you seen my daughter?" Prince Shamir asked. "She's here, you know. I'm sure she'd be delighted to see you."

"In fact, yes. I was sat across from her at dinner and I… we… have just spent several hours with Princess Asanna. She and Princess Maagy have met and we are all great friends. She has retired for the night."

"Yes, we've had a lovely time and, Your Majesty, Queen Haideh, your daughter is a gracious lady. I am grateful for her friendship."

"What a nice thing to say, Darling Princess Maagy. I'm completely charmed by what a mature young woman you are at only thirteen. I'm sure she is fond of you, as well. I hope this is the beginning of a long and healthy friendship."

"Thank you, Your Majesty," she responded as she curtsied, politely. "I have a request, if it's acceptable to all of you. Princess Asanna and Prince Rudolpho have asked if they might accompany me to the barn tomorrow morning whilst I muck stables and milk cows. They also want to meet Cupid, my… the… palomino filly I'm training. I'll ask Estelí to wake them quietly so as not to disturb anyone else and they can eat breakfast early with us. I'm sure Grandma Polly has boots that will fit Asanna… excuse me, Princess Asanna. Would that be acceptable?"

The adults seemed to conspire to make her uneasy for a few moments, as they whispered among themselves and looked back at her, occasionally. Then King Henry turned toward them with an air of authority.

"Are you quite sure you can handle being observed so closely whilst performing menial tasks?"

"Menial tasks? I think what I'm doing is important work. I don't consider it menial at all!"

She realized her tone might be impertinent* and didn't want to embarrass him further, so she apologized quickly.

"I'm sorry, Father. I didn't mean to speak rudely. I just like caring for the animals, milking the cows and training Cupid. It's all been so enriching and I just wanted to share that with my new friends. I hope you will forgive me for speaking harshly."

"Where is my daughter, the Impetuous Princess Maagy, and who is this mature young woman standing in front of me? Can anyone tell me that?" He said, jokingly as he looked round as if to search.

"Daddy! Don't be silly. I'm right here! You're teasing me!"

"Yes I am teasing you, my dear child!" he said, as he threw his arms round her and hugged her close, rocking her from side to side. "And yes, your friends may accompany you as long as all of you do exactly as Jorge tells you. Now, it's been a long day and tomorrow will be here before you know it, so, off to bed with you! Sweet dreams, Child."

He kissed her several times on her cheeks and forehead and let her go.

"I shall bid you all good night, as well," said the exhausted prince. "Duchess, may I escort you to your door?"

"If my father approves."

"Of course, of course. Off with the both of you and I'll see you early."

"You called me Duchess. No one ever calls me Duchess."

"Sorry… was I out of line? I certainly did not mean to offend."

"No! Not at all… I rather like it… for a change."

"Then I shall call you Duchess… occasionally… in the appropriate situation."

They quietly discussed the plan for morning as they made their way up the long staircase to the second floor.

"This is my room," she said as they crossed the hall. "I'll see if Estelí is awake."

She tapped lightly on the service hall door. Estelí opened it and peeked out.

"Estelí, I'm so sorry to disturb you, but could you please wake Princess Asanna and Prince Rudolpho in the morning, in time for breakfast with Father and me?"

"Of course, Your Grace. I will be happy to and you are not disturbing me at all. Is there anything else you need, Mademoiselle?"

"No, nothing at all. Have sweet dreams, Estelí, and thank you."

"It is my pleasure. Adieu, sweet dreams, Your Highness."

She closed the door and Maagy returned to Rudolpho.

"It's all set then, she'll wake you. Goodnight, Rudy. I'm glad we're friends."

"I, as well."

"And… thank you… for the lovely dances."

"It was my pleasure, I assure you. I'm looking forward to morning and meeting your other friend, Cupid. Goodnight, Princess Maagy… Duchess… sweet dreams."

He took her hand and kissed it gently. She shivered and her heart raced.

"Good night… sleep well."

He crossed to the third floor stairs and ascended out of sight. As she closed the door, she caught a glimpse of herself in the full-length mirror and saw a young lady, where a little girl had always been. She stood for a moment and closed her eyes to reflect. She thought about her conversation with Asanna and how it had been like no other. She thought about Rudy and got that warm, flutter in her stomach. She opened her eyes and smiled, as she began to take out hairpins and prepare for bed. She saw Princess Maagy… Young Lady… Future Queen… looking back at her and *knew* her dreams would be sweet.

Chapter 7
The Summit

Five-thirty in the morning came much earlier than Maagy had anticipated, but once awake, she threw back the covers and stretched toward the ceiling, anticipating the fun, which was about to begin. She needed an early start, since King Henry had told her she would be sitting in on the League of Kingdoms Summit and she was giddy with excitement, feeling oh so important. Estelí had awakened her, with bath drawn, and arranged her hair in a dignified chignon*, before going to waken Rudy and Asanna. Maagy was in and out of the tub in no time and threw on overalls for chores and breakfast. She flung open her door to find the hallway completely dark. She was so busy she hadn't notice the daylight had not yet dawned. She immediately burst into laughter and had to stifle the noise, as no one else was awake! She ran down to the family dining room and slipped inside. Once safely behind closed doors, she couldn't stop laughing out loud. Surely, the anticipation of the up-coming events heightened her emotions and laughter was the perfect release. Finally, as she emerged from her giggle-fest, she realized the smell of bacon frying was creeping into the dining room. She looked toward the kitchen, and sure enough, there was light under the door. She peeked in to see Grandma Polly, Josephine and an army of helpers already well under way with meal preparations.

"Good morning, Gram-P. Good morning, Josephine. You're both awake early. Do you always begin cooking before daylight?"

"Well, well, look who's awake already!" Grandma said.

"Good morning, Your Highness, Princess Maagy." Josephine added, with a bow of her head.

"Yes, we begin before dawn. It's the most peaceful time of day," Grandma Polly replied, with a smile and a twinkle in her eye.

"I had to laugh at myself for not noticing it was still dark. I hope I didn't awaken anyone with my outburst."

"Oh, don't worry about that, Dear. All the guests are asleep on the third floor and most of the staff is awake already. The only one you could have disturbed would have been your father, and he sleeps like a rock, if I remember correctly. So I'm sure your sweet little giggles wouldn't have interfered with his slumber. Are you hungry? We've just started cooking. Breakfast won't be ready for a bit. Can you last?"

"Of course, I'm hungry. I'm always hungry. But I'll be fine. Can I help you do something?"

"Well, those apples over there need to be sliced up for frying. Would you like to do? You may snack on a slice or two if you like."

"Yes, Josephine showed me how to handle a sharp knife properly. I'd love to test my skill."

"Good. Be careful, then."

Maagy sliced and snacked on the apples until all were done. Then she watched as Josephine fried them to perfection with sugar and cinnamon. Grandma Polly finished cooking the bacon and made stacks and stacks of pancakes. She scrambled a mountain of fluffy eggs and filled the huge silver urn with hot coffee. There were muffins, croissants and scones. There was a large bowl of berries and cut peaches. Maagy took the dishes of butter and various cheeses into the dining room and placed them on the buffet. Josephine had followed with a tray of jams and jellies and a pitcher of fresh fruit juice. A flurry of constant activity and workers in and out of the kitchen had chaffing dishes of piping hot food set in no time.

Without her notice, daylight began streaming through the windows. The rising sun bounced light off the western tower wall and the lingering mist on the lawn to give a golden glow to the dining room. She stood back for a moment to appreciate the picture, knowing as soon as the sun rose higher into the sky, this particular phenomenon would be gone. It occurred to her there were probably many things like this, which only exist for a moment and should be enjoyed for as long as possible. Just as all the food was in place, the door opened and in strode the handsome Prince Rudolpho. He was in full uniform, sword and dagger on either side. This was his real military dress, equally as sharp, but fewer tassels and less gold than the one he'd worn for opening ceremonies. He looked more like a man of authority, rather than a boy prince, and seemed to have got even taller overnight.

"Good morning, Duchess. I must say, you look stunning in overalls."

She wasn't expecting anyone so soon… least of all, *him*… she thought breakfast would be private with only her father. She lost her breath, for a moment. Her heart pounded like a drum and felt as if it would jump out her mouth. The day before had been so pleasant and Maagy felt as if she had got to know Asanna and Rudy so well… she didn't expect the reaction. She was sure her knees were rattling, as they felt like the bowl of strawberry jelly on the sideboard.

"Oh! Hello! Good morning! Yes… hello… top of the day!" She stumbled, as she struggled to control her mouth and her emotions at the same time. "Yes, good morning, Rudy… Prince Rudolpho. You look… rather… much… like… you look stunning, as well! I mean handsome… I mean… are you hungry? Breakfast is almost ready."

She ducked into the kitchen to take a deep breath. She had thought all these funny feelings were gone after spending the entire day with him on Sunday. She thought she was under control and she could behave like a normal person, but here she was telling him he looked... *stunning*!

"*Oh bother*! He must think I'm daft*," she mumbled. "Maybe he didn't hear what I said."

"Pardon, Dear?"

"Oh... nothing... Gram... nothing."

She grabbed a basket of bread from someone's hands and went back into the dining room to face her fears.

"Good morning... again. Breakfast will be ready soon and I helped prepare it. Did you know Grandma Polly and Josephine Penning get up well before dawn to begin cooking? I didn't... I only just discovered it this morning. I've been up since before dawn," she rattled at breakneck speed. "When the sun rose, it reflected off the west tower wall and gave the room a golden glow. You should have seen it... it only lasted for a few minutes... oops... talking too much, right? Would you like a croissant?"

"Not yet, thanks... just getting a cup of tea," Rudy said with a grin. "Why up so early?"

"I just woke up... I mean... Estelí woke me... so I'd have plenty of time to do chores... and visit Cupid before the Summit... so I got up... and took a bath... and dressed... and came down... to find them in the kitchen busy working, already, so I helped... and now... I guess I should be quiet... and let someone else... get a word in edgewise."

She was embarrassed at her enthusiastic tongue rattling and took a deep breath to calm herself, as she put the basket on the sideboard.

"I'm sure the sunrise was quite the show," he responded, amused by her ramblings. "I wish I'd seen it, too."

"Wasn't that whole exchange with the letter hilarious, the other evening?" She continued, making nervous small talk.

"Indeed, it was," Rudy agreed with a chuckle. "I've not seen that side of Father. He's always so serious when dealing with state matters. It's nice to see such affection between the three of them, after all these years. They're like brothers. So… I'll see you for breakfast in a bit?"

"Yes… I'm going to do my chores… now… so… in a bit…"

Rudolpho took his tea and swept out of the room as quickly as he swept into it, leaving Maagy speechless… and almost lightheaded.

As she walked alone to the barn… smiling in the warmth of her infatuation… her mind drifted back to every detail of the day before and the budding camaraderie between Asanna, Rudy and her. Maagy learned Rudolpho had an older, married brother named Raul and a sister named Consuela. They were twelve and ten, respectively, when Rudolpho was born, which put him second in line for the monarchy behind Raul. However, Rudolpho had secured a valuable place in his father's administration with his intelligent negotiation skills. Asanna told her about collecting porcelain dolls, each of which had a name. She had made up stories about their lives and written them down in a book she planned to give to her children, someday. She invited Maagy to come and visit and meet her "friends". Maagy shared with them her sadness at never knowing her mother and talked about the images that haunted her dreams. She told them about her birthday party disaster and the tantrums, which prompted King Henry to bring her along on the trip. She admitted how unhappy she had been, three weeks ago, when he had awakened her before dawn, but how the experience had changed her life.

Sunday had been a perfect day. There was a pick up game of *Creckett** on the lawn, egg hunts and pony rides for the children and lazy afternoon naps for the adults. The evening haze, which hung low over the mountaintops, yielded an unusually spectacular show of colors. The frogs and night bugs delivered their customary serenade and the fireflies blinked as if in time with the music. The evening had ended early, as the next day… today… and the next week… would be full with meetings and much work. Rudy had walked her to her door and, once again, kissed her hand... and once again... made her heart skip and flutter. She had watched him ascend round the third floor staircase... until he was out of sight.

Her dreamy thoughts carried her through her chores and she returned to the moment, as she entered through the mudroom, kicked off her smelly boots and washed her hands for breakfast. She arrived at the table promptly at six-thirty, as instructed, and was pleasantly surprised to find Prince Rudolpho already there with her father. When she opened the door and laid eyes upon him, her heart pounded wildly, her breath was taken away and she couldn't repress a great smile.

"Hello, again," she gushed.

"Always a good morning with you in it, Duchess."

He stood quickly, stepped boldly forward and took her hand before she could blink and kissed it as he bowed, and then pulled out the chair for her to sit... next to him.

"Your father and I have a few strategic details to discuss before the meetings begin. I hope you don't mind. May I get your tea?"

"No... yes... I mean, no... I... I don't mind a... a bit... not at all... it's... I'm... I mean... of course... discuss whatever you like. Tea would be lovely... sugar only, please," she stammered as she gazed at him.

As he delivered a cup of piping hot drink, their eyes locked. Rudolpho actually blushed a little.

"Good morning, Maagy, Dear," the King interjected, smiling at his daughter's foibles*. "Sleep well?"

"What? Sleep? Oh! Yes, Father, I slept quite well, thank you," she said as she got hold of herself and went to the buffet.

As they ate, Henry and Rudolpho discussed what seemed to be important matters. She felt left out of the conversation, but didn't mind much, since it gave her the opportunity to sip tea and stare at the handsome guest. When they had finished eating, Prince

Rudolpho excused himself, kissed her hand, again, bowed and took his leave. She was still basking in the warmth of the moment when her father broke the spell.

"Now Maagy, you're not wearing overalls to the meeting are you?"

"Sir? Oh... overalls... no... of course not, Daddy. I'll change clothes. I ran to the barn for chores and to say hello to Cupid first."

"Good. I want you at your best and at my side in the meetings. It's important you learn to conduct yourself in these sorts of negotiations. This will be your responsibility in a few years... nine o'clock, sharp."

Maagy had never seen her father in such a way. He seemed on edge, nervous. The meetings were obviously more important than she'd realized.

"Don't worry, Daddy, I'll be dressed appropriately and on time... I promise."

"Good, good... and, Maagy, please remember for the rest of the week, if we are in the presence of anyone else, you must follow protocol when addressing me."

"Yes... Sir," she said, a little intimidated. "I shall."

"Very well, then, I'll see you shortly in the grand ballroom."

He exited without any familial* affection, leaving her alone and stunned. He had never left her without some sort of kind word or kiss on the forehead... even in her most impetuous moments. She felt uneasy and lonely. Her heart pounded, again, but this time in *not* such a good way. She ran back to the barn as quickly as her feet would carry her and flung herself into Cupid's stall. The spirited horse jumped and whinnied, startled by the intrusion. Maagy wrapped her arms round Cupid's neck and sobbed quietly. She really couldn't identify what had injured her feelings so badly. All she knew was she wanted to cry and Cupid seemed the most logical choice for a sympathetic ear.

"Oh, Cupid, Daddy was cross with me and I don't know what

I've done to deserve it. My heart will surly break any moment," she sobbed.

The filly seemed to comprehend her friend's emotions and stood quietly. She nudged the weeping girl gently as if to reassure her. Finally, Maagy wiped her tears on her sleeve and took a deep breath.

"Thank, you, My Sweet Girl. I feel much better."

She gave Cupid a quick currying before leading her to the pasture. She ran to the castle, into the mudroom and kicked off her boots; then dashed through the kitchen and ducked into the shortcut in the coat closet. She flew up the stairs and found Estelí with clothes laid out on the bed. She had become more than a chambermaid. Maagy considered her a Lady-in-Waiting… though she was not aristocracy… and a friend. Estelí had been reluctant to cross the line between service and familiarity, but Maagy had convinced her she genuinely enjoyed her company. These arrangements were kept discrete, of course, as such a relationship would be quite improper under normal circumstances. Maagy really didn't care. She just wanted a friend.

She dressed hurriedly and ran down the grand staircase, ducked into the service hall and through the magic doors into the main dining room, which was already set for the midday meal. She saw her father standing outside the ballroom among the other heads-of-state and sidled* close to him. She took his arm and he instinctively put his hand on hers, but didn't look at her with his usual warm smile. Instead, he remained deep in his own thoughts. Again, she felt the urge to cry, but knew this was not the time. The pocket doors were pushed open as far as they would go. Maagy was shocked to see an enormous round table set precisely in the center of the ballroom with chairs placed at equal intervals. She had never seen a table so large and was curious as to how people would speak to each other across it without shouting. Smaller desks and chairs were placed round the perimeter of the room for the many assistants to the delegates.

"Daddy, why is the table so big?" She whispered.

"Shh!" Came quickly.

She was stunned by the abrupt response and shrank behind him, motionless, watching the scene. Finally, everyone seemed to be present and in place. The trumpets sounded and the entrance procession began.

Since Emperor Zinrahwi of The Empire of Terrasicus was the focus of the negotiations, he was an honored guest. He was introduced first and could choose which chair he preferred. He and his entourage had arrived late the previous evening, with another Darhambian chieftain, and had gone straight to their quarters, so this was Maagy's first look at him. She surmised he must have been the one all the whispering was about. She had never even heard of him until that week and didn't know what to expect, but immediately got an uneasy feeling, as she watched him move. She thought he looked rather like a buzzard stalking a rotting corps. He was not excessively tall, slight of build and his shoulders were hunched forward. She knew he was relatively young… round the same age as Queen Haideh… but appeared much older and weathered. His dark eyes were beady and close together and his skin ashen. He looked as if he had lived underground for a long time… like a mole.

"What's the matter with him, Father? Is he ill?"

"Shh! No!"

The two Darhambian chieftains accompanied the emperor. They were large, muscular men with brightly colored robes and hats to match. Their very dark chocolate skin was smooth and shiny, as if oiled, and their heads… what she could see of them… were bald. They were Chief Obuku of the southern region, father of Owanu… the strangely quiet boy who huddled in the corner at the ball… and Chief Nandu of the northern region. It was clear the emperor was in charge, though she could not, for the life of her, figure out why.

The chieftains were confident and powerful looking, while Zinrahwi seemed weak and mousy. He slithered into the room and walked round and round the table several times, with his henchmen close in tow, as if they were eyeing a fine horse for purchase. He looked at each corner of the room and up toward the ceiling. The other two followed suit. It was actually comical and she thought they behaved rather arrogantly. She couldn't help but smile at the folly.

"It's round, for goodness sake. What difference does it make?" She mumbled under her breath.

She felt the warm hand on hers squeeze firmly and realized she must have spoken out loud.

"Sorry," she whispered.

Zinrahwi finally settled on a position and stood behind a chair. The other two men flanked him with Owanu accompanying his father. King Henry was the host and was introduced next. He and Maagy walked in together and the king immediately… decisively… almost defiantly… chose the seat directly across from the emperor. She moved to the next chair, right of her father, but he reached out and drew her back to his side. A page appeared with a tufted stool and placed it close to his, being careful not to move the chairs on either side.

Prince Rudolph was the third introduced and moved quickly to the chair on the other side of King Henry. She tried to catch his eye and smile, but he never glanced in her direction. Queen Haideh positioned herself beside Maagy, but she, too, did not divert her eyes from the emperor. Maagy was delighted Asanna had joined her mother and, once again, a stool appeared for her and was placed on the far side of the only female head-of-state at the table. Father-King Afarnae and Prince Shamir took positions on the other side of Asanna. Maagy tried to discretely peek round the queen to catch her friend's eye, but the king took her hand and squeezed. She frowned and straightened up. The rest of the participants followed the same protocol until no chairs remained empty. Another layer of assistants stood or sat behind their respective delegates.

She looked round the table and thought she understood the strategy in the arrangements. Her father was in direct eye line of the one about whom the Summit had been called, a show of strength, on his part. Zinrahwi's allies were flanking him, so King Henry's allies flanked him. The other leaders chose seating in a similar manner with the Commonwealth delegates together. Premier Chamberlaine of Senecia seemed caught in the middle. Martha was sat *in a chair* beside her father… several spaces away from Rudolpho… and was watching him… too intently for Maagy's taste.

"Daddy, why can't I have a chair?" She leaned close and whispered.

"You're not here to negotiate or advise, you're here to observe. Now please be silent and observe… and when you address me, do it properly," he chided under his breath.

"Martha Chamberlaine has a chair," she mumbled… unfortunately, loud enough for her father to hear.

"*Shhh!!*"

She felt a lump rising in her throat and she couldn't stop the tears from welling. She looked down and wiped them away with her handkerchief and folded her hands in front of her. Her instinct was to run, screaming from the room and bury herself in pillows on her bed, but she set her jaw and stared at the center of the table, determined not to let the situation get the best of her. The trumpets blared again and the opening ceremonies began with the customary '*welcomes*' and '*thank yous*'. It seemed to drag on for hours as everyone stood in place behind his or her chair. Her feet were hurting, so she stepped out of her shoes and stood in stocking feet. The pins in her hair itched, so she unceremoniously rearranged them. She scratched her nose and her leg… and her arm… and fidgeted… and sighed loudly. Again, the king's hand squeezed hers.

Finally, the speeches were done and the last part of the formality was at hand. As a gesture of good will and trust, each participant was expected to lay down his… or her… weapons on the table and leave them for the duration of the Summit. King Henry started the process. He drew a formidable sword and laid it in front of him with the handle toward the center of the table. Maagy had never seen the instrument out of its housing and was amazed at the sheer beauty of it. She'd always thought the shiny silver scabbard was the sword. What could she possibly know about such things? The hilt was intricately carved gold and silver, inlaid with Mother-of-Pearl. The pommel was ornate with a large emerald encased in gold. The guard, also of gold and sliver, was wide and curved down away from the grip. The broad double-edged blade was forged steel with gold inlay, glistening and razor sharp. She was spellbound.

Emperor Zinrahwi was next. The blade of his sword was oddly curved and narrow with a black onyx hilt and guard. It reminded her of the thing Grandpa Kris showed her in the barn used for cutting tall grass and hay. He called it a sickle*. He had warned her not to touch it as it was quite sharp and could cut off her finger with one swipe. She was loath to think how lethal the emperor's ominous weapon might be. He positioned it slightly sideways in front of him so the handle pointed toward the center of the table. His fellows followed suit… in blind obedience. The humor was not lost on the princess. Rudolpho drew his sword… a one-handed, double-edged Claymore with a basket hilt… a formidable weapon… and a dagger and followed the same procedure.

Maagy's jaw visibly dropped as Queen Haideh produced an ornately embellished dagger from underneath the folds of that delicate silk garment she wore so elegantly. The hilt was full and carved from jade in the shape of a horse's head, adorned with a halter of inlaid gold, rubies and emeralds. The blade was considerably long and wavy. Forged from Damascus steel, it too was inlaid with gold. Her Royal Highness couldn't suppress her amazement and admiration.

"Brilliant!"

"Shh!"

She looked round embarrassed, and then back at the table. This bit of business took another several moments before it was time to sit and presumably begin negotiations. She had looked forward to seeing her father and Prince Rudolpho in action, but nothing happened and no one said anything. She looked round the room to see who might speak first. What she saw, instead, were clusters of two and three huddled together, whispering with their assistants. Premier Chamberlaine was going back and forth between the Terrasican camp and the Commonwealth delegates, Martha in tow. The Ministers of Trade for Poseidonia and Aquatain and Marinia's Prime Minister were in hushed dialogue with the Aradinian Foreign Minister. King Henry, Prince Rudolpho, Queen Haideh, Prince Shamir and Father-King Afarnae were sending hand written messages back and forth and Maagy was charged with relaying them. At least she had something meaningful to do, but she was dying to know what was being discussed. She craned her head over her father's shoulder in hopes of catching a glimpse of one of the notes, but his eyes met hers, went sharply to her stool and then back to hers. She frowned and plopped down with her arms crossed and a pouty grimace.

"Oh horse feathers!"

The king snapped round and glared at his daughter.

"Did I say that out loud?"

"You did."

"Sorry."

The hushed meetings continued as she tried her best to maintain dignity, but once again, she began to wiggle in boredom. She tapped her toe on the stool rung.

"Shh! Princess Maagy!"

She drummed her fingers on the table while the other hand held up her head.

"Princess Maagy, please!" Her father discretely admonished, as his impatience grew.

She sighed loudly and stood to stretch. The king cleared his throat… deliberately. She sneezed and the room fell even more silent than before.

"Excuse me," she said timidly.

"Bless you," was the response from several.

She looked up to see all eyes trained on her and some of the expressions were not pleasant, especially Zinrahwi and his two followers. They all had the exact same scowl and she was amused.

"They remind me of three blind mice, each following the other for fear of getting lost," she ruminated*, this time… *thankfully*… silently.

Asanna and Rudolpho had exchanged passing glances during Maagy's calamity and could hardly contain themselves. While the prince found it all wildly entertaining, he could not be a foolish boy, so he never looked back at Asanna nor did he look at King Henry, directly… and certainly not at Maagy… for fear he would burst into laughter. There were several who found the child's behavior delightfully refreshing and were working to suppress their smiles… one being King Afarnae with his unique sense of humor.

"Oh for goodness sake… why don't they just get on with it?" She whispered, impatiently.

"Princess Maagy, be quiet!" Her father instructed under his breath.

King Afarnae could refrain no longer and snickered out loud… and then covered it with a cough. Henry glanced his way and they made eye contact, which was the last thing either of them needed. Just as both were about to burst out laughing, the luncheon bell tinkled and saved them. King Henry quickly stood and announced a casual buffet would be served in the main dining room and the conference would reconvene at three o'clock. He and Afarnae beat a hasty retreat as everyone else slowly exited in small groups, leaving Maagy standing alone.

Chapter 8
Fishing Lessons

She had hoped for personal time with her father, but not so. He was sitting at the head table in the grand dining room with Father-King Afarnae, Queen Haideh and Prince Shamir and it looked as though they were involved in serious conversation, as Rudolpho joined them. Even Asanna was engaged in the conference. Maagy looked round the room at all the others and a sudden wave of panic overtook her. She bolted through the dining room, into the coat closet and through the service hall. She burst into the kitchen and found a buzz of activity, as she located Grandma Polly and rushed to her side.

"There you are," she said breathlessly. "I need a friendly face!"

"Oh My Dear, Your Highness Princess Maagy! You cannot be in here. You must leave at once."

"But *why*? I come in all the time."

"But not this week… not while the meeting is in session… Your Darling Highness. Your presence in the kitchen is highly inappropriate."

"I don't care! I hate it out there! No one has time for me and Daddy is ever so cross. I want to hide."

"Oh my. I'm sorry you're so miserable, but you cannot hide in the kitchen. Now scurry along. Slip out through the service hall and into the ballroom, and then double back into the dining room. I'm sure you're hungry and it's putting you at *sixes and sevens**."

"I don't want to eat with the adults. They're all stuffy and… *busy.* Can't I eat in the family dining room with the children?"

Grandma Polly's heart was aching for the sad little girl.

"No, Your Precious Grace. You're the Official Hostess. You must eat with His Royal Majesty King Henry."

Even Grandma Polly was using all the formal designations… though somewhat modified.

"Oh goodness, you are in a bad way, aren't you?"

"Please Gram-P?"

"I'm sorry. You must go now… but…" then she whispered as she brushes a bit of stray hair from the child's face, "come back later when there's no one about and we'll have tea and a good talk… I promise. All right, Your Dear Highness?"

"All right… I suppose."

The woman gave an affectionate wink and Maagy returned to the foyer by way of her secret route… intending to do as she was told… but slipped into the family dining room, instead, where she fixed a plate of food and took it outdoors to a secluded area on the lawn next to the pond. She found a good spot in the grass and took off her shoes and stockings. She ate slowly and picked at her food as she pondered the days events. She was just about to melt into tears when Estelí appeared with a fishing pole and bucket.

"Oh! Your Highness, I apologize for interrupting your *repas**. I will leave you alone, *tout de suite**."

"No! Wait! Please don't leave me alone. I've been alone all day."

"But, Your Highness, I should not be here with you in such a casual way. Someone might see us. It is highly inappropriate."

"*Highly inappropriate*!" She mocked. "I don't care! I want you here and I'm the Crown Princess! Do my wishes mean nothing?"

"I am sorry, Your Grace. I did not mean to make you angry."

"Oh… you didn't make me angry, Estelí. I'm so frustrated. No one has time for me. My father only snaps at me and he *never* does that. The meeting is *mind numbingly* boring and the Emperor of Terrasicus keeps looking at me and scowling as if he's going to cook me for dinner. I just want friendly company."

"Well then… I am at your service, Your Highness."

"Oh call me Maagy… and that's another thing. My father insists I address him formally when anyone else is present. I have to call my own father, 'Your Royal Majesty'! Unbearable!"

"I see your dilemma. Perhaps you need a distraction… like… fishing."

"What's in the bucket?"

"*La pollo piel**"

"What?"

"Chicken skins. It sounds better in my language."

"Eeewww! What on earth for?"

"Bait!"

Estelí proceeded to take a glob of the slimy mess and tie it to the end of the string attached to the pole. She gathered the string in her hands and threw it and the bait into the water. She took hold of the pole and sat on the grass beside the princess.

"Now what?"

"Now, we wait."

"Wait for what?"

"For a fish to grab the morsel and swallow it and then we pull him ashore."

"Oh… How long will it take?"

"As long as it takes."

"As long as it takes for what?"

"You ask too many questions, Your Highness… Maagy."

"So I've been told!"

Suddenly, The pole bent almost in half and the line zipped out across the pond.

"You've got one! *You've got one!*"

Both girls shrieked with joy. The fish was pulling so hard Estelí almost went into the water headfirst.

"I cannot hold him! I am going to lose the pole! He is pulling me in!"

"Hang on! I'll help you!"

Maagy jumped to her feet and wrapped her arms round the angler's waist. She pulled with all her might, both girls hysterically laughing and squealing. Their feet dug into the mud and both slid to the edge of the bank. Suddenly, the tension on the line gave way. They flew backwards and landed on the ground on their backsides, still giggling.

"What happened?" Maagy asked as she gasped for air.

"The string came untied and our catch got his belly full, I suppose!"

"Was that a fish?"

"Whatever it was it was big! That is all I know!"

"That was the funniest, most exciting thing to happen in a long time. Let's try for another."

"Oh dear, my free time is over and we are all muddy. I shall need to wash up before I go back to work. I am sorry, Madam."

"Not to worry, you gave me a good giggle and I needed it. Thank you for the distraction."

"It was my pleasure, Your Highness… I mean… Maagy. *Adieu*."

"See you soon."

Estelí hurried back to the castle. Maagy gathered her plate and utensils in one hand, her shoes and stockings in the other, and walked slowly through the soft grass. She was looking down to make sure she didn't step on a bee, when a familiar voice interrupted her thoughts.

"Maagy, The Barefoot Duchess."

She looked up to see Rudy standing in front of her.

"Oh, hello! Where did you come from?" She asked, flustered.

"The question is where did *you* come from? You have grass in your hair. Here let me get it for you."

He stepped closer and reached out toward her. She shivered and closed her eyes. She had never felt such a strong wave of... something... she didn't know what. She wanted to lean against him, as he removed a blade of grass. He gently brushed a few hairs off her face and tucked in an errant pin.

"There, good as new," he said smiling. "Wait, weren't you wearing something on your head earlier?"

"What?" She said. "*Oh no!* My tiara! Here, hold these!"

She shoved the contents of her hands at Rudolpho's chest. He instinctively caught it all as she flew back to the pond in a panic.

"Where is it? *Where is it?*" She muttered as she searched.

She found the precious headpiece several feet behind where she and Estelí had crashed to the ground. The tiara was her mother's and was a birthday gift from her father. She plopped it on her head and ran back to the prince. He could only chuckle at the entertainment. She noticed Captain Sistrunk a discrete distance away, but ever watchful.

"Does he follow you everywhere?"

"Yes. It's his sole job... to follow me... everywhere."

"How annoying."

"You didn't eat much," he said, as he looked at the plate in his hand. "What's this... the royal bottomless pit, not hungry? Are you ill?"

"No... just... not hungry."

"Are you going in? May I walk with you?"

"Yes, and you may," she said as she took her belongings.

"So, what did you think of the morning session?" He asked.

"Are you interested or just being polite?"

"Oh... I'm *quite* interested," he reassured with an ironic grin.

She was oblivious. They entered through the main door and ducked into the family dining room. No one was there except the cleaning staff, so she placed her dish on the tray with the others and sat down to put on her footwear.

"Oh bother. My feet are caked with mud. I can't put my shoes on over that. I'll have to wash up."

"There's plenty of time. It's just one. We have until three. Are you trying to avoid answering my question?"

"No… but I'm not sure how honest I should be."

"Be brutal, I can take it."

"I've never been so *bored* in all my life. Did I say that out loud?" She mocked herself. "Yes, I think I did. How's that for honest?"

"I could tell it wasn't your cup of tea," he replied as he poured each of them one. "Sugar and milk?"

"Sugar… how do you do it? I would go positively batty if I had to do that all the time."

"I'll be honest, this time. I actually love the excitement of brokering deals," he said, as he brought their drinks to the table and sat. "This morning was just the beginning… the posturing phase, where each is calculating what the others are thinking and what they might offer in compromise. It's a game, really, like cards, only the stakes are much higher."

"It seemed as if nothing happened in all that time. No one said a thing out loud… except me… and I was chastised for it. And, that Terrasican Emperor gave me chills. He glared at me the entire morning."

"Shh, Maagy, careful what you say. If I've learnt one thing from this process, it is there are always people about listening," he whispered, as he sipped his tea. "I don't mean to chastise you, as well. You've had enough of that today. Take it as friendly advice."

"I will… and you're right… I do know better. I'm just so cross today I don't know what to do. My father is acting completely unlike himself and I don't know what to make of it."

"Maagy, there's a tremendous burden on his shoulders. Don't judge him too harshly. You've probably never seen him in this setting, have you?"

"No, I suppose not… but… even you and Queen Haideh were different," she said softly, then quickly changed the subject. "*Speaking of*, did you see that enormous dagger she pulled from… I don't even *know* from where… and laid on the table?"

"I did! I have a whole new respect for the gentle queen.

"I, as well!"

"I'm sorry if I hurt your feelings… we're all… a bit… apprehensive."

"Oh… it's fine… no worries…" she replied, somewhat embarrassed, as they sipped tea. "Rudy… or should I address you as Your Highness Prince Rudolph?"

"In this setting, Rudy is fine," he chuckled fully understanding the reference.

"Rudy, how is it you are representing your entire kingdom? You're so young. Your father must have great faith in you. I can't imagine being in the same position."

"I began accompanying him to meetings when I was twelve. He does trust me, but he would be here himself if… I shouldn't speak further."

His voice trailed off and he became serious. She knew she had touched a nerve. They finished their tea.

"Rudy, is there something wrong? What is it?"

He drew his chair closer and whispered, "You must never *ever* speak of this. It could have repercussions throughout the region."

"I won't, I promise. I'm good at keeping confidences. What is it?"

"My father is not well. He has been ill for some time, but no one knows, save the family and King Henry… and now you. I'm worried out of my mind. My brother is grooming to take the throne and elected to stay with him. Since I've always shown a keen interest in military strategy and diplomacy, Father sent me. I fear something terrible will happen… and I won't be with him."

"I'm sorry," she said gently. "Will Raul be a good king? Oh, I shouldn't have asked such a personal question."

"Nonsense, nothing is off limits to you. Yes, he will be, but he has no interest in military issues. That will be my job. He will lead by example and I will lead the troops into battle. Together, we'll be an excellent team."

"Do you and he get on well?"

"Surprisingly well, considering he's twelve years older."

"I don't know what I'm going to do. My father wants to retire and give me the crown. Can you imagine me at the head of the table… being diplomatic? I haven't the first clue what's going on in there. I want to smack some of them, but I'm quite certain it's not acceptable. I'm never going to be ready… and I don't want to be. It sounds nice saying, 'I'm going to be Queen!' But actually doing it is another whole ball of yarn. It's too much. I don't want to be responsible for an entire kingdom. I want to play hide-and-seek and have adventures. It's all too overwhelming!"

"Would you like some help sorting it out?"

"I didn't mean to rant at you, Rudolpho. It must be nice having siblings. What about your sister? What is she like?"

"My sister… my sister… Consuela is a bit hard to define, really. I suppose she's like… a sprite… a free spirit… she doesn't conform to any of the normal expectation of being a royal. You're a bit like her, actually. She isn't at all interested in the pomp and ceremony. She is happiest working in the garden or carrying food to a family in need. You could pass her on the street… or in a confectionary… and not know who she was," he said, smiling at the memory. "I admire her, really. She's one of a kind."

His words were steeped in *double entendre** and Maagy blushed, as her heart raced. He continued to smile and absorb her with his eyes.

"What can I do to help you through the meetings this afternoon, Maagy?"

"I… don't actually know why… the Summit is taking place. Why is everyone so serious and secretive?"

"Well, no wonder you're bored. Let's see, where to start… first of all, your instincts about Emperor Zinrahwi are dead on the mark," he murmured, as he drew closer to her. "I assume he is one you'd like to smack?"

"Absolutely! And the other two blind mice following him."

Rudolpho snickered and continued in a hushed tone. "Are you familiar with the geography of the region?"

"Of course… yes… well… we studied it this past quarter… but honestly… I didn't pay attention. So the answer is no… I'm not familiar."

"Let me see if I can explain it to you. The Ascondia and Crying Wind rivers are vital to the prosperity of the valley nations. The two rivers… a map would be nice…"

"A map? You want a map?"

"Yes, a map would help."

"Come with me."

"Where?"

"Just come with me… discretely… be nonchalant."

As Maagy went to the door to make sure the way was clear, Rudy noticed the back of her skirt and chuckled.

"Maagy, your skirt is covered with mud and grass stain. What in the world were you doing on the lawn?"

"Fishing… in the pond," she retorted, indignantly. "That's why my feet are muddy. Follow me."

She led Rudolpho up the stairs to the second floor and round to the science library. She opened the doors with a flourish and pointed to the large map[4] hanging on the wall.

"Will that do?"

"Oh, wonderful! Yes, it will definitely do. What is this place?"

"It's a library devoted entirely to science, complete with a laboratory. Isn't it fascinating?"

"Indeed it is. This is a beautiful map… one of the most detailed I've ever seen," he said as he perused it.

4 Please see Glossary; Maps

He had been careful to leave the library doors open, with his ever-present guard, Captain Sistrunk, just outside. It would not have been proper etiquette for him to be behind closed doors in the presence of such a young girl and certainly not the Crown Princess.

"You think that's good, come see this!"

Maagy led him to the steps, which spiraled upward to the observatory. She took them, two at a time, and he had no choice but to follow.

"How about this? Isn't this just extraordinary?"

"What is it?" He asked, looking at the enormous thing in the center of the room.

"It's a machine called a telescope. It makes the moon and stars look as if you could reach out and touch them."

"A telescope… I've heard of such, but have never actually seen one. It is, indeed, extraordinary! Why is it here?"

"Why not? It's the farthest north of any manmade structure in the kingdom and the highest elevation possible without being on a frozen mountain peak… according to Grandpa Kris… and he knows how to use it. I discovered it while exploring the castle and asked him to show it to me and he did, last week. I swear I could have touched the moon."

"How does it work?"

"The way he explained it, there are lenses and mirrors inside this tube. The lenses are shaped such that they magnify the image and each additional one magnifies it more. The image is reflected into the mirrors… and bounced… round… in there… until it reaches the eye. Or something like that… I think… I don't really understand it, but it works… so I love it! Unfortunately, it only works at night. You can't look at the sun… it's far too bright."

"I'd love to see it in action."

"I'm sure Grandpa Kris would happily demonstrate."

"So shall I continue with your geography lesson, Princess Grass Stain?"

"Oh, Rudy," she said, blushing. "Yes, please continue."

The two descended the stairs and went back to the map. She climbed onto a stool and gave her full attention to her instructor, as any good student would do. He found a pointer and began the lesson.

"First, I'll tell you, in order to understand the delicate nature of the talks, you must know something about the geography and history of the kingdoms in attendance. Here is Berensenia, the largest and most prosperous of the valley kingdoms."

"That one, I know."

"And these are the kingdoms of the Commonwealth."

"I know that, too."

"Now, you see here to the south, Aradinia, Senecia and my home, Estadore. All our borders are friendly with an open trade policy…"

She began to drift off into fantasy, as she watched every move the handsome prince made and barely heard a word.

"… Senecia and Estadore have ports to the Sea of Melania… shipping access to Greco, Italania, Franciné and Hispania… through the Aegean Sea into the Mare Medio Terrae. The tricky part… strait between Adriaca and Ottoman… access to open water… trade with Isle of Reland, Reland Main and Skodinovia. Questions?"

"No," she responded, dreamily, "I follow you, so far."

"Good. So, trade and shipping are two significant reasons for the Summit, as they affect all the valley kingdoms."

"I see…" noticing the silence, she snapped back to reality and added, "I overheard something about water rights. What is that about? It seemed awfully important."

"Well that's the rub," he said with authority. "Several major rivers run through Berensenia and on into the southern kingdoms. Those rivers are critical to agriculture and as shipping lanes. It all starts with the Ascondia River, which originates far north in the frozen region, here, you see?"

"Yes. It begins in a rather large lake, isn't that right? I forgot the name of it."

"You are correct. The river flows out of Frost Proof Lake in the Depopulos."

"What a funny name for a lake surrounded by snow covered mountains."

"Well, the Berensen Sea just a few mile north is completely frozen over, but the lake never freezes."

"That's odd."

"Indeed. It is believed the lake is fed by a hot spring deep inside the inactive volcanic crater, which forms the bowl of the lake. The water bubbling from the depths is quite hot so it never freezes. It's fresh water rather than salty, like the sea."

"That's interesting," she said genuinely engaged, again. "My tutor never said that when we studied it before. How do you know all this?"

"Because explorers from Estadore discovered the lake and the mouth of the river. It's all well known at home."

"Oh… I see," Maagy said with a great yawn.

"Have you had enough? Am I boring you?" He asked, completely charmed by her.

"Oh… no… so sorry! Continue, please," she responded, slightly embarrassed, as she propped her chin on both hands and smiled sweetly. "Five thirty came quite early."

"Indeed it did. So the Ascondia runs east and slightly south to here…"

She could hear the dulcet tones of his voice, but the words meant nothing, as she watched him adoringly, her thoughts lost in her own head.

"Can you see that? Maagy, did you hear me?"

"What? Oh… yes, then what?"

"Then it branches, with the Crying Wind turning southwest… Rainbow Falls… Dragon's Den Canyon… Berensenia and Terrasicus… a sort of no-man's land…"

His words were dancing round her like a butterfly ballet. She tried to pay attention, but it was difficult to hear past her eyes.

"The canyon… natural barrier… treacherous rocks and raging currents… impossible to navigate… Maagy, are you listening?" He said abruptly, noticing the dreamy look on her face.

"Yes…" she whispered, through a far away grin, then caught herself. "Yes! Of course… I'm listening… the canyon… a barrier… raging currents… something about a dragon… Dragon's Den Canyon…"

"Hmm… you had a strange look on your face. Anyway, the river follows the entire length of the canyon to where it dumps into Buzzard Lake, then out the other side… through the most strategically vulnerable area… Buzzard Lake Gap back into Berensenia toward Estadore."

"I love that name, Buzzard Lake!"

"You know how it got the name, don't you?"

"Of course… no, not really," She said, too curious to pretend to be knowledgeable.

"It's also a volcanic crater and is said to be deeper than anyone has ever measured. There are legends the lake is under some sort of spell," he said mysteriously, leaning on his elbow eye to eye with her. "Many have tried to cross the lake, but few have succeeded, thus the name *Buzzard… Lake*!"

She couldn't breathe… her heart pounded from the closeness… her eyes widened. She was totally taken in by his charisma*.

"Oh stop! You're not scaring me," she finally managed to admonish, playfully. "It's just legend, which means it's not true."

"Not so. Some legends are based in fact… does make for a good story, though, doesn't it?"

"I suppose, but keep going," she said, sitting up straight and being more serious about the business at hand. "I still don't understand what this has to do with the Summit."

"Ah, now for the good part. You see here, the mountains on the Berensenian side of the canyon are colored green?"

"Yes..."

"That's because they're heavily forested and are teeming with plant and animal life. Now, on this side of the canyon is Terrasicus."

"It's painted brown."

"That, my barefoot lady, is because it is a desert wasteland. Nothing grows there, not crops or animals or even many people, thus, another important piece of the Summit puzzle."

"Water rights! So it has to do with Terrasicus needing water!"

"Brilliant! You're beginning to get the idea. Look back here at Buzzard Lake Gap. The Jaldahr River originates at the lake, and flows east into Terrasicus, but goes deep underground before exiting the mountains. It's theorized the sandy desert is too porous for the riverbed and the water sinks into the aquifer. There is not one other river flowing through Terrasicus."

"How does anything live there with no water?"

"Nothing does. The entire population of Terrasicus lives along the southern borders with Darhambi and Nihmrobi or the eastern border with Asiana. Estadore is somewhat protected by the mountains. Those areas are the only places with water, so even though the total population is small comparatively, there is extreme overcrowding and resources are stretched to the limit. One hundred thousand people are crammed into cities where only a few hundred once lived."

"One hundred thousand? You call that a comparatively *small* population? That seems like a lot of people to me!"

"Maagy, how many people do you think live in Berensenia?"

"I have no idea. I never thought of it."

"Well over five hundred thousand."

"Half a million people? My father is king for half a million people? Oh... I think I feel sick!"

"And that number is just Berensenia... there are four other kingdoms in your Commonwealth of Realms, over all of which you will preside... well over a million people."

"Oh lord… I'll never… *ever*… be fit for the job."

"I think you will. I think you'll be just fine when it's your turn. You're smart, strong willed and the most unique individual I know. I have faith in you, Princess Grass Stain… Duchess of Barefeet."

"Unique? Strong willed? I do hope those were compliments."

"Most assuredly."

"Do you really think I'll learn enough in five years to lead all those people?"

"I do. Shall we continue?"

"Yes," she answered, now fully engaged in the conversation.

"The emperor is constantly crossing into one or the other of the bordering territories to plunder."

"Well, that's a rather sad existence. I suppose he's trying to feed his people."

"I would agree with you if it were anyone other than Zinrahwi. He has twice dammed the major rivers in attempts to divert water to Terrasicus. The first time was far north in the mountains. He attempted to dig a new riverbed that, in theory, would have changed the course of the Ascondia into his kingdom completely. The work went on for years before it was discovered. A small volcanic eruption in the area destroyed all their clandestine achievements. Lava flowed into the trench they had dug and filled it up, again. It was then the plan was discovered. Your father led a military assault and drove them back into Terrasicus. It was an ugly confrontation called the Battle of Ascondia River… look it up when you go back to Avington."

"I never knew that… I will…"

"The second time was last year. He managed to get into Dragon's Den Canyon and do the same thing. He has, so far, diverted almost half the water flow from the Ascondia toward his nation. The water level in the lake is declining and the river into Estadore is well below its banks. If he continues this quest, Estadore will lose its major fresh water supply and Nihmrobi will lose its only river."

"Why can't we drive him out of the canyon and tear down the dam?"

"Because the canyon is not within your borders or his. It's a sort of neutral zone between the kingdoms, so there is no jurisdiction to force him out. The only alternative is to offer him something he wants in return for more water. Do you understand, now?"

"I do. I'm beginning to realize the complexity of the problem, but I don't see why we have to allow him to continue. If he can go into the canyon, why can't we? It seems simple enough to me."

"It's anything but simple. Historically, Terrasicus has been led by a legacy of vicious, aggressive rulers. Wars with their neighbors to the east have raged on for decades throughout the centuries, with only brief periods of calm. Your father managed to broker a peace years ago, with the western kingdoms and now that peace is threatened."

"But you said the population is small, so how formidable could their forces be? Can't we subdue them?"

"Again, not so simple. Here's the real irony. While the flat land is barren desert, the Sagamathias are rich with precious ore and gems. Zinrahwi possesses wealth beyond imagination from the sale of those resources, but he keeps it for himself rather than use it for the good of his nation. He could easily trade for goods and services his people need. Instead, he hoards personal riches while he steals from all of us. When his victims have had enough and push him back, he hires mercenary* soldiers to fight his battles and increases his forces by a hundred fold with an unlimited number of combatants to go on forever. He's an evil man, pure evil, as was his father before him and his before him. And now you know."

"Now I know… but I'm not sure it does me any good."

Chapter 9
Diplomatic Tutorial

The geography and history lessons were food for thought. Maagy returned to her room to clean up and change her clothes before the afternoon session.

"Oh, crumbs, I'm a mess," she muttered as she caught sight of herself in the mirror.

There was mud on her feet and legs; grass caught in her petticoat and her tiara was sideways. When she removed her skirt and saw it ruined with grass stains, she threw it under the bed. Her hair was disheveled. She paused for a moment to recall his gentle touch, when he removed some twigs and brushed hair from her face. She shivered again. Back to the problem at hand… she had no alternative except to take it down and start all over. She had washed up and dressing, while pondering the gravity of her future, when she heard strange noises coming from the fireplace. She leaned into it and listened. It was the faint sound of crying coming from Estelí's room through the shared chimney. Maagy went even closer and realized it must be her friend in anguish on the other side. She rang the bell cord. The chambermaid tapped on the door and Maagy was ready to welcome her.

"I need some help with my hair, if you have the time," she said, nonchalantly.

"Of course, Your Highness," the girl responded, not looking up and discretely wiping her eyes with her apron. "I always have time for you."

"Estelí, what is the matter? Why are you crying?"

"I am not crying, Your Grace. I have dust in my eyes."

"That's nonsense and you know it. I heard you crying on the other side of the wall. I demand you tell me now, *and truthfully,* what has made you cry," she said as she folded her arms and took an authoritative stance. "I am still your Crown Princess and, as such, I demand honesty. I am also your friend and I want to help, if I can."

"Thank you, but it is nothing… silly, really. I do appreciate your concern."

"If it's nothing then tell me what it is."

"No… really… it is not necessary…"

"Let me be the judge of that. Now, why were you crying?"

"Your Highness, I…"

"Tell me!" She demanded, stomping her foot.

"I was assisting on the third floor… one of the girls is ill… and I was cleaning the room of the son of one of the Darhambian chieftains when he walked into the room. We are not allowed to be present with anyone of the opposite gender while working. So I excused myself, quickly, and was about to leave, but the room was not finished and the bed was not yet made. He demanded I finish and make his bed. I told him I was not allowed to be there with him and I would come back and finish later. He demanded again and, when I respectfully declined to break the house rule, he picked up a crystal paperweight from the desk and threw it at me. It smashed against the wall and glass flew everywhere. He said now I could clean up that mess, too, when I returned. I ran to my room and did not know what to do next. I cannot lose this position, Madam. *Ma mère** is ill and I care for her with the money I make here. I am so sorry to cause such an incident."

"You poor dear. You didn't do anything wrong. In fact, you did exactly what you should have done and you need not apologize."

"I should have done as he told me and finished the room. No one would have been any the wiser for my breaking the rules… and the paperweight would not have been broken… and I would not have cried… and upset you."

"Stop right there! First of all, *you* would have known you broke the rule and would have carried the burden of it. Second, you handled the situation precisely according to protocol and did absolutely nothing wrong. Third, the fault for this sits squarely on the boy's shoulders. He is the one who was rude and even violent. I shall take care of this and you will not lose your position because of it. What would I do if you were gone?"

"Oh, Maagy… Your Highness… I am so sorry for the trouble… really. Just let it lay. I do not want you to be inconvenienced."

"Look here, I've had a huge wake-up, today. I'm going to be the queen in a few years. I'll have much more than this to deal with soon enough. I can handle this small problem."

Maagy knew immediately it was Owanu Obuku who had committed the offense. She marched up the stairs to the third floor and knocked loudly on his door. He opened it with a sour look on his face and it didn't get better.

"Are you Owanu Obuku?"

"I am."

"I am Princess Melania Abigail Alice Grace, Duchess of Wentworth, Crown Princess of Berensenia and the Commonwealth of Realms. Might I have a word with you please?"

"I know who you are. You may come in," he said as he stepped aside and gestured.

"Our protocol dictates unmarried young women and young men are not allowed in a bedchamber together without chaperons present," she stated firmly, but respectfully. "Since there are none, I would appreciate your stepping into the hallway."

"I'm resting," he said indifferently. "I'd be more comfortable sitting in my room than standing in the hall."

"Be that as it may, I must insist you come out here. I wish to speak to you concerning this same protocol or… rather… *your breach* of it," she said deliberately, with her hands on her hips.

"Excuse me?" He responded indignantly*, as he stepped out of his room to confront her.

She was not the least bit intimidated… even though he was several inches taller and much heavier than she… and stood her ground, looking up at him. She spoke calmly, but was positively seething inside.

"My chambermaid, Estelí Barrineau, was the young woman at whom you threw a crystal paperweight. I don't appreciate your treating our staff with disrespect. She was only following the rules, which you demanded she break."

"I don't appreciate you treating me with disrespect! I am the son of a tribal chieftain!"

"And I am the daughter of a king! That has nothing to do with this discussion. You owe her an apology."

"I owe no one anything. She disobeyed my command. She is but a lowly servant girl, so what do you care and why are you involved at all?"

"We do not consider our staff to be servants. They are paid a fair wage by the Commonwealth, and as such, deserve respect… *and your regrets* for your rudeness."

"You are just a female. I do not have to listen to you."

He tried to step into his room and shut the door in her face, but she reached out and pushed the door further open.

"I say you do! This is my home and you've disrespected our staff and therefore me. So you will hear this!"

"This is not your home. You do not even live here. You are visiting."

"*As are you*! It is my summer home; therefore, my home and you are a guest in it. You should have better manners!"

"Your *'staff'*... as you put it... should have better manners and so should you!"

"You arrogant, obnoxious *brat*! Don't you dare speak to me that way! And do not ever speak to anyone who lives or works here with disrespect again... or... I'll tell my father... and he will... *invade your kingdom*!"

She whirled round and stomped downstairs to her room and slammed the door. Estelí was still there waiting for her.

"That boorish brute! I cannot believe his behavior! How can he be so discourteous?"

"Oh no! *Mon dieu**! I knew it! I knew this could not end well. I am so sorry, Your Grace."

"It's not for you to be sorry about anything. He's the offender. Oh dear, look at the time. I have five minutes. Can you do something with my hair, Friend?"

Estelí worked her magic with the hair and Maagy was out the door in three, down in two and back in the meeting on time, even if her tiara was slightly askew. As with the morning session, the afternoon was more posturing and whispering, but Maagy was more engaged. She glanced, occasionally, at Rudolpho, who smiled and winked. Finally, King Henry called the group to order and suggested all participants present their proposals and begin discussions. Emperor Zinrahwi took offense at the idea and stood for several *very long* minutes ranting about the injustices imposed upon his kingdom and then stormed out, leaving everyone in the room scratching their heads in wonder. The meeting adjourned for the day and a light dinner buffet was served.

Later that evening, King Henry called Maagy into his room and shut the door.

"What is this about words between you and the son of Chief Obuku?"

"You heard about that?"

"I did. Would you care to explain?"

"He was rude to Estelí… and I told him it was unacceptable… and he should apologize."

"The way I heard it, you threatened to invade his kingdom!"

"Not exactly. I threatened… *you*… would invade," she said sheepishly. "Daddy, he made her cry! I heard her sobbing on the other side of the wall, so I pulled the bell cord and sure enough she had been crying. At first she wouldn't tell me, but finally, I got it out of her. He went into his room while she was cleaning it. She tried to follow protocol and leave, but he demanded she finish. When she started to leave anyway, he threw something at her. I will not tolerate such behavior, Father!" She explained, as she finished her rant and took that defiant stance he had seen so many times.

"So you interceded on her behalf… is that when you threatened invasion?"

"Yes Sir… but not before he was rude and dismissive of *me*! He said because I was *a female*, he didn't have to listen to me. That's when I got really angry and threatened…"

"Maagy you cannot confront people in such a manner! He is the son of an extremely important individual in these negotiations. You must make amends to the boy."

"I'm sorry to disagree with you, Father, but I shall not do anything of the sort. He is an arrogant brat and I told him such."

"Maagy, you've no idea what you're doing here. Your behavior could undermine this entire effort."

"Yes I do know, Father. Rudolpho gave me a tutorial on the geography and politics of the region. I understand the water rights negotiations are critical… but so are principles. And I will not apologize for doing the right thing… and standing up for Estelí *is* the right thing."

"Zinrahwi is looking for an excuse to leave the Summit and go build his dam even higher. He would love to justify an invasion and that is the last thing any of us needs. Maagy, you must back down on this and tell the boy you were wrong."

"Father… I… I… *cannot* believe my ears. I cannot believe you would ask me to compromise my ethics, and go against what I *know* is right and honorable, to appease those barbarians!"

"Oh, Maagy… you make it so hard to find fault with your reasoning," he admitted as he paced the room. "The fact is… life is not always white or black. Sometimes it must be shades of gray in the middle. Sometimes we have to *swallow our tongues** to keep from speaking our minds in order to achieve the greater good. This conference and the water agreement with Zinrahwi is the greater good, Maagy. This mess is endangering the entire negotiation."

"I *am* sorry… but only for making your job… and Rudy's… much harder. Perhaps, I shouldn't have confronted Owanu, but having done so, I will not go back on what I said. He was mean spirited and violent toward one of our own. That cannot… and *will* not be tolerated by me… and shouldn't be by you. Daddy, you've always encouraged me to be brave and stand up for what I believe. Now, you're asking me to abandon all that and give in to a tyrant. I just cannot."

"Oh, Child…" he said, sinking onto a chair, "what am I going to do with you?"

"There must be a way round this… to save face for all concerned. I'm sure something will come to mind, Daddy. May I go to my room now? I'm frightfully tired and I'm sure you are."

"Yes, you may go. Good night."

She turned and walked slowly to the door, hoping to have a small bit of the father she recognized come through the gruff exterior of the *King* in her presence.

"Sleep tight. Don't let the bedbugs bite."

She spun round on her heels and ran to him. She hugged him and kissed him on the check, as he did to her.

"I love you Daddy. I'm so sorry. Sleep well."

As she was walking to her room, Rudy came up the stairs headed to the third floor.

"Rudy, You're just the person I need to see."

"Now, Maagy? It's late and we're all worn out from this difficult day."

"Please? Just a quick word?"

"I suppose, but it must be quick. I'm dead on my feet."

"Follow me," she whispered.

She led him round toward the railing overlooking the grand ballroom. Mak took his place a respectful distance away to give them privacy.

"Look down. Look at that enormous table and all those weapons on it. Isn't it bizarre?"

"What a vantage point. It certainly is a different perspective from here. Why do you need to talk to me?"

"I have a… *tiny* problem… I need to sort out."

"Yes… I've heard."

"What have you heard?"

"Only that the Impetuous Princess and Owanu Obuku had a… shall we say… *tête* à *tête**… and it didn't end well."

"What else?"

"Nothing."

"So you don't know what *actually* happened?"

"Not really… no… but I'd love to hear your version."

"Suffice it say, he was insolent to someone in our household and I confronted him on her behalf and demanded an apology."

"There's the girl!" He smiled and said admiringly. "Who was it?"

"My chambermaid… and friend."

"I see."

"Are you judging me?"

"Not at all."

"Now, Father wants me to apologize for the good of the Summit and I've refused… on principle."

"On principle, is it?"

"What's that supposed to mean?"

"Only that you have been known to be stubborn… from time to time… for the sake of being stubborn."

"That's not the case, this time," she scowled, wondering where he got that bit of information. "He threw a crystal paperweight and almost hit her. It smashed and glass flew everywhere. She could have been hurt."

"Now that's a different story. Violence against one's household… or friend… cannot be allowed. So you confronted him and what happened?"

"He dismissed me as a lowly female and told his father *his* version of the story, I suppose. Now, I'm a *pariah** and he's a *victim* of my impetuousness! Brilliant!"

"Shall *I* speak to this fellow?"

"Heavens no! I think I've done enough damage."

"He made several mistakes, as I see it, the biggest of which was to dismiss you. He obviously didn't know to whom he was speaking."

"Then… I lost my temper and… sort of… *threatened*… to tell my father to invade Darhambi."

"Ohhhhh! Now I see the rub! My dear Maagy, you do have a knack for digging a trench, don't you?" He said laughing out loud, and then whispering, "I'm glad you're not on Zinrahwi's side or else none of us would have any water, at all!"

Rudy held his sides laughing at her precarious* predicament. She folded her arms, pouted her bottom lip and sulked until he was ready to talk.

"I hope you enjoyed that, at my expense."

"I'm sorry, Duchess, but you never cease to amaze… or amuse me."

"Well? What am I going to do about it? I need to find a way to smooth things over without telling that lout* I'm sorry… because *I'm not* and I *won't* give in!"

"Think about it for a moment. Someone, who was *not* in a position of power, was insulted by someone she perceived to be more powerful. But then someone… you… *in* a position of power defended her. What does that tell you?"

"That… hmmm… I've no idea… what are you saying?"

"Look at it this way. She came to you…"

"Not really. I had to pry it out of her. She would have never told me, had I not heard her crying."

"The point is she went above *his* head with her grievance. Perhaps… you…"

"Could go above *his* head with mine! Rudy, you are a genius!"

"You never heard that from me," he whispered, as he took her hand to kiss it gently. "Now, I must go to bed. I'm done. Good night, My Lady."

"Good night, Friend," she chortled, as her heart fluttered and she tried to take a breath. "Thank you for your wisdom… and good humor. By the way, her name is Estelí… Estelí Barrineau… and she is a dear person."

"I'm sure she is… and she's lucky to have you as her friend."

Exhausted, he slowly climbed the stairs to the third floor as she walked to her door. She looked up in time to see him glance back at her and smile, before he rounded the last step and disappeared. She entered her room with renewed resolve.

The second day of the League of Kingdoms Summit started as early as the first for the host family. King Henry and Maagy were at the breakfast table by six-thirty, as was Rudolpho. Asanna joined them soon after.

"Good morning all. Another fun filled, exciting day ahead," Asanna greeted with a bit of sarcasm in her tone.

They chuckled and made small talk as they ate. The king and the prince, as before, were embroiled in serious whispers. The two princesses caught up on some gossip and Maagy relayed her side of the Owanu debacle.

"It was nice to have breakfast with you, Asanna," she said. "Yesterday was a lost cause. I didn't see you at all."

"I know what you mean. Mother had me tied up in strategy planning when we weren't in the meeting. I found it excruciatingly boring. Speaking of Mother, I really should find her and Father for last minute instructions. Breakfast tomorrow, then?"

"Lovely, I look forward to it."

As Asanna left, Maagy went to her father's side.

"Pardon me, Father. May I have a moment?"

"Yes Maagy, what is it?"

"I'd like to be excused, please. I have something to attend. I'll see you at the door at nine, sharp."

"I suppose. Don't be late."

She exchanged smiles with Rudolpho and left, closing the doors behind her. She took a deep breath and slipped quietly into the main dining room, pausing to locate the right person and then made a beeline for him. She slipped a hand written note on the table beside him and was gone before he knew who had done it. The note read:

Your Excellency,

Please do me the honor of having audience to discuss the events of yesterday. I will be in the first floor library for the next half hour, if you will be so kind.

My humble appreciation

Chieftain Obuku folded the note and concealed it in the pocket of his robe. He finished his last sip of coffee and moved through the room, making sure he was not being watched by anyone. He found the library and Maagy waiting for him. She took a deep breath and stood to face him. She nodded her head as a sign of respect.

"Your Excellency, Chieftain Obuku, thank you for meeting me. I feel I owe you a personal accounting and explanation of the incident between your son and myself."

"You are the Impetuous Princess Maagy of whom I have heard much. What do you wish to say?"

"I deeply regret handling the situation as I did. However, I do not regret interceding on behalf of my chambermaid, who was doing nothing more than following the rules of etiquette with regard to unmarried young men and women being together in a bedchamber without proper chaperons. The protocols are for the guest's protection, as well that of our household. Surely, there are similar requirements in your culture, so I'm certain you understand."

"According to my son, the young woman refused to make his bed and when he chastised her for it, she smashed a piece of crystal on the floor and stormed out. Is there anything you would like to add?"

Maagy was furious that the boy had told such a blatant falsehood. Her instinct was to scream at the top of her lungs what a liar he was, but since her goal was to resolve the dilemma and not make it worse, she did as her father had said and "swallowed her tongue". She maintained her composure and continued respectfully, as she chose her words carefully.

"All I can say is… my chambermaid is an honest person… who cares for a sick mother with the money she earns in humble service to our household. I do not believe she would jeopardize her position… or her mother's welfare… to behave in such an irrational manner. She told me it was *he* who threw the paperweight *at her* and she ran out in fear. I went to your son on her behalf to illicit an apology and he *dismissed me* as a lowly female, not worthy of his respect," she said, seething under her skin. "I'm afraid it was this last straw that broke the camel's back and I allowed my anger to get the better of me… and… I threatened invasion. Fortunately, my father, His Royal Majesty King Henry, is a fair and wise man… and has a much more tranquil temperament than his daughter. I would never *actually* ask him to commit an act of war for such a small offense… neither would he do it… even if I did. That, Sir, is what I wanted you to know."

Obuku stood looking at the plucky girl, who was standing straight and as tall as her tiny frame would allow. She, likewise, looked him squarely in the eye, never diverting her gaze.

"You are a brave young woman to speak to me this way. I know my son all too well. I, also, know your father and agree he is a wise man and has raised an equally wise daughter. Things are not always as they seem, are they, Princess Maagy?"

She got the distinct impression, from his tone, the chief was trying to tell her something without actually saying it… a sort of coded message. '*Things are not always as they seem*'… she thought she might have understood.

"I suppose… sometimes… perception is its own truth, Your Excellency."

"No truer words were ever spoken. What is it you wish from me?"

"The only thing I've ever wanted was an apology for my chambermaid."

"And if you get it… you will not ask your father to invade us? And you will give him the message… all is well?"

"You have my word."

"Then things are truly *not* as they seem."

She was sure now this was the message… not for her… but for King Henry.

"How shall we accomplish this apology? Tell me when and where and I shall see to it my son is there."

"On the west lawn, down the hill in front of the castle, there is a pond partially obscured by shrubs. The spot is adequately secluded for privacy of this matter. Everyone seems to take their leave after luncheon and go to their rooms for some quiet time. One o'clock beside the pond, if you will, Your Excellency."

"We shall be there."

"Thank you for your kind understanding and willingness to resolve this matter peacefully, Sir," she said, with a slight bow of her head.

"You *will* give your father my regards, will you not, Your Highness?"

She was positive she was right.

"I shall, indeed, Sir."

The chieftain left the room and she stood for a few moments sorting out what had just happened. She was giddy with joy at the outcome of her bold move. She raced through the ballroom and up the stairs to her bedchamber and tugged frantically on the bell cord. Estelí was there immediately and Maagy told her the news and she was to be at the pond at one o'clock. It was a few moments before nine when she checked her appearance and proudly placed her mother's tiara on her neatly coiffed head. She flew down the stairs, two at a time, and into the ballroom, where she found her father ensconced in hushed conversation with the usual group.

"Your Majesty, may I have a word with you?" She asked breathlessly.

"Princess Maagy, can't you see I'm in the middle of something? You'll have to wait."

"Excuse me, Your Royal Majesty King Henry, but I *must* speak with you… *now*!"

"Your Highness Princess Maagy, I am busy with important matters of State. Please mind your manners."

"I am minding my manners, Your Royal Majesty. I have something to tell you, which is important, as well."

"Your Highness, your role here is to observe, so observe, *quietly*!"

All of this back and forth was done in whispered tones, which were becoming increasingly louder until finally…

"Daddy, you must listen to me, *now*!"

Fortunately, the only ones to hear the commotion were close friends, who were rather amused at her persistence.

"What is it, Maagy, for Heaven's sake?"

"I have a message for you…" then she whispered in his ear, "from His Excellency Chieftain Obuku."

"What do you mean, a message from… him? Maagy, what have you done?"

"Do you want the message or not?" She said defiantly.

"What is it?"

"He said, '*Things are not always as they seem*', and '*all is well*', and to *give you his regards*."

"When? When did he say that?"

"Not more than thirty minutes ago… in the first floor library… *to my face*," she crowed proudly.

"Prince Rudolpho, please come closer. Queen Haideh, if you please. You all should hear this," he whispered. "Repeat the message, Maagy."

"Chieftain Obuku said, and I quote, '*Things are not always as they seem*', and '*all is well*', and to *give his regards to His Majesty*."

"Maagy, tell me exactly how you came to be in the library with His Excellency."

"I regretted the run-in I had with Owanu over Estelí, but I was not about to apologize for it either. I knew it was causing some concern for the future of the negotiations," she explained to the group, "and something had to give, but still save face for everyone. Since I am Estelí's superior… in so much has her work is concerned… I thought I should go to Owanu's superior, *his father*."

"Oh, Maagy! You didn't," the king groaned.

"I did. I slipped him a note to meet me in private, which he did. He listened to my explanation of the incident and my reasoning. Then, he said what I told you and reiterated it. I took it as clandestine* communication. He told me he knows his son all too well. When he asked me what I wanted from him, I told him all I wanted was an apology for Estelí. He promised to meet us at the pond at one o'clock with Owanu. Then he asked, if I got the apology… would I give you the message, quote, '*all is well*'. By this time, I knew we were no longer talking about the incident. He was clearly sending the message he is not in Zinrahwi's pocket, as we all presumed, and I don't believe Chieftain Nandu is either. They are willing to work with us!"

"And you're sure those were his exact words?" Rudolpho asked.

"*Pre-cisely.*"

He smiled at Maagy and gave her a subtle wink when no one was looking.

"Maagy, this is good work... *good work*, indeed," King Henry complimented. "You turned an ugly situation round and made contact where we couldn't have. I am proud of you, My Dear."

"Thank you, Your Royal Majesty," she said, bursting with satisfaction.

King Henry, Prince Rudolpho, Queen Haideh and Father-King Afarnae quickly planned a new approach to the morning session. Maagy was only too happy to pass communiqués to the allied representatives. Terrasicus was out of the loop completely. Even as the Darhambian chieftains seemed to show solidarity with Zinrahwi, the occasional glances toward Maagy insured they were playing a game to protect their own interests, but were aligned with the valley kingdoms if push came to shove.

She had absorbed the lessons of the last twenty-four hours like a sponge. She found negotiating to be intuitive and her command of sophisticated vocabulary aided her immensely. She could find the words to say what needed saying, without saying it, at all. She had always been direct in her communication, but this newfound skill was exhilarating. She realized diplomacy was a balancing act, which sometimes pits what is right and fair against what is necessary for the benefit of everyone. She began to understand the complexity of her father's job and discovered she loved it.

Berensenia and Estadore had the most to gain or lose, so King Henry and Rudolpho took the lead in brokering a mutually beneficial arrangement for trade. Estadore was particularly vulnerable, as it bordered Terrasicus. However, Rudolpho was prepared to make the greatest concessions on allowing both land and shipping routes through his kingdom, provided he had a pledge of protection from

Berensenia and Nihmrobi. Once those issues were agreed upon, the other Commonwealth nations and Aradinia came on board quickly.

Finally, the proposal was hammered out and ready to be presented to the Emperor. All participants had agreed to open trade with Terrasicus and Darhambi. In addition, they agreed to allow Terrasican and Darhambian cargo transport vehicles to cross their borders, with restrictions in place. The possibility for ships under the Terrasican flag sailing into ports in Estadore and Nihmrobi was briefly mentioned, as was a shipping route from the Sea of Aragon through Poseidonia, Aradinia and Senecia to the Sea of Melania, but no firm commitment was made. Prices for goods were set at reasonable rates and a council to ensure fair trade practices would be created with representatives from each kingdom. In addition, the valley and coastal sovereignties pledged to prevent all future hiring of mercenary soldiers, from inside their borders. In return, Zinrahwi must open the dam and allow water to flow freely again. The terms of the document seemed fair and equitable for all concerned, but no one knew how the emperor would react. He was unpredictable at best and down right nasty at his worst. King Henry stood and called the general session to order. He addressed the Terrasican and Darhambian delegations formally.

"Your Excellency's, Emperor Zinrahwi of Terrasicus, Chieftain Obuku and Chieftain Nandu of Darhambi, I am pleased to inform you we have come to agreement on a proposal, which we believe will be in the best interest of all our kingdoms, not the least of which are your great sovereign nations. We sympathize with the difficulties you face living in a desert region. Therefore, we have proposed generous trade routes and fair pricing to effectively move much needed food and other staples to the good people whom you represent. The document is being drawn up officially as we speak and will be ready by afternoon session. I would like to suggest we break early for luncheon and resume our exploration of these matters at three o'clock. Is there anyone who opposes that plan? Good, then three it is. Enjoy your leisure time."

Maagy, Rudolpho and Asanna ate together in the main dining room; also at the table, King Henry, Queen Haideh and Prince Shamir. Premier Chamberlaine, his wife and Martha were directly across from Maagy and her friends. Martha's blatant fixated on Prince Rudolpho invoked in Maagy feelings of jealousy she had never felt before. She recognized the need for some alone time to sort things out and was anxious to see Cupid… since she hadn't been to the barn all day… so she excused herself and changed into overalls. She had to carefully time her escape from the castle to avoid encountering any of the dignitaries. She peeked out the barely open door. No one was on the steps either up or down, so she made a break for the staircase. Rather than running down and making noise, she flung her leg over the rail and slid all the way to the bottom at break-neck speed. She dismounted and disappeared into the coat closet… safe from spying eyes… raced through the kitchen and past Grandma Polly, who was about to speak.

"I know… 'Highly inappropriate'… I'm not here! You didn't see me!" She said, as she grabbed an apple from the basket.

She was gone in the blink of an eye, leaving the elder woman smiling in appreciation. Maagy ran to the pasture and called. Cupid raised her head from grazing and whinnied.

"That's the girl. Come get your sweetie!"

Cupid kicked up her heels as she galloped. The two enjoyed a visit while she held the apple for the filly to take bites. She had forgot about the one o'clock appointment, until Rudolpho appeared at the fence.

"Isn't there somewhere you're supposed to be?"

"Oh, hello. What? Oh no! What time is it?"

"A few minutes to one."

"The pond!"

"Run and you can make it!"

Maagy took off as fast as she could round the lower part of the yard to the front lawn. It was farther to run, but she had less chance of being seen by anyone. She reached the pond just as the chieftain and his son were arriving. Her face was red and beaded with sweat and she was out of breath. Her hair was falling down and bits were hanging in her face. The tail of her blouse was crawling out of her overalls and she was barefooted. She was not at all the well put-together young woman Chieftain Obuku had been so impressed with that morning. Estelí was already there and had been waiting long enough to become nervous.

"What a mess! This is to whom I am supposed to apologize, Father… a servant girl and a stable hand?" The sarcastic boy remarked. "Surely you must be joking."

Maagy wanted to pounce on him and take him to the ground. Instead, she, once again, remembered her father's wisdom and *swallowed.*

"I do realize my appearance is shameful, but I'm training a young horse and, as you know, Your Excellency, it takes a lot of time and patience," she said deliberately.

She glared at Owanu and brushed back her hair. He glared back, knowing full well the double entendre she intended.

"And you spend all the time you can accomplishing that task, no doubt," the senior Obuku returned.

"I do, Sir," she acknowledged with a slight smile and dip of her head.

"Owanu, tell the chambermaid… what is your name, young lady?"

"Estelí, Your Excellency… Estelí Barrineau."

"Tell Mademoiselle Barrineau you regret your impolite behavior and will never again ask her… or anyone else… to break the house rules."

The boy stood defiantly looking down at the ground. His father put his arm round him firmly, as he whispered close to his ear, and then let him go.

"I regret I put you in a compromising situation. I regret I lost my temper and threw the paperweight. I will never again do such things," he said almost inaudibly.

Maagy felt the apology was half-hearted, at best, and had hoped for much more, but realized she had pushed her luck as far as it was going.

"*Merci, Monsieur**. I accept your kind words," Estelí replied, as she curtsied respectfully.

She could hardly breathe for trembling. Maagy stood close and gave her a reassuring nod.

"Now to Princess Maagy… go on, boy."

"I deeply regret speaking to you… in a condescending* manner… Your Highness. I hope you will accept my… humble apology," he said, choking on the words.

"I do… accept."

"Your Highness, we will let you get back to your horse training… and I will get back to mine," Obuku said. "May we all have much success in our ventures."

He nodded politely and put his arm round his son's shoulders, as they walked back to the castle.

"How did you make that happen, Your Highness? I thought I would come to pieces shaking."

"All a matter of knowing to whom one should speak… and what they want in return. I think that… is the business… of negotiating."

It was only half past one when she got back to the barn. She found Rudy and Asanna there talking to John Miles. They were saddling horses for a ride. Rudolpho had Sunrise, a big dark bay with black stockings. A former dressage* competitor and high-spirited, he was the largest riding horse in the stable. He was a lot of horse for most people, but Rudolpho handled him with authority. Asanna, who was also an accomplished rider, was on Dinah, the black mare with a white blaze on her face.

"Maagy, just in time. Have a ride with us, won't you?" Rudy said cheerfully.

"Oh... a ride... um... I'm not sure..." she stammered, embarrassed to tell the two she had never been on a horses back. "Um... well..."

"Mister Miles, who do you have for the Duchess?"

"I believe Carmela would be a good fit, Sir."

Carmela was a chestnut color with flaxen mane and tail. She was patient and responsive with a smooth gate, which made her an excellent choice for a first time rider. She was also smaller than the other horses and would fit the diminutive* novice*.

"She's Cupid's mother. I think she and Her Royal Highness will get along famously."

"I... know Carmela... yes," Maagy said.

John knew she had never ridden, but was chivalrous enough to save her admission of such. He, also, knew Rudolpho had surmised the same and their unspoken words were communication enough.

"Shall I saddle her for Your Highness?"

She was desperately afraid, but just as desperately, wanted to ride with them. She gave John a terrified look.

"Yes... please. Carmela is quite acceptable. Wait, I'm barefooted. I can't ride without boots."

"Where are they? I'll send someone for them and he'll be here by the time I have her saddled," Mister Miles said.

"In the mudroom, outside the kitchen."

He sent one of the stable hands, who was back in no time with her boots. She had no more excuses. As she walked toward the horse, John turned the mare round so she would be on the proper side to mount, without anyone knowing she was clueless. She approached the horse and panic set in, but he, once again, came to her rescue.

"Your Highness, Let me give you a leg up," he said.

He whispered close to her ear, as he cupped his hands for her foot.

"Relax, Your Highness. Follow my lead. Take hold of the front and back of the saddle firmly and use it to pull up. Put your left foot in my hands and swing your right leg over the horse and sit in the saddle. Take the reigns in both hands."

She did exactly as she was told and executed a perfect mount, her heart pounding out of her chest.

"Thank you for the assist, Mister Miles," she said.

"My pleasure, Your Highness. She's a sweet girl… no need to use the heels or speak loudly. She responds to a gently tap of the crop on her withers. Her mouth is soft, so no hard pulls on the reigns. A gentle touch is all you need with this one."

"Thank you."

"We'll take it slow for a while and have a good chat," Rudy said, picking up on John's continued clues.

"I'm all for that. It's been a whirlwind for days. We all need a quiet moment," Asanna added.

"How was your… meeting… Maagy?" Rudolpho asked.

"Quite good, thank you… excellent, in fact," she replied with a proud smile.

They had a slow ride through the meadow and round the fields behind the castle as they discussed the day's events. She watched the other two more experienced riders and tried to mimic their posture and actions. By the time they were back at the barn, she felt comfortable in the saddle and looked forward to the next ride.

"I say we should do this everyday after luncheon, what do you ladies think about that?" Rudolpho asked.

"I'd love to," Asanna said as she dismounted. "How about you Maagy?"

"Yes, I'd love it, as well. I'll be honest with you both. That was the first time in my life I've been on a horse. It was incredible! I want to do this every single day!"

"I never would have known. You did very well, Maagy," Asanna complimented. "The first time I tried to mounted a horse, I went over the other side right onto the ground."

"Really?"

"Very well done, Duchess. You're a courageous one," the Prince said, as he took her by the waist and helped her down.

"Thank you. Perhaps I should have a few lessons. What do you think, Mister Miles?"

"It would give you confidence I'm sure."

"Rudy is an excellent equestrian," Asanna added, with a mischievous smirk. "You could give her some pointers this week, couldn't you?"

"I'd be happy to if you'd like, Maagy."

"That would be fabulous. This may be my new favorite passion!"

Time was moving quickly. The new horsewoman was in a frightful state of untidiness in need of washing, dressing and coiffing* of the hair. She excused herself and ran back to the house, in the door and kicked off the boots in the mudroom. She retraced her earlier escape route through the kitchen, again, crossing paths with Grandma Polly.

"I know! You're not here! I see nothing!" The lady snickered.

Maagy giggled mischievously, as she grabbed another apple… this one for her… and raced through the coat closet. She stopped at the door and peeped out, as she munched on the snack. The coast was clear so she scurried up the stairs and into her room, once again, undetected.

"I'm getting good at this stealth business," she mused proudly.

Her afternoon clothes were laid on her bed complete with shoes and clean stockings. A fresh face cloth and towel were waiting on the basin, as was warm water, just right for a refreshing wash. She pulled the bell cord and Estelí was at her service immediately to rearrange the royal hair, while the proper princess finished her apple.

"Thank you, Friend. I don't know what I would do without you."

She had but seconds to get to the ballroom on time, but somehow managed. As expected, the proposal was ready and each participant had a copy. Protocol was for the representatives to read, discuss and sign the document. That process could go quickly, since all of them… except Zinrahwi… had already agreed on the terms, or it could take the rest of the week if he chose to argue every point. Most everyone anticipated the worst.

The meeting was called to order and the business began. Zinrahwi was the first to speak and went immediately on the offensive, accusing the other delegates of conspiring to overthrow his reign. He had not even read the document, but he was sure it was unfair. Chiefs Obuku and Nandu seemed to try calming the Emperor and mitigating the terms. Oddly enough, he listened to them. King Henry did a masterful job of diffusing the situation and preventing anyone else from over reacting. Rudolpho assured the Emperor the proposed routes through Estadore were legitimate and guaranteed, as long as the Terrasicans followed the guidelines. Other representatives, likewise, assured him of their sincerity. The discussion continued, sometimes heated, for almost two hours. Finally, King Henry stood again and called order. He suggested, since the hour was late, it might be best to adjourn for dinner and give His Excellency the opportunity to read and digest the proposal in private. The majority agreed and the meeting ended.

Dinner was served formally in the grand dining room and the quiet evening ended early for most of the guests. However, Maagy had a surprise up her sleeve for her friends. She had asked Grandpa Kris to demonstrate the telescope for Rudolpho and Asanna sometime that week if weather permitted. He had whispered to her during dinner it was a perfect night and to bring them to the observatory at ten thirty. It would be dark enough by then and the moon was in the right position for a grand show. She found the Prince and her father in the foyer saying goodnight and joined them.

"Goodnight, Daddy. Have sweet dreams."

"You too, Darling," he answered as he hugged her and headed upstairs.

"Be in the science library at ten twenty-five. Don't ask questions," she whispered as she brushed by Rudolpho.

He picked up on the clue, immediately, and gave her a subtle nod. He enjoyed her newfound sense of intrigue. Asanna was on the third floor landing bidding her parents sweet dreams. Maagy waited until they went down the hall to approach Asanna.

"Psst... Asanna," she beaconed from the top step. "Come with me."

"Oh, Maagy Dear, I'm quite exhausted. I was just headed for bed."

"Trust me, you'll want to see this. I promise, it won't take long and it's well worth the lost sleep."

"If you insist. It better be spectacular."

Asanna followed her down the staircase and round to the library. Once again, she opened the door with a flourish and stood with arms wide.

"Isn't this a magnificent library? It's devoted entirely to science. Look at that map and all those bottles and beakers and... things. What do you think?"

"It's... interesting... I suppose... but not so much that I'd rather lose sleep for it," Asanna replied, somewhat cross.

"Oh, no, this is not what you're losing sleep over..."

"I'm here. It's ten twenty-five. Oh, hello, Asanna. I see she pulled you in, as well," Rudy said as he entered.

"You know what this is about, do you?"

"I have a guess."

"You'll both thank me later. Now come on."

She led the way up the winding steps to the top of the tower where they found Grandpa Kris. He had already turned the complicated maze of pulleys and cables and the entire roof of the observatory was wide open to the sky. That view, alone, was spectacular, but promised to get even better.

"There you are, Children. Right on time. It's almost in focus… ah… there she is. Come, have a look."

Rudy and Asanna were spellbound. Maagy was about to burst out of her crown, she was so excited to share her discovery with them.

"How did you get the roof open like that? What is that machine? I'm positively overcome!" Asanna gushed.

"Amazing! Brilliant! Maagy, what a treat. Thank you Grandpa Kris. I can't imagine anything more spectacular," Rudy added.

"It's my pleasure, Your Highnesses. Look, the moon is within arms length. This is a telescope, Princess Asanna. It brings the moon and stars close enough to touch… at least they look that way. Here, see for yourselves."

The young ones took turns looking at the heavens and marveling at such a wonder. They giggled and asked questions and looked some more, as Grandpa Kris showed them several constellations and explained basic navigational secrets. Finally, he brought the session to an end.

"It's getting late, my dears, and you all have an early morning. The show is over for this evening, but I'll do this again when time permits."

They thanked him profusely and offered to help close the roof. He declined and assured them it was no trouble to do alone. They suspected he wanted to keep the exact mechanism secret. The three descended the stairs still talking about the telescope and how extraordinary the experience.

"Maagy, thank you for asking Grandpa to give us this treat," Asanna said. "You were right. It was worth losing sleep over!"

"I told you…"

"You are a woman of your word, Princess. Thank you is not nearly sufficient, but it's all I can say."

"It was my pleasure. I'm the lucky one here… for having met such nice friends. Goodnight to you both. Sleep well."

Day three began as days one and two, with family breakfast. Maagy took time to care for Cupid before dressing for the morning session. She was punctual, as usual, and was curious to see what the irascible* emperor would do today, besides glare at her. The meeting came to order and the first business was to read aloud the entire trade agreement in case there were errors. The Document was titled *The Valley Fair Trade Treaty.* Once the official reading was done, the participants placed their personal seals in wax to certify authenticity. Next would be the arduous* task of signing it.

Zinrahwi stood, immediately. The others were waiting for his bombast to begin, when he abruptly announced he would sign the document, as it was, and then, did so. The room was silent with amazed glances hopping like frogs from one to the other. King Henry rose... and without speaking a word... took quill in hand, and wrote his name quickly. Queen Haideh looked to her father and then to the king. She and Prince Rudolpho followed suit* simultaneously, starting the chain reaction for the rest of the representatives. Maagy guessed they all wanted to sign as quickly as possible, before Grumpy Gus changed his mind. The process continued, as the documents were passed to the left and signed, again and again, until each had gone completely round the table and ended with its original owner. These identical documents became official records once King Henry's Royal seal was affixed. The process took the entire morning. He thanked the Emperor and chieftains for their cooperation and asked if anyone had other business to discuss, but no one dared. The League of Kingdoms Summit officially ended early. Everyone was cordially invited to stay and enjoy the rest of the week on holiday, before returning home.

Emperor Zinrahwi and his entourage left almost immediately after a quick repast*. It was as if their bags were packed and the horses hitched before the day began. Maagy couldn't be sad about that. He had given her a foreboding feeling whenever she saw him. The Darhambian delegations departed together, but not before Chief Obuku had a private moment with King Henry and Prince Rudolpho. She was ever so curious to know what was said, but chose to ask later. She had been gracious to Owanu as it was her duty as Official Hostess to see all the guests off, but he knew her smile was paper-thin. Several other representatives left soon after eating, due to their long journeys, including the Senecians. Maagy was pleased to see Martha Chamberlaine leave.

The Nihmrobi delegation decided to stay until Friday, as did Rudolpho. Maagy was thrilled, as it would give her more time to visit with them and have a few riding lessons. She thought about the bizarre turns and twists she had encountered and the strides she'd made in just a few days. It was a bit dizzying as she began to comprehend the enormous future, which lay ahead of her. After dinner and some warm goodnights, she sat on her bed and pondered it.

Chapter 10
Fourth Floor

It was Friday morning already and Asanna and her family had got an early start on their return home. The only one left was Prince Rudolpho, who was saying good-bye. He had well represented Estadore and had made a good impression on the other heads-of-state. King Henry dispensed with formalities and gave the young man an affectionate hug, which he was happy to return.

"Rudy, my boy, it's been a pleasure watching you handle yourself this week. Please tell your father I said he has nothing to worry about. You're a fine negotiator. Tell him, also, he owes me a visit, as soon as he's well enough… and… give your mother… my dearest regards."

"I will, indeed, Your Majesty. I know he missed seeing you this time. Perhaps you and Princess Maagy will visit us this summer, if your schedule permits."

"Perhaps we shall. Godspeed, Son, and by the way, please let Captain Sistrunk know he and his family are welcome to visit here anytime."

"Thank you, Sir, I will. Take care and so long, until we meet again. And Princess Maagy, I hope you'll continue riding."

He had given her several lessons and she was a quick study. She and Carmela had become fast friends and worked well together. Asanna had accompanied them and they had grown close. She would miss them terribly.

"I will, I promise, but you must promise to come back and teach me to jump. I'm sure I'll be ready soon."

"I promise to return… perhaps next month. Hopefully, the emperor will have begun de-construction of the dam and water will be flowing more freely. I'm sure my father will want me to see the project through. Perhaps I can convince my parents to come for a visit, as well. We'll see."

"I'll hold you to it."

"That sounds like a fine plan!" King Henry added.

"We must be on our way. The sun is high in the sky and we have a long journey ahead."

He knelt on one knee in front of her and extended his hand. She lived for these moments. She placed her hand in his palm and he kissed it softly. She shivered and felt her face flush.

"Until we meet again, Dear Lady, you will be in my thoughts often."

"And you in mine."

He continued to hold her hand as he stood, and then let go… reluctantly… and boarded his carriage. She felt a sudden panic as he closed the door, but stood stoic as tears filled her eyes. The rush of emotion took her by surprise and she looked away momentarily to wipe them. Captain Sistrunk and several other guards were on horseback flanking all sides. He gave her one last smile and a lingering wave. The driver gave the gee-up and the entourage began descending the cobblestone path. She missed him already.

He missed her, as well. He had realized an instant attraction and discovered, throughout the week, how much joy her presence brought him. He knew, full well, she was smitten with him and found it both flattering and amusing. However, he also realized he was practically a grown man and she was still a child. Any action on his feelings or encouragement of her infatuation would be extremely unsavory and unwelcomed by her father. He would keep his distance and remain ever the gentleman. He would settle for friendship and be a trusted confidant and wait for her to grow up. As they watched his carriage disappear from sight, she pulled herself together and changed the subject.

"Father, who is Captain Sistrunk? I get the impression there's more to him than meets the eye."

"Very perceptive, My Dear. Captain Sistrunk is an interesting man. He is Darhambian, you know."

"No, I didn't know, but I did see him once or twice discretely speaking with the chiefs. I pretended not to notice."

"Good of you to do. Your instincts are excellent, Maagy. He is actually Darhambian royalty. His grandfather was the last king."

"Really? What happened?"

"Mak was a small child. His tribe is the Shimborazi from the southern area called Shimboran. For generations, his family had ruled peacefully. Zinrahwi's father, whose name will never cross my lips, convinced the Chericini's, in the north, they should take control and ally with him. There was an ongoing drought, much like the one now, and the Shimborazi were vulnerable. With help from the Terrasican emperor, the Chericini invaded and took over. Mak's father took his young family and fled in the night to Estadore, where King Rafael gave him asylum and a position in his Royal Command. King Sistrunk… Mak's grandfather… was killed. Mak followed in his father's footsteps and actually trained at our Academy with Raul, Rudy's brother. Raul wasn't much for the military, but Rafael insisted he at least complete the course. When Rudy trained here…"

"Rudy trained at our Academy?"

"Well, of course. Maagy, our Academy of Her Majesty's Royal Guard is the foremost military training facility in the entire known world. We have applicants from as far as Reland Main and Skodinovia."

"I had no idea..."

"Anyway, Rafael saw right away the talent and skill his younger son possessed and decided he would be the military genius. He knew Rudy would be in a powerful position, therefore, in constant danger. He assigned Mak as his personal guard. Since the take over, Darhambi has had no centralized government. Mak hopes, with the help of King Rafael and Prince Rudolpho, to negotiate a peaceful return for the royal family and the restoration of their parliament. He hopes one day, to unite the country under one government. Obuku is currently the Shimborazan Chieftain, but has always been loyal to his friend, Mak's father, who died in battle when Mak was at Academy."

"What battle?"

"The Terrasicans tried to invade Estadore. Your mother sent troops... under my command... to stand with them. We were successful in driving them back, but many good men were lost... including Prince Amador Sistrunk."

"When was that?"

"Not long before you were born. The Terrasicans ravaged Darhambi... again... during that skirmish. Obuku would like nothing more than to avenge Amador's death and to see Mak take his rightful place. I believe that's why he was willing to work with us this week."

"Now I understand why Owanu is as he is... he doesn't want to lose his position of power if his father gives up control to Captain Sistrunk someday. How very intriguing it all is. I never would have guessed."

"Well, well, well," sighed the king, as he put his arm round her shoulder and they started up the steps. "I believe I see a queen peeking round the corner!"

"Oh, Daddy, I don't know about that. The one thing I've realized most clearly this week is I have way more to learn than I ever dreamt. I don't think I'll be ready for the crown for at least ten more years."

"Well that's a problem. You *must* be ready by your eighteenth birthday. There's no choice in the matter."

"What do you mean, 'No choice in the matter'? Where are you going when I turn eighteen?"

"Nowhere, I hope, except retirement. You see, Dear, I am only the guardian of the monarchy until you are old enough. The royal lineage is through your mother."

"Oh… really… I was meaning to ask you about that…"

"She was descended from Queen Kathryn, the first queen of the New Commonwealth."

"Do tell… I didn't know…"

"Yes… by rights… I should have stepped aside and the next in line should have assumed the crown… that would be you… but she died when you were just a baby. It posed a tricky situation. You were next in line, but so young. Rather than seek out some obscure cousin, who had nothing to do with the intricacies of diplomacy and politics of running a nation, Parliament chose continuity. Since Melania and I had worked well together for many years… and she had assigned command of the armed forces to me, already… they *voted* and *elected* me the temporary monarch… or Regent*, if you will… until you were ready. I was His Royal Highness Prince Henry… Prince Consort*… Duke of Covington, until that time. They also believed the title of King would have more… influence… with our… neighbors… to the east."

"I see… No… *I don't see*," Maagy said, as she stopped abruptly and faced him. "I'm very confused, Father…"

They sat on the steps looking down the hill… watching the carriage, which was only a tiny speck, as they talked.

"Your mother was the unwitting heir to the throne of Berensenia. My lineage is actually Aradinian. I was born and raised in Aradinia. My Father was a prince, but not in line for the throne."

"So we have ties to the Aradinian monarchy, as well?"

"Very diluted ties… many generations removed cousins. One of my great, great… there are several more 'greats'… grandmothers was the daughter of the king and queen of Aradinia. She had two sisters, and one brother, who became king, leaving her descendants destined to be princes and princesses. I think my father was actually bitter about it. He wanted me to marry a crown princess so at least his progenies would have a chance at a throne. He was a rather vain man…"

"But he would be proud of you now, wouldn't he? You did marry a crown princess and you became a king."

"There's the irony… Melania wasn't the Crown Princess. Her older sister, Abigail, was… another long story…"

"Tell it to me, Daddy. I love long stories. How did you meet Mummy?"

He put his arm round his daughter and pulled her close. She rested her head on his chest.

"My mother and Melania's mother were childhood best friends. I first met her here, at the Summer Castle, when we were both just small children. That's how I came to know the place. My mother recognized how unfeeling my father was… so she brought me with her to Whitmore Castle each summer to visit her best friend, who had two daughters, Melania and Abigail; thus, the reference, The Summer Castle. As we grew up, we were all best friends… Abigail, Melania and I… but Melania and I fell in love… and when she was of age, we married."

"I never knew you and Mummy met as children… So I was named for my aunt, Mummy's sister?"

"Yes, a dear, sweet girl Abigail was. But your mother was the most beautiful woman I'd ever seen. Your grandfather wanted me to marry Abigail, who was in line for the throne. He was furious that I married Melania. Since neither of us was to inherit either throne, we went back to Aradinia and lived in complete obscurity at Auburndale, my family's country home. Those were some of the happiest times of our lives. Abigail was to marry Tarin, the chosen successor to the Imperial Rule of Terrasicus, and join the two kingdoms into one. A terrible storm, the likes of which had never been seen in the world, ravaged the valley. Abigail and Tarin were both swept away by the swirling winds… and their bodies were never found."

"That's horrible!"

"That's when we came here to care for Melania's parents, who were never well after that terrible loss. Sadly, both died soon after. Your mother assumed the throne and I was the lucky one by her side. The irony of it all… had I planned to marry Abigail, as my father wished, I would have been here when the storm hit and the one swept away with her. Also ironic, Tarin was a decent man, unlike his brother, Zinrahwi's father. Had he and Abigail lived, the history of our entire region would have been much different."

"How did I never know this, Daddy?"

"I suppose… I never told you. I chose to allow you to be a carefree, happy child. Suddenly… you turned thirteen… the time has flown by so quickly… your coming-of-age is too close… I want you to be my child a little longer," he said, as he kissed her on the forehead and hugged her even closer.

"I'll always be your child, Daddy, no matter how old I get."

"It all happens in five years, ready or not."

Her mind was flooded with this new, stunning information and she didn't know what to say. She had never thought of her father as anything but the most powerful man in the kingdom, perhaps the entire region. Now to learn he would be forced to give up that power… and he would give it up to *her*! She was bewildered, to say the least. There was a long silence as they slowly climbed the stairs to the portico. Finally, King Henry spoke in an effort to take her mind off such weighty contemplations.

"It was a busy week, My Dear. What do you think?"

"I think you're right."

"I'm going to my room to read a little and rest a lot," he said with a chuckle. "What will you do the rest of the day?"

"I don't know... perhaps... I'll explore some more of the castle. I quite enjoyed it when we first arrived, but I've been so busy I've left much undiscovered. Besides, I've had enough politics for a while."

"Excellent idea. I remember when I used to crawl round in the passages and play detective games," he said, knowing it would send her on a new tangent.

"Passages? What passages? Tell me, Daddy. I must know!"

"Ho, ho... not on your life! I'll not give away secrets. You must find them on your own or it doesn't count."

His strategy worked. She was beside herself with curiosity.

"Count? Count for what?"

He made a gesture as if to seal his lips.

"Come on, Daddy, spill it... spill it out... I promise, I won't tell anyone where I heard it!"

He threw back his head with a belly laugh and tickled his daughter.

"Go, go, go, My Sweet, and explore on your own! I'll never give away my secrets!"

With that, he bounded up the steps into the castle and continued to the second floor with her hot on his heels. He disappeared into his room, as she reached the second landing. He was still laughing, which peeved her, and she wanted to stomp her foot and bang on his door, but thought better of it. Now alone, she spun round and sat down on the top step, looking out the rotunda windows. So many things were swirling round in her head. There was the handsome prince she couldn't stop thinking about; the monarchy would be dumped into her lap; the sadness on her father's face when he spoke of her mother; the namesake aunt she had never... and would never... know; the foreboding she felt when Zinrahwi's name was mentioned. There were still so many questions. It was all too much… too much for a little girl to handle at once. Curiosity and exploration were the answer.

She climbed the stairs to the third floor, where the guests had stayed, but since the entire floor had been occupied, the staff was busy cleaning. She thought it might be rude to explore those rooms while the chambermaids were working. Sure enough, there was much activity with piles of bed linen and towels in the hallways, brooms and dust mops going in every direction. She thought it prudent to pursue other adventures.

She decided to address the mystery of the missing steps to the fourth floor. She had determined, on the first day, the spiral stairs above the foyer stopped at the third level. She had watched Rudy go up them enough to be familiar. There was at least one more story in the main center of the castle and two more above it between the towers on either side. She surmised there must be another staircase to those upper stories. The castle was roughly in the shape of an "H" and faced southwest. She could tell all that by looking at it from outside and noting the position of the sun. She had paid attention to Grandpa Kris' lessons. She continued along the rotunda railing and into the west corridor where she discovered a door oddly tucked round the corner above the science library she'd not noticed on her previous search.

"Oh horse feathers… another door… probably locked…"

However, when she tried the knob, it turned freely to reveal the missing stairs, but her elation turned to anxiety when she ventured upward. This landing was not like those below. The hallways looked longer and narrower and there were many more doors… all closed. There was barely any light. She could find no access to the southwest tower with the observatory. It was spooky and a little frightening, but she was determined to be brave. She saw no one, but heard the muffled sounds of voices beyond the doors, the *locked* doors. She moved from one to the other, trying each, but couldn't find a single one kind enough to open. This was both frustrating and intriguing. The dilemma only served to stimulate her curious nature, even as her heart raced with a tad bit of fear. What she found even more fascinating was the muffled voices didn't seem to come from any of the rooms she tried to enter. Whenever she tried one door, the noise seemed to come from the next. But when she tried that one, the sounds emanated from the next. There was definitely something amiss.

She tried looking through several of the keyholes. In one room, her limited view yielded only dusty furniture stacked hap-hazardly, as if the room were for storage. In another, she saw musical instruments gathering dust, as they waited at the ready for a chamber ensemble. Yet another tiny portal revealed what looked like a nursery with the furniture covered in white sheets to keep off the dust. None of the rooms looked as if anyone had entered them in a long time. Yet, the sound of voices persisted. She, also, persisted in her quest to find the source of the noise and to discover the mysterious "passages" her father had mentioned. She turned down another long hallway and continued on, courageously pursuing her adventure. She moved cautiously along the wall, listening for sounds. Again, she peeked into a keyhole, but the key must have been in it, because she saw nothing. So she gathered her fortitude and grabbed the doorknob. She gave it a mighty twist and to her great surprise, it turned and the door opened. She was so shocked she squealed and slammed the door shut.

"Oh, drat," she thought. "I shouldn't have done that."

She gave the knob another twist and the door opened, again. She discovered it didn't conceal a room, but yet another hallway, which went on forever. In addition, there were narrow corridors along it that went off in both directions and, as she learned, even more locked doors on either side of them. How could this be? There were no comparable hallways on the lower levels. Then she remembered the children's library occupied the entire center portion of those floors, with its two-story windows, floating staircase and reading balcony.

"This must be just above the library," she reasoned.

Still, something didn't add up. She had a keen sense of direction and, frankly, she was lost. However, the mystery was too juicy to turn back, so she moved cautiously down the passageway, but stopped dead in her tracks and went absolutely quiet… almost not breathing… when she heard more voices. They were whispering, but she thought she heard her name being spoken. Her heart raced and pounded until she was sure the owners of the voices could hear it. She began to shake. Suddenly, a door flung open. She jumped and screamed at the top of her lungs as she turned to run.

"Maagy, Dear, what's the matter? Did I scare you?" Asked a familiar voice.

It was Grandma Polly who had emerged from the room. Maagy stopped short and whirled round.

"Sc… sc… scare… me? N… n… no… not at all. I knew you were there… I did… no I didn't. You scared the life out of me! Hello, Gram-P. What are you doing up here?"

"*I'm* working up here. What are *you* doing up here?"

"I'm exploring. Is that all right?"

"Of course it is. I'm so sorry I frightened you. I didn't realize you were outside the door."

"You're working here? What are you doing?"

"All the shops, which keep the castle and the farm round it operating smoothly, are on this floor. There is a wood working shop, a dress shop, a leather shop, a cobbler's shop, a tinker's shop, a silversmith and a pottery shop with a kiln; in short, we can produce or repair just about anything you'll find in the house or the barns or the tool sheds."

"Whoa! I had no idea!"

"There is even a toyshop where we produce toys for needy children in the towns and villages that surround the castle. You know, Maagy, this is not just a wonderful summer home. It's also a working enterprise that employs many, many people, some of whom live on the grounds and some of whom live elsewhere and only work here. So we have to support them and their families."

She was riveted by the fact there was so much going on behind locked doors. No wonder she heard voices; there were lots of people up there going about their usual business. She *was* a little disappointed it wasn't something more mysterious.

"In addition to all the shops," Grandma continued, "There is a music room where an entire orchestra may practice for performances."

"Yes, I saw it."

"There is a dance studio with mirrors and ballet bars. Oh, perhaps you'd like that room opened and aired out. You do take dance lessons, don't you, My Dear?"

"Yes I do. I'd love to practice."

"There is an art studio next to the pottery shop, as well, with any medium you want at your disposal. You could throw a few pots and fire them when the kiln is hot. Oh, but have the artisan help you. It's much too dangerous to do alone."

That made her happy. She loved all types of art, visual and performance, and was looking forward to making good use of the studios.

"It all sounds exciting, Gram-P. I'll definitely use the art studio to paint. Where is it?"

"Go to the end of the hall, opposite where you came in. Turn to the left and go down three doors and the studio is on the right. The lighting is best in the morning, as the sun comes in through the tall windows. Enjoy! But now, I must get down to the kitchen to supervise luncheon."

Before Maagy could say anything, Grandma was gone.

"Thank you," she said to the air, in the direction of the disappearing woman.

She wondered what Gram-P had been doing before she emerged from the mysterious room. She reached for the knob, gave a turn, and to her extreme dismay, found it was locked tight.

"Drat! Horse feathers! Locked!"

She could feel her temper heating up and wanted a good foot-stomp, when she heard voices resume chattering. She forgot about bratty behavior and, instead, turned her full attention to seeking out the source. She continued to the end of the interior hallway and exited into another long, dimly lit corridor. She crept along listening and was pleased the voices were getting louder. She stopped at a door she felt certain was hiding the owners of those voices and peered through the keyhole. She could barely keep from squealing when she saw what was on the other side. She had found the toy workshop Grandma Polly mentioned. Even from her limited perspective, she could tell the room was enormous. There were shelves of toys, floor to ceiling, all sparkling new and brightly painted. There were blocks, tea sets, stilts, Jack-in-the-boxes, dolls, wagons, rocking horses; every treasure a youngster could imagine was right in that room. She thought there must have been a lot of needy children in the towns and villages, because she had never, *ever* seen so many toys in any store.

In addition to the toys, there were people. They were all busily working and didn't seem to know someone was watching. She decided to ease the door open and get a better look without disturbing anyone. She took hold of the knob and slowly turned. It moved freely and the latch let go without making a sound. She felt a wave of excitement wash over her. She had never had such a wonderful adventure. She took a deep breath and slowly pushed. The door gave way easily and cracked a tiny bit. No one noticed. She pushed again... just a tiny bit more. Suddenly, it flew out of her hand and flung wide! Bells rang, buzzers buzzed!

"Alert, intruder! Alert, intruder!" Repeated over and over again.

She stood fully exposed... so startled her feet were glued to the floor. Her mouth dropped open. Everything in the shop abruptly halted and all eyes were fixed on her. No one moved a muscle for an interminable* length of time, as the alarm kept repeating its refrain. Finally, a little man in a long white coat spoke.

"May I help ya, lass?"

The alarm silenced, but not a single person moved, except the little man. He calmly walked toward her.

"Is there anything I can do for ya?" he asked again, in a heavy Isle of Reland accent.

"No…" she squeaked. "Just… looking… just… um… I'm… um… sorry… for… intruding…"

She could feel all the eyes in the room peeled* on her. She felt as she had that very first morning at the barn, when she became aware of eyes watching her every move. Her face went red and tears welled up. The man was now in front of her… and she could see just how short he was… actually… so were all the others.

"Are ya lost, Child?" He asked.

"Um… no… not really… at least, I don't think I'm lost. I… I'm just… exploring."

"Do ye have a name, My Dear, or shall I call ya Magellan?"

"You're close… actually. It's Maagy… Princess Maagy… I mean Princess Melania Abigail Alice Grace, Crown Princess, if you please."

"What? Ye are Maagy, little Maagy? I have not seen ya since ya were a baby. How is, Henry? Is he here with ya?"

She was stunned by this familiarity. He called her father by his first name without the title and he knew her, but she didn't remember him.

"Yes… I am… Princess Maagy and yes… my father is here… at the castle and is… quite well, thank you. Who are you? How do you know my father well enough to call him by his name?"

"I am McTavish, at your service, Your Highness."

He bowed elegantly and clicked his heels together.

"Pleased to make your acquaintance, Mister McTavish. You know my father and me?"

"McTavish, just McTavish. Aye, for your whole life… and his. Ya have not been here in at least… oh… about… ten years, though. Too bad. We have missed ya. We have missed Henry, too. He used to be a regular visitor here in the summertime."

"Really? I don't remember you and I don't recall ever hearing of you either. Oh dear, I didn't mean to be insulting. Please pardon me."

"Oh, not to worry, no offense taken. So, what do ye think of the toyshop? Is there anything ye can think of that is not here?"

"It's… magnificent! I've never seen any toyshop with as many toys. There must be a lot of needy children in the area."

"We aim to please," he beamed. "But I must ask ye to leave now, as it is mealtime and we must have a full two hours for eating and resting. It has been a pleasure seeing ya again, Dear Princess."

He escorted her from the room and quickly closed the door behind him. She must have looked puzzled, because he asked if she knew her way back to the first floor. She *was* puzzled, but not about directions; more accurately, she was curious about this person and his odd behavior, calling her father "Henry" and ushering her out of the toyshop so quickly.

"I'm… not sure… I think I can find my way."

"Would ya like a short cut?"

She forgot about the toyshop and, instead, became intrigued by the idea of a short cut and the possibility of another adventure.

"Is it a secret passage? My father says there are secret passages in the castle, but I've not found one yet. I'm ever so anxious to and see where it takes me."

Without her realizing it, he had skillfully walked her down the hall, round one corner and down another hallway, well away from the toyshop door.

"Come here," he said moving a little further down the hall. "Push on that panel in the wall."

He took her across the hall and showed her a spot on the wainscot. She pushed and, low and behold, a door popped open to reveal a staircase that spiraled downward.

"There ye are. Just go down those steps. They dump ya in the coat closet on the first floor… or in the cellar, if ye go too far… but either way, ya will be downstairs."

"How will I know if I've gone too far?"

"Ya will be at the end and the end is too far… so, do not go all the way to the end."

"But how will I know where the end is unless I go all the way there?"

"Uhh… hmm… geewilikers … I do not know… no one has ever asked me that. They just go… and figure it out… I guess…"

"Has anyone ever got lost in there, I mean, lost forever?" She wondered out loud, as she peered down the dimly lit cavern. "Has everyone who's gone in, come out the other end?"

"I believe so, aye. At least, eventually… they always turn up… sooner or later."

"How sooner… or later are we talking?"

"Usually by dinner time they all find their way to the table. I suppose they follow their noses."

"So… I should follow my nose to luncheon, then?"

"Hmmm… do not know about luncheon… only know about dinner… luncheon might work."

She was skeptical about going into a dark stairwell with an uncertain destination for an unknown period of time. She wondered if she should seek out the more conventional way. Then she thought about her father saying he had loved, "*crawling round in the passages and playing detective games*". She was, after all, exploring and looking for adventure; and here was a secret passage right in front of her. Dinnertime wouldn't be so far off she couldn't stand it, although she would be ravenously hungry. No… the adventure would be worth the possible hunger pangs. She resolved to be brave and give it a go. She had conquered stable mucking, cow milking, horse riding, and sewing needles; how much worse could it be descending these stairs?

She had been looking at McTavish for some time, without realizing it, while reasoning through her dilemma. As she made her decision and her thoughts returned to the moment, she found herself fascinated by his diminutive size. She was a petite girl, for thirteen, and he was smaller than she. He must have noticed her stare.

"Ye are wondering why I am so small, are ye not?"

"Pardon me?"

"Ye think it strange I am so small, correct?"

"Oh… ahh… no… heavens… no… not at all… I wasn't thinking… um… thinking… yes, I must be honest. I was thinking I've never seen a grown man who was shorter than I… begging your pardon, again, for my rudeness."

"It is perfectly fine to be curious. My ancestors are from Polacia, as are my colleagues. It is a much colder region… an island far north of here…"

"I'm familiar… one of the Commonwealth states…"

"That is correct. The entire population is small of stature, as we are descended from a group of Leprechauns cast out of the Isle of Reland for their shenanigans* many centuries ago. Our ancestors had to work together and be kind to each other… completely against their nature… in order to survive the bitter cold. As a result, they changed their naughty behavior and found a new way of life. Many generations ago, the population officially changed its identity from Leprechaun to Polacian. A small band of explorers decided to leave the bleak barren north and migrated south, across the frozen sea and mountains to the valley. The occupants of this castle took the lot of them in and taught them a new occupation as master toy makers. A few set out on their own and went farther south, settling in the foothills and becoming miners. After all, Leprechauns are cobblers by trade… and are inherently skilled with all sorts of tools. That is why my colleagues and I are of small stature. So off with ya, then, upon your adventure… happy exploring! Top o' the mornin' to ya!"

As he gave his cheery encouragement, he turned and went round a corner. She had more questions and moved quickly to follow him.

"McTavish? McTavish? McTavish… where are you?"

He was gone… disappeared… in the blink of an eye. She was left alone with her decision to either brave the secret staircase or find her way back to the first one. The cubbyhole was the obvious choice, so she crawled in and closed the panel behind her. She was pleased to see it was wider and more spacious than it looked from the outside. It was, also, not a continuous spiral, but a series of steps and landings. There was a handrail and a small bit of light shone in from a tiny window above so it wasn't as dark as she had anticipated. As she cautiously descended an endless number of steps, she noticed the light was growing dimmer. Down, down and round… she worried she might be the first person lost forever in the vortex, when she noticed delicious aromas penetrating the stairwell.

"Food!" she thought. "I smell Food! Luncheon works, too, not just dinner!"

She was thrilled her journey could be at an end, as she was becoming claustrophobic*… and hungry. She couldn't tell which way she was facing or what level she had reached, since cooking odors can travel quite long distances. Was she on the first floor or had she only made it to the second? Was she already in the cellar and possibly further down? She spotted a tiny bit of light round an area in the wall in front of her. She thought it must be an entry panel. It was the right height to be part of wainscoting, but how did it open? From the outside all that was necessary was a tiny push. What if that didn't work from the inside? She realized she should have asked more questions about the portal and been less enamored with McTavish's stature. She felt for a knob or latch. Like magic… and for no reason she could figure out… a door popped open. She poked out her head.

She was both relieved and amused to recognize she had landed in the coat closet; relieved she had emerged from her adventure on the first floor and amused she was where her father had taken her, along with Rudy, to address her embarrassing outburst. Amused also, with all those shortcuts to and from the kitchen, she never knew this wonderful door existed. She thought it fortunate no one saw her crawl out of the woodwork… literally! She closed the entrance panel to keep the secret. She could barely see anything, as the service hall door was only slightly ajar, letting in the tiniest bit of light. She pushed through the heavy fur coats, winter capes and many pairs of boots she had encountered so many times. By now, she had her own trail blazed through the maze. When she reached the entrance, she stopped and listened. She exited smiling nonchalantly, undetected once again, her adventure all her own. She reflected on her fourth floor discoveries and eagerly anticipated future visits.

Food was very much on her mind, now she was back in familiar territory, and she went to find Grandma Polly. With the company gone, she looked forward to sitting in the kitchen and chatting with the two elderly ladies. She found them where she knew they would be.

"Hello, Maagy, Dear. Have you had a wonderful adventure?"

"Oh, my, yes… I have had an amazing time! I met McTavish."

"Really? You actually met him? He actually spoke to you?"

"Yes and he's ever so tiny… I mean… ever so nice! Oh, my, I didn't mean to be rude. I seem to be obsessed with his height. I'm afraid I embarrassed myself with him, too."

"Nonsense, Dear, McTavish is a forgiving sort. I'm sure he thought nothing of it. So… does that mean you saw the toyshop?"

"I did, indeed! It was incredible! I've never seen so many toys in one place. You must have a lot of needy children round the castle. Perhaps Father should look into helping their families with better wages."

"Are you ready to eat?" Grandma asked, smiling to herself.

"Oh yes! I'm ever so hungry."

"And how did you get downstairs?"

"I… um… I… came down… steps…"

Grandma leaned close and whispered, "The ones in the coat closet?"

Maagy was bursting with excitement and felt as if she were *the cat that ate the mouse**. She instinctively knew to keep this communication private, so she nodded and turned her face away so no one could see her smile.

"Sit and have this peanut butter and honey sandwich. I have a sliced apple for you and some peach tea. How does that sound?"

"Delicious! I'm famished."

As she ate and the two women bustled round the kitchen, they told wonderful tales about Grandpa Kris and the king when young *Prince* Henry would visit. It seems he was quite the mischievous lad. This knowledge only increased Maagy's admiration of him.

"Where is Father?"

"He took his meal in his room. He said he wanted to read and rest, but I think he may be napping."

"Napping… that sounds like a wonderful idea."

She finished her food, thanked Grandma and was excused to her room. She crawled among the fluffy pillows and laid a sleepy head down and drifted off to dreamland.

Chapter 11
Library Secrets

It had been another busy and rather contentious week for the king and allies of the Commonwealth... in particular Berensenia. There had been another round of informal meetings to address water issues. Representatives from Aradinia and Senecia, Queen Haideh, Prince Rudolpho and King Henry were present and Maagy had sat in on them. They had come together, again, to discuss the water restriction imposed by Emperor Zinrahwi. He had reneged on his part of the agreement and surprised them by sending his emissary with a new list of demands not included in the original treaty. There was dissention among the delegates... specifically, the Senecians wanted to give in to the demands... the other delegates would have rather impose trade sanctions. All the dignitaries, including Prince Rudolpho, had left with little resolution to the problem. His presence had been bittersweet for Maagy in that, even though he and Asanna were there, they had no time to ride horseback or catch up as friends. It had been an exhausting exercise in frustration.

Fortunately the seasonal rains had finally arrived. For the last week, everyday, the storms had begun in late afternoon and continued until early evening. This was the normal pattern for summer weather in the valley; however, due to the drought over the entire hemisphere the rains were long overdue. This gift from the skies was a welcome friend to the farmers, but often put Maagy at sixes and sevens. She had become so accustomed to spending time outside, she was bored with inside tasks. So, to amuse herself, she continued to explore the castle and had discovered a few more of its secrets. Having revisited the fourth floor several times, she found some of the workshops Grandma Polly had mentioned. She had spent time in the dance studio and painted a self-portrait… nothing of the comedic quality of Wesley's, however. Curiously, she had not been able to relocate the toyshop since the initial accidental discovery. She got lost frequently, but somehow always managed to find her way out of the maze.

One of the most intriguing secrets was the room undoubtedly used for training in the ancient combat arts. There were all types of bladed weapons carefully polished and hung on the walls. There were protective garments and headgear for fencing. Padded mats lined the center of the room. She had gone in, but hadn't touched anything. She had meant to ask her father about it, but it always seemed to slip her mind until she was there, again, alone.

Her favorite place, by far, was the children's library. She had enticed Estelí to sneak away with her, on a few occasions, for private tea parties under the steps. She eagerly anticipated climbing the floating staircase and gazing out over the meadow toward the mountains, where the storm clouds hung low and lightning danced. She cozied down on the balcony, with the many volumes of the most wonderful adventure books, and read while the storms roared. She enjoyed hearing the rain pound against the windows and watching the wind carry sheets of it across the courtyard. She cherished the solitude, also, and used it to reflect on the enormous changes she had experienced since coming there almost two months earlier. She actually looked forward to the afternoon rain so she could get back to reading the adventures of a young girl who had fallen down a rabbit hole and was meeting the most extraordinary characters. As she read, she became completely engrossed in the images the words created. She was reading the part where the girl was just about to meet another strange creature when… from the corner of her eye… she saw something move. She was startled and looked quickly in the direction to discover there was no one there.

"That's odd," she thought. "I could have sworn I saw movement."

She kept looking just in case she was right, but when all was still, she returned to her book and continued the adventure. Again, movement in the same place as before… again, she looked quickly, to see no one… nothing out of the ordinary.

"Now this is strange, indeed," she pondered.

She fixed her eyes on the area of the disturbance. Without looking, she placed a marker in the book and put it on the ottoman. Keeping her eyes peeled on the spot in question, she wiggled out of the chair and onto her hands and knees. She slinked toward the corner, like a cat stalking its prey and maneuvered round the table and lamp that stood in her way.

"Perhaps it's a mouse… or maybe a bird has got inside and is hiding in fear," she thought.

Her heart pounded and she was a tiny bit frightened. Curiosity, however, out-weighted fear and she crept onward. As she drew nearer the corner, she noticed a small crack in the otherwise solid wall. The dark wood paneling of the wainscot below the chair rail was definitely in question. Upon closer inspection, she saw there was an opening, an almost undetectable door reminiscent of the fourth floor. She was elated.

Estelí had mentioned a network of passages throughout the walls of the castle, but didn't know or was unwilling to share, the exact locations of them. Her father was mum on the subject and the one McTavish had pointed out was the only one she knew about, thus far. When adults were asked about the passages, they only laughed and explained there were service hallways, allowing discrete access to various areas, but there was nothing secret about them; the stories were old wives tales… *they said.* Nevertheless, in front of her, there was most certainly a hidden door and surely a secret passage beyond. She could hardly contain her emotions. She almost shrieked with joy, or perhaps fear… maybe excitement… her own great adventure, just not down a rabbit hole. The realization the door probably had not cracked open on its own interrupted her wild thoughts of exploration. The movement she saw from the corner of her eye was most likely the reason for her discovery. Who… *or what…* had come through the door and where was *he… she… it…* now?

"It was a mouse looking for a crumb or a bit of fluff for her nest," she rationalized. "When the little creature saw me, she retreated to the recesses of the wall."

Surely, this was a plausible explanation. Still, what if it wasn't a mouse? She sat back with a sigh, unsure now, if she should show someone the opening or keep the information to herself.

"Suppose everyone already knows about it," she reasoned. "Maybe they'll laugh at what a foolish child I am… thinking I have discovered something marvelous… and all the while, it's just a cleaning closet or book storage."

Then she wondered if she left and came back with someone, would it have magically disappeared? Would she look even more foolish? She concluded the best way to proceed was to muster her courage, open the door and go in for a look.

"After all, I'm not afraid of mice. I've encountered many of them in the barns and fields. They are more afraid of me than I could possibly be of them."

So with that thought, she took a deep breath and reached for the opening.

"Maagy! Maagy, Darling! It's time for dinner. Wash up and come down," shouted the king from the bottom of the stairs.

She was so startled she bumped the door and it snapped shut tight. She could hardly see the seam in the wood panel.

"*OH NO*!" she cried out.

"What do you mean, 'Oh no'? Grandma has prepared another of her award-winning meals and you say 'Oh no'?"

"Oh… no… I mean… oh… yes! I'll be right there, Father. I… I was in the middle of… an adventure."

"Well, mark your place and it will be there after dinner. Come along, now."

She heard the library door close as he made his exit. She madly felt for a button or a knob or anything that could open the portal. She pushed on the panel, as on the fourth floor, but nothing. It was shut tight without the slightest hint of movement or any trace of the opening that had been right in front of her just seconds earlier.

"Oh, fooey! Horse feathers!" She exclaimed in frustration. "It's gone! The door is gone!"

She sat for a few more moments in utter disbelief, but became more determined than ever to find the way in and explore what lay beyond. She realized, however, she was hungry and decided to act promptly upon her father's instruction. She washed her hands and face, changed into a dress and descended to the family dining room. King Henry was right. The evening meal was one of the best. It was quiet and intimate with just the family. The rain was, by then, only a drizzle and she could feel drowsiness creeping upon her. She made polite small talk at the table, then excused herself, said her goodnights and went to her room.

Once inside, her thoughts turned again to the children's library and the secret door. She thought about going back to the scene of the mystery and examining it further, but yawned instead. She realized it was time to sleep; the mystery could wait. So she put on her nightgown, cleaned her teeth, unpinned her hair and crawled into bed. The fluffy pillows felt especially good. Tomorrow was another day… she could work with Cupid… she could look for the secret door. She yawned one last time and drifted off to sleep.

Although she fell asleep quickly, she did not stay asleep long. She woke with a start, as if someone had called her name. She sat up and looked round the room bathed in moonlight. Nothing seemed out of place and there was no one else in the room… that she could see. She thought she must have had a dream that woke her, but could not, for the life of her, remember any part of it.

"That's strange," she thought. "I could have sworn I heard someone whisper my name, but there's no one here."

She lay back down on the pillow, but sleep was not with her anymore. Her thoughts soon turned to the children's library and the secret door. She threw back the covers, climbed out of bed and put on her slippers and robe.

"I must find a way to open it and see what's on the other side. I need something to pry it open… something sharp… something strong."

She spotted a letter opener on the dressing table. It was silver with an ornate handle, probably a family heirloom. Nonetheless, it was all she had with which to work, so she would take care not to damage it. The hallway was dark, except for the moonlight spilling through the windows of the rotunda. She crept to the library doors and eased one open. She peered in to check for visitors and then slithered through the crack as quietly as a mouse, allowing the door to close behind her without a sound. Her heart pounded so hard and fast she was sure it could be heard outside her body. She put one hand on her chest to silence the noise as she gripped the letter opener in the other. The darkness cast an eerie pall over the library that did not exist during the daylight. As she stood there mustering her courage and planning her next move, she, again, heard faint whispering that seemed to come from the reading balcony this time. Her heart pounded even faster, as she considered calling out, *who is there*… but then… thought better of it… since she didn't want to scare away the owner of the mysterious voice. As nervous as she was, she was even more curious.

Maagy took a deep breath and let it out slowly, as she began her quest toward the floating staircase. She slinked along the right side of the library wall, carefully avoiding the streams of moonlight pouring through the windows, and stayed hidden in the shadows of the curved bookcase until she reached the edge. She knew she would have to expose herself to the moon's rays for a brief time while she sneaked round the corner to the base of the stairs. She crouched close to the floor, using the large newel post to provide cover and was on the bottom step. One by one, she crawled up, all the while, listening for the voice or voices emanating from the top. She was so giddy with excitement she almost laughed out loud, at one point, and had to stop for a moment to regain control. A deep breath later, and she was on her way, again. She reached the balcony and laid completely still on the stairs, looking a bit like a big, white, furry lizard, in her fluffy robe and slippers, peering from floor level.

There, in the shadows… barely visible… was a rather strange little being with its back toward her. This little person… *creature…* Maagy wasn't sure which… was even tinier than McTavish. It almost resembled a large rat… or perhaps a small dog… *wearing clothes*! It appeared to be reading aloud, which accounted for the whispers… the same book she had been so engrossed in, earlier that day. The book was open and propped on several other books, as it was too big for the rat-person to hold in its lap. The sight of an actual living, breathing *being* took her by surprise and she let out a tiny gasp, and then quickly slapped her hand over her mouth, as her eyes widened in disbelief. This startled the little thing and it jumped straight up and spun round in mid air, landing in a martial arts-type… rather brazen… defensive pose. She screamed and dropped the letter opener. The creature squealed and they both retreated… she down a few steps… it behind the stack of books.

Cinderella
ART
Classic Music
Goldilocks
Jack & the Beanstalk
The Princess
Wizards
Spells & Hexes
Romeo & Juliet
ENCHANTED
Happily Ever
Once Upon A Time
Little Red Riding Hood

"Hi-i-i-ya!!" It uttered. "Goesen whotle therein? Intrumer! Showen, now!"[5]

She couldn't help but laugh at the sight of this critter and his squeaky voice. From the front view, he did seem to possess human features, odd that they were. Maagy estimated his height to be roughly several inches higher than her knees. He had short, dark fur, which seemed to cover most of his body, although, she could only see his head and face and his hands and feet. He was wearing the cutest little waistcoat and vest, and ankle-length pants with no socks or shoes. His feet were more rat-like than human, with no fur. His tiny hands each had four fingers and a thumb… also without fur… that moved with human-like dexterity, as he waved them at her, threateningly. His face was somewhat more human than rodent, in that there was no hair on it, either. His ears were set on the sides of his head like a human, but were round… and stuck out… like a rat. His nose was long and slender and his cheeks were chiseled. His eyes were deep-set and definitely human, as he looked directly at Maagy, seemingly, to anticipate her next move. She was not at all intimidated, but more curious than ever. She came back to the top of the stairs on her hands and knees and moved slowly across the floor. She was cautious to avoid frightening the little creature, since anyone backed into a corner and feeling vulnerable can be dangerous. She stopped a reasonable distance from him and sat down.

"Hello… hello there," she said gently.

The little rat-man stood stone still as if to pretend he was a statue. He did not move a muscle or blink an eye.

"Hello… I know you're real… I heard you reading and then you shouted at me. What are you?"

"*What*?" He said, holding his ground. "Nonen *what*. Whotle."

"What?" She replied.

5 Please see Glossary, Huggermugger Vocabulary. Huggermugger spelling used for Winnsbo's dialogue.

"What? Nonen what. Whotle. Winnsbo whotle," he said, turning his head curiously, but maintaining his bravado. "Nonen what."

"What? Whotle? What's whotle? What's Winnsbo?"

"*Nonen what*! *Whotle*! Winnsbo whotle. Winnsbo! What youtle? *Intrumer*!" He shouted, pointing an accusatory finger at her.

"What, me? No, who… Oh dear! 'Nonen what whotle', what is that? I don't understand you."

"Winnsbo! Winnsbo whotle! Winnsbo I! Namy… uh… umm… hugan… name… Winnsbo name!

"Oh… oh, I think… I understand! You're Winnsbo! I see, now. Namy must be name… whotle is who… youtle is maybe… you? I have no idea what intrumer is, but you pointed at me. I hope it wasn't insulting. Well, now that's cleared up, I am Her Royal Highness Princess Melania Abigail Alice Grace… Covington… Duchess of Wentworth… Crown Princess… soon-to-be queen of this fair kingdom, Berensenia… and the Commonwealth of Realms. Pleased to make your acquaintance."

She paused for a moment to allow him to realize he was in the company of royalty and properly acknowledge her status. Instead, he dropped his hands to his sides and stood with a puzzled look on his face.

"Hello… did you not hear me? Did you not hear that I am your Princess? I am royalty! Does that not mean anything to you?"

"Ro-yal-ty? Youtle?"

"Yes! Royalty meetle… uh… me! I am Princess Maagy!"

"Mag-gy? Nonen Megonia Nightingale Isie Fase Cumbering? Dutshess Wentout?"

"WHAT? Nonen Meg… whatever… you said. How dare you! I am soon-to-be your queen! You can't even say my name properly?"

"What… namy… name? Maagy? Megonia Nightingale Isie Fase Cumbering Dutshess Wentout?"

He seemed truly perplexed. She realized they were not speaking the same language… exactly… even though some of the words sounded similar. She thought she must have confused him with so many names. He wasn't trying to be rude, at all.

"Oh my, this is confusing for me, too, Kind Sir. Let's start again. You are Winnsbo. I am Mel... Maagy... just... Maagy. Call me just Maagy."

"Just Maagy, youtle. Winnsbo, meetle. Yem, yem, yem!"

"Yem... no... not yem... I mean... yes! That's almost right. But it's not Just Maagy. It's Maagy... just Ma... no just... oh dear, now I'm doing it! Let's start again. I am Maagy!"

"Said Winnsbo... yem... yes... that. Maagy, Just Maagy, yem?"

"Yem?" She muttered under her breath. "Oh... perhaps 'yem' is the word for 'yes'. That makes sense... I suppose... yes, I do think you got it right that time... sort of! Whew! That was a chore! Now, is Winnsbo your first name or your surname?"

"Yem, Winnsbo."

"Yes, that's right, Winnsbo. Is it your first or last name? Are you Winnsbo Something or Mister Winnsbo?"

Again, the bewildered little person stared at her.

"W-i-n-n-s-b-o," he spoke the name slowly, as if to make her understand.

"I know... your name is Winnsbo... but do you have another name?"

"Oh! Winnsbo no! Yem!"

"Yes... yes... yes... what?"

"Winnsbo."

"All right, let's try this another way." She said slowly, as she pointed to herself. "Maagy... Duchess of Wentworth."

Then she pointed to the little man and looked as if to ask a question.

"Winnsbo..." she said, trailing her voice, as if expecting him to add something.

"Yem."

"Okay, this is getting us nowhere. So Winnsbo it is, just Winnsbo."

"Non. Just Maagy, nonen Just Winnsbo. Winnsbo Yem. Just Maagy, youtle."

"Fine! Fine! Just Maagy, I… I mean me… I mean… oh my goodness! This is going to be a real challenge!"

"Challenge? Winnsbo Yem? Non. Winnsbo licum Just Maagy. Yem non challenge friend."

"Winnsbo likum just Maagy… I think I understand that part…. I think it means you like me… That's nice, thank you. Yem, non challenge friend. Yes… no… challenge friend. What does that mean?"

He sighed deeply, seeming to realize he only confused her even more. He began to speak slowly and carefully.

Winnsbo Yem licum Just Maagy. Non, nonen challenge. Friend, new."

"Wait! Winnsbo yem… yem means yes… your name is… Winnsbo Yes! I'm Just Maagy and you're Winnsbo Yem… which means yes! Yes?"

Yem! Yem! Yes, yes! Just Maagy right! Winnsbo Yem!"

He jumped in the air and did a backward somersault, as pretty as you please. Maagy leapt to her feet and danced round in a circle. They both laughed and clapped their hands as they celebrated the breakthrough. She suddenly realized someone might hear them, since it was the middle of the night. She stopped short and sat down with her hand over her mouth. It startled him and he dove behind the stack of books to hide. She began to giggle, again, while pondering the strangeness of the situation. She had often fantasized about meeting tiny people, but never thought it would happen outside sleep. He peeped out from behind the books and she motioned for him to come out.

"Shh, someone might hear us."

The inquisitive girl was full of questions for her newfound friend. She wanted to burst forth with all of them at once, but knew that, with the communication difficulty, there would be more confusion than answers, so she decided to start small.

"Mister Yes, what are you?"

"Non Mister Yes... Mister Yem... Mister Yem for nonen friend... Winnsbo... just Winnsbo... for friend. Just Maagy, friend."

"That's kind of you. So Winnsbo... just Winnsbo it is. No Yes, Yem... but no Yem... just Winnsbo."

She realized she might be getting the hang of his language. 'Non' was his word for no, 'nonen' meant not. Some words were the same, like 'what' and 'friend'. So she tried again.

"Winnsbo, what? Maagy, human. Winnsbo, what?"

"Winnsbo, Huggermugger-Polasian. Mamarc, Polasian. Patarc, Huggermugger. Winnsbo more Huggermugger. Polasian, nonen mutsh."

"Huggermugger, I've never heard of Huggermuggers. Of course, I'd never heard of Polacians, either until I met McTavish."

"McTavish! Maagy, McTavish friends, yem?"

"Well, I've met McTavish, but I'm not sure we're exactly friends, yet. You know McTavish?"

"Winnsbo eberboly no. Winnsbo friend all. McTavish, Winnsbo flabely. Mamarc Polasian."

"Mamarc?" She questioned. "Oh... wait... Mamarc... Patarc... Mamarc Polacian... Mother! Mamarc must be mother and your mother is Polacian, yes?"

"Yem, yem, yem!" He squealed and giggled. "Patarc Huggermugger! Mamarc Polasian! Winnsbo Yem, Hugger-Polasi-mugger!"

She giggled along with him as he rolled round on the floor like a roly-poly. She thought now might be a good time to ask about the door in the wainscoting. The conversations were getting more understandable... strangely enough... and she was still curious about the possibility of another secret passage. If he would take her in willingly, there would be no need to damage the letter opener. She thought carefully before she spoke.

"Winnsbo, Just Maagy see you, reading earlier, here... yes?"

"Winnsbo solly. Disburb, nonen mean. Winnsbo, licum read. Mamarc Yem tutel Winnsbo."

She understood what he had said; he was sorry, he hadn't meant to disturb her; he liked to read and his mother had taught him. She was proud of her linguistic* skills.

"Just Maagy reads, much. Reading, love. Just Maagy door saw… in wall… yes? Winnsbo… through door… in wall… see Just Maagy read… yes?"

"Yem. Winnsbo trudle dooran libon, Just Maagy see? Winnsbo haben trudle dooran."

"Ummm… Just Maagy… nonen… understand. What 'haben trudle dooran'?"

"Haben… um… libon… um… haben… home. Trudle dooran Winnsbo libon."

"Oh, your home… haben… is that correct?"

"Yem… trudle dooran libon."

"I… don't understand… trudle… dooran… libon?"

"Um… hugan…" he muttered as he searched for the words, "door… hugan."

"Hugan?"

"Youtle… hugan."

"Oh… human… hugan is human, yes?"

"Yem."

Finally, she thought she understood… Winnsbo's home was through the door in the wainscot panel. Libon… she surmised was live… he lived… his home… was on the other side of the door. She knew she should tread lightly, as he might not want to share his home and would flee in fear if she were too insistent.

"I didn't mean to intrude. More Huggermuggers, yes? Winnsbo… family… yes?"

"Just Maagy nonen intrume. Flabely, yem. Many Yem Huggermuggers. Friends. Just Maagy nonen intrume. Just Maagy meet, yem?"

This was it! This was her chance. He had extended the invitation to meet his family and friends and to do so, she would, most assuredly, be allowed through the secret door.

"Yes, oh yes! Just Maagy… I mean I… would love to meet your family and friends. When shall we go?"

"Now. Winnsbo, Just Maagy now go, yem?"

"But it's the middle of the night. Won't they mind being awakened? Wait, I should say that so you understand…"

"Winnsbo ubenstam… um… under-stand-ing. Rebumbering… uh… remembering… hugan languaje* more. Huggermuggers sleem when sunlight, worc, play in darc."

It occurred to her that… perhaps… just perhaps… this little fellow was much more fluent in "human" language than he was letting her know… after all, his mother was human… well, Polacian… which was almost human. She suddenly felt apprehensive. Now the opportunity to actually go through the door was in front of her, she was not so sure she should do it. What if it was a trick to steal her away and keep her from becoming queen? Would she find her way back if she got lost? What about the time? Surely, the Huggermuggers didn't actually live in the walls of the castle… it was, most likely, a passageway to some other place. Would she be back in time for breakfast and chores? Was this forbidden? Was he deceiving her? All these things were swirling in her head when he moved toward her and reached out his tiny hand.

"Just Maagy, non frygan. Winnsbo tagomcore Maagy… umm… tace good care Maagy. Nisem flabely. Nisem friends. Just Maagy safe."

The adventure was too enticing…

"Fine. Let's go. Will I be back before morning?"

"Yem. Winnsbo sleem morning."

"Lead the way!"

He turned to the wall and sat down on the floor with his back to her. She tried to look over his shoulder to see what he was doing, but before she could, the wainscot door popped open. He must have done something to a spot on the floor that triggered the door's latch from the inside. Her insatiable* curiosity would demand she figure out exactly what he did, but the pressing issue in front of her was he had already disappeared into the dark abyss. Without another thought, she dove, headlong, into the opening. The door clapped shut behind her and she found herself in pitch black. She turned quickly and pushed where she thought the opening must have been, but the wall was as solid as the stone in which it was set.

"Winnsbo? Winnsbo! Where are you?"

There was no response. She could see nothing in front or behind her. The walls on both sides were cold and solid and she dared not reach out to feel her way along for fear she would disturb a large spider lying in wait for just such an opportunity.

"Winnsbo, this is not funny! Where are you? Are you still here? Winnsbo? *Winnsbo*? Oh bother!"

After a few long moments, she realized her eyes had adjusted to the darkness and there was a glimmer of light, which seemed far away. She blinked and squinted to focus, but the light was too faint to see her surroundings. Since she could not get back into the library and she was completely alone, she figured the only thing that made any sense was to move in the direction of the light. So with trepidation*, she began inching forward on her hands and knees.

The tunnel was unremarkable. The floor was smooth and the walls were of the same stone as the rest of the castle. The passage seemed unusually long, but she thought it might be her own interpretation from not knowing what lay ahead. She tried to envision where along the wall on the side of her father's bedchamber she might be, but realized she was way beyond. She calculated she must be at least half way down the second floor corridor. As she was processing these thoughts, she became aware the light was slightly brighter than before. She reached her hand forward to take another step and down she went, face first on the slickest surface she had ever experienced. Down, down, down she flew like the wind, on her belly, arms outstretched in front. She started to scream, but was too focused on where she might land to make even the tiniest sound. The downward motion ended and she rolled and tumbled forward, finally coming to a halt, feet in the air, fuzzy slippers against the ceiling. Once she caught her breath and realized she was unhurt, she giggled out loud and turned upright, resumed her hands-and-knees stance and looked round to get her bearings.

"That was really fun! But where on Earth am I?"

"Finbeleese!"

She whirled round to see Winnsbo standing behind her.

"Youtle finbeleese herein comen!"

"Winnsbo! Where have you been? You left me all on my own. I was frightened… except for the wonderful slide down, that is. It was delightful."

"Slow, youtle. Winnsbo fabs. Youtle catsh ut."

"I'm slow because it's dark in here and I can't see where I'm going. Yes, you move quite fast. That must mean you can see in the dark better than I. How about slowing down a bit so I can keep up?"

"Oceydocey! Winnsbo slow. Youtle ceem ut."

"Fine! So… which way now?"

Without a word, Winnsbo leaned forward and took off down yet another tunnel. This time though, she was close at his heels. The passage was getting smaller and smaller. She was now on her belly crawling, sometimes on her elbows and knees, as the passage had the occasional rock to surmount. He, however, moved easily and quickly, sometimes rounding a turn and leaving her temporarily alone in the dimly lit caverns. It soon dawned on her she was much too far along to find her way back without his help. She couldn't even turn round in the narrow tunnel. She would have to figure out her initial path backwards. This was the first time, since the journey began, she had stopped to think of the gravity of the situation. She had told no one where she was going. It was the middle of the night and, as far as anyone in the castle knew, she was fast asleep in her bed. Imagine how awful it would be for her father to discover she had disappeared without a trace. Her heart raced and she felt fear creeping upon her. Suddenly, it was as if her robe was tightening round her and she was having difficulty breathing as she inched her way forward.

Finally… and just before full-blown panic attack… the tunnel ended and she crawled into a room carved out of stone. She could actually stand up, although her head was touching the ceiling. The area was spacious, with corridors leading off in several directions. There were stone benches, with brightly colored cushions and pillows lining the round walls. Tiny lights, that seemed to have no source of power, provided a dim, but welcome glow to the darkness. She realized the light she had seen in the tunnel must have been a similar to the one in Winnsbo's hand, but she was too flustered to notice it, at the time. A large, well-constructed fire pit, with cast iron cooking spits and grates that looked well used, was in the center of the room. There were popcorn baskets and skewers lying about and propped against the pit wall. This was obviously some sort of common area used for cooking and socializing.

She could feel a rush of fresh air and it felt good to breathe deeply after such a long time in the dank caves. She looked up and saw stars through a large hole in the ceiling, a skylight, directly over the pit. It was a chimney to draw smoke out when a fire was lit. This was the source of the fresh air and it was drawing from several directions, indicating there were other openings to the outside. Her panic quickly subsided, once she realized she could go above ground at anytime. She had been so focused on the fire pit, the lights and the stars above she failed to notice Winnsbo was nowhere to be found. Now realizing she was completely alone, she stood still and listened for any movement, but heard nothing. She hesitated to call out, not knowing how the other residents would react to a stranger in their midst. She had no choice but wait for his return. In the meantime, her curiosity, about the tiny lights round the walls, got the best of her.

She inspected them up close, since she was tall enough to see them straight on. Still, she could find no source of power. There was no flame, no fuel, nothing she knew of, that could cause them to light, yet they were glowing. The color was strangely familiar, but she couldn't place where she had seen it. It was a mystery, indeed, on which she would surely question Winnsbo, when… *and if…* he ever returned.

While she waited, she also inspected the cushions and pillows covering the stone benches. They were of a fine quality of cotton material. Some were floral patterned, some were gingham… a few were plaid… all of vibrant colors. Many were edged with hand crocheted lace of a high degree of craftsmanship. She was impressed these creatures… that mostly resembled rodents… were so skilled in domestic arts. She wondered what other surprises were in store for her, as she continued to wait… and wait… and wait… for Winnsbo's return.

She lay down on one of the benches and discovered the cushions and pillows were quite soft and comfortable. The next thing she knew, she heard birds singing overhead. The stars were gone and daylight was breaking. She had no idea how she would get out of… or where she would emerge from… the cavern. He had tricked her, as she had feared. Now, her only thought was to get back to her bed as quickly as possible, so as not to be caught. She looked round the room, trying to remember which tunnel she had followed. All of them looked the same. She decided the tunnel would take too long, anyway, and she had a better chance of finding her way if she was above ground. So she lifted her robe to her knees and stepped up onto the edge if the fire pit.

Maagy could see iron bars, like handles, protruding from the stone and dirt walls of the skylight. She reached up as high as possible and grabbed hold of one. It was solid and sturdy, so she grabbed another with the other hand. Now she was swinging above the ashes in the pit and there was only one option; she had to climb out on her own. She pulled herself up with all her might. She let go one hand

and grabbed a higher bar. She pulled up more and did the same with the other hand. She continued to ascend slowly, hand over hand, until she could swing up and get a foothold on one of the bars. Her slippers made it hard to grip, so she kicked them off, leaving them on the floor of the room, and used a bare foot. She pulled with her arms and pushed with her leg until she got the other foot on a bar. She stopped for a moment to rest… now she was no longer swinging above hot coals. She still had a good distance to climb to reach the top and dawn was getting brighter. She took a deep breath and carefully ascended to the top. Once there, she pulled herself just high enough to peer through the grass and see there was no one round. She climbed the rest of the way out and crouched on her hands and knees in the tall grass. She stretched upward and immediately recognized she was at the very bottom of the hill in the meadow, but still inside the wall, fortunately for her.

The sun was not up, but would be soon. She knew she would have to stay close to the wall and in the shadows of the gardens to get inside without being seen by the early morning staff, who would surely tell Grandma Polly. She darted from tree to tree… hiding behind each… making sure no one was about. Finally, she reached a back entrance to the castle. She crept through small sitting rooms and into the grand dining room, feeling along the wall until she found one of the hidden service doors. She stepped in front of it and couldn't help but smile, as it slide open like magic. She moved through the service hallway undetected, and into the coat closet. She cracked the door open and peeked out into the foyer, still fairly dark. She listened to hear if anyone was there, then slithered out and stayed close to the railing, as she crept up the steps and into her room successfully undiscovered. She leaned against her closed door and breathed a sigh of relief.

As Maagy crossed to the lavatory, she caught sight of herself in the full-length mirror. To her surprise, she was covered in dirt and soot. Her fluffy, white robe was now dingy gray and grass stained. Only then, did she notice the dank, musty smell emanating from her person. Her face was smudged and her hair was tangled, with bits of ashes from the skylight and grass from the meadow. She looked down to see her feet were blackened from the fire pit and skylight walls and she had left a trail of footprints behind.

"*Oh crumbs*! It's all for naught! I've left a trail! I'm doomed!"

She ripped off the nasty robe and gown and rolled them into a ball, which she promptly threw under the bed.

"So much for that."

She went into her lavatory and bathed and washed her hair. It took several times lathering to remove all the dirt and grime. Finally clean, she toweled her hair and dressed. She was quite tired and wanted, desperately, to sleep, but it was time for breakfast and chores and she knew Julie and Cupid were expecting her attention. She combed her hair, pulled it back into a ponytail and made up the bed, as usual. Then she got a wonderful idea. She would sneak out and mop the black footprints from the white marble floors with the wet towel she used on her hair. She eased the door open to find still no one in the corridor. She threw down the towel and began skating from footprint to footprint, erasing any trace of her clandestine adventure. She followed the trail down the steps and back into the coat closet, through the service hall and into the grand dining room, through the dining room into the smaller rooms and to the door... done. All the evidence was gone. She retraced her path back to the foyer to check for any sooty prints she might have missed. She was so focused on the floor she didn't notice her father descending the stairs.

"Good morning, Maagy Dear! How are you today?"

She threw her hands and the towel in the air and screamed.

"Daddy! You scared me to pieces!"

"So sorry, My Dear. What are you doing with that towel?"

"I... I'm... practicing... my coronation! It's my coronation robe. I'm taking it back to my room. I'll be down in a moment."

She grabbed the towel and raced past him up the stairs and into her room. She slammed the door and burst into tears. She had fibbed to her father… *again*. She felt as if her heart would break. She had tried so hard to stop telling these made-up stories, into which her curiosity and adventuresome spirit always seemed to lead.

"This was Winnsbo's fault. He made me tell a story."

She resolved to find the little beggar and give him a piece of her mind. In the meantime, she had to go down to breakfast and face her father, while keeping her secret. She dried her tears and threw the towel under the bed with the robe and gown. The only saving grace to the morning was the delicious food waiting. Cheery hellos were exchanged and her day was underway. Still, there was the issue of the mischievous Winnsbo and his dirty trick. The thought of it made her angry and she was even more determined to find him, again, and discover his secrets. She was clearly preoccupied throughout breakfast, but when asked why, she shrugged it off as being not quite awake yet… another misleading statement for which she heaped on another pile of guilt.

She rushed through her chores and even Cupid's ring training, still obsessed with the idea of finding Winnsbo. She spent the entire day searching the meadow for the chimney hole to the Huggermuggers' burrow, reasoning if she could find it during the day, the residents would be asleep and the fire pit would be cold. She could climb back inside and surprise him and give him his comeuppance* for his chicanery*, but she never found the chimney hole in the huge expanse of the meadow. Finally, she gave up the search and went back to the barn to accomplish her evening chores.

Maagy was unusually quiet during dinner; to the point King Henry asked if she were feeling well. She assured him she was fine… just tired… and she would like to retire early… this time, the absolute truth. She couldn't bear to look him in the eye with the burden she carried for lying to him, so she said her goodnights and went to bed.

Chapter 12
Festival Finery

Maagy arose especially early that morning. In fact, she had awakened every hour throughout the night to make sure she didn't oversleep. It had been several days since her fateful adventure with Winnsbo and she was still plotting ways to get even with him, but it was the third Festival Day of the summer, a day of fun, food and relaxation enjoyed by all the residents of the towns and villages surrounding Whitmore Castle. She decided a parade and picnic were more important than her vendetta*. She could take care of the little trickster anytime.

Festival Day celebrations were on the third Saturdays of each month, May through August. Her birthday was on the first one and she and King Henry had arrived at the Summer Castle the day after. The second Festival Day had been the day after the League of Kingdoms Summit ended. She had experienced it with some lack of enthusiasm, as Prince Rudolpho and Princess Asanna had left the day before, but once she discovered how much amusement and delicious food were involved, she eagerly anticipated the next. Last time, she had braided Cupid's mane and tail and walked her in the parade, but soon found out she was sorely underdressed. Apparently, the tradition of children "dressing" the animals had been going on for some time and had become quite the art form. There were geese on leashes wearing tuxedos and bow ties. There were dogs with hats and vests and cats in tutus. The horses and cows that walked the parades were gilded to the nines.

There was even a pig in last month's festivities. She was a huge sow, led by a little girl from Summer Valley, the village at the base of the hill southwest of the castle. The sows name was Miss Trinny McBride and she held the unique title of having given birth to more piglets than any other sow in the area, perhaps even the kingdom. She was not a particularly handsome pig, but was dressed as if she were. Someone had gone to a great deal of trouble to craft a frilly, pink party dress for Miss Trinny, which hung low enough to cover her unsightly teats*, but high enough off the ground she didn't step on it. There was no covering her giant derrière*, but a satin ribbon tied in a bow adorned her curly tail. Miss Trinny's costume was finished off with a little pink bonnet on her head, tied round her neck with a big bow on the side. She was a paradox, to be sure! The proud owner of the pig, Sydney McBride, was sporting a matching outfit and was leading her with a rope of braided pink ribbons.

Not wanting to be outdone by a village girl and a pig, Maagy arose earlier than usual to have plenty of time for grooming, polishing and dressing Cupid. The unknown factor in all the planning was how the filly would react to the commotion. Maagy washed her face and hands, cleaned her teeth, fixed her hair and got dressed for morning chores. She could already smell bacon and coffee from the kitchen. As she thought about breakfast and the day ahead, she also thought about the fib she had told her father a few days earlier. She had reasoned it wasn't a big one and it was harmless, since no one was hurt and it hadn't led to further untruths. She tried to find some solace in that reasoning, but to no avail. She felt guilty for sneaking out in the night to follow such a shady character. It was completely against everything her father had taught her. She went off with someone she didn't know, to a place she'd never been. Not only did she not know where she was, no one else did either. The result of such action could have been tragic and devastating for the king. It still weighed heavily on her and was beginning to dampen her joy at the day's activities. She resolved to fix her mistakes after the parade and picnic.

She ate quickly and headed straight for the barn. She was quite proud of her skill and ingenuity in designing and executing a costume for Cupid. She had tied together and braided ribbons of red, yellow, green, purple and blue to make a long, rainbow colored rope. John Miles had taught her to tie the rope in such a way as to fashion a halter with a lead. She had found a piece of fine brocade fabric in the sewing room and Grandma Polly gave her blessing to make a blanket for Cupid's back. She had hand stitched gold fringe round the edge and put tassels on each corner to weigh it down. She had sewn long ribbons on two sides to tie round Cupid's girth. She had, also, made fringe and tassel leg decorations and attached tassels on each side of the halter.

Now, she had to "dress" the frisky filly and hope she would tolerate it. She bathed and curried Cupid, then polished and painted her hooves. She braided her mane and tail and intertwined individual pieces of the same colored ribbons as the halter. She added tassels in her mane and one long tassel was draped down her tail. Maagy left her in the stall with an extra bit of hay while she ran back to the house to dress for the day. She had found a skirt in the wardrobe she didn't recognize, but which fit her well. It was mid-calf length with rainbow colored scarves draped round it from the waist to the hem. She thought it was a nice match to Cupid's costume, so she wore it with a white linen blouse. Rather than dressy shoes, she cleaned and shined her leather boots, thinking they were a more practical choice. She checked her hair in the mirror and decided at the last minute to tie some of the same ribbons she used for the costume round her ponytail and let them stream down her back. She gave one last look in the mirror and ran to the barn.

One by one, Maagy put the pieces on Cupid and waited for her to become accustomed to each. She tied the tassels round her legs and switched the regular halter for the fancy one, and then walked the horse round the barnyard a few times to calm her. Finally, she gently placed the brocade blanket on her back. Cupid shook her head and quivered her skin, as if it itched. She stomped her feet and switched her tail. She'd had a blanket on her back only a few times and wasn't too keen on it. Maagy carefully tied the ribbons round her girth and then walked her again to familiarize her with the strange sensations. She regretted not being more attentive to her training responsibilities the last few days, and wished she'd been less focused on getting even with Winnsbo. She might have better prepared the horse for this experience. Cupid kicked and bucked and flung her head a bit, but nevertheless, calmed down and seemed to accept her new finery and bits of carrot and apple were her reward. It occurred to Maagy that she had not spoken a word to her beloved pet through the entire process.

"You must think I'm angry with you, my darling friend. The irony is, you're probably the only one in the world I could actually talk to about this. If only you could talk back and tell me what to do. I really need someone to give me guidance, but I can't tell anyone about the Huggermuggers or that I've told my father a false story. That's why I've been so quiet and cross, lately. At least, you'll keep my confidence."

Oddly enough, Cupid seemed to genuinely understand, or at least her emotions. She nuzzled gently and whinnied.

"Thank you for your kindness. I'm not sure I deserve it."

"Ah, Your Highness," John Miles said, as he came round the corner, "I see you and the little one are getting ready for the parade."

"Oh, yes, what do you think? Is she dressed enough?"

"I think you've done a fine job. She's even more beautiful than usual. Now, hold on to her firmly and don't let her get the best of you with all those other strange looking creatures round today.

Remember, she can't reason they're just ordinary animals with a lot of fancy things hanging on them. She sees a completely different thing. She might get skittish… if so, hold her tightly and keep her head down so she can't rear up and hurt you. Cover her eyes and speak softly… close to her ear… so she can hear your voice over the other noise. If that doesn't work, you should bring her here, straight away, and put her in the stall for her safety and yours, do you understand?"

"Yes, I do. I'll be careful. I know she's young and inexperienced… sort of like me… I understand how all the commotion might upset her. Thank you, Mister Miles, for your advice."

"It is my pleasure, Your Highness," he said with a slight bow. "Have a pleasant day, Princess Maagy."

Maagy was leading Cupid out of her stall when she got an unexpected treat.

"Is this where I have my horse done up for the parade?" The familiar voice asked.

She looked up and almost fainted. There stood handsome Prince Rudolpho with a charming smile on his face. Her hands began to tremble, her mouth went dry and her face turned beet-red.

"Rudy! What are you doing here? I… I… di… didn't know you were coming today!"

"Neither did I until last evening. Hello, Duchess," he returned, as he extended his hand for hers.

She placed a clammy, shaky, somewhat soiled hand in his and he kissed it. She felt the rush of blood to her face, again.

"I'm… so surprised… I can hardly speak. What do you mean you didn't know you were coming? Why are you here? More meetings? Is something wrong? Does my father know?"

"I was in Montclair monitoring the progress at Buzzard Lake Gap when I remembered this was a Festival Day. I wanted to stay last time, but the Summit business was too pressing. I knew my father was anxious to hear and so…"

"How is your father? Better I hope."

"Much better, thank you. He's recovered nicely. As I was saying…"

"How are things at Buzzard Lake Gap?"

"Um… there is progress… are we going to talk politics?"

"I… just thought… I should know… that's all."

"There's the right attitude… but… as I was saying… I remembered the day, so I decided to ride up… and surprise you. Yes, your father knows. I just saw him at the castle."

"Surprise… *me?* Not my father… or business?"

"No… just you… and the festivities… and way too much food… of course."

"Of course…"

"Besides, I have to check on your riding progress."

"I… don't… know what… to say."

"Now, that's a first. Princess Grass Stain… speechless."

"Oh… my… that skirt never came clean. I think it got ripped up for rags."

"What a funny sight you were that day. I shall never forget it. My goodness, Cupid is decorated. I think she's grown since I saw her last. I've heard of this business of dressing animals, but have never witnessed it."

"Oh, just you wait. It's the most hilarious thing you'll ever see. Last time, Cupid was woefully under dressed and you're right; she has grown. So this time, I went all out. There's a pig you simply must see to believe! You'll never get that image out your head, either."

"Shall we go, then?" He said as he extended his arm to escort her and her prized pony to the parade line.

"Are you here alone?"

"No, never alone… sadly. Captain Sistrunk is here and two other guards."

"Where are they?"

The captain is with your father. I believe they've become friends. And the guards are in the crowd enjoying a bit of holiday… but always with eyes on me."

"Is it awkward having another prince as your personal guard? Oh, that came out of nowhere. I didn't mean to be indelicate."

"How do you know about Mak?"

"Daddy told me. He said his grandfather was the last and *late* king of Darhambi. I noticed the captain discretely communicating with Chief Obuku at the Summit. I didn't let them know I saw and I asked Father about it after everyone had left. He told me the whole story. He said your father assigned Captain Mak to you… because you would always be in danger… is that true?"

"I… hope not… it's true I have a great deal of responsibility."

"How is that possible? You're so young."

"Tutankhamun became Pharaoh at the ripe old age of nine."

"That's ridiculous…"

"And you'll be a queen when you're eighteen…"

"That's frightening!"

"You never cease to amaze, Princess!"

There were all sorts of animals in outlandish outfits and the prince and princess laughed until their sides hurt. Cupid walked quietly in the parade, but Maagy could sense she was becoming agitated so she and Rudy took her back to the barn. Miss Trinny McBride and Sydney were in attendance again and were dressed all in yellow. Maagy made a point of telling Sydney that Miss Trinny looked even more elegant this time than last. The little girl was most appreciative and was completely enamored with Rudy and Maagy. She followed them round for most of the morning with Miss Trinny close behind, which didn't bother either of them one bit.

The food was abundant and delicious and everyone shared their best recipes. Sydney was thrilled they invited her to enjoy a picnic in the shade with them, as Miss Trinny stretched out on her side in the sunshine and slept. They ate until they thought they might pop like bubbles. Sydney and her precious pig left soon after and Maagy and Rudolpho decided to saddle Carmela and Sunrise and go for a nice long ride. His horse, Remington, was having a rest and bite to eat in the barn. One of the things Maagy found most intriguing about him was the ease with which they conversed. Although considerably older and more educated and worldly wise, he never made her feel her thoughts were less important than his. She felt as if she could discuss anything with him… and she did.

"Rudy, you said once you thought I'd be ready to take the crown in five years… do you still think so?"

"Of course. Why would I think differently?"

"Well… now you've known me longer. Maybe you've changed your opinion."

"Nonsense, Silly Girl! Considering how far you've come in just two months, I think you'll be well prepared for the job."

"What should I call myself, 'Queen Maagy'? I'm not sure that's appropriate."

"Why not? You've been *Princess* Maagy since you were born. Why confuse them now?"

"Well, most queens use their first given name, but mine is Melania. My mother was Queen Melania. I don't want to be 'Queen Melania… the Second'."

"Do you know what Melania means?"

"Do you?"

"I do. It's from the ancient Greek word for black. It means, 'dark-haired'."

"Really? Do you *know* that or are you guessing?"

"I know it for sure. I like studying the origins of names. I've looked up all of yours. Want to know what they mean?"

"I'll call your bluff! Tell me what all of my names mean."

"Well, I just told you what Melania means. Abigail is from Hebrew and means, 'source of joy', and you are certainly that. Alice is Teutonic and means, 'noble and of good cheer'. You're that, too! Grace is from Latin and means, 'blessing from God'. Your parents named you aptly."

Maagy blushed. She was overwhelmed. Rudolpho had, indeed, researched her names and was exceeding complimentary. She wasn't sure what to say next. They rode in silence for several minutes.

"So? Which is it? Melania, Abigail, Alice or Grace?" He said after the long pause.

"I wonder why my mother was named Melania," she finally said, her mind now on a completely different curve.

"What?"

"Melania… my mother… she was as blond as I am. Why would she be named, "Dark-Haired?"

Rudolpho burst into laughter and almost fell off his horse.

"Duchess, you are hilarious! You've completely gone off the road!"

"Why are you laughing? Don't you think it odd?"

"I think Melania is a beautiful name and your grandparents obviously thought so, too! Most people give their children names they like or name them for relatives. I'm sure it has little to do with the actual meaning of the name. So what will the future impetuous queen be called?"

"Maagy… I think… just Maagy… Queen Maagy."

They had ridden round the entire estate and were back at the barn. Mister Miles was waiting and took over unsaddling and cooling down the horses. She had been riding everyday under his supervision and had progressed quickly. Rudy was impressed with her skill and had given her some pointers on jumping. He promised to continue the lesson later in the summer.

As they walked up the lane to the house, she noticed the sword on his side was not the one-handed Claymore he had at the Summit.

"That's not the sword you had before," she mumbled under her breath.

"Pardon?"

"Oh… I'm sorry… I just noticed your sword is different. Why?"

"How observant of you. This is my actual utility, defense weapon. This is the sword I trained with and would use in battle. It has a more balanced hilt and guard and a much more substantial blade, not as ornate as the other. I only wear that one when I want to *look* impressive," he said with a wry grin.

"Well, it did that," she muttered.

"Pardon?"

"Nothing! I… nothing. It's just that… well… I've become enamored with weaponry ever since looking down on the Summit table from the balcony and seeing all those blades. Is that odd, do you think?"

"For you, a bit… I see you much more smitten with fashion… or… astronomy… or… ice cream."

"Oh, stop. Now you *are* teasing. I'm serious."

They had reached the back of the castle and were about to enter when she grabbed his hand and pulled him toward the kitchen door.

"Come this way. I want to show you something."

She dragged him through the mudroom and into the kitchen where Grandma Polly and Josephine were washing dishes.

"Hello, Gram-P, hello Josephine. This is my friend, Rudolpho. Oh, that's right, you know him already."

Both women immediately curtsied and bowed while quickly drying their hands.

"How do you do, Your Highness Prince Rudolpho," was their unison reply.

"Very well, thank you, Ladies. Please, don't let me disrupt your routine."

"Want an apple? They're crisp and tart," Maagy added, completely unaware of the awkward situation she had created.

"No, thank you," then he whispered, "Duchess, what are we doing in here?"

"We're taking a short cut," she whispered back. "Good-bye, Gram, Josephine. Have a lovely afternoon."

She dragged him through the service hall and the coat closet, which he recognized, into the foyer and up the stairs. They climbed to the third floor and then round the corner and up to the fourth floor. She was oblivious of any protocol or decorum she might have breached in her intense determination to show him her secret room.

"What's up here?" He asked in wonder at the maze of doors and hallways.

"All the shops, which keep the entire estate and surrounding farms working like a fine time piece. There are shops for woodworking, leather working, seamstress and silversmith; there's a shop for everything. There's even an enormous toyshop, which I stumbled upon once... but can't seem to ever find... again. There is a music room, a dance room and an artist's studio with a kiln. I've had so much fun up here. The most intriguing room, however, is this one," she said as she opened the door to the combat training room.

"Holy mother-of-pearl! This is magnificent. I've not seen some of these blades since Academy training."

"And speaking of... why didn't you tell me you trained at our Academy?"

"You never asked... this is incredible, Maagy. You haven't touched any of them, have you? You could be serious injured if you don't know what you're doing."

"Of course not. They scare me to death... but at the same time... I find myself totally intrigued. I want Father to train me and teach me about every single one."

"It doesn't look like anyone has been in here for quite a long time. We're leaving footprints in dust."

"Would you show some of them to me? You're a qualified swordsman."

"I should need your father's permission, first, Dear Duchess. It would be a huge overstep for me to take that responsibility without his knowledge."

"I was afraid you'd say that. He'll never let me train with them. Oh well, I wanted you to see it, anyway."

"Most impressive!"

As the sun inched its way closer to the mountaintop, the townspeople slowly descended the hillsides in every direction. It was after the midpoint in the year and already, the sun was setting a little earlier and rising a little later than a month ago. The two friends had a small bite to eat and found King Henry and Grandpa Kris on the veranda watching the sunset. They joined them and chatted until dark. It had been a wonderful day and she was sad to see it end. Rudolpho had told her he would leave before dawn the next day and she wasn't looking forward to it. The King bid the prince good-bye and Godspeed, kissed his daughter and was gone. Grandpa Kris also took his leave.

"I must say goodnight as well, Princess. My day will begin before your dreams are complete. It's been a wonderful day and I'm glad I made the journey," he said as he stood. "May I escort you up?"

"Yes, I'm turning in as well. Thank you for this lovely surprise. I thoroughly enjoyed spending the day with you."

They walked slowly not saying a word. As they climbed the stairs, she thought about running sooty footprints up those steps. She wished she could turn back the clock and erase what came after. If only she had told her father about Winnsbo… if only she hadn't fibbed about the towel… if only… if only. By then, they were at her door.

"When will I see you again?" She asked.

"I'm not sure, but I look forward to the next time."

"I, as well..."

"Goodnight and the sweetest of dreams, Princess."

"And to you the same. Goodnight, Prince."

She was about to go in and he was on the way to the third floor.

"Maagy!"

"Yes?"

She turned to see him running down the stairs toward her with boyish exuberance, a silly grin on his face.

"I forgot something..."

"What?"

"This!"

He dropped to his knees and slid in front of her, took her hand and kissed it gently.

"Goodnight, again!"

She was breathless. He stood and laughed and ran back up, taking the steps two at a time.

"Sweet dreams, Duchess," he called over his shoulder.

She giggled, as she watched him round the last step and disappear.

Chapter 13
Fuzzy Slippers

She was still enjoying the glow of her crush and had shut the door, when she saw her bed and became weak in the knees. There… sparkling clean and folded… were her towel, nightgown, robe and fuzzy slippers… *her fuzzy slippers*… the ones she had kicked off and left behind while climbing out of the Huggermuggers' burrow. How… who… someone had found the towel, nightgown and robe under the bed. She had planned to dispose if them, but had forgot about it. The cleaning staff would have found them, but the slippers? There was only one way the slippers could have found their way back to her room.

"That little stinker!" She shouted. "Now, he's mocking me!"

"Maagy, Darling? Is everything all right? Who is in there?" King Henry inquired, as he tapped on the door.

She was startled out of her skin. She jumped clear round and faced the door.

"Ah… ah… ah… no one, Father! Just um… just um… me… I'm… I'm… alone with myself… just singing," she stammered as she opened the door.

"I was on my way to tuck you in and I thought I heard you shout. Just making sure you're all right."

"Yes, Father… just fine… I'm just fine, thank you," she said almost in tears. "Goodnight."

"Goodnight then," he said, as he leaned in and kissed her cheek. "Sleep tight, don't let the bedbugs bite, My Darling! I'll see you in the morning… if you don't see me first!"

He chuckled as he scurried to his room. She listened to him still laughing, as she closed her door. She felt her heart would surely break. She had to get this burden off her chest. She was about to go to her father and confess when someone knocked. Her heart pounded as she opened the door, expecting to see King Henry on the other side.

"Daddy, I'm so glad you… oh!"

She stopped short as she saw, not her father, but McTavish.

"Hello… Mister… I mean… Mc… um… Mac…"

"McTavish, just McTavish, Your Highness," he said politely, as he bowed. "So sorry to disturb ya, but I was wondering if ye could give me a moment for talking."

"Talking? About what? I mean, of course, Sir. Please forgive my manners. Shall we go downstairs?"

"If ya do not mind, we could go to the fourth floor parlor where we will not be overheard by anyone."

"Of course, lead the way, Sir. I'll follow."

She was so flabbergasted by this turn of events she didn't even question his motives. She hadn't seen him since that first excursion when she found the toyshop by mistake. Her instinct told her he was an honorable person. She followed him round the rotunda to the third floor and then up the stairs in the southwest tower. They chatted as they went.

"McTavish, I've been back up here several times to use the art and dance studios. I found the combat training room and most of the other shops… but I've never been able to find the toyshop, again. Have you moved it?"

"No Mam. It is still up here, right where it has always been."

"Then why can't I find it?"

"I suppose ya are not looking in the right place!"

"Where *is* the right place?"

"On the toyshop hallway. Right where it has always been."

"You said that already… which hallway is it?"

"The big one… with the toyshop."

She could see he was a master of double-talk and realized she was getting nowhere, so she gave up… for the time being. He led her straight into a brightly lit parlor, next to the tower staircase, she had never seen.

"Please have a seat, Your Highness. May I serve ya a cup of tea?"

"Thank you, I'd love one. Sugar, please. This is a lovely parlor."

"Thank ya, Mam," he returned, as he poured them each a cup. "May I sit?"

"Oh yes, of course! Where are my manners? Lovely tea, Mister McTavish."

"McTavish, just McTavish. No mister. I will get right to it, Your Highness. I wanted to speak to ya on behalf of my cousin, Arundel. She is most embarrassed at her son's actions and wishes to send ya her deepest and most sincere apology."

"Thank you, I'm sure, but I'm a little confused. Who is your cousin and what has she done? Why is she apologizing to me?"

"Her name is Arundel Yem. She is Winnsbo's mother and is quite upset at what he did to ya the other night. She hopes returning your slippers and washing the soot out of your night clothes will make up for his indiscretion."

"Wait, Winnsbo's mother did that? She is your cousin? You told me you were Polish or Leprechaun or…"

"Polacian, we are Polacian. As I told ya before, we are, indeed, descendants of Leprechauns of the Isle of Reland."

"Oh yes… of course… I remember now… so sorry… he said his mother was Polacian… I had no idea… you were related."

"She is married to Nemtuc Yem, a Huggermugger, and Winnsbo

is her son. She has punished him for leaving ya on your own in the burrow and hoped to make amends by washing your things and returning them."

"That little rat-creature made me tell my father a lie!"

"Oh no… ye did that on your own. Winnsbo only played the trick, ye made the choice to bend the truth," he said in a matter-of-fact tone, as he sipped tea.

"I beg your pardon?" She snapped back indignantly.

"Winnsbo is a trickster, not a wizard. He did not *make* ya do anything. He played a trick… that is for certain… but ye made the decision to tell the fib."

"Oh dear, you're right, McTavish. I didn't think of it that way until you just said it, but it's absolutely true. I had a choice and I made the wrong one. Why did I do that?"

"It seems to me ye do not trust Henry to accept the truth. After all, Princess Maagy, ya are only human and a young one at that."

"You think I don't trust my own father? How dare you?"

"Well, why else? Remember, he grew up here every summer until he was almost an adult. He probably knows all the secrets already. He has more than likely done the same thing, but ya do not trust him enough to tell him the truth. What did ye think he would do if ya told him ya went into the Huggermugger's burrow, got left there and had to find your own way home? Did ya think he would be disappointed in ye? Did ya think he would stop loving ye? Ye did not trust him enough to be honest with him."

"Thank you, McTavish… I think," she said, as she took the last sip of tea. "What you've said *does* make sense. I suppose, since my father is the only parent I have, I'm keen on not disappointing him. I suppose I didn't trust him enough to accept me being less than perfect. I should talk to him about this. Thank you for the tea… and your wisdom, Sir."

"My pleasure, Your Highness. What about Arundel? Is all forgiven?"

"Of course."

As they were leaving the parlor, they encountered a Polacian woman walking toward them.

"Your Highness, Princess Maagy, this is my cousin, Arundel Yem,"

"Lovely to meet you. Thank you kindly for washing and returning my things."

"The pleasure was all mine, Your Highness," Arundel said as she curtsied. "I hope ye will forgive my naughty son for his trickery. He is only a child and his father and I are working diligently to teach him right from wrong."

"I'm sure you are. All is forgiven," she said, her mind quickly turning in another direction. "If you'll excuse me, I really need to speak with my father. Lovely to meet you."

She rushed down the stairs. Once at his door, the butterflies returned to her stomach. She was trembling and her hands were clammy. She knew she had to deal with this issue and put it behind her, once and for all. She tapped lightly on the door.

"Daddy,... may I talk to you?"

"Of course, Dear. Come in. Is everything all right? What's troubling you? I can see it all over your face."

King Henry was sitting in the tattered chair by the window, reading. She took a deep breath and began to speak as she went closer and sat on the arm of his chair.

"No, everything is not all right. I need to tell you something, but first I need to ask... Daddy... what did you do as a child when you were here all those summers?"

He closed his book, realizing the conversation could be involved.

"I played, I worked, I explored; all the things you're doing now."

"Did you have... adventures? Were you curious by nature?"

"Oh my, yes! I had a wonderful time," he said smiling at his memories. "I learnt to be a man, to be strong, resilient... resolve my own problems... make good decisions... be patient, be forgiving, be honest, be kind... I learnt it all... right here."

"What sorts of adventures did you have?"

"Why? Is there something in particular you want to know?"

"Are you familiar with… Huggermuggers?"

The King playfully feigned concern and drew closer to his daughter.

"Oh no! Not the Huggermuggers. Which ones and what did they do?"

"So you know about them?" She questioned, completely drawn in by his ruse.

"Of course I know about them," he chuckled as he sat back. "They're little rodent-type creatures that live in large packs and some of them are annoyingly messy, but they're fiercely loyal to their own and fairly harmless. There are several colonies of Huggermuggers on the premises. Some live underground, some in treetops…"

"In treetops? Where?"

"Well, there is one such clan in the big tree by the meadow gate. Did you not meet them when Grandpa Kris showed you the silk worm farm?"

"No… why would I… why would they be there?"

"Oh… no… of course you didn't… they only work at night, being nocturnal creatures. Their tiny fingers unravel the chrysalises and spin the delicate threads. They are exceptionally hard working and skilled individuals."

"Really?" She questioned in wide-eyed amazement.

"Really… quite valuable to our economy… I'm surprised Grandpa didn't tell you. There are colonies, which live along the riverbanks, some on the ground in the forest. They speak their own language… each colony has its own dialect… some wear clothes like humans… some do not. They like humans, but are mischievous, by nature… and often cause trouble… for the fun of it. They're paradoxical little rascals."

"That's for certain!"

"They're innately curious and highly intelligent… and most

are productive and reasonably responsible… but… like every society, there are *ner-do-wells** amongst them all. They eat the most disgusting things, like fried cockroaches and mealworm stew… they love anything that smells rotten. They can be quite naughty, but also quite kind. When my mother… rest her soul… passed away during a summer trip, the Huggermuggers were the first to gather flowers for her service and they dug her grave and chiseled her headstone… all without a single request."

"My grandmother died here? Is she buried here, as well?"

"Yes. She rests in the family plot down the east lawn in front, by the wall."

"Oh… I haven't seen that… Huggermuggers did all that for her? For you?"

"Yes… paradoxical, indeed. Why? Have you encountered Huggermuggers?"

"Yes."

"Who… which colony?"

"Just one, so far. His name is Winnsbo. Do you know him?"

"Winnsbo! Heavens, yes! I remember when he was born. His mother is not a Huggermugger, you know. She's one of McTavish's distant cousins, I think. You remember McTavish, don't you, the fellow from the fourth floor? Anyway, she is Polacian, a dear lady."

"I know. I just met her. How did you know I met McTavish? Did I tell you?"

"I believe Grandma Polly may have mentioned it."

"Oh… I see… he's an odd little man, isn't he?"

"Who? Winnsbo?"

"No… McTavish. He's quite adept at double talk… don't you agree? When asked a question he never quite gives a straight answer… have you noticed?"

"Hmm… can't say I have. He always answers my questions."

She was clearly trying to illicit information on McTavish in order to solve the toyshop mystery, but her father's answer left her no where else to go at the time.

"Anyway, it was quite the buzz round here for some time… a Polacian and a Huggermugger… there were those who… didn't approve… it all blew over, though. Nemtuc Yem is her husband. He's one of the highest achievers… quite a brilliant scientist. You came in to talk about something. What was it?"

"Winnsbo."

"Ah, yes, how did you meet Winnsbo?"

"He was reading a book, in the children's library."

"I see… as I said, they are smart and curious… and what happened?"

"A few evenings ago, when I was on the balcony reading, I saw movement in the corner. I noticed a crack in the wainscot and discovered a hidden door. I was about to open it when you startled me, calling me for dinner. I hit the door and it shut and I couldn't pry it open. I came back later and found him sitting and reading amongst the books. We talked and oddly enough, I began to understand his language. He invited me to meet his family."

Maagy stopped for a moment and looked at her father to discern his reaction. A tiny hint of a smile crossed his lips and he raised his eyebrows… as if he might have known what was next.

"I went with him through the door," she continued slowly as she watched his face, "and followed him… into underground tunnels… I could hardly pass through."

As her accounts drew her closer to the point of the story, her voice grew louder and her demeanor became defensive. His expression never changed.

"Then he left me alone in a big common room in his burrow, underground. He never came back for me. I fell asleep and morning birds awoke me just as dawn was breaking. I couldn't figure out how to get back the way I came, and besides, it would have taken too long. I would have been missed and no one knew where I was. So I climbed out the fire pit chimney into the meadow. I sneaked back in and washed up. Then I discovered my sooty footprints leading all the way from the door to my room. I used a towel to clean up the footprints and… and… Daddy…" she continued, as she crumbled into tears, "I lied to you about it. I told you I was pretending it was my coronation… and the towel was my robe. I lied to you… again. I'm so sorry, Daddy. Winnsbo played an awful trick on me and I was afraid you'd be angry with me for following him, so I told you a fib."

King Henry sat for a moment watching his daughter *stew in her own juice**. He finally spoke…

"What made you think I'd be angry with you?"

"Because going off on my own… isn't safe… and you've always told me so… but I did it anyway," she sobbed.

"Maagy, the whole reason I brought you here was for you to go off on your own. When you're at home, it isn't safe. Not even I do it. There are some truly evil people in the world, Maagy, but the Huggermuggers are not some of them. Mischievous, yes; naughty, yes, but evil… no."

"But he left me there… *all alone*! I could have died!"

"No you couldn't and you didn't. You used your head and your strong will and resourcefulness to get back home safely and undetected. Besides, Winnsbo was only playing with you. He would have never let you be harmed or lost."

"So you've known about them all along?" She asked as she sniffled and wiped her eyes. "Why didn't you tell me to beware? I'd never have followed him."

"What fun would that have been? You'd have missed a great adventure!"

"I wouldn't have fibbed to you."

"That's not the fault of the adventure… or Winnsbo. That's a choice you made, Maagy. Why do you think you keep making that choice?"

She hung her head, embarrassed at the answer.

"McTavish says… I don't trust you enough… to tell the truth."

"Ah… McTavish… a wise man. What shall we do about this?"

"I suppose… I should trust you more… to understand when I make mistakes… and not feel I have to tell tales."

"That sounds like a good place to start. How about trusting your own instincts more, as well?"

"Are there more secrets round here I should know about?"

"If I tell you, you won't have the fun of discovering them and figuring out how to handle them. It's why I brought you here, Maagy… for you to have adventures… make discoveries… make choices… all in a safe environment so you learn and grow. Now that doesn't mean there are no real dangers here. There certainly are, but you are a smart girl. Listen to that little voice inside you. It always tells the truth and *you* decide what to do about it. If you trust the little voice, you'll always know the adventures from the dangers."

"What about Winnsbo? What should I do about him?"

"You do whatever you think is right with Winnsbo. You know… all Huggermuggers appreciate a good prank and can take as good as they give. I've had a few played on me… by Winnsbo's father, no less."

"Really?"

"Oh yes… Nemtuc was quite the jester, in his younger… more carefree days. I hear they're not too keen on getting wet. You might want to think about that. Anyway, they know they're living inside the castle grounds at my discretion. They would never do anything to jeopardize that or you. We live a peaceful… mutually beneficial… coexistence."

"I'm so sorry for being untruthful. I promise I'll try and do better. I love you, Daddy. Thank you for bringing me here."

"You're welcome. Now, it's getting late and I'm quite exhausted. I imagine you are, too. By the way, you and Cupid made a grand showing today in the parade. You did a wonderful job of making her costume. Congratulations!"

"Thank you."

"Nice to see Rudy, don't you think?" He said mischievously.

"It was nice… and unexpected…" she replied bashfully, as she quickly changed the subject. "Did you see the sow all dressed in yellow frills? Wasn't she just the best? Her name is Miss Trinny McBride. Her owner is Sydney. She's a sweet girl… younger than I… but quite precocious."

He smiled to himself, knowing full well he had touched a nerve.

"Yes, I know the McBrides. Sydney's father used to be in the Guard, but we can talk about this tomorrow. Goodnight, my darling girl."

"Goodnight, Father. Sleep tight, don't let the bedbugs bite!" She giggled as she ran out and down the hall, calling over her shoulder, "I love you, Daddy!"

When she arrived at her room, she saw, again, the pristine, neatly folded nightclothes and slippers. She marveled at how thoughtful it was of Arundel to make such a kind gesture. She put on the nightgown and climbed into her bed, as she reflected on the events of the day. She slept better than she had all week.

Chapter 14
Fire! Fire!

Maagy awoke suddenly and sat up in bed, startled at a sound she recognized. *Clang, clang, clang, clang…* it was a fire alarm bell. *Something was burning*! She jumped out of bed and flew to the open windows. She threw back the lace sheers and peered out in every direction, but could see no hint of trouble. The castle towers obstructed the view of any other structures on the grounds, but she could smell smoke. Then she heard the most horrible screeching and realized it must have been the horse barn on fire. It was still the dead of night and the moon was the only light. She grabbed her robe, as she ran barefoot for the door. Once in the corridor, she could hear the household staff in the service hallway banging on door after door and calling frantically, "*Get up! Get up! Fire! Fire!*" Then rushing down the back steps. King Henry emerged from his room just after Maagy, still in pajamas and robe.

"Maagy!" He exclaimed, as he sprinted toward her. "Stay in your room, Child! This is no place for you!"

"No Father! I can help! I'm going with you!" She shouted back, as she threw on her robe.

He must have known it would be harder to convince his headstrong child to stay put than to extinguish the fire, so he said nothing further as he followed her down the stairs. They cut through the service hallway and the kitchen to the mudroom, where they put on boots. Grandma Polly, Josephine and several others were already filling large baskets with rolls of snow-white material and jars of cream.

"What's all that?" Maagy asked.

"It's bandages and burn salve," Grandma Polly answered.

"We must be ready for anything," Josephine added.

Maagy's blood ran cold as she watched them prepare for possible injuries. Her hands shook as she tugged on her boots.

"Is it bad?"

"It's the horse barn. It could be devastating!" The king replied.

She had never been so close to an actual emergency. She had watched out her window at Avington Palace as the fire brigade battled flames in the town below, but it always seemed a safe enough distance that it wasn't quite real. Now, she was about to come face-to-face with a real, live, dragon. They exited the mudroom together without another word and were joined by the rest of the household staff, as they sprinted down the long path toward the burning building. The smell of acrid smoke grew stronger as they ran and she could see the orange glow of the flames dancing against the night sky. She could hear the frantic cries of the dozens of horses housed in the burning barn. She was overwhelmed with anguish at the possible fate of her beloved Cupid, Carmela, Sunrise and Dinah; also, her father's prized jumper, Prince Charming, and all the carriage and field horses she so lovingly fed and groomed daily.

They reached the barn and she froze in her tracks. It was in the hayloft above the stalls and flames were licking out into the night sky. The hay was dry and fire was spreading fast and furiously. She could see through the open loft door sparks jumping and running like hundreds of scared mice. The orange monster was already lapping at the roof overhead. She could hear people shouting things like, *"Get the horses out!" "Form a line, form a line!" Someone, man the well! Get the buckets!*" Her heart pounded as she took in the sight of people and horses running in every direction.

Jorge was battling on the front line by pushing burning hay out the loft door onto the ground where others were dousing it with water and dirt. Tongues of hungry flames licked at him, but he stood his ground. She marveled at his bravery. John Miles and Claude Wickem were already releasing horses from their stalls and shooing them out into the paddock. The poor creatures still trapped inside were kicking and pawing the ground as they gave up their desperate cries for help. She recognized Cupid's frantic screams above the commotion.

Without a second thought, she took off her robe, threw it into the water trough and tied her nightgown in a knot above her knees. Suddenly, one of the freed horses bolted back toward the passageway and Maagy was caught in the middle. The huge field horse reared up on his hind legs, his massive hooves flying in the air. She squealed and stopped short to avoid being hit, just as Mister Miles stepped in front of her.

"Whoa, there, big fellow!" John said, as he approached. "Easy, boy, easy."

He removed his vest and covered the horse's eyes, and then gently took hold of his mane.

"Thank you, Mister Miles. You saved me... why did you do that... cover his eyes?"

"I knew it would calm him..." he responded, as he walked the horse to out of danger. "He would then hear my voice and trust me... when horses can't see danger, they usually settle down."

"Why did he run back in?" She asked, as she followed him.

"Panic... he was confused and frightened... he lost the instinct to run *from* the danger and, instead, ran to what was familiar... his stalls... where he's always been safe."

"I see..."

"With respect, Your Highness, this is not the place for you," he advised as they returned. "It's much too dangerous."

"I want to help, Mister Miles... please."

As the smoke and heat intensified, more horses refused to leave the passageway and began circling aimlessly in the middle.

"All right then... I suppose we can use all hands... help Claude and the others take them to the riding ring down the hill. Tie them to the railing."

"Yes, Sir!"

Maagy was terrified, but she grabbed the sopping robe, draped it over her head and dashed into the barn. The process was taking extra time and there were still horses to be rescued, among them, Cupid and her mother. A bucket brigade had formed and water had begun passing efficiently from person to person into the barn and up the stairs to the burning area. However, the scene was still chaotic and the smoke was getting thicker and harder to see through. She went to a stable and threw open the door, untied the halter rope and gave an authoritative "*gee*" to a carriage horse. Surprisingly, he complied and walked behind her, as did the next one, and she led them both to the ring. More fiery debris was falling from the loft into the passageway and stray bits of hay were catching up. The smoke was chokingly thick. She knew there was little time to get everyone out safely. She kicked dirt on some burning hay as she retrieved two more carriage horses and led them out. Next, it was Cupid's turn. When she opened the stall door, the filly reared up, her hooves flailing wildly. She was panic-stricken.

"Cupid! It's all right! It's me, Girl! Easy, easy!"

Maagy tried to calm her, but she was inconsolable* and continued to screech and paw the air. Maagy could hear Carmela in the next stall calling frantic whinnies to her daughter. She remembered the trick John Miles had used. She took the wet robe off her own head and climbed the railing to get a better vantage point. She knew if she missed her mark, the robe would be lost under the stomping feet and she would have no chance of retrieving it. She said a prayer and made a perfect throw. Time slowed to a crawl as she watched the robe fly open and land precisely over the horse's entire head. Her panic subsided, as she stood trembling. Maagy climbed down and untied the rope.

"There's the girl. You're all right, now," she said gently, as she gave a reassuring pat on the neck.

They walked out of danger and into the riding ring. She raced back into the barn and retrieved Carmela the same way, reuniting mother and child. The smoke inside had become almost unbearable, but there were still horses in grave danger. She took a deep breath of fresh air, held the wet robe over her face and went back into the inferno. Her eyes were stinging and it was becoming more difficult to see which stables were empty, as some of the doors had swung shut and latched. She tried several, only to find the occupants were already rescued, but pressed on from one door to the other. Just as she was beginning to feel her efforts were in vain, John called to her from the other side of the passageway.

"We have these four! Get the one in that last stall. That's all of them!"

"Yes, sir!"

She flung open the door and found the horse was starting to lie down.

"No! No, don't do that!" she shouted at him.

She knew when a horse goes down because of illness or injury, it's almost impossible to get it back up, again, and it's often lost. She grabbed him by the mane and pulled just as his hindquarters were about to go to the ground.

"No, no! I won't let you die here!" She screamed, "*Help! Help! Help me!* He's going down! Help me! Please, someone, help me!"

Just then, several stable hands reached the scene. She had kept the horse from getting all the way to his side by pulling on his mane and halter. The men were strong enough to get behind him and use their backs to lift his haunches and push him forward as she pulled. The old fellow wanted to give up, but she would have none of it. She continued to pull on his halter with all her might, as she shouted encouragement to him.

"Come on, old man! You can do it! Get up, get up!"

The horse, finally, rose to his feet, but pulled back and refused to leave the stall. She threw her robe round his eyes and the men took hold of him… all leaning against him to hold him up… and were successful in coaxing him to walk out into the fresh air.

They all breathed huge sighs of relief, but the job was far from done. Farmers who lived down the hill had reinforced the firefighting crew. McTavish and the workers from the fourth floor had also joined them. They had appeared from all sides and jumped in to help with buckets, rakes and shovels to battle the blaze. With all the living creatures safely out of harm's way, efforts turned to the carriages and tack equipment still in the burning structure. Embers had fallen between the loft floorboards into the area where the carriages were garaged in the front of the barn. Bits of hay and wood shavings were burning near the king's personal carriage. It was a fine piece of craftsmanship, with mahogany paneling, solid brass running lamps… still full of flammable oil… and gold-gilded wheels. The quick action of the volunteer brigade gave Mister Miles and Mister Wickem just enough time to pull it and two other smaller carriages and the supply wagon out into the yard before several flaming boards came crashing down.

Maagy ran round the side of the barn and entered the tack room from the outside door. Smoke had begun to invade and she could see the orange glow of the monster overhead through the cracks in the ceiling. Any moment, flaming debris could have come crashing down, as she carried saddles and bridles out and laid them on the ground. She loaded her arms with blankets, saddle pads, work collars, hames, grooming equipment; in short, anything she could carry to safety. She worked feverishly until she had almost emptied the tack room, all the while, mindful of the imminent danger from above.

Finally, a cheer went up from the other side of the building. The fire-breathing dragon had been slain. She collapsed on the ground… completely exhausted… and took a moment to catch her breath… and offer up a silent prayer of thanks. The barn was saved, as was most of the hay. This was a good thing, too, as it was the entire first cutting of the spring and summer crop. It accounted for more than half the winter feed for the horses and cows. There would be another fall cutting, but it would not be nearly enough to sustain all the animals for the winter. There was still a huge task ahead in the aftermath of what could have been a devastating tragedy. There was water everywhere in the loft and it was pouring through the cracks into the stables below. She heard Mister Miles and Mister Wickem discussing with Jorge what lay ahead for them.

"Most of the hay that did not catch fire is wet," Jorge said. "We will need to throw it out in the sun and spread it to dry right away."

Maagy had learned that wet hay was dangerous. Not only was the mold… that would likely grow in it… bad for the horses to eat, it was an indicator of changes within the stack. The moisture caused chemical changes, which gave off heat and the hay could actually combust, spontaneously, and cause another loft fire.

"If nothing else, we can use it for bedding," John said.

"We will most likely throw it all down. It smells like smoke. The animal will not eat it that way," added Claude. "We will start first thing after daybreak to spread it and turn it several times a day in the fresh air and see if it can be saved."

Jorge was confident this procedure would be successful, as other farmer had done the same. However, all the extra work couldn't have come at a worse time. The summer crops were at a peak and lots of fieldwork was necessary. Everyone would have to pitch in longer hours. The extra volunteers began cleaning up the charred bits of hay and debris inside the barn. Almost all the stalls had wet bedding, even if no embers fell in them. McTavish and his crew were raking and using the pitchforks and wheelbarrows to carry the soggy mess away.

"All of these stalls need new bedding. Get clean feed hay from the loft over the cow barn," Jorge instructed. "It's leftover from last year and should be used up entirely, anyway."

No one complained about the difficult chores or the wee hour of the day. Everyone worked in harmony to restore order and provide a safe, clean place for the traumatized animals. Maagy was surveying the damaged area when she saw her father coming toward her. She wanted to run and greet him, but saw Jorge walking toward him and realized he was on a mission. The two men went into the loft, but she could hear them talking.

"Tell me, Jorge, how bad is it?"

"Fortunately, the oak beams, holding the loft in place, are charred, but still sturdy, Your Majesty. Boards will need replacing at the opening, but the door is only blackened with soot. The roof suffered the most damage. Look here, Sir. There is a gaping hole above the door."

When she moved closer to get a good look from the ground outside, she could see right through to the stars.

"You may hire additional workers to replace the roof as soon as possible."

"As you wish, Your Majesty. Thank you."

They came down to the main floor. A few boards had burned through and fallen into several of the stables and caught feed boxes on fire. The brigade had done a fine job of extinguishing those flames before they got out of hand and preventing anything else from catching up.

"The horses who occupy these stalls will be relocated, temporarily, to the other barns while repairs are made," Jorge continued.

In all, the damage was much less severe than it seemed when fire was raging and smoke was swirling. She was relieved no one was seriously injured. Then she saw Jorge's left hand. King Henry saw it, too.

"My lord, Man, you're injured! Go immediately and take care of that hand! And sit down for a while! That's a royal directive!"

"Yes Sir, Your Majesty. Right away, Sir!"

Grandma Polly and Josephine had administered salve and bandages to a few minor burns. They washed out eyes, stinging from smoke, with mild salt-water solution. Jorge got his entire left hand bandaged and Grandma Polly insisted on washing out his eyes, as his face was entirely blackened with soot. He had been the first one into the loft and had fought the entire battle from his command post at the door. Now it was time for him to rest and others to take over the reins of the clean up.

Maagy wanted to help as much as possible so she was carrying saddles and other equipment back into the tack room, when she was joined by Sarah Miles and her younger sister, Cornelia. They were the children of John and his wife, Rebecca, who was a chambermaid with the household staff. Sarah was eight and Cornelia six. They were sweet little girls and Maagy had read book with them in the children's library several times. She thought they would be fast asleep at that hour, but soon found they, too, had a great sense of responsibility. They were eager to help with the cleanup effort. She gave them smaller things like grooming tools and brooms to carry in, while she carried the heavier tack. Once most of it was replaced, she instructed the girls as to where the remaining blankets and saddle pads were kept and turned her attention to the horses still in the ring. She went round the corner and saw John leading two of the big field horses back toward the barn.

"Mister Miles, what can I do to help?"

"Oh, Your Highness… Princess Maagy… nothing… I can do this. You've done enough, tonight. And may I say you were brave and resourceful… the way you used your robe and kept going back into the smoke. We couldn't have done it without you, Your Highness. Thank you for your help."

"Please, Mister Miles, you were the brave ones… you and Mister Wickem and the other workers. You got the old horse back up on his feet and coaxed him out the door. Then you pulled all the equipment out and saved my father's prized carriage. It is I who should be thanking you for your heroic efforts. Please, may I help you with the horses?"

"Well, if you wish, Your Highness. These two lost their feed boxes. I'm taking them to stables in the cow barn. They all have to be checked and cleaned. I'm concerned about the last ones out. They breathed in the most smoke."

"What shall I do?"

"If you're sure you want to help, we need to bring each one to the washing station. Most all need baths to get the smoke off them. That smell is a source of anxiety. It reminds them of the fire."

"Right away, Sir."

Maagy, John, Claude and several other volunteers washed all, but the first twelve horses evacuated at the beginning of the fire. They were taken out before the smoke traveled down into the stalls and didn't have the unpleasant odor. They were looked over carefully, blanketed and taken into clean, dry stalls. The other horses, including Cupid, were thoroughly washed down to remove the soot and smoky smell. The volunteers used a mixture of mild, natural, fragrant soap and lemon oil to cut through the black film on the hair. They were then rinsed and toweled dry. Sarah and Cornelia helped by bringing blankets, which were placed on all the horses, to keep them from getting chilled in the cool night air. Maagy and the others gave them much tender loving care. She was especially attentive to Cupid and Carmela and got them settled and secure in the same stall, as Mister Miles suggested.

"Princess Maagy, if you please, go to the tack room and find the large jar of salve with the black top and bring it to the cow barn. That's where we'll do the treatments while the horse barn is being cleaned."

They treated ten horses for smoke inhalation. He told her the salve was his own mixture of aromatic oils, mysterious herbs, Eucalyptus, Menthol and tallow, which opened the horses' airways and helped to prevent the accumulation of fluid in their lungs during the critical hours after exposure to smoke. He rubbed it just inside their nostrils so they breathed in the medication.

"It also has a soothing effect on them. I'll administer it twice, daily, for five days and that should prevent them from developing breathing problems."

"How did you learn all this, Mister Miles?"

"I watched my father and he watched my grandfather, before him. They trained and treated horses all their lives. I took what they taught and learnt more on my own."

She was amazed at the wealth of knowledge he possessed. She had grown fond of all the horses; Cupid was, of course, her personal favorite and kindred spirit, but she found she enjoyed just being round them. She thought she might spend more time now assisting and learning all she could about horse medicine. She even thought about becoming a farrier and horse medicine specialist, herself, one day, but then remembered her future was decided. She was the Crown Princess. She envied ordinary people, just a bit, for their freedom to choose their own paths in life.

"The injured horses must stay quiet and in their stalls for several days until the danger is past," John said. "They can be walked for short periods and taken to the trough for water, but none can work in the fields or pull the carriages for at least a week. They will need to be closely observe for breathing difficulty, fever or signs of distress, like not eating, excessive pawing, swaying or head-shaking. They have all suffered a terrible trauma and are not out of danger yet. Breathing difficulties could still flare up and it's critical my instructions be followed to the letter."

"May I help with their care? Please, Sir?"

"If you wish, Your Highness. The older horses are in more danger of complications than the younger ones and those who were the last out and closer to the front are at greatest risk, like the last old fellow."

Maagy found out he was twenty-nine years old, which is elderly for a horse. His name was Parker for his talent of backing a carriage into perfect position at the curb. He taught every horse he was paired with, over the years, to do the same. No one taught him the skill; he instinctively knew how close to get and how to move the carriage backwards into place. His name was Sampson, originally, because of his size and strength, but Parker is the name that had stuck for the last twenty years.

"Mister Miles, might I take the responsibility for Parker's care for the next few weeks? I'm concerned for him and I want him to know he has a friend."

"It's a lot of responsibility. Are you sure you're up to the task?"

"Oh, yes, I promise. I'll be diligent."

"All right, then. Report to me, morning and evening, on his progress. You're to walk him, observe him and medicate him twice daily. If you notice anything out of the ordinary, find me immediately. Do you understand? Oh, dear, forgive me, Your Highness. I forgot I was speaking to my princess. Forgive me."

"Please, Mister Miles, think of me as your assistant, not royalty. I insist."

Once the stalls were cleaned and the horses were offered water and safely housed, she began to feel extreme fatigue. It was still dark and she had no concept of the actual time. She also realized she was cold. Her robe was long since gone and her flannel gown was wet and offered little protection against the chilly night air. She set out in search of her father's warm hug. King Henry and Grandpa Kris were the two men who lowered the buckets into the well to fill them and then handed them off to the next persons. The two had worked in perfect harmony to keep the water flowing as fast as empty buckets appeared. She found them both sitting on a log congratulating each other for a job well done. As she approached, her father rose from his seat and met her with open arms.

"There you are, my dear," he said, as he hugged her. "You're all wet… you're shivering, Child."

"I'm freezing!"

"Here, take this," he offered, as he removed his robe and put it round her. "I hear you are quite the hero. Mister Wickem and the little Miles girls can't say enough good things about your bravery, rescuing the horses.

"I wasn't brave at all," she said, as she hugged him back. "I was positively frightened out of my wits every time I went back in."

"But, you went back in. That's what makes you brave. If you weren't afraid… well then… that would make you foolish," he said with a chuckle. "How are our four-legged friends?"

"All survived, I'm happy to report. Cupid, Carmela and Sunrise are well. Prince Charming is virtually unscathed. He was the first one out, before the fire really got going. Most of the other horses are fine and didn't need medical attention, although they needed good baths. I helped Mister Miles treat ten for smoke. They're doing well, but none of them can work for at least a week and must stay in their stalls, except for short walks to get water and mild exercise. That's going to make it difficult to work the fields or get supplies, isn't it, Grandpa Kris?

"Oh, my, yes. It will present a challenge for a while. Perhaps, we can borrow some work horses from the valley folk."

"Parker, however, is somewhat more critical. You know, he's the really old fellow. He was the last one out, and oh, Daddy, it was so scary! I opened the stall gate just as he was about to go down. I grabbed his mane and halter and screamed for help. Mister Miles and Mister Wickem and a couple others came running and got to him just in the nick of time. They pushed and I pulled and together we got him back to his feet. Then he wouldn't move. There was fire dropping all round. I threw my wet robe over his eyes and they got him to walk forward and out just as a burning board fell into the stall. It was awful, Daddy! I was ever so frightened he was going to die, right there!"

The enormity of it all finally crashed down and she buried her head in his chest and sobbed.

"There, there, my precious girl. Everything will be fine. Everyone is safe. You just let it all out, now."

She sobbed and sniffled for a few more moments, then took a deep breath and dried her eyes.

"Daddy…"

"Yes, Darling?"

"I think I'm going to need a new robe," she said, as they both burst into laughter. "Mister Miles is trusting me to take care of Parker for the next few weeks. I'm going to feed him, medicate him, walk him, take him for water and observe him for any signs of illness. Isn't that wonderful, Daddy? He's my responsibility."

"Oh my, yes, Darling. That's a huge vote of confidence… for John to give you such important work. He must trust you a great deal."

"What time is it, anyway? I'm hungry!"

As they congratulated her on her newfound passion, Grandpa Kris told her the fire bell had rung at one o'clock in the morning. It was now four-thirty and they were hungry, too. They recounted for her how they had worked to fill buckets. She was surprised to learn the fire brigade did not happen by accident. The procedure had been well practiced for just such an emergency and had paid off in saving the barn and everything in it. The three were still exchanging stories when they heard the bell ring again. This time it was a summons ring, not an emergency. Everyone made their way back to the barn and found Jorge standing in the open doorway of the loft. He had a badly charred corncob pipe in his hand. It was barely recognizable. Once everyone was assembled, Jorge spoke.

"I believe I have found the source of the fire. I found this pipe here, near the doorway. I believe someone was up here smoking it. Now, all of the adults who smoke pipes know better than to come into the hayloft. That means it was most likely a child hiding from parents and sneaking the smoke. I hope the person who did this understands what could have happened here tonight. It should serve as a lesson. I hope parents will talk with their children and make them understand the seriousness of this action. Thank you, everyone, for your hard work. It could have been much worse."

Jorge turned and left the stunned crowd below to ponder who might have done this foolish thing.

"May I have everyone's attention, please?" King Henry announced. "I would also like to thank everyone who pitched in and worked so hard here tonight, not the least of which are the kind souls who came from the villages to help us. Please, all of you, join my daughter and me for breakfast in the family dining room of the castle."

Grandma Polly found Maagy and gave her a hug and compliments, as she, too, had heard the good deeds. They laughed at her smudged face and soot filled hair.

"My robe is ruined."

"Not to worry, Dear. I'll make you another one by the end of the week. You earned it!"

"I'm starving! When is breakfast?"

"As soon as everyone is cleaned up and to the house. We'll have a feast. Come, Josephine, we have work to do."

The two elderly women and the rest of the kitchen staff sprinted up the lane toward the castle. Grandpa Kris, King Henry and Maagy walked together. She left her boots in the mudroom and slowly climbed the stairs, arm in arm with her father. Once in her room, she stripped off the smoky, wet gown. Dear Estelí had prepared a hot bath. She took her time relaxing and washing her hair three times to get rid of the smell. She chuckled at remembering the last time she washed smoke and soot from her hair in the wee hours of morning. She still owed Winnsbo payback for that one.

She put on a day dress and went down to the family dining room barefooted. The guests trickled in one and two at a time, once they had cleaned up and changed clothes. As they gathered and chatted in the dining room, each had his or her own story to tell, and would still be telling it for years to come, about the night the horse barn caught fire and they all helped save it. True to her promise, Grandma Polly and her crew prepared a delicious buffet, as they had each taken turns washing up and changing clothes, as well. On that morning, everyone at the castle ate together as one big extended family, and in fact, she felt as if they all were family, related or not. As the sun crept up in the east and reflected off the western sky, the light streamed in through the dining room windows. They shared a meal and their stories one more time. She climbed the stairs… belly full… crawled back among the soft pillows… still wearing her day dress… and fell sound asleep.

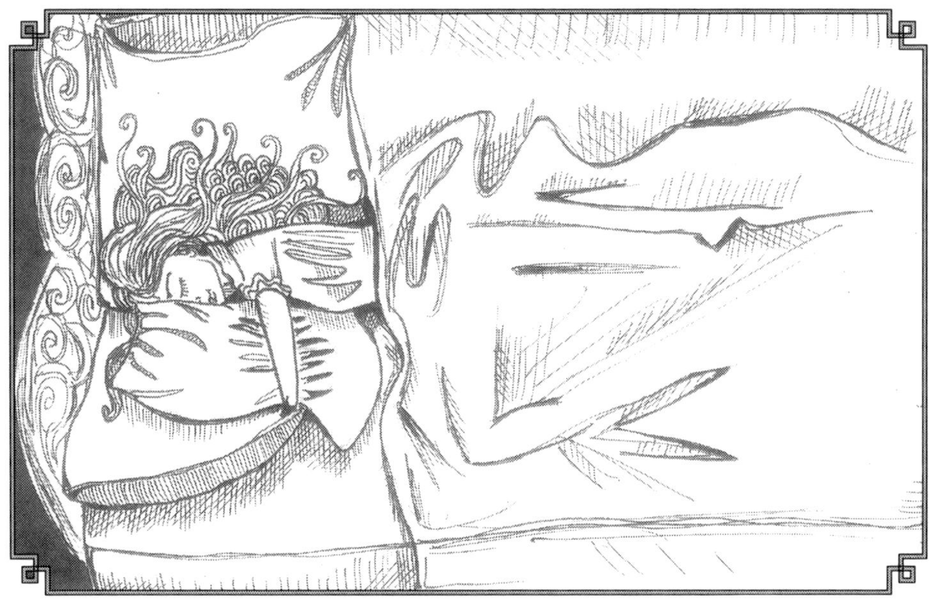

Chapter 15
Saying Goodbye

August had been an eventful month. King Henry and Maagy had taken a ten-day trip to visit the royal families of Estadore and Nihmrobi. They were the guests of King Raphael and Queen Marisol at *Palacio de los Santos*, the royal palace, in the capital city of San Jose, Estadore. This was her first experience traveling outside of Berensenia and she loved every moment of it. Father-King Afarnae, King Henry and King Raphael had a rollicking reunion and she had never laughed so much in her life. All three families spent most of the days together and she thoroughly enjoyed meeting Asanna's younger siblings and Rudolpho's family, Raul, his wife, Gabriela, and Consuela. They were exactly as he had described them. They seemed to like her, as well, she thought. There was some discussion of politics and the Valley Treaty, but it was holiday and no one wanted it bogged down with business.

On the return trip, they stopped at Lake Helga and spent the night at Edgewyck, the Greymiller's estate, a secluded compound on the lakeshore. She was happy to see Lady Cecily and her mother, Lady Madelaine, with whom she felt an odd connection. They left midmorning and made another stop at a small town livery where the king was having another carriage built and wanted to check on the progress. This was a brief stop, just long enough for the horses to rest and have water. Maagy waited in the carriage. When King Henry climbed back in, he had a basket full of roasted chicken, a loaf of bread and berries. There was also a jug of apple cider and sweet cakes for dessert. The food hit the spot and the ride home went quickly as father and daughter recounted pleasant moments from their holiday… and napped a bit.

She was happy to be back at Whitmore. She had missed Cupid and went immediately to the barn to tuck her in for the night. She returned to the house and went into the kitchen where Grandma Polly was busy. She gave her a hug and kiss on the cheek.

"I missed you Gram-P. I missed our talks in the kitchen."

"I missed you too, Dear Princess Child. Did you enjoy your travels?"

"I did. The three kings are quite hilarious together. Each feeds off the other for their humor. I laughed until I cried! Queen Marisol, on the other hand, was a bit…"

"What? A bit what, my dear?"

"Oh dear… I don't wish to be rude, but she was aloof and absent most of the time. It seemed a bit awkward."

"I see… and what of Prince Rudolpho and Princess Asanna? How were they?"

"Lovely! We had a brilliant time. We rode horses, hiked the grounds and played croquet. Their families are very nice people. Palacio de los Santos is magnificent. It was a fabulous holiday. How were things here?"

"Lonely and quiet with you gone. I much prefer your presence!"

"And I much prefer being here with you and Poppy. Where is he? I'd like to say hello."

"On the west veranda, I think. He quite enjoys listening to the night birds. Call him to dinner, won't you?"

The sun was almost down and the sky was colorful. She found her grandpa where Grandma said he would be.

"Hello, Poppy, I missed you," She said, as she gave him a hug and a kiss and sat beside him on the bench.

"Well, there's my best horsewoman! How are you? Your girl missed you, you know. She looked for you everyday."

"I missed her. I don't know what I'm going to do this fall and winter until I come back in the summer. I'm afraid she'll forget me. Oh… dinner is ready. Grandma says to come."

They walked slowly toward the dining room as they talked, his arm round her shoulders.

"No, Cupid won't forget you. You're fast friends. A horse never forgets the person with whom it bonds. She'll remember you, no matter how long it is between visits."

"I hope so…"

It was good to be back at the table with the family, but Maagy had been preoccupied throughout the meal. She had been thinking about something for a long time, but wasn't sure how to approach it with Grandma. She had been riding horseback at Whitmore wearing her overalls and boots, but on holiday, she had ridden in skirt and petticoats and found it cumbersome. She didn't think it proper to take her work clothes. So after dinner, she decided to address the issue directly.

"Gram, I have a problem and I need your help."

"What is it, Dear?"

"When I ride Carmela here, I'm usually in my overalls and boots. When I go home, I intend to continue riding, but I'm loath to do in skirt and petticoats… as I did on holiday. I don't believe my overalls will go over too well with the stuffy courtiers."

"Probably not. What do you have in mind? Men's riding pant?"

"Yes, I'd prefer… but, again… probably not the best fashion idea. It's going to be hard enough to fit back in… I shouldn't want to fly too much in the face of decorum*. I need something comfortable, practical, but somewhat ladylike. Can you help?"

"Hmmm… the comfort of pants, but looks feminine… pants,

which look like a skirt… a skirt, which functions as pants… I think I have it!"

She did indeed. In no time she made Maagy a slightly below knee-length garment, which looked like a flared skirt when she stood or walked, but was divided down the middle and sewn like loose pant legs. It fit perfectly with her riding boots and was comfortable and ladylike when she was on the horse.

"We'll call it culottes after the knee-length breeches worn by men in Franciné. They're fitted at the top and a bit bloused at the knees, although men wear the legs buttoned at the bottom. I thought leaving them loose… and a bit longer… looked more feminine. What do you think?"

"I think they're brilliant and ever so comfortable. Could you possibly make several more in various materials and colors for all year round? I shall set a whole new fashion trend."

Grandma also made her matching jackets to wear with them. Maagy couldn't wait to show off her new style.

The fourth and final Festival Day of the summer had come and gone and had been bittersweet. The food and parade were as rewarding as before, the highlight being Miss Trinny McBride in the most ruffled frock thus far, in shades of purple and lavender. However, Maagy couldn't help but think of the last one when Rudolpho surprised her for the entire day. She half expected him to pop round the corner and when he didn't it took some of the joy. Also, it was the last until next May, a long time to wait. The best memory of that day, by far, was giving Winnsbo his comeuppance. He and the princess had actually become great friends. She, however, had not forgot the trick he played on her and how much it frightened her. She had been plotting and waiting for just the right moment and it came in the early evening.

It is well known, among those who know Huggermuggers, they

are notoriously afraid of water. They take only sponge baths… when forced… and never, *ever,* go out in a rainstorm. No self-respecting Huggermugger would intentionally go swimming. She knew, also, Huggermuggers prefer warmer weather. In fact, they almost hibernate from just after Krispen until the first of March. She had prepared him for several days with some well-placed fiction about a certain rare plant, which grew close to the edge of the pond and only bloomed for one day in August. She told him it was the stinkiest flower on earth and it smelled worse than a dead skunk. She also told him the unpleasantly odoriferous* blossom was considered a delicacy in the Orient, like kimchi*. Now, in actuality, the plant she was calling "*la fleur rare*", which was Francinése for "the rare flower", was nothing more than a common weed, which grew in the edge of the water, with a bud at the top of a long stem. She knew he slept all day and would never consider venturing alone close enough to the pond at night to check her story. It was dusk and there was a slight chill in the air. The last of the visitors had gone home from the picnic and she knew he would be awake and foraging for leftovers on the lawn. She found him easily.

"Winnsbo, guess what? The stinky flower…I mean… la fleur rare is about to bloom! Come with me to the pond. If you miss it the flavor is gone. Come on… hurry."

"Pond? Winnsbo pond nonen lobel. Huggermuggers waler nonen lobel. Frygan Winnsbo."

"Don't worry, I'll be there with you. You don't want to miss having a bite of that lovely flower, do you? From what I hear, it's quite sought after by those with the most refined palates."

"Winnsbo flower nonen hear. Find non referense in boocs."

"Well, if you don't trust me… to keep you safe at the pond… I guess a silly flower isn't *that tasty.*"

"Maagy blossom picen. To Winnsbo bringen, yem?"

"I think you have to bite it right from the stem at the moment it blooms to get the full taste sensation bursting in your mouth. It's nothing… I'm sure there will be another one… next year… or is it every two years…?"

"Oceydocey, Winnsbo pond go. Mouth wantum yummy. Taste… delicasy… hugan word."

He bolted down the hill and she followed, feeling a little guilty for what she was about to do… but only a little. It *was* payback. He got within a few yards of the pond and stopped. She caught up and went closer.

"There it is, Winnsbo! That long stem, there! The flower is opening now! Come on… before it wilts! Reach out and grab it!"

"Winnsbo non waler!"

"You can do it! Hold my hand and I'll keep you from falling in. You can reach it!"

"Non! Winnsbo nonen wet get!"

"You won't get wet. I'll be holding on to you. Just lean out. Here, take my hand."

The little creature crept as close to the edge of the water as any Huggermugger had ever dared. He reached back and took her hand, his eyes fixed on the "*tasty bloom*" atop the tall stem just in the pond. He stretched himself to the limit, closed his eyes and opened his mouth wide anticipating the luscious flavor. *Maagy let go*! He flopped face down in the muddy, cold water. All his appendages flailed and splashed wildly. His head bobbed up and he gasped for air. She grabbed him by the waistband and lifted him easily out of the water, his arms and legs still waving. He was screeching and howling as if he were on fire.

"Winnsbo, it's all right! I have you. You're safe. You're not in the water. Did you get a bite?"

"Wet… wet… wet! Winnsbo wet! Non yummy… only wet!"

She plopped him in the grass on his belly, still wiggling. She had hidden a towel near-by earlier.

"Here's a towel. Dry yourself and wrap up. It's getting chilly. Now we're even. I got you! How does it feel to be scared half out of your mind?"

"What? *What*? Maagy purpose dranum Winnsbo in pond? Guilen Winnsbo? Non flower yummy?"

"Non flower yummy! I gave you your comeuppance for leaving me in your burrow alone and scared to death! How does it feel?"

"Wet… mutsh wet… Winnsbo… nonen wet licum. Clothes wet… ruined… Maagy got Winnsbo… *mutsh good*! Done nisely, Princess!" He said in his best human language.

"Why, thank you, Winnsbo. My father said you'd appreciate a good prank," she laughed as she rubbed his head with the towel. "He said you could take as good as you gave… and you have! Don't worry, your clothes will dry. I'm sure your dear mother will take care of them."

"Guilen non more. Friends, just friends… Winnsbo… Just Maagy… foreber… oceydocey?"

"Oceydocey!"

Maagy usually woke in a happy mood, but today was different. She and King Henry were leaving the Summer Castle and traveling back to Avington Palace. Her first thoughts were of Cupid and how much she would miss her friend. She had noticed the filly's growth during the three months she had been there and knew John Miles would soon be training her with more tack. She hated the thought of not being present for that learning experience. Maagy had grown, too. The overalls she put on at the beginning of the summer were above her ankles. The straps had been let down as far as possible, but they were still too short. Her boots cramped her toes and her blouses wouldn't stay put in her waistband. She knew she would need an entirely new wardrobe for fall and winter, which pleased her.

One of the large windows was open and the breeze blowing in was decidedly cooler. Daylight was barely breaking. She thought the sun should be up, but remembered it was already the beginning of September and summer was quickly giving way to autumn. The leaves were already turning and the corn stalks were drying and turning brown. They'd soon be cut for fodder to augment the winter food supply for the farm animals, especially with the shortage of hay. Corn from those stalks had been sweet and plentiful just a month ago, but now was fit only for cattle and horses. School would start in a few days and she was not looking forward to it. It seemed so long ago when she and her father had arrived for a visit. Now, this seemed like home and she was sad to be leaving.

"Maagy Dear, are you awake? We should get an early start. It's going to be a long day."

"Yes, Father, I'm awake. *Must* we leave today? Can't we wait until tomorrow?"

"I'm sorry, no. There will be a lot of catching up to do when we get home and you begin school in just a few days. Come, come, now; breakfast is waiting."

She turned back the covers and rolled to the edge of the bed.

She sat for a few moments lamenting the day. Finally, she mustered her energy and freshened up, dressed for the barn and went down to the dining room.

"Good morning, Your Dear Highness. How are you on this crisp, lovely morning?" Grandma Polly greeted.

"Good morning Gram-P. I'm fine… I suppose."

"Oh my, that sounds most un-fine! What's the matter?"

"I don't want to leave. I want to stay here forever."

Big tears streamed down and she buried her face in the old woman's apron. She wrapped the child in loving arms and gently rubbed her back.

"I know, Dear. I'm going to miss you, too. But think how much fun it'll be when you return next year? We'll start all over again, having a wonderful summer holiday."

Maagy dried her eyes and ate breakfast.

"Hurry with your chores and goodbyes at the barn. We should be on the road by nine, else we'll be arriving home in the dark," her father instructed.

She couldn't stop crying the entire morning. She bid Jorge, Mister Miles, Mister Wickham and the other stable hands goodbye. She kissed Julie on her soft brown nose and checked on Parker one last time.

"You did a fine job of rehabilitating the old boy, Your Highness," John said. "He's fit as a fiddle and will be pulling carriages for many more years, the way he's going!"

She was proud of that. She went to Cupid last. The filly seemed to know something was different. She bobbed her head and nudged the sad girl. Tears flowed freely as they said their goodbyes. She couldn't bare the thought of not seeing her horse for nine months, but finally had to accept the inevitable and trudged up the lane to the castle. She entered the kitchen and found Josephine at the sink.

"I'm going to miss you, Josephine," as she gave the woman a hug.

Josephine was overwhelmed at such affection and wasn't sure

whether to hug back or remain stoic. She hugged back as a tear crept down her cheek.

"I shall miss you, too, Your Highness."

She ran through the service hall and coat closet one more time and up the stairs to her room. Estelí was closing the last case and all was packed and ready to be loaded onto the carriage.

"Your Highness, I did not pack these dresses and shoes, as they no longer fit you. What shall I do with them, Madam?"

"I don't care… no wait, divide them and send some to that darling little Sydney McBride, who brightened my whole summer with her lovely sow. Give the rest to Mister Miles' little girls. They might like to dress as princesses. What do you think? Is that a good plan?"

"I think it is a brilliant plan. I am sure they will feel ever so special, wearing their Crown Princess' dresses."

"Wait… take all but the red taffeta one. Just… leave it there, will you… in the closet."

"Of course, Madam. That one is… special."

"I wish I could take you with me, Estelí. You've been a great help and a better friend."

"I wish I could go! I could not possibly, though, because of *ma merè*. She needs me, as well. I shall miss you terribly. Things will not be the same without you."

"I shall miss you even more. I can't wait for the winter to be done so I can return to this enchanted place."

She noticed a stunning travel outfit spread on the bed.

"Where did this come from?"

"I do not know. It was here when I came in to pack. I thought you had laid it out."

"I've never seen it, but it's exquisite!"

She picked up the calf-length, A-shaped, tweed skirt and put it to her waist, then saw the note on the bed and read it.

Dear Princess Maagy,

I hope this skirt and jacket are the right size and to your liking. Thank you for your patience, good humor and friendship with my son, Winnsbo. He has never had such a good friend. Godspeed and safe travels home. We look forward to seeing you next summer.

Your Humble Servant, Arundel Yem

"How nice of her!"

"Who?"

"Arundel Yem, Win… McTavish's cousin. She's a generous and kind woman."

"Oh, of course. Yes."

"You know her, then?"

"I know *of* her. She works on the fourth floor in one of the shops."

Maagy thought it prudent to carry the discussion no further. She had got the sense there were mysteries surrounding the toyshop, of which most household staff seemed unaware. Perhaps, their own children were the recipients of the toys and Grandma Polly and Grandpa Kris wanted to keep the production discrete to save them embarrassment. At any rate, she changed the subject.

"Estelí, will you wait here for a few minutes? There's something I must do!"

"Of course, Your Highness."

She dashed out the door and up the hall to the children's library. She knew Winnsbo would be sleeping, but she wanted to tell him goodbye, so she wrote a note:

Dear Winnsbo,

I wish I didn't have to leave without saying a proper goodbye, but Daddy says we must leave today. I hope you're not holding

a grudge for the prank I played on you. You must admit it was a good one! I shall miss you terribly until next summer when I return for holiday. Give your mum my best regards and thank her for the lovely traveling outfit. Try to behave yourself until I see you, again.

Your Friend,
Just Maagy

She replaced his bookmark in the book he was reading with the note, knowing he would find it that night, then raced back to her room.

"Will you help me with my hair? I suppose I should do it up properly and wear my tiara to arrive home. I'm not sure it would be taken too kindly for the Crown Princess to emerge from the royal carriage with bare feet and a ponytail!"

They giggled and their mood was somewhat lifted as they joked about her wearing overalls to school and sliding down the balustrade of the grand staircase at Avington Palace.

"I'm *really* going to grind the gossip mill when I show up to equestrian class in my new riding outfits," she quipped, referring to the culottes and matching jackets Grandma had provided.

Estelí shook things up when she reached under the bed and pulled out the portrait Wesley had given Maagy for her birthday.

"And what about this, Madam? Surely you want to take it with you and hang it over your mantel!"

"Oh, lord! I had completely forgot about that monstrosity! Quick, put it back before it comes to life!"

Laughter was just the medicine to cure their ills. The morning flew by and it was nine o'clock before she knew it. The luggage was loaded and Grandma Polly had packed a delicious picnic basket and placed it in the carriage. There were more baskets for the entourage of royal guards and Mister Fenster, the King's personal driver. Leave it Grandma to think of everyone.

"Maagy, are you in there?" King Henry said as he tapped on the door. "It's time, Darling. We must go."

"I'm on my way, Father."

She opened the door slowly, stopping for a moment to look back, and sighed deeply.

"I'm ready."

As they walked down the staircase, arm in arm, for the last time that year, she thought of the first time and the handsome prince who had been waiting at the bottom. She tried to take in every detail of the scene to hold in her memories. They walked out onto the portico and found the entire estate residency lining the steps. She burst into tears as she saw all the dear faces. They were cheering and waving them on as if it were a grand parade.

"*God save the King*! *God save the Crown Princess*! *We love you*! *Come back soon*! *We'll miss you*," were the shouts as they descended the steps.

Grandma Polly and Grandpa Kris were waiting to be the last goodbyes. After many more hugs and tears they boarded and Mister Fenster closed the door and climbed onto the seat.

"Get up there, boys," he called to the team of four. "Gee-up!"

As the carriage rolled down the cobblestones, she leaned out the window as far as she could, for as long as she could, and waved to them all. Finally, she sat back on the seat next to her father and rode in silence until they stopped for luncheon.

"Are you all right, Maagy?"

"I will be."

"I've never seen you so quiet. What are you thinking?"

"There is so much… I don't know where to start."

"Start anywhere you like. I'll catch up."

"I've been thinking… most of all… about how different I feel. I've spent all this time doing ordinary chores with wonderful, ordinary people… by that I mean *real* people… who treat me like I'm a real person… not some mythical… royal… pain-in-their-neck they're nice to only because they're required."

"You've grown up, Maagy."

"I have. Others at the palace my age… how many of them have ever mucked a stable? Not one, I'm sure. I've woven fine silk; I've fought fire; I've studied veterinary medicine and treated a horse for the last month. I've learnt to find my way at night by looking at the stars. I've been involved in complex political negotiations. I've trained a horse and learnt to ride. How will I be able to relate to their frivolous goings-on… after the summer I've had? I could better relate to the stable hands and gardeners. Take Lady Millicent and Lady Elizabeth… they detest me, and I them. I don't want to sit through classes with them and watch their wicked glances and hear their snide* whispers. Wait until they see my riding outfits. I'm not at all looking forward to school."

"I'm sorry to hear, Maagy. You've always been so gifted. I don't want to see you slack in your studies. A good education is important, even for a monarch… *especially* for a monarch."

"The instructors are so boring. I gleaned more from Rudy's geography and political instruction during the Summit than I did the entirety of last year."

"What do you suggest we do about this dilemma?"

"What if I went to school… outside the palace? I understand there are some excellent private schools with extraordinary professors in the smaller towns."

"Oh, Maagy, I think that's out of the question. The security, alone, would be quite a feat*. Perhaps we could find these extraordinary professors you speak of and bring them to the palace as private tutor."

"Boring! Daddy, that would be horrific. I'd lose my mind. I want to be round people my own age, but people who are interesting and friendly… like Estelí. You know, we became good friends. Did you know she is the sole provider for her mother and herself?"

"I didn't know that, no. She's a nice young lady. You consider a friend, do you?"

"Yes, I do. She's smart… and clever… and funny… and not at

all intimidated by my position. I like that about her. Anyway, back to the subject, why can't I go to the school in Montclair?"

"No! Absolutely not! There are too many factors you're not aware of to allow it. There are those who would… shall we say… want to have leverage against me. You could become a target. It's too dangerous."

"There must be something you can do, Daddy. I'll be miserable otherwise."

"Let me think about it. Give me a day or so. What else is bothering you, Dear? We have several more hours of travel… I'm all yours."

"I'd like to redecorate my bedchamber."

"Well… that wasn't what I expected… but let's hear about it."

"At Whitmore, my room is bright and airy. The bedclothes are white and crisp. The duvet is even white linen. The feather comforter is fluffy. The curtains are lacey and flow freely. At home, everything is heavy and dark. I love the brocade and the gold gilding, but it's so… overbearing. I'd like my walls to be much brighter than the dark stone. What say, Daddy? May I spruce it up a bit?"

"I see no reason why not. Yes, speak with… well… I'm not sure who to speak with about this. The décor is as it's always been… start with Lady Periwinkle. I know she's your Social Mistress, but she's quite well educated. Perhaps she can guide you."

"Oh, thank you!"

"Anything to see you smile again, My Darling. What else?"

"Well… since you're in the mood to listen… I've been thinking a lot about the toyshop. First, I want to discuss why I never found it again after that first excursion to the fourth floor. What do you know about that?"

"I don't know anything about it. As far as I know, it's on the fourth floor on the long hallway off the main one. I can't help you there."

"Hmmm… never mind, then… second, Grandma Polly said the

toys were for needy children in the surrounding villages. There must be a lot of needy children, Daddy… judging from the number of toys on the shelves. Perhaps you should investigate working conditions… and wages for the parents."

"Oh… hmmm… perhaps I should. I'll look into it at once. That was an easy one… what else?"

"Is there any way you could bring Cupid to Avington? I'm going to miss her training. I can't bear it."

"My goodness, you have been doing a lot of thinking. Avington Palace is not the ideal place for her development. Mister Miles is the best trainer in the kingdom. I couldn't pull him away from Whitmore. It's where all our horses are developed for royal service. Perhaps I could arrange for her to visit… for a week or so… hear and there. John could bring her down… I'll consider it. Next?"

"The last thing is… and I hope you won't be angry… I found the combat training room."

"You did what?"

"I never expected it, but I'm positively *fascinated* with blades! It started when I looked down from the balcony over the ballroom and saw all those swords and daggers on the Summit table. I've never seen anything like it… so when I found that room, I wanted to learn about every blade on the wall. I took Rudy there and asked him to show them to me…"

"*What*? Did he?"

"No Sir! Don't worry. He chastised me and told me not to touch a single one. He said he could never do such a thing without your knowledge and permission."

"Good! My faith in the boy is well placed."

"Will you teach me, Daddy?"

"Absolutely not. Not under any circumstance. They're nothing to play with, Maagy. They're lethal weapons used in war, not something for your curiosity."

"Daddy, I know what they are. This isn't idle curiosity. I'm going to be queen in just five years… as you point out, I have no choice in the matter… shouldn't I know about these things?"

"You have plenty of time to learn about them later."

His mood had changed and she decided not to press him further. They packed up the baskets and climbed back into the carriage and rode quietly until she thought enough time had passed.

"Tell me more about my mother," she said decisively.

"Not now, Maagy. I'm tired. We'll talk later."

He leaned back and closed his eyes as if he were going to sleep. Anger swelled in her throat and then tears filled her eyes, but she said nothing more. Instead, she turned toward the window and watched the countryside go by. The royal entourage rumbled through Montclair to the base of the road leading to Avington Palace and began the arduous trek up the narrow winding road toward home. It was getting close to dinnertime when they finally arrived at the top of the mountain. She heard the familiar creaking and clanking of the mammoth wooden bridge being lowered across the gorge. She leaned out the window and watched as the pulleys and chains did their work. Finally in place, the carriage rolled forward through the opening into the courtyard. As she listened to the chains closing the hole in the wall behind her, she suddenly felt as if she were entering a prison. Whitmore Estate was open… surrounded by rolling, green fields… an inviting home. Avington Palace was build on cold, gray rocks… a fortress. She'd never thought of it that way before, perhaps because it was all she'd ever known… until that summer. It was staggering how much her life had changed.

Maagy was barely inside the palace when the very first person to greet her was none other than Lord Wesley Applegate, the last person she wanted to see.

"Your Highness Princess Maagy, it's so good to see you! I hope your trip was pleasant."

"Oh, Lord… Wesley… yes it was… thank you."

She tried to duck into a room to escape him, but the door was locked.

"Did you like the birthday present I gave you?"

"The present… um… why, yes… Lord Wesley. I… can honestly say that… I… smiled when I opened it. It brightened my day. I'm sure I sent a note."

"A note… of course you did… I remember."

She hurried down the long corridor trying desperately to escape him, remembering how ghastly the portrait and how much she laughed at it.

"I'm so pleased! I painted it myself, you know?"

"Indeed, I gathered you must have done. I believe it… has… your… style."

She was about to come loose at the seams. He was still in hot pursuit.

"Mummy said it would be risky business to give you my very first work of art, but I wanted you to have it."

"That was kind of you, Lord Wesley," she reiterated, working hard to keep a sincere face. "Thank you for your generosity."

"You're entirely welcome. It was my pleasure. Where did you put it? In the parlor? In a hallway?"

She remembered Estelí pulling the thing out from under the bed at just the right time to give them both the humor they needed. She giggled out loud and then pulled herself together, hoping his next words were not, "*Over the mantel?*"

"Actually… I took it with me… to the Summer Castle. We left so suddenly… **giggle**… I hadn't finished opening my gifts and I saved yours for last… **giggle**… It was so… enjoyable… I decided to leave it there in my room… which… was… in need of… some art work!"

"Ducky! I'm glad I could add to the décor!"

"It definitely adds… something…"

She turned down another long hallway with no particular destination in mind except away from him. He was persistent!

"By the by, Your Highness, I do want to apologize for the dreadful mess at your birthday party. The food fight was entirely my fault. I was a clumsy oaf and ruined your stockings. I take full responsibility. When I told Mummy about it she said I should apologize."

Maagy was no longer laughing nor was she running away. She stopped and faced him, realizing what a genuinely nice person he was, and focused on the actual conversation rather than the pathetic artwork.

"Lord Wesley, you are forgiven, but it was an accident. What I did, however… with the spumoni ice cream… was a deliberate act, for which I owe *you* the apology."

"Very kind of you to say. I humbly accept if you accept my regrets for my awkwardness."

"Done and done!"

"And while we're on the subject, I think the magician was out of line to be so put out with you. After all, it was *your* birthday party. He could have been a bit more tolerant."

"Well, I did ruin all his tricks."

"Nonsense! I've seen him ruin those same tricks by himself. He's not a very good magician. Mummy had him to my twelfth birthday two years ago and he wasn't any different."

"Thank you for that, Lord Wesley. I feel better about it."

"And just between us, I thought your party was one of the most fun parties I can remember. Most of the others our age round here are stuffy and oh-so full of themselves. That's why I like you so much. You're real and spontaneous. You laugh easily and aren't afraid to say what you think. Most of the young ladies want to giggle and bat their eyelids, but you like to engage in real conversation and… oh dear… did I overstep my bounds?"

"Not in the least, Lord Wesley. I think you and I could be great friends."

"That would be ducky with me, Your Highness."

"When it's just the two of us talking, let's drop the formalities and be just Maagy and Wesley, what say?"

"I say… just ducky!"

Returning to Avington was just as she had expected. The other young aristocrats were the same arrogant, petty people she remembered, only they seemed to be even more boring and judgmental. She could feel their stares and hear their whispers behind her back, as she tried to settle into the palace routine. She didn't help matters by refusing to conform to the standards of attire. She showed up to school the first morning in a casual skirt and blouse. Her hair was in a long ponytail down her back and her tiara was askew. She marched through the courtyard every day, in front of everyone, in her custom designed riding outfits and boots, as she insisted on going to the stables.

"Where on Earth is she going?"

"What is she wearing?"

"How disgraceful! Not at all ladylike!"

"That is our future queen?"

"Who could respect a woman who dresses that way?"

The whispers and snickers were relentless, but it seemed as if she were trying to provoke them. Knowing her, it was *precisely* what she was doing. She missed Grandma Polly and Grandpa Kris terribly and it put her in a mood to be obstinate*. Her friendship with Wesley settled into a comfortable place and she enjoyed his humor and humility. She discovered they had much more in common than originally thought, when she ran into him one day at the stables and found he enjoyed riding and caring for the horses. His father had taught him to be self sufficient and resourceful, completely the opposite of her first impression of him. They rode together almost every day.

She was glad Lady Cecily had returned from her visit with her mother, but felt the tiniest bit envious she *could* visit her mother. Their relationship improved, as well. They became close and Cecily became a valued confidant. Together, they completely transformed Maagy's entire suite. It turned out Cecily had an eye for design. They had the furnishings removed and the dark stone walls washed down to discover the dinginess was due to years... centuries... of dust and dirt. The lighter, beige stonework made the dark wood stand out. When they had the floor scrubbed, they realized the beauty of the intricately inlaid tiles and had them polished. The winters were extremely cold so the heavy velvet drapes were a must for warmth, but Cecily suggested the drapes be on a pulley system, which could be opened easily during the day. They hung lace panels behind them to soften the look when the drapes were open.

Once the furniture was moved back in and rearranged, they exchanged the heavy brocade bedcover for a feather comforter inside a royal purple duvet. All the sheets and pillow covers were white. Maagy had found a patchwork quilt in the trunk she had never bothered to open. It resembled the one on King Henry's bed at Whitmore and she discovered her great-grandmother had made it, as well. They had the chaise lounge, vanity stool and the couches in the parlor reupholstered in brighter more vibrant fabrics. Everything was dusted and polished and it gave Maagy the boost she needed. In fact, she set Lady Cecily and Lady Periwinkle on a mission to supervise the cleaning and refurbishing of the entire second level of the palace before winter holidays began.

The King had been quite busy since returning home, as Parliament was back in session and rumors abounded about Zinrahwi's activities and his on-again-off-again cooperation with dismantling the dam at Buzzard Lake. There had been no more mention of Queen Melania and Maagy was growing increasingly more curious... and angry. She understood, however, it was physically painful for her father so she kept her questions to herself, which only fueled the fires of her discontent. Finally, after weeks of tantrums and complaints about her classroom behavior, King Henry gave in and made arrangements for her to attend school outside the palace. Her mood improved dramatically. Attending school as a "normal person" also took her mind off those she missed… and the burning in her heart for knowledge of her mother. With her surroundings more pleasant and the new school situation, she seemed much happier… and that made *everyone* much happier.

Chapter 16
Civics Lessons

Maagy was well into the fall quarter at her new school in Clementine and was accustomed to the daily journey, which began before dawn. It was necessary to give her the complete anonymity* she desired to be fully ensconced in everyday life as an ordinary person. So far, no one knew she was Her Royal Highness Princess Melania Abigail Alice Grace, Crown Princess of The Commonwealth. To her classmates she was Grace Covington. Her Civics professor, Lord Dardmore, was a particularly gruff man whom she found a bit scary. He was about the same age as her father. The irony was not lost on her that Lord Dardmore would be her subject when she became queen. The knowledge amused her when his behavior was especially pompous.

"All right, Pupils," Lord Dardmore began his dissertation, "does anyone know why we celebrate Founders' Day?"

Timothy Mottistone raised his hand timidly and offered, "Because somebody found something?"

"Put down your hand, Timothy. Is that the best anyone can offer?"

The room was silent. Maagy neither wanted to seem presumptuous*, nor did she want to draw attention to herself, so she kept quiet though she *did* know the story of the great explorer, Bjorn Berensen.

"Chickens, we celebrate Founders' Day on the eighth day of October in commemoration of the expedition by Bjorn Berensen and his men, who were the first western explorers to conquer the dreaded Depopulo Mountain range, which is our western border with Skodinovia, Marinia and Poseidonia. Depopulo is a Latin word meaning to lay waste, ravage, devastate. Does anyone know anything about this harrowing expedition?"

"I do!" Maagy chimed, positively bursting to speak. "It happened many centuries ago, I think. Bjorn Berensen was Skodinovian. No one had ever been brave enough to try and find out what was on this side of the mountains. So he did. There were a lot of men who started the journey, but only a few actually made it."

She stopped short and looked at all the eyes upon her.

"That's all I know."

"Well done, Miss Covington. You seem to know more about it than anyone else in the room... except for me, of course. The mountain range is called Depopulo for a reason. Prior to Berensen's brave trek, no one in the known western world had ever been successful in surmounting the treacherous, craggy peaks, which, in some places, reach over twenty thousand feet toward the sky. The peaks are steep and snow covered. The temperature can reach into the double digit minus range at worst, and still below freezing in the heat of summer. There are crevices into which many explorers have disappeared and never been heard from since. So to undertake this journey was brave, indeed, and some even called Berensen fool-hearty. But undertake it, he did and he assembled a team of one hundred of the strongest, bravest, most adventuresome men from all over the known world. It is written in history from the times, the planning alone took more than seven years and Berensen, himself, designed special clothing for warmth and sleds for transporting large amounts of supplies."

Lord Dardmore's enthusiasm was unmistakable. He obviously loved teaching this particular part of history and this story held a special place in his coffer of knowledge. Perhaps he fancied himself a bit like the courageous explorer, daily braving a classroom full of adolescents. Perhaps he wished he had been more adventurous in his own life, now living vicariously* through the likes of Berensen. Either way, she was quite enjoying his account of history.

"The journey began in the early spring, reasoning the most difficult part of the expedition would be during the heat of summer, so they would reach the highest, coldest peak during the warmest time. In preparation, to lessen the initial load, smaller expeditions had carried supplies to designated points along the route they planned to take. These smaller attempts were not without difficulty. Since they wished to leave in early spring, some of the supply runs took place in the dead of winter. Several lives were lost and supplies were buried in snow, which would not be melted in time for the explorers to find and make use of them. It was a tremendous task to complete. But I digress from the actual lesson at hand… Founders' Day in Berensenia."

"Oh please continue, Sir. It's ever so interesting the way you tell it."

She realized she had spoken out of turn and felt her face flush with embarrassment.

"Begging your pardon, Lord Dardmore, Sir. I didn't mean to interrupt."

"Yes… Miss Covington… you did interrupt. Thank you for recognizing your mistake. Now where were we… oh yes, Founders' Day. The journey lasted three months longer than anticipated due to unforeseen circumstances. In the few journals recovered from the experience, storms, animal attacks and particularly difficult terrain took a heavy toll. By the end, there were only twenty-five men, in addition to Bjorn Berensen, who made it to the top of Widow Peak of the Depopulo range. Some turned back; some were lost to the elements, but twenty-five indomitable* souls, led by the courageous Berensen, stood on the peak on October eighth. It is said, when they reached the summit and looked out over the valley below and east to the Sagamathia Mountains in the distance, they were overcome with emotion at the sheer beauty of it. It took them two more months to pick their way down the mountain into this valley we find ourselves in today, Berensen Valley. Three kingdoms of the Valley Region were named for explorers; Berensenia… well, that's obvious; Estadore, for Berensen's right-hand man, Ferdinand Estadore, who haled from Hispania and Senecia for Bulwar Senecia, third in command who was a native of Franciné. This is why all three kingdoms celebrate October eighth simultaneously for a period of one week. Does anyone have any questions about Founders' Day? This will be on week's end exam."

Maagy's hand shot into the air.

"Yes Miss Covington, you have a question?"

"What about Aradinia? It's a Valley Region nation, is it not? How was it named?"

"Very astute of you… yes Aradinia is a Valley Region nation, but with a much different history. We'll go more in depth later in the class, but suffice it to say, Aradinia was named for King Aradin, the man who saved it from invasion by the Adriacan Empire. Those events happened before the expedition into Berensen Valley, but the exact timeline is muddy."

Another hand popped up. It was the freckled faced girl with the shock of curly red hair. She sat in the back of the class and Maagy didn't know her name.

"Miss Gray, you have a question?"

"Was anyone in the band of explorers named Clementine?"

"Interesting you should ask; in fact, our humble village of Clementine is named for the first born child of Bjorn Berensen and his wife, Helga. Once the trail was blazed and a route was cleared, many settlers from the western kingdoms made their way here.

Helga was eager to accompany her husband and settle in a new land."

"Is that where Lake Helga got its name?"

"Again, astute, Miss Covington, but please raise your hand next time."

"Sorry, Professor."

"Yes, you are correct in your assumption."

"What about the people who were already here? Did they like the idea of so many new settlers from all over everywhere?" Annabelle Crumkey chimed in, also without raising her hand.

Lord Dardmore was not expecting such lively discussion. In fact, he usually had to thump at least one or two to wake them up. He was delighted at the interest.

"Hands, please! Remember your hands! Actually, what the band of explorers found was a sparse population of unhealthy people living in abject poverty. A plague had devastated the region some time before Berensen's expedition arrived. Those who were left had endured a drought, not unlike the one we have endured. However, the indigenous* people had few farming and no irrigation skills. They depended largely on the plants and animals they could forage and most of the population lived along the riverbanks. The drought had devastated the vegetation and, therefore, the animal population. The influx of new blood and farming skills was actually a Godsend to those already here. The transition and colonization went smoothly and was peaceful, to be sure. Most all of us today, are of mixed blood between indigenous and settlers. It was the best possible outcome for the expedition and the known world, at the time. Hmmm… this, too, shall be on the exam. Thank you for your interest and enthusiasm, students, but I see it's already time for luncheon. Go children, and eat… back in forty minutes. Off with you, now… lovely morning…"

Maagy was fascinated with Lord Dardmore's accounts of history. She had never been interested before, but between Rudy's geography and political lesson in the summer and the professor's bombastic* delivery, she decided history and civics might be her new favorite subjects. She reasoned knowledge of both would be of great help to her in the future. She also decided he was not as scary as she had once thought.

The children stood and stretched. It had been a long morning. They took their luncheon buckets and sacks and made small talk as they drifted out to the shady courtyard. The stone tables and benches in the cool, autumn air were a welcome change from the stuffy schoolroom. The trees were now full into fall colors and she marveled that leaves could display so many variations of red, gold and brown. Maagy was by nature, a shy girl, even though she seemed bold and brazen when her temper got the best of her, so she had not made friends with anyone. Also, because of the unusual circumstances, she didn't want to put herself in the position of having to tell stories about her identity, so she kept mostly to herself.

She chose a seat at a table where no one else was sat and began to unpack her food. The kitchen staff was, obviously, much happier with her more polite behavior, since returning from holiday. They gave her an abundance of choices each day, which she really couldn't finish in one sitting. She always had plenty for a snack on the long carriage ride home and even shared with the driver, Mister Fenster. Today was no different. She found a peanut butter and honey sandwich; a huge apple, cut into slices; several generous hunks of cheese; two thick slices of sourdough bread; three strawberry pastry puffs and four large oatmeal cakes. She was pleased to have such variety, but as she looked round, it was obvious she had much more than anyone else in the class. In fact, most had a small sandwich and a piece of fruit. Some didn't have even one sweet cake. She was embarrassed at her own bounty, so she left all but the sandwich and apple inside the sack. Several children had sat at the table and were in various stages of unwrapping their food... among them, the red haired girl… who was now sitting next to Maagy. Dark auburn curls encircled a face highlighted by big, blue eyes, which sparkled when she flashed a contagious smile. She was a wisp of a thing, but carried herself confidently.

"Hello. I'm Mary Louise Gray."

"Hello. I'm Ma… Mel… Grace… call me Grace… Grace Covington."

"You're new here."

"Yes… I… I am…"

"Where do you live?"

"Um… east of town… a bit…"

"I live square in the middle of it. That's Timothy Mottistone on the other side of you. Say hello, Tim."

"Hello," he said, not looking up.

He was the thinly built boy who had tried to contribute to the Founders' Day discussion. He was sitting on the other end of the bench, but with his back to the table and he never turned round when he spoke. His elbows were on his knees, his hands drooped toward the ground and his head was down. No one seemed to take notice… except Maagy. By now, Mary Louise was engaged in conversation with Annabelle and another girl and wasn't paying attention.

"Aren't you eating?" she asked quietly, but got no response.

It was then she noticed he had no pail or sack.

"You must have forgot yours," she said a bit louder, as she leaned in his direction.

"What? Are you talking to me?"

"Yes. I see you don't have a luncheon sack. Did you forget yours today?"

"Forget… umm… no… I never eat in midday. I eat too much breakfast to be hungry now," he said quickly, as he turned slightly away from her.

"Oh, I see. I eat a huge breakfast, but I'm famished, anyway. I could eat all the time."

He seemed to pay her no mind. It was her first attempt to make conversation with anyone since she had been there and she was being met with silence. She was insulted at the dismissal of her social interaction and felt like stomping her foot at him, but knew it would draw unwanted attention, so she controlled the urge. Now, however, she looked at him more closely and decided his demeanor was more of sadness than rudeness. She tried another tactic.

"This apple is much too large for me to eat and it'll only turn brown and go mushy by the end of the day. I hate to throw it away. Could you help me eat it… so it won't go to waste? Please?"

"I suppose… I could have a piece or two… just so it won't go to waste."

"Oh, lovely… what about this piece of cheese? It'll get too warm and dry out if someone doesn't eat it."

"I suppose I could manage it, too."

This game continued as she shared bread, pastries and sweet cakes, in addition to the apple and cheese. He ate as they made small talk, mostly about the lesson and the colors of the trees. She was sure he hadn't eaten breakfast. She concluded his family was of modest means, judging from his clothing. Perhaps they didn't have enough food to give him. She wondered, as she looked round at the others, what secrets they were keeping as carefully as he was keeping his… or she was keeping her identity from them. She realized, in the weeks she had shared their classroom, she had not really looked at any of them. She was so absorbed with herself she hadn't stopped to consider them or what she, as Crown Princess, could do to help people in need of basics, like food and clothing. She resolved to have a conversation with her father as soon as she got home. There was still plenty left in her sack to share with the driver. The end-of-luncheon bell rang and the children began putting their leftovers away and moving back into the classroom. She was still pondering what to do with her new sense of civic duty, when Timothy walked beside her.

"Thank you," he whispered, as they entered the room.

"You're welcome."

She felt as though she would burst. A simple "thank you" was the greatest reward. Somehow, he knew she would keep his confidence. They went to their respective seats and didn't look at each other for the rest of the day.

"I saw you share with Timothy. It was kind of you. He's had a difficult time of it," Mary Louise whispered discretely as she passed Maagy and sat down.

A shared meal… a shared secret… it could be the foundation of a great friendship.

"Let us return for a moment, to our lesson on Bjorn Berensen. Does anyone have any further questions before we move on to mathematics?"

"Yes, Sir, I do," Maagy said as she raised her hand.

"You may ask."

"Where did the royal family originate?"

"My, you are full of all sorts of questions, today, Miss Covington. Let me see if I can answer that. The new monarchy was established due to a marriage between Princess Kathryn, Duchess of Wilster of Aquatain, and Prince Randolph, Duke of Burlington, from Marinia. Together, they formed what was known as the House of Wilington, which is not used in royal title anymore. The monarchs of both kingdoms had contributed money and supplies to the original expedition and requested their children be given a place of honor in the newly colonized valley. The existing government, such as it was, was primarily tribal rule with no cohesive central government. Since the indigenous people were so scattered by disease and drought, the colonists had to go from village to village to explain how they wished to form a central monarchy government with a parliament, in which the citizens would be represented by individuals chosen by each locale. It was a difficult process and took years to accomplish, but it was met with little opposition and Kathryn and Randolph were the first king and queen of the Berensen Valley Region. As time went on and the valley was divided into smaller kingdoms, the Commonwealth of Realms was formed. The seat or home of the monarchy remained Berensenia. Does that answer your question, Miss Covington?"

"Yes, Sir, and thank you for explaining it so thoroughly."

"You are entirely welcome. Now on to mathematics..."

The rest of the afternoon went by quickly and she was glad to hear the bell signaling school was done for the day. The students packed their books and chatted as they made their way out into the schoolyard. There were other students of all ages scurrying to leave. She had a long walk to the livery stable, where she would duck inside the back door and board her carriage. She would draw the curtains closed until well away from Clementine before she could open them, again. Sometimes, she wanted to dispense with all the cloak and dagger foolishness and just be herself. Then she would remember being ordinary was her idea. As she walked along the path toward town, she saw three of the boys in her class walking in front of her. She had heard others call them Digger, Badger and Chuck. They were a band of toughs who intimidated and harassed their classmates. Everyone mostly avoided them. She could, also, see Timothy walking alone in front of them.

"Hey, Timmy, I saw you sitting with the new girl. Is it love, Timmy Boy?" Digger mocked.

Timothy paid no attention to them and kept walking. The boys quickly caught up and surrounded him. They pushed him from side to side as they continued to taunt with derogatory* verbal jabs. Maagy couldn't believe what she was witnessing. She had never seen such a thing. She felt an overwhelming surge of anger and had the impulse to scream the code word "*Raven*" for her guards, who were in disguise. She did *not* want to see her new friend being abused.

However, she realized if she did so, the guards would be on her in an instant and her identity would be revealed. She could never return to the school. She decided to confront the aggressors herself, giving no thought to her personal safety. She ran into the midst of the gaggle, threw down her books and took a stand.

"You want to talk about *me*, do you? How about you talk *to me*!"

"Oooooo…I think I'm *really* frightened, now," Badger said.

"Yeah, me too! Not very *graceful*… I'm scared to death! Aren't you, Chuck?"

"Grace, what are you doing? Get out of here before you get hurt!"

"Hurt? Me? You let them touch me and see who's going to be hurting by the end of it!"

Her guards were close at hand and watching every move the boys made. She knew if one of them became physically aggressive and actually touched her, they would all be in shackles before they could say Bjorn Berensen. She was feeling brave.

"Take a stand, Timothy! Don't let people shove you round. These boys have no right."

"No right? Surely you jest. You make me laugh, Miss *Graceless*. Who do you think you are?" Digger taunted.

"I think I'm the person who is going to teach you to be a gentleman, *Digger*! How did you get that name, anyway? Digging worms to eat?"

"You insulting my name?" He said with red-faced fury.

"You did the same to mine. How does it feel to be humiliated?"

She stepped right in front of him and stood on her toes to be face-to-face with him. To her surprise, and Timothy's, he began to tremble and backed off slightly. She had faced down the tormentor and he was just a boy, after all. The other two, Badger and Chuck… short for Woodchuck… slithered sheepishly away. A little blond girl had dethroned their fearless leader. They, too, were just scared little boys. She continued her piercing stare until the entire scene de-escalated. The guards, the one dressed as an old man with a cane, the fellow with the vegetable cart and the woman with the baby pram, all smiled and remained in place, as the scene played itself out.

"You need to apologize to my friend for mocking her name," Timothy said unexpectedly, taking a posture of strength.

"And you need to apologize to my friend for trying to intimidate him," she said, as she continued to stand her ground. "Why would you do such a thing, anyway? All of you, what do you think gives you the right to behave that way?"

"I didn't do anything," said a deflated Chuck. "I was just walking home. I like you, Tim."

"Yeah, me too. I like you, Tim. Sorry if I gave you the wrong impression," added Badger, as he gave him a friendly slap on the back.

"That's a farce! You two are cowards! You were teasing him just as much as I was!" Digger exclaimed. "It's not fair!"

She had a sense of empowerment and walked from one to the other staring each in the eye.

"What's not fair is you picking on people who are alone and appear vulnerable. You're like a pack of stray dogs looking for prey, something smaller and weaker so you can pounce. Well, small isn't always weak, and sometimes the predator becomes prey. That's a lesson I learnt while at the Summer Cas… never mind where I was… or what I was doing! Just remember that lesson, and be more thoughtful of other people's feelings. You never know what they might be going through. You could be missing an opportunity for a great friendship. Kind and polite and gallant… that's who *real* men are. You're just ruffians!"

She was shocked when there was spontaneous applause. She looked round to see a number of her schoolmates encircling them and expressing their apparent approval of her diatribe*. She was instantly embarrassed and could feel the familiar red face, but pride replaced embarrassment when she saw Timothy with a whole new demeanor and the rest of the children pleased someone finally stood up to Digger and his lackeys. Her regret was using insults to get the point across. Everyone began to drift away toward their destinations, as she picked up her books. Timothy helped her.

"Thank you, Grace. You were brave. I have to get home and help my mother with the chores. And you're right about the other things, too. See you tomorrow."

He ran toward home. Badger and Chuck had made their hasty retreat, leaving only Digger still dumbfounded he had been so challenged.

"You're quite plucky, Grace Covington. Where did you learn it?"

"So I've been told… actually, I'm rather shy, but when I see someone being treated badly, my anger gets the best of me. I've been known to be *quite* temperamental at times and have learnt the bitter consequences of bad behavior. So now I'm on a mission to teach others my lessons."

She started to walk away toward her rendezvous when he began to follow her.

"I've never known a *girl* so outspoken. Why have we not become friends?"

"Because you have never once, said hello to me or tried to make me feel welcome here. Maybe if you tried being nice to people rather than taunting them, you'd have more friends. Why do you behave so rudely? I've seen you do it before."

"I don't know… it's what I've always done. I suppose it's how I have my own way."

"Well you didn't have your way today. And I don't think that behavior is going to work for you in the future, either. I think most of your classmates are full up with you. How *did* you get the name Digger? Surely, it's not your given name."

"My father is the town grave digger. The other kids gave it to me.

She stopped abruptly and faced him.

"Oh… well… that explains a lot. Persecute them before they

have the chance to do the same to you, right? Let them think you really like the name, even though you hate it, right? Don't let them see it hurts your feelings. Am I right? What's your real name?"

"Chauncey Patrick McDougal."

"That's a fine name. What do you prefer, Chauncey or Patrick?"

"My Mum calls me Patrick, sometimes Patty Boy. I like it when she calls me Patrick."

"Sooo… shall I call you Patrick… or Digger?"

"Patrick would be good."

"All right, then… so long, Patrick. I should be on my way. See you tomorrow."

"Sure… tomorrow, Grace."

He went home to chores and she to the livery for the long ride home. As she rode and shared her snacks with Mister Fenster, she thought about the events of the day and especially the history of her kingdom and knew it was important information to know as she prepared to become queen. However, the more important lessons in civics were the one's learned at luncheon and on the way home. These life experiences would do more to mature her and mold her into a responsible woman than anything she could possibly study in a classroom. She was exhausted and fell sound asleep by the gentle sway of the carriage.

Chapter 17
Dame Spitfire

Several weeks had gone by since the incident with Timothy and the naughty boys. Digger, Badger and Chuck were behaving much better and were sticking together, although Digger and Maagy had exchanged pleasantries, upon occasion. Timothy, Mary Louise and she sat together most days for luncheon and several others had begun to join them. The old saying, "*There is safety in numbers*," seemed to be the mantra, since all the students at the table were the classroom misfits.

There was Grace Covington, the cheeky, blond, new girl with a keen interest in history and a big temper; Timothy Mottistone, the skinny, shy boy with shabby clothes; Mary Louise Gray, the precocious redhead and Ravi Parminder, the math genius who spoke with a slight stutter. Then there was Marseille, a rather large boy who spoke only Francinése and whose last name no one could pronounce. Maagy had continued to bring plenty of food, in case someone didn't have enough. They shared and no one seemed to notice who did or did not contribute toward the bounty. They were a motley bunch and were happy to have each other's company.

All the leaves had fallen and cloaks, scarves and mufflers

were necessary for warmth during the mealtime gathering. It was November and Harvest Festival was just round the corner. The entire valley observed the holiday in celebration of successful harvest of the crops. It had been slimmer this year because of the drought at planting, but it was a time to be grateful for any and all blessings. Even those who had little managed to do some small thing to observe the holiday. The friends began to chatter about Harvest Festival and what each household was planning. Ravi related his parents and three older sisters had recently immigrated to Berensenia from Nihmrobi and would most likely make the long journey back to spend the week with family. Unfortunately, it had taken him most of the luncheon period to tell the story with his stutter, but all were patient and polite. Ravi had transferred in even later than Maagy and had just begun to speak at all. She found it interesting his stutter was completely gone when he answered math questions. She surmised the stutter might have been due to nerves and since he was comfortable with mathematics, he concentrated on it and spoke quite well.

"My entire family goes to my grandparents' house in Buckleberry," Mary Louise added. "They're my father's parents. He has seven brothers and one sister. I have thirty-seven first cousins. Can you imagine? I, also, have four older brothers. There are so many of us, all the children sleep in the hayloft with the cats. It's the most fun ever!"

Marseille wanted to add to the conversation, but since no one spoke Francinése… even though Maagy had learnt a bit from Estelí, she was at a loss… they all smiled and nodded their heads as if they enjoyed his account. They didn't want to hurt his feelings.

"What about you, Timothy?" Maagy inquired. "Will you celebrate with family?"

"I don't really have any family. My father died this past August. My mum and me brought in the harvest by ourselves."

The table was quiet for an uncomfortably long moment. It was the first time most of them had heard of Mr. Mottistone's passing. Mary Lu, who obviously knew but kept it private, put a reassuring hand on Timothy's shoulder. Maagy finally understood the source of his melancholy and was helpless.

"I'm so sorry about your father, Timothy. I don't have my mother. I understand."

Then, out of the blue, Marseille began speaking in broken Berensenian with a heavy Francinése accent.

"I… am… too… so sorry. Mon… um… um… what… pere… um… mere… inviter… invite… vous et votre mere… ah… you… et… your… mere… mama… pour… Moisson, no, no… Harvest, yes?"

"H-h-he s-s-said h-h-his f-father and m-m-mother invite h-h-him and h-h-his mother for H-h-harvest d-dinner."

Another surprising fact about Ravi; he spoke Francinése!

"Yes, that's what he said… I think… I recognize some of the words. How kind of you, Marseille," Maagy said. "Timothy, he is inviting you and your mum to join them for Harvest Festival, right, Marseille?"

"Oui, oui! Ma maison, ma maison! Pour le diner!"

"I don't speak much Francinése, but I think he said 'my house, my house for dinner'. *N'est-ce pas*, Marseille? Is that right, Ravi? Is that what he said?"

"Y-Yes, th-that's wh-wh-what h-he s-s-said."

"Oui, oui, ma maison pour diner!" Marseille shrieked.

Everyone in the courtyard turned to look in the direction of the table. The five at the focus of the ruckus were laughing and clapping, as they had finally broken through his language barrier and communicated with him. Somehow, he seemed to understand Berensenian, but it was the first time he had successfully spoken it. The other students began to laugh and it was unclear whether they were laughing *at* or *with* the group. It really didn't matter, since they were all having a good time of it. The end-of-luncheon bell rang and everyone scurried inside to the warmth of the classroom and continued with afternoon lessons.

The days were considerably shorter and the sun was much lower in the sky by the time the ending bell rang. Maagy's walk to the livery stable seemed even longer with the sun chasing her every step of the way. She bundled up against the cold and began the long journey. Timothy left her at his usual place at the path toward his farm and her pace quickened, as she was now alone. She had become aware, recently, someone was following her, but could never catch anyone when she turned round. It made her uneasy. Nevertheless, she didn't want any suspicious behavior to give her away. She reached the livery and ducked into the alley behind it so as to go in the back door, as always. Suddenly, who should pop right into her path, but Mary Louise Gray?

"Hello, Grace," she said, cheerfully.

"Oh, good heavens! Mary Louise, you scared me to death. What are you doing here?"

"My father owns the livery. What are you doing here?" she asked, as if she already knew.

"Me? I… I… I take a carriage home… I meet the driver here…"

She was flustered. No one had ever come so close to learning her secret. She had got comfortable with the routine and never expected Mary Louise, of all people, to be the one to undo her mission. She had tried to be careful not to tell lies and so far had succeeded, but what if this curious girl pressed her further for details?

"It's all right… *Grace.* I know who you are. I've always known. I won't tell anyone."

Maagy took her by the arm and they slipped into the back tack room of the stable and closed the door.

"What do you mean, you know who I am? Who do you *think* I am?"

"Really, *Grace? Grace Covington?* I've studied the Royal Family since I was old enough to talk… Princess Melania Abigail Alice

Grace… Duchess of Wentworth? His Majesty is the Duke of *Covington*? I am your humble servant, Your Royal Highness, Princess Maagy," she said, as she curtsied perfectly and bowed her head.

"You've known all along? Why did you keep my secret?"

"Because it is your secret to tell… or keep… as you wish, Your Royal Highness. It isn't my place to betray your trust."

"Stand up, Mary Louise. You're making me uncomfortable. Who else knows?" She asked, as she paced back and forth.

"Only Father and I. He doesn't know I know. I even kept that secret from him. I kept Tim's secret when he asked. You see, Your Royal Highness, I am most trustworthy. My dream in life is to be… perhaps I shouldn't say."

"Mary Louise, please stop calling me that. Call me Grace or Maagy… no, call me Grace here… but please, not Your Royal Highness. Now, what is your dream in life?" She demanded, as she stopped pacing and folded her arms in front of her.

"I wish to be… your personal guard… when you are queen. I wish to be knighted and take the name *Spitfire*."

Maagy was taken aback by this whole conversation, especially since Mary Louise really *did* know her identity. But when she announced she would be called Spitfire, Maagy erupted into irrepressible* laughter, completely forgetting for a moment her precarious situation.

"Spitfire?" She said, as laughter tears rolled down her face. "*Spitfire*! Where did that come from? You're the quietest little thing in class. Why would anyone call you spitfire?"

By now, even Mary Louise was laughing and could hardly speak.

"My father calls me that because of my red hair and hot temper when my brothers tease me. Don't Knights of the Realm take arcane* names? That would be mine."

"Spitfire sounds more like me! That should be my arcane name, The Impetuous Princess Spitfire!"

The girls held their sides as they laughed even more.

"How do you, my carrot-top friend, intend to save me if I am attacked? You are no bigger than I, and a girl, as well!"

"I've studied the ancient martial arts since I was six years old. I've already achieved the second highest level and have the silver belt to prove it. I lift hay bales every day and I can hit the bull's-eye with an arrow at one hundred paces nine out of ten times. My father is an accomplished swordsman. In fact, he was a Knight in Her Majesty's Royal Guard for many years, until he lost his leg in battle and…"

Maagy abruptly stopped laughing.

"Your father is a Knight of the Realm? Are you telling the truth, Mary Louise?"

"I absolutely am telling God's truth. You've noticed his limp, I'm sure. He fashioned his own artificial leg out of forged steel and wood so as to continue working and riding a horse. He's a clever man, my papa. But he was forced to retire from HMRG."

"What is his given name?"

"William… he is Sir William Gray, though he doesn't like when people call him 'Sir' anymore. His arcane name was Blackthorne," she whispered. "I'm *not* supposed to know *that* detail."

"He was in service to my father? Wait… *your father* is the infamous Blackthorne? I've heard stories of his bravery… he's legendary at the palace."

"Yes, Papa was Elite Guard Service*… His Majesty's most trusted protector… and friend. He lost his leg in the Battle of Ascondia River protecting him…"

"Ascondia River… the battle over water…"

"Yes… you know about it?"

"I… learnt of it… this past summer."

"When he was injured, your father was generous to our family and pledged to take care of us as Papa had taken care of him. This livery stable was a gift and he pays Papa a yearly stipend, as well. You were with your father this past August, when he stopped to check on the carriage he ordered from us. You never got out, though. Mama made your luncheon basket. It was no coincidence he sent you here and our school. He knew you would be well protected."

"We were here… in Clementine? I had no idea…"

"Papa has been teaching me to handle a blade since I was big enough to hold one."

Maagy burst into laughter once again at the thought of the wisp in front of her wielding a battle sword.

"It's true! Papa has taught all of us. Two of my brothers are Horsemen, but they plan to leave as soon as their obligation is done. None of them is interested in a military career, but I am. By the time you wear the crown I will have grown considerably. All my brothers are quite tall, so I should be as well. I will be a formidable opponent for anyone who would wish you harm, Your Highness… I mean Maagy… I mean Grace."

"Has no one ever told you all Knights are *men*?"

"I shall be the first woman."

"You're serious about this, aren't you?"

"Yes. It's what I've dreamed of as long as I can remember."

"Then, there's nothing to do… but dub you. From this moment forward, Mary Louise Gray, you shall be known as Her Majesty's loyal defender and lifelong friend, Sir… or as the case may be… Dame Mary Louise Gray, *Spitfire*, Royal Personal Guard, to Her Royal Majesty Queen, Melania Abigail Alice Grace. Kneel before me and be knighted."

As both girls giggled, Maagy looked round the tack room for a suitable object to perform the sacred right of dubbing. Mary knelt on one knee and threw her cloak over her shoulder like a knight's cape and bowed.

"Oh dear… I need a sword."

"You can use mine," Mary said, as she sprang to her feet.

She went to the corner of the tack room and reached behind a rack of tools. Her hand emerged with a scabbard. She unsheathed a gorgeous blade and presented it to Maagy, handle first across her arm. She was flabbergasted, as it all became absolutely real.

"*Yours*? This is *yours*? You have your own sword? You really are telling me the truth."

"Of course."

Maagy had seen the weapons on the Summit table and in the training room, but had never actually held one, despite her attempts to coax Rudy and her father into it. She was breathless as she took the hilt in both hands and lifted the point into the air in front of her. She stood in stunned silence admiring it. Something in her changed. Mary Louise had knelt, again, and was waiting.

"Are you going to do this or just stand there, looking at it? You can't have it… it's mine… Papa made it for me."

"Yes… of course…"

She was back, but it was a much more sincere moment. She ceremoniously, tapped Mary Lu on each shoulder.

"I dub thee Dame Mary Louise Gray, Spitfire. Rise up, oh brave and trustworthy Knight of the Realm. *Take your place at the table**."

The sound of the large livery doors opening interrupted the girls' solemn moment. The carriage rumbled inside. They fell silent as Maagy handed Dame Mary her sword and she put it back in its hiding place. As the doors closed, Maagy heard the driver speak to the man she now knew to be Sir William.

"Has she arrived, yet?"

"I haven't seen her."

"I'm here," she said stepping out from the shadows. "I'm actually here with my friend, Mary Louise."

She grabbed Mary's hand and pulled her out of hiding and both girls huddled in giggles, again.

"Mary Lu, what are you doing here?" Sir William said, surprised and afraid of what might happen, now the secret was out.

"Please Mister Gray, she is my friend. She has kept my secret

all this time and will continue to keep it as long as I ask her to, I'm quite sure. Don't be angry with her."

"I beg your pardon, Your Highness, Princess Maagy. I had no idea my naughty daughter knew of this plan. I shall punish her impudence and see to it she tells no one."

"Didn't you hear me, Sir? No punishment is necessary. She has known all along and has kept my confidence. She is a true and trustworthy friend, to be sure. You have taught her well and should be proud of your accomplishment. I know you're her father and I would never presume to tell you how to parent your child, but I assure you, I hold no grudge and would ask you to do the same."

"You are most kind, Your Highness. I do sincerely apologize."

"Excuse me, my lady, but we really should be on our way," Mister Fenster said. "As it is, we will be traveling most of the journey in darkness and it is not as safe as the light. Your security detail is waiting on the outer edge of town."

"Yes, of course, Mister Fenster. I know you're right. Friend, I'll see you tomorrow. Pinky-swear you'll keep my confidence now and forever." She whispered.

"I swear, Your Highness. I will remain faithful to the end."

They giggled, again, as they threw their arms round each other, now bonded in their secret pact. Maagy jumped into the carriage, as Mister Fenster stood at attention with the door. He climbed to the seat on top. Mary Louise jumped onto the running board and waved one last time. Maagy playfully pulled the curtain closed and jerked it open, while making a funny face. Both laughed even more. She jerked the curtain closed, again, and then open.

"Mary Lu, get down. They must go. It's getting late," Mister Gray chided.

She did as told and they said more goodbyes, as Maagy closed the curtain for the last time. He opened the stable doors and Mister Fenster gave the gee-up to the horses and off the carriage went toward home.

THE END

See how Maagy's adventures continue in

Krispen

The world round Maagy turns dark...
Her faith in all she has known is shaken to the core...
Nothing seems right...
Go with her on her quest to save Krispen...

Glossary

Characters in Order of Appearance or Mention

Princess Maagy—*(pronounced MAG-e; hard G sound as in "good")* Melania Abigail Alice Grace, Crown Princess of the sovereign kingdom of Berensenia and the Commonwealth of Realms; Duchess of Wentworth; daughter and only child of King Henry, Duke of Covington, and deceased Queen Melania, former Duchess of Wentworth; typical entitled royal child

King Henry—His Royal Majesty King Henry David Charles Edward, Supreme Monarch of the Commonwealth of Realms including Berensenia, Marinia, Aquatain, Poseidonia and Polacia; Guardian of the List; Duke of Covington of Aradinia; Knight of the Commonwealth of Realms; Presiding Parliamentary Officer for the Commonwealth of Realms; Chief Ambassador of the Commonwealth of Realms; Knight of Aradin; Aradinian prince not in line for the throne of Aradinia; elected King of Berensenia when wife, Queen Melania, died; born and raised in Aradinia; doting elderly father

Queen Melania—Maagy's deceased mother; formerly, Princess Melania, Duchess of Wentworth; became Queen upon the deaths of her older sister, Abigail, and subsequently, her parents

Persephone Fendlwart—"the kind voice" from the kitchen; the head chef of Avington Palace; cousin to Sir William Gray

Samantha Payne—Maagy's chambermaid at Avington Palace; a sweet natured, timid girl two years older than Maagy

Lady Periwinkle—Avington Palace Social Mistress

Lady Cecily Greymiller—Maagy's Lady–in-Waiting; daughter of Lady Madelaine Fleming Greymiller, Queen Melania's Lady-in-Waiting, and the late Sir Warwick Greymiller, a Knight and fallen soldier

Lord Wesley Applegate—friend of Maagy; one year older; Son of Lord Walter Applegate and Lady Harriett Applegate, Duke and Duchess of Burlwood who are friends of King Henry; on Court at Avington Palace

Lady Millicent and Lady Elizabeth Smythe—daughters of Baron Bullington and Baroness Jacqueline Smythe, members of the King's Court and his close friends; Baron Smythe is financial advisor to His Majesty; Millicent is the same age as Maagy and Elizabeth is one year younger

Merlin The Great—mediocre magician hired to perform at Maagy's thirteenth birthday party

Grandpa Kris—elderly caretaker of Whitmore Castle; Astronomer; Silkworm Farmer; Equine expert

Grandma Polly—elderly wife of Grandpa Kris; also caretaker of Whitmore Castle; kind, generous and a fabulous cook

Estelí Barrineau—upstairs chambermaid at Whitmore Castle; Francinése girl two years older than Maagy; expert angler

Julie—a gentle cow with big brown eyes

Cupid—a palomino filly; Maagy's special friend

Jorge Corrales—stable manager at Whitmore Castle

Claude Wickem—stable hand at Whitmore Castle

John Miles—farrier, horse trainer and veterinarian at Whitmore Castle

Rebecca Miles—chambermaid at Whitmore Castle; wife of John and mother to eight-year-old Sarah and six-year-old Cornelia

Josephine Penning—Grandma Polly's elderly kitchen assistant

Prince Rudolpho—Rudolpho Eduardo Rafael Valente of the house of Santiago, Prince of the sovereign kingdom of Estadore; youngest of three children; not in line for the throne; diplomatic envoy representing Estadore

King Rafael and **Queen Marisol**—King and Queen of Estadore; lifelong friends of King Henry; Prince Rudolpho's parents

Makubar Sistrunk—Captain in Royal Command of Estadore; personal guard to Prince Rudolpho; grandson of the late king of Darhambi; brought to Estadore with family as a small child when they escaped invasion by the Terrasicans

Gilles Chamberlaine—Premier of Senecia; father of Martha Chamberlaine

Martha Chamberlaine—daughter of the Premier of Senecia; three years older than Maagy

Queen Haideh—Queen of Nihmrobi; descendant from the ancient Mughal Dynasty through her father; became Queen at age fifteen when her father abdicated; mother of five, including Princess Asanna

King Afarnae—"The Father King" of Nihmrobi; Haideh's father; became King as only child (Royal line passed through his mother); abdicated when his wife, Queen Ajeera, died in a riding accident; close friend of King Henry; still influential in valley politics

Prince Shamir—husband of Queen Haideh; father of five

Princess Asanna—daughter and oldest child of Queen Haideh and Prince Shamir; Heir-Apparent to the throne of Nihmrobi; three years older than Maagy; childhood friend of Prince Rudolpho

Emir Sistrunk—son of Makubar Sistrunk; four years older than Maagy

Ohno Sistrunk—son of Makubar Sistrunk; two years older than Maagy

Lamalah Sistrunk—daughter of Makubar Sistrunk; same age as Maagy

Owanu Obuku—son of the Darhambian chieftain; one year older than Maagy

Chief Obuku—Darhambian; tribal leader from the southern region of Shimboran

Chief Nandu—Darhambian; tribal leader from the northern region of Chericini

Prince Amador Sistrunk—Makubar Sistrunk's father; Son of the late king; fled with his family to Estadore in the middle of night to escape Terrasican slaughter; officer in Royal Command of Estadore; killed in battle when Mak was at Academy

Prince Raul—Rudolpho's older brother by twelve years; the Crown Prince of Estadore; married to Gabriela

Princess Consuela—Rudolpho's older sister by ten years; humanitarian and philanthropist; not interested in royal pomp

Emperor Zinrahwi—Emperor of Terrasicus; son of Aftanisbahr and brother of Tarin; last of ancient line of The House of Terras

McTavish—Polacian; works on the fourth floor of Whitmore Castle; runs the workshop, which makes toys

Winnsbo Yem—mischievous; adolescent Huggermugger

Arundel Yem—Winnsbo's mother; Polacian; cousin of McTavish

Nemtuc Yem—Huggermugger; Winnsbo's father; brilliant scientist; the Keeper

Sydney McBride—little girl from Summer Valley near Whitmore Castle; owner and handler of Miss Trinny McBride, prize winning, piglet-prolific sow; always dressed to the nines

Professor Lord Francis Dardmore—bombastic professor at Clementine School

Mary Louise Gray—best friend of Maagy from Clementine; same age as Maagy; youngest child of five with four older brothers; life's goal is to be knighted and serve as Maagy's personal bodyguard

Sir William Gray—Mary Louise's father; owner of the livery stable in Clementine; legendary Knight of Realm, retired; arcane name, Blackthorne; close friend of King Henry

William Fenster—King Henry's personal carriage driver; former soldier in the Royal Horsemen

Timothy Mottistone, Annabelle Crumkey, Ravi Chandrashekar, Marseille Vadeboncoeur, Digger (Chauncey Patrick McDougal), Badger (James Christian Larsen), Chuck (Charles Patterson)—Maagy's classmates from Clementine School; some friends, some not

Princess Kathryn—*(historic figure)*; Duchess of Wilster of Aquatain; became the first queen of the new Commonwealth of Realms, Berensenia, Aquatain, Marinia, Poseidonia and Polacia

Prince Randolph—*(historic figure)*; Duke of Burlington of Marinia; married Kathryn and became first King of the new Commonwealth of Realms

Bjorn Berensen—*(historic figure)*; Skodinovian explorer whose expedition crossed the Depopulo Mountain range to discover the valley, which became Berensenia

Ferdinand Estadore—*(historic figure)*; Berensen's right-hand man; from Hispania; Estadore named after him

Bulwar Senecia—*(historic figure)*; third in command to Bjorn Berensen; a native of Franciné; Senecia named after him

Words and Terms*

Abdicate—resign position, as in a monarch stepping aside; renounce; relinquish; step down from

Academy of Her Majesty's Royal Guard—world's most elite military training center for Knights of the Commonwealth of Realms; located at the Crittenton Military Compound at Mason's Lake in the southwestern plains region of Berensenia, at the foot of the Depopulo Mountains; not eligible for admission to AHMRG before sixteenth birthday; intense program, which includes equestrian skills, archery, swordsmanship, hand-to-hand combat, knife skills, ancient martial arts, leadership and strategies of warfare

Accentuate—draw attention to something; emphasize; highlight

Adieu—Francinése (*French*) for good-bye; farewell

Anonymity—freedom from identification; state of being unnoticed

Arcane—mysteriously obscure; secret; hidden

Arduous—difficult and tiring; steep or demanding

Ascertain—determine something; discover; establish

Assuage—relieve something unpleasant; ease; soften

Asymmetric—not symmetrical; not equal; uneven

At sixes and sevens—a state of confusion or disorder; a disagreement between parties

Audacity/Audacious—daring; bold; impudent; cheeky

Banter—teasing; joking; repartee; mocking

Bewildered—befuddled; disconcerted; baffled

Bombastic—pompous language; verbose; pretentious

Bowled over—overcome with amazement; boggled the mind; surprised

Cajole—persuade gently; coax; entice

Catacombs—network of tunnels below ground

Caterwaul—loud harsh noise; yowl; squall

Cat That Ate the Mouse—an expression of self-satisfaction from a secret accomplishment; smug demeanor, having achieved a goal; similar to *the cat that ate the canary* or *the cat that swallowed the canary*

Cavernous—like a cavern; hollow-sounding; vast; hollow

Cendrillon—Cinderella

Chagrined—angered at being let down; displeased; bothered

Chaise longue—Francinése *(French)* long chair on which one may lie

Charisma—personal magnetism; divine gift; charm; allure

Cheeky—Sassy; mischievous; bold

Chicanery—cheating or deception; trickery; nonsense

Chignon—roll of hair; Francinése pleat; bun; twist

Chivalrous—considerate and courteous; relating to knighthood code; gallant; noble

Chrysalis—insect between larva and adult; insect cocoon

Clandestine—secret; covert; concealed; undercover

Claustrophobic—confined or cramped; enclosed; stifling

Coiffing—arranging attractively; dressing the hair

Comeuppance—deserved fate; retaliation; reward

Condescending—patronizing; disdainful; haughty; pompous

Confection—something sweet; elaborate creation

Consternation—amazement or dismay that causes confusion; bewilderment

Contrite—arising from a sense of guilt; repentant; apologetic

Coronation—ceremony of crowning

Creckett—precursor to modern-day Cricket; a ball and bat game dating back to the mid 1500's in the British Isles; game played strictly by the rules and the "Spirit of the Game"; requires high degree of personal integrity and sportsmanship

Crescendo—increase in loudness; intensification; climax

Crown Princess—Royal woman in line for the monarchy

Daft—not sensible; frivolous; foolish; silly

Decorum—appropriateness of artistic element; propriety; correctness; respectability

Derogatory—disparaging; critical; insulting; pejorative

Derrière—buttocks; posterior

Despondent *(despondency)*—discouraged; hopeless; misery; depression

Diatribe—bitter criticism; tirade; rant

Dilemma—a situation with unsatisfactory choices; impasse; predicament

Diminutive—very small; little

Disillusionment—the freedom from a belief or idealism; disenchantment; disappointment

Double entendre—figure of speech; phrase spoken to be understood in either of two ways; first (more obvious) meaning is straightforward; second meaning is less obvious, but implied, nonetheless

Dressage—competitive equestrian sport; demonstrates highest degree of training and horse athleticism; horse and trainer work as one to demonstrate a series of predetermined moves and are scored from zero to ten; sometimes called horse ballet

Duvet—comforter; coverlet; quilt

Elite Guard Service– Knights of the Commonwealth; only those with most distinguished service records; serve as personal security detail to ruling monarch; stationed at Avington Palace; women who serve as personal guardians for the princess or queen are covert and appear to be on Court; while functioning as EGS, none has attended the Academy; not considered official military service personnel

Ensconced—settled in comfortably; entrenched; concealed; shielded

Enthralled—fascinated; engrossed; captivated

Entrepreneur—risk-taking businessperson; tycoon; impresario

Escargot—edible snail; may be served a variety of ways

Et cetera—from Latin meaning "and other things"

Exasperate/exasperation—to irritate to a high degree; annoy extremely; frustration; irritation; vexation

Familial—common to family

Famished—hungry; ravenous; starving

Farrier—specialist in equine hoof care; including trimming and balancing of horses' hooves; shoeing, if necessary; combines blacksmith's skills (fabricating, adapting, and adjusting metal shoes); veterinary skills (knowledge of the anatomy and physiology of the lower limb) to care for horses' feet

Feat—*(pronounced "feet")* achievement; notable act; accomplishment

Firefly—*(lightning bugs)* winged beetles in the Cleopatra family; use bioluminescence to attract mates; "cold light" chemically produced in the lower abdomen; no infrared or ultraviolet frequencies; over 2000 species found in tropical and temperate regions

Foibles—weaknesses; quirks; eccentricities; imperfections

Followed suit—each did the same as someone else had just done

Fortuitous—happening by lucky chance

Francinése—descriptive term for anything from Franciné; language spoken in Franciné

Frock—dress; loose outer garment

Gentleman of the Bedchamber—man of noble blood; personal companion of the king; responsible for personal needs; cares for his clothes; assists in dressing; correspondence; serves meals in private; assists with bodily functions and hygiene; only person allowed in the kings private quarters

Glean (Gleaned)—accumulate something; gather; garner

Guardian of The List—the ruling monarch; holds the only key to the Hall of Honors where The List is kept

Gunnysack—coarse cloth sack made of burlap

Hall of Honors for Knights of the Commonwealth—a sacred place of honor for recognition of service for all Knights of the Commonwealth; fallen Knights' swords and shields are mounted with plaques bearing their names and dates of birth, service and deaths; no one may enter the Hall except those already knighted or candidates for dubbing; the ruling monarch holds the only key

Hapless—unlucky; unfortunate; ill fated

Her Majesty's Royal Guard—Knights of the Commonwealth; elite warriors; command units of Royal Horsemen; direct service to the monarchy

Hors d'oeuvre—(*French*) Francinése; singular or plural; small bites of food served before a meal; usually meant to be eaten with the fingers

House of Domestic and Foreign Affairs—Branch of Parliament; oversees relations with other kingdoms, both trade and diplomatic; oversees trade and financial affairs of Berensenia; members appointed by and serve at the pleasure of ruling monarch and are trusted advisors; similar to president's cabinet

House of Judiciary—Branch of Parliament; equal to the Supreme Court; panel of judges and legal scholars; review and determine legality of laws passed by the House of Legislature based on Constitution of Berensenia; neutral in political affiliation; appointed by and serve at the pleasure of ruling monarch; approved by the House of Legislature

Houses of Legislature—Branch of Parliament responsible for laws of the land; laws passed by two-thirds majority vote of both divisions; constitutional review by House of the Judiciary; back to House of Legislature for revisions; to ruling monarch for Signature of Enactment into law; two legislative bodies; *House of Lords*—Duke or Baron (which ever is present) of each county is the representative; *Senate of Commons*—two working-class representatives sent by each township and village within each county; meets September to mid November and again January to May; working-class representatives serve one year terms with no financial compensation; Lords serve as long as they hold the title, also, with no financial compensation

Immaculate—spotlessly clean; neat and tidy; faultless

Impenetrable—impossible to get in or through; impassable

Impertinent—brash; insolent; disrespectful

Impetuous—hotheaded; impulsive; reckless; unthinking

Impudence—Impertinence; sassiness; boldness; nerve; audacity

Inanimate—not alive; inactive; inorganic

Incensed—enraged; angered; infuriated

Incognito—in disguise; pretending to be someone else; unrecognizable as self; anonymous

Inconsolable—too distressed to be consoled

Inconspicuously—not obvious; unnoticeably

Indigenous—belonging to a place; natural; native

Indignant—angry at unfairness; outraged; incensed

Indomitable—unconquerable; determined; resolute

Insatiable—always wanting more; greedy

Interminable—never-ending; endless; perpetual

Irascible—grumpy; irritable; cantankerous

Irrepressible—not restrainable; uncontrollable; wild

Kaleidoscope—complex scene or pattern; complex set of events

Keister—slang term for buttocks; behind; derrière

Kimchi—Far Eastern (*Korean*) pickled vegetables, usually cabbage; extremely odoriferous and spicy hot

Knights of the Commonwealth of Realms—most elite, highly trained soldiers; graduates of Academy of Her Majesty's Royal Guard; dubbed by ruling monarch; take arcane names for security of family when on the battlefield; candidates must be recommended by a trusted elder and approved by ruling monarch; must pass upper levels of early education; candidate must accomplish feat of bravery and self-discovery called Faith Quest; upon graduation and dubbing, are awarded rank of Lieutenant; may achieve highest rank of Commander; exceptionally skilled knights handpicked to serve in ruling monarch's personal security force, Elite Guard Service, the highest honor achievable; serve as long as able-bodied

Krispen—holiday similar to Christmas in modern day

Le Petit Poucet—Francinése *(French)* fairytale; the youngest of seven children in a poor woodcutter's family; his greater wisdom compensates for his smallness of size; when the children are abandoned by their parents, he finds a variety of means to save his life and the lives of his brothers; threatened and pursued by an ogre; Poucet steals his magic seven-league boots while the monster is sleeping

Lady-in-Waiting—female of noble ancestry who looks after a queen or princess; personal assistant and confidant

La pollo piel—Francinése (*French*) for 'the chicken skin'

Lavatory—washroom or toilet

Linguistic—of language

List (The)—books containing all the names of all Knights dubbed in the Commonwealth since the beginning of knighthood; held in the Hall of Honors; includes given name, ancestry, birthdate, dubbing date, battle experience and bravery, medals awarded for service, date of death and arcane name; the ruling monarch is the Guardian of The List

Loath—reluctant; opposed; against; averse

Lout –offensive term; deliberately insults the behavior and attitude of someone, especially a young man; hoodlum; ruffian

Ma mère—Francinése *(French)* for "my mother"

Malaise—general feeling of discontent; illness; disorder

Meandered—wandered slowly and aimlessly; strolled; rambled

Melancholy—pensive sadness; gloomy; despondent; miserable

Mercenary—*(adj.)* motivated only by money; *(noun)* somebody interested only in profit

Merci, Monsieur—Francinése *(French)* "thank you, Sir"

Mon dieu—Francinése *(French)* term; my goodness; my god; good heavens

Muse—*(Muses)* from Ancient Greek mythology; goddesses of inspiration for music, literature and art; the seven daughters of Zeus;

considered the source of the knowledge, related orally for centuries in the ancient culture that was contained in poetic lyrics and myths; in modern language, used to describe a woman who is the object of ones obsession

Ner-do-wells—"never do wells"; irresponsible individuals; under achievers; always waiting for someone else to take care of them

Nonchalant—indifferent; casual

Novice—someone who is new at something; beginner

Obstinate—difficult to control; stubborn; determined

Odoriferous—having strong odor

Ornate—excessively decorative; lavish

Ostentatious—rich and showy; flamboyant; grandiose; pretentious

Palpable—able to be felt; tangible

Pariah—outcast; somebody rejected from caste

Passel—a group of undetermined number

Peckish—British informal term for wanting food; hungry

Peeled—*(keep one's eyes peeled)* to be alert; observant; Sir Robert Peel established the first organized police force; officers were known as 'peelers'; expected to be particularly observant and to keep their eyes '*peeled*'

Penance—self-punishment; atonement; reparation; amends

Peruse—read something carefully; read something quickly; inspect

Personable—amiable; friendly; pleasant

Pestilence—epidemic of disease; plague

Petit fours—*(Francinése; pronounced "petty four)*; tiny iced and decorated cakes of various flavors

Phenomena—plural for phenomenon; marvels; wonders; miracles

Pinnacle—highest point; summit; peak

Placate—to pacify or appease by concession or conciliatory gesture

Portico—covered walkway; porch

Precarious—unsafe; not well founded; risky; hazardous

Prestidigitation—sleight of hand; conjuring

Presumptuous—unwarrantedly or impertinently bold; rude or arrogant; audacious

Pristine—immaculate; unspoiled

Proficient—very skilled; capable; expert

Quandary—dilemma; predicament; difficulty

Repas—Francinése *(French)* for repast; food provided for a meal

Repast—meal; feast; banquet

Repose—sleep; rest

Rotunda—round room; dome; tower

Royal Horsemen—rank and file soldiers; required, two-year enlistment for young men at age sixteen if not attending school; not required to complete upper level education; may defer if applying to AHMRG or completing upper levels; all males are required to do military service

Rudimentary—basic; undeveloped; fundamental

Ruminate—mull something over; ponder; cogitate

Sarsaparilla—sweet soda-type drink, originally made from *Similax regelii*; a perennial, trailing vine with prickly stems; native to Central America; found elsewhere as in Berensenia; taste similar to Root Beer; used by Native Americans for medicinal purposes; introduced to Europe by colonists from the New World

Shenanigans—questionable acts; tricks or pranks

Sickle—curved bladed farm implement used for cutting grass; usually a hand tool

Sidle—move furtively; move sideways; edge; slither

Sleight-of-hand—skill in feats requiring quick or clever movements of the hands for entertainment or deception; skill in deception

Snide—derisively sarcastic; nasty; mean

Sobriquet—*(so-bruh-key)* humorous epithet; assumed name; nickname

Spumoni Ice Cream—ice cream made with variety of different colors and flavors; usually contains candied fruit and nuts; typically three flavors with a fruit/nut layer between; ice cream layers often mixed with whipped cream; cherry or pistachio fruit and nuts with chocolate and vanilla ice cream layers

Steeplechase—long distance horse race through the countryside with various obstacle and jumps to surmount; originally named from the course running from church steeple to church steeple.

Stew in her own juice—worry about something bad she has done; think about how foolish her actions; bask in her own guilt

Stripling—ancient word for *teenager*; adolescent; youth; dates back to fourteenth century; in Maagy's world, boys became striplings at age twelve and girls at age thirteen; a right of passage toward adulthood; most boys were considered men at sixteen and girls had their *Debuts* at fifteen in Berensenia (various cultures differed), where they were eligible to be courted for the purpose of finding a suitable mate.

Superfluous—more than necessary; inessential; extra; redundant

Surmised—idea or thought of something as being possible or likely; guessed; deduced

Surreptitious—secret or unauthorized

Swallow our tongues—same as bite our tongues or bite our lips; a phrase used to indicate staying silent when the instinct is to speak up; keeping one's opinion to one's self; sometimes, considered the same as "swallow our pride", as if keeping our thoughts to ourselves somehow belies our principles

Take your place at the table—in Berensenian tradition, means, "you are family"; "welcome to the club"; "we are one"; when someone is invited to the dinner table, they are accepted as part of the fold

Tacit—implied, but not expressed; unspoken; inferred

Teats—body parts for producing milk; same as nipples

Tempestuous—emotional; turbulent; stormy; uncontrolled

Tête à tête—*(French)* Francinése; head-to-head; face-to-face; private meeting; indicative of confrontation.

Trepidation—apprehension; trembling; fear

Tout de suite—*(French)* Francinése term for immediately.

Tutelage—supervision by a tutor; condition of being tutored; instruction; guidance

Unflappable—composed; unflustered; self-possessed; unexcitable

Unobtrusive—inconspicuous; discreet; low profile

Vendetta—prolonged feud; blood feud among families; quarrel; dispute; grudge

Vicarious—felt or enjoyed through imagined participation in the experiences of others

Voilà—*(French)* Francinése; an exclamation meaning right or there; presto!

Voraciously—very hungry; especially eager; insatiably; ravenously

Well heeled—wealthy or well provided for; comes from reference to shoes; good shoes are never available to the poor, consequently do not have good soles or heels; well heeled shoes belong to the wealthy

Whip-poor-wills—nocturnal birds found in Northern and Central America and also Berensenia; medium sized, well-camouflaged bird, which nests on the ground in dry leaves and usually lays two eggs at a time; the birds' call says their name, whip-poor-will

Huggermugger Vocabulary

Huggermugger language probably developed from misunderstood human language, thus the similarities. Many words are the same (what, friend, challenge). Many sound similar (yem for yes, whotle for who, therein for there, etc.).

Quirks of Huggermugger Spelling:

1. S is used to spell the soft C sound, as in sentury (century); pronounced the same
2. CH sound is spelled with TSH, as in breatsh (breach)
3. Words spelled with G always take the hard pronunciation, as in Go; gibe (give)
4. J forms the soft G sound, as in jigantum (gigantum); languaje (language)
5. No symbol for K; replaced with hard C, as in come; Catrin (Katrin)
6. No symbol for Q; replaced with CW, as in cween (queen)
7. No symbol for V; replaced with B, as in gibe (give)
8. No symbol for X; replaced with CS, as in ecsellent (excellent)
9. No symbol for Z; replaced with SS, as in wissardry (wizardry)

Each Huggermugger clan or colony (Woodland, Tree-dwelling, Burrowing, etc.) has its own dialect; all Huggermuggers are at least familiar with most of them. Winnsbo's dialect is Burrowing. This list is by no means a complete vocabulary of Huggermugger language.

Abingtion—Avington

Allyboly—anybody

Allyding—anything

Allymore—anymore

Allyway—anyway

Alsome—also; too

Apprentise—apprentice

Aromanse—aroma

Aromansel—*(v.)* to smell

Arribe—arrive

Asc—ask

Awace—awake

Bac—back

Balley—valley

Bault—vault; crypt

Beliebe—believe

Bery—very

Bigil—vigil

Biolet—Violet

Blinc—blink

Booc—book

Brabe—brave

Braselet—bracelet

Breatsh—(*v.*) breach; break; violate

Bringen—bring

Broddur—brother

Cabi—carry away; take; steal

Cannonen—cannot; can't

Castum—castle

Catsh -catch

Ceem—keep

Cleber—clever

Comen—come

Crispen—Krispen

Cumbering—Covington

Cween—Queen

Cwestions—questions

Cwic—quick

Cwiet—quiet

Darc—dark

Deserbe—deserve

Ding—thing

Disburb—disturb

Discober—discover

Donnur—daughter

Dooran—door

Dranum—drowned; throw into water

Dutshess Wentout—Duchess of Wentworth

Eatsh—each

Eben—even

Ebentumly—eventually

Eber—ever; every *(depends on usage)*

Eberboly—everybody

Eberdare—everywhere

Eberday—everyday

Eberding—everything

Eberwhere—everywhere; wherever

Ebil—evil

Ecspectation—expectation

Ecstractions—extractions

Fabs—fast

Fabum—favorite

Falenaler—climbing vine; weed; Rain's real name, Climbingvine

Falum—fall (falling)

Fanem—fine as in very thin (fanem thread)

Fanum—fine as in a state of being (feeling fanum)

Fase—Grace

Fatam—faithful; loyal; trustworthy

Fics—fix

Figen—figure as in number or shape

Figun—figure *(verb)*; reason; conclude

Finebeleese—finally

Firestic—firestick

Flabely—family

Foggel—*(v.)* to think

Foggen –*(v. past tense)* thought

Foreber—forever

Forlegioners—foreign mercenaries; soldiers-for-hire from other countries

Freesse—freeze

Frygan—frighten; scare

Gibe—give

Goesen—goes

Grandonnur—granddaughter

Grantshics—Grandchildren

Guilen—guile; to trick; trickery (noun and verb spelled the same)

Habe—have

Haben—home; habitat

Habing—having

Habenhaben—home to home; place to place; transporting something between locations

Hi-i-i-ya—exclamatory sound of warning

Hobel—hovel; shed; shack

Hugan—human

Inbention—invention

Infamtion—information

Infantem—baby

Intrumer—intruder

Intshes—inches

Isie—Alice

Jigantum—gigantic; excessively large; huge

Laboratome—laboratory

Languaje—language

Leabe—leave

Libon—live

Licem—like; as; as if; similar to; used as comparison (Winnsbo licem Patarc means Winnsbo is like his father)

Licum—like; enjoy; approve

Lobel—love

Locem—location; place

Mace—*(hard 'c' sound)* make

Mally—many

Mamarc—mother

Meetle—me

Megonia—Melania

Memorisse—memorize

Mersenary—mercenary

Mics—mix

Mistace—mistake

Mistshief—mischief

Mutsh—much

Naced—naked

Namy—name

Neclase—necklace

Necst—next

Neesie—necessary

Nisem—nice; kind; pleasant

Nightingale—Abigail

No—know

Non—no

Nonding—nothing

Nonen—not

Noneneber—not ever; never

Nonone—no one

Nonenone—neither one; not one

Nowledje—knowledge

Nown—known

Oceydocey—okay, all right, satisfactory

Patarc—father

Picen—pick

Placen—play

Plase—place

Plegin—pledge; oath; promise of loyalty

Rebeal—reveal

Reberse- reverse

Rebumbering—remembering; *(rebumber)*—remember

Recumguise—recognize; know

Reserber—research

Reterb—return

Rethal—lather; soap

Sabe—safe; save

Sabeceem—safekeeping; custody; protection

Santum Nich—Saint Nick; Santa Claus; Saint Nicholas; Kris Kringle; Father Krispen

Scill—skill

Scin—skin

Servise—service

Shac—shack

Showen—show as in demonstrate

Sics—six

Sicsteen—sixteen

Siense—science

Sisem—sister

Slagen—kill; murder

Sleem—sleep

Smilen—happy; joyful

Snac—snack

Snoosse—snooze

Solbe—solve; solved

Solly—sorry

Sorserer—sorcerer

Sourodo—sweet; fragrant; perfumed

Spicenbalen—jacks and ball set; child's game

Stuben—study

Stubener—student

Tace—take; carry; remove *(Note: active verb form)*

Tagom—take *(Note: inactive verb form; does not indicate movement, but rather take care, take an oath, take a look)*

Tagomcore—take good care

Teatsh—teach

Thanu—thank you

Therein—there

Thinc—think

Thribe—thrive

Til—until

Toutsh—touch

Trics—tricks

Trucum—trust; believe

Trudle—through

Tshecing—checking

Tsheem—cheese

Tshic—(chick) child

Tshoise—choice

Tshosen—chosen

Tshums—chums

Tummel—tunnel

Tutle—teach

Tutler—teacher

Uben—under

Ubencober—under cover; hidden

Ubenmousolem—underground vault; safe storage in underground system

Ubenstam—understand; comprehend; know; grasp

Ubentummel—extensive underground network of tunnels; covers the entire kingdom; extends to most other valley kingdoms; through the Sagamathias to Terrasicus; deeper underground than Terrasicans tunnels

Unenlibon—dead; "un-live"; (*may be used as verb, "to die"*)

Uniberse—universe

Unloc—unlock

Usen—us or we (*depending upon context*)

Ut—up

Waler—water

Wanten—want; would like to have

Watsh—watch

What—what

Whotle—who

Wissardry—wizardry

Witsh—witch

Worcs—works

Wrapun—coat or jacket

Yem—yes

Youtle—you

Yummy—exquisitely tasty; exceptionally good flavor

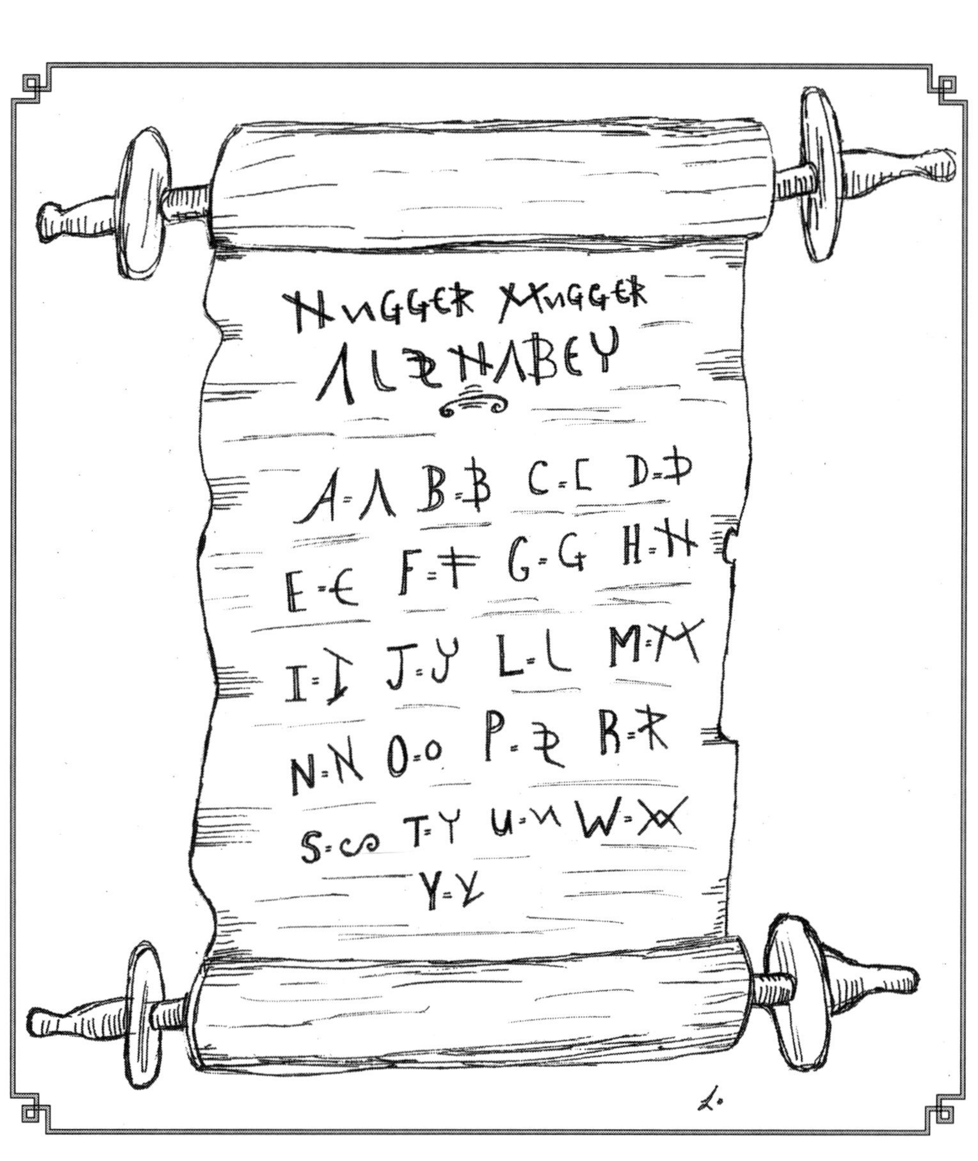
A = B = C = D =
E = F = G = H =
I = J = L = M =
N = O = P = R =
S = T = U = W =
Y =

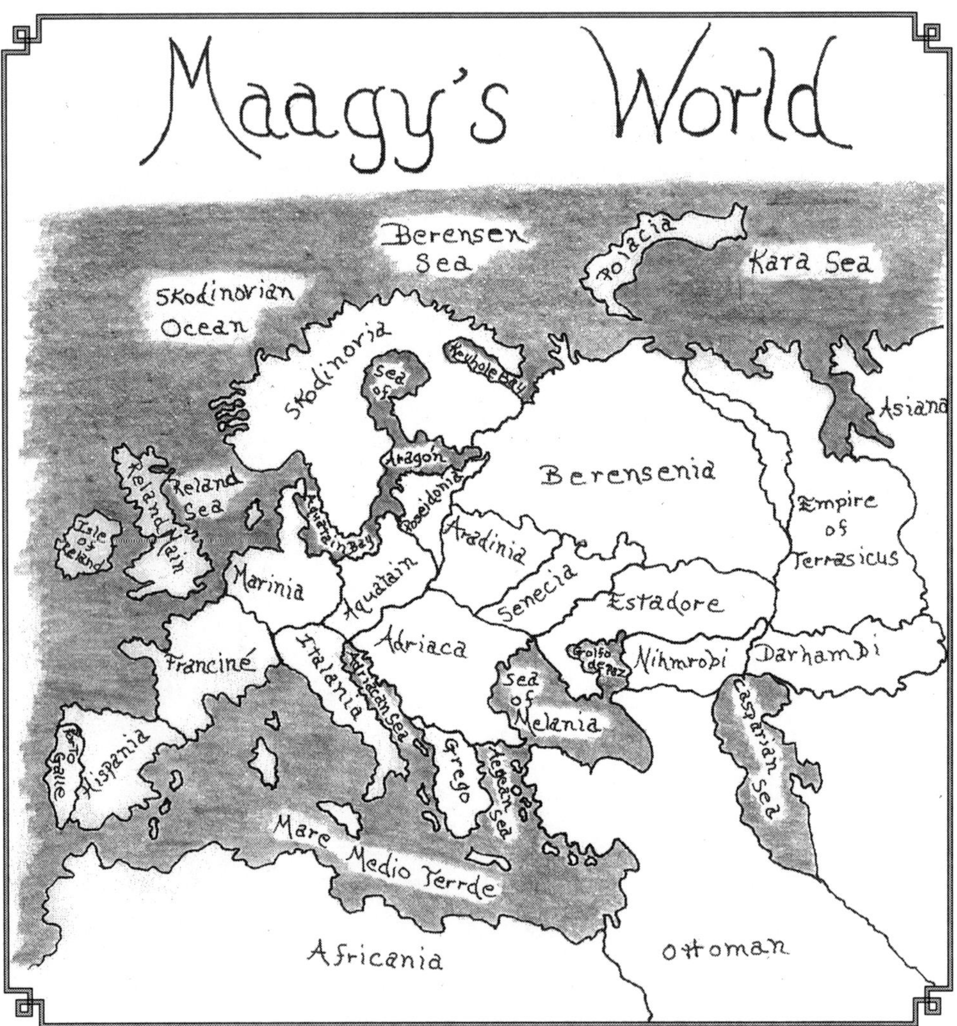

Maagy's World
Berensen Sea
Skodinorian Ocean
Polacia
Kara Sea
Skodinoria
Sea of
Keyhole Bay
Asiana
Aragón
Berensenia
Reland Sea
Reland Main
Isle of Reland
Poseidonia
Aquatain Bay
Aradinia
Empire of Terrasicus
Marinia
Aquatain
Senecia
Estadore
Italania
Adriaca
Golfo de Paz
Nihmrobi
Darhamdi
Francíné
Adriacan Sea
Sea of Melania
Caspanian Sea
Porto Galle
Hispania
Grego
Aegean Sea
Mare Medio Terrde
Africania
Ottoman

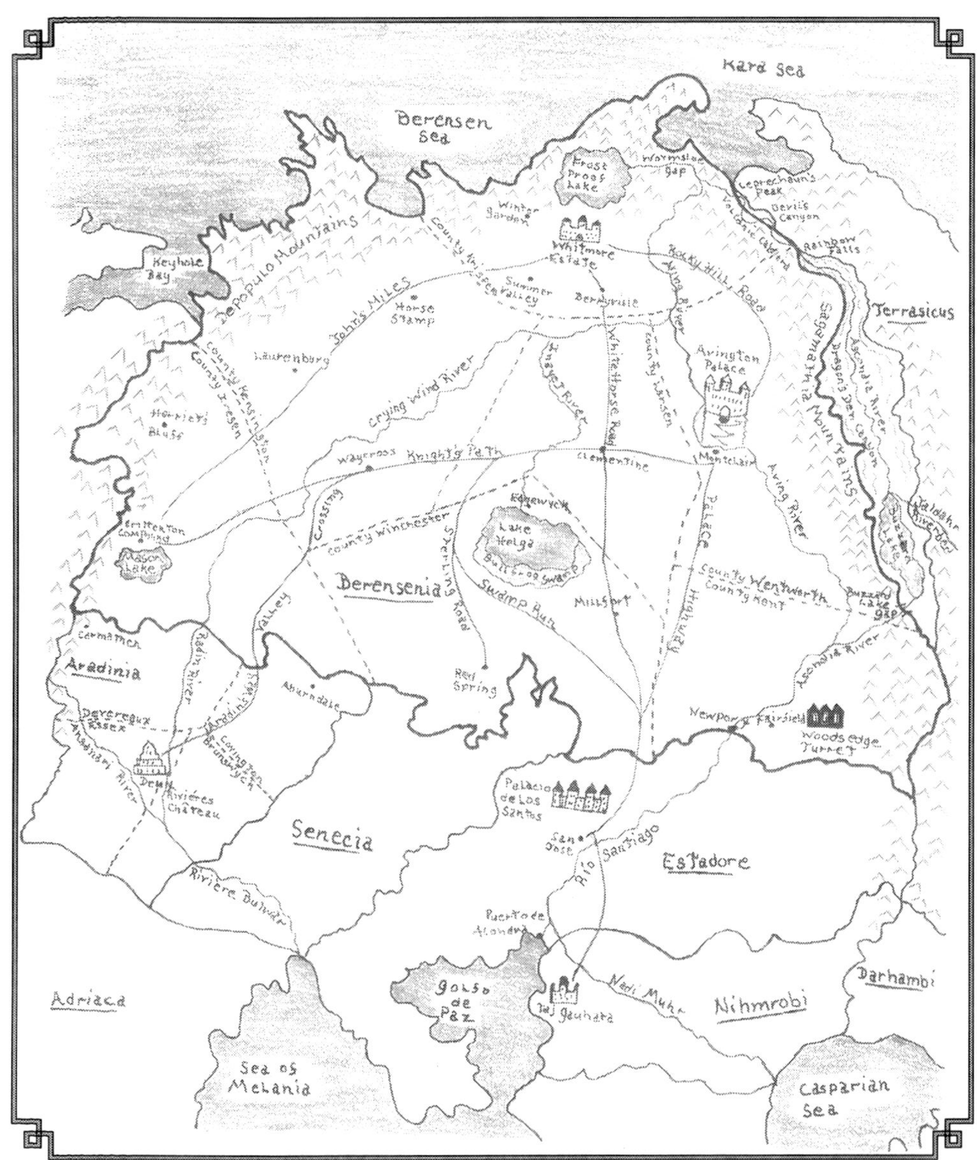
Kara Sea
Berensen Sea
Frost Proof Lake
Wormsloe Gap
Leprechaun's Peak
Devil's Canyon
Volcanic Caldera
Rainbow Falls
Winter Garden
Whitmore Estate
Keyhole Bay
Depopulo Mountains
Summer Valley
Horse Stamp
Berryville
Rocky Hill Road
Aving River
John's Miles
Terrasicus
Sagamatha Mountains
Ascendia River
Lautenburg
County Kensington
Crying Wind River
Sunset River
White Horse Road
County Larsen
Arington Palace
Harriet's Bluffs
Waycross
Knight's Path
Clementine
Montclair
Aving River
Crossing
Edgewyck
Lake Helga
Bullfrog Swamp
Emmerton Compound
Mason Lake
County Winchester
Sterling Road
Palace Highway
County Wentworth
County Kent
Buzzard Lake Gap
Berensenia
Swamp Run
Millfort
Valley
Carmathen
Aradinia
Radin River
Red Spring
Ascendia River
Newport
Fairfield
Woods Edge Turret
Devereaux
Essex
Covington
Brunswick
Palacio de Los Santos
Rivières Château
Senecia
San Jose
Rio Santiago
Estadore
Puerto de Alondra
Golfo de Paz
Nadi Muhr
Nihmrobi
Darhambi
Adriaca
Sea of Melania
Casparian Sea

CPSIA information can be obtained at www.ICGtesting.com
Printed in the USA
LVOW07s0527161014

408917LV00004B/4/P